T0369267

The Light Voyager

The Light Voyager

Mardi Orlando

Order this book online at www.trafford.com
or email orders@trafford.com

Most Trafford titles are also available at major online book retailers.

© Copyright 2010 Mardi Orlando.
All rights reserved. No part of this publication may be reproduced, stored in a retrieval system, or
transmitted, in any form or by any means, electronic, mechanical, photocopying, recording, or
otherwise, without the written prior permission of the author.

Printed in Victoria, BC, Canada.

ISBN: 978-1-4269-2244-2 (soft)
ISBN: 978-1-4269-2245-9 (hard)

Library of Congress Control Number: 2009941107

*Our mission is to efficiently provide the world's finest, most comprehensive book publishing
service, enabling every author to experience success. To find out how to publish your book, your
way, and have it available worldwide, visit us online at www.trafford.com*

Trafford rev. 1/20/2010

 www.trafford.com

North America & international
toll-free: 1 888 232 4444 (USA & Canada)
phone: 250 383 6864 ♦ fax: 812 355 4082

Contents

1

Calatia

Amber halls of twilight fell through the tall pines of the Caletian Plains as Tarl strode home. With each step he tried to piece together fragments of a dream that had been troubling him for several days. This morning he had woken from the reverie with such a start that for a moment he felt as if he was still drowning in the images of his subconscious. As he woke to reality, a sting of disappointment surprised him. Even now, the sense of loss wouldn't lift. He belonged back in that dream and that was what was changing him.

■　■　■

Tarl squinted into the radiance of the blood orange sun as it began to dissolve into the horizon. The warm light fell across his tanned skin and straight shoulder-length black hair. There was just enough time to get home and cook his father's evening meal, if he didn't waste time. He did have a habit of losing himself in thought, especially lately.

Breathing in the evening air and relishing in its freedom, Tarl tried to shed the visions that seemed to follow him like ghostly shadows. At least long walks allowed him to remove himself from the ordinariness of life. His curiosity was unquenchable but nothing here gave him satisfaction. In the fields at least, there was always something new to investigate. It helped balance the monotony.

The most recent season-cycle had passed by without much interest but Tarl appeared to be the only one concerned by this. His friends were content to go to morning school, do their daily chores and play sports. The people of the town even appeared to relish the quietude of late. Industry was going well; there was plenty of work for everybody; and even the usual town gossip had failed to kindle the imagination.

His uncle Rembeu, a Keeper, apparently had no reason to call for him either and Tarl missed his company and infectious enthusiasm. It was the longest spell that they had been apart and he craved his uncle's insight.

The cycle had just drifted onward and over itself punctuated only by the day to day events of the town. It amazed him that life could be so dull. Perhaps that's why he dreamed so vividly.

A cool breeze breathed under Tarl's loose cotton over-top. He tied up the thin cream straps at the front and tightened the gold-skin traveling wrap dangling at the waist of his loose black pants. Above him the early evening moon was waiting to take its shift in the darkening sky.

As he strode on, the sky began to reveal the familiar formations of the stars. Tarl turned his gaze toward the constellations as they unfolded and tried to remember their names as his uncle Rembeu, had taught him. All those perfect, silver, sparkling points of light, thousands of moonspells away never failed to amaze him.

Star-gazing always reminded him of the Viewing Tunnel in his uncle's mountain home. It was the planet's ultimate monitoring station. Rembeu's brilliant design had created the only place on the planet that every star formation in the universe could be viewed. Each would be picked up eventually: Northern formations; Southern formations; and of course those of the Center Sky. Like the colored patterns of a kaleidoscope, the beautiful frameworks of the stars would sit in wait always ready to take their turn on the center stage and spread their crystalline wings across the sky. Tarl realized he was lost in thought again.

The evening was settling in but he was not far from town now. The tall pines were far behind him and he was now descending Still Hill, the town's cemetery. He always stopped here for a moment to admire the ancient grave-plates that circled up the hill like glistening memories. Many different stones had been used: Mauve amethyst; metallic-gray hematite; crystal quartz; and occasionally, for the graves that housed Protectors, halved agate crystals cradled both ends to guard the occupier.

Tarl's favorite however, was the smallest: A fine pane of transparent yellow citrine secluded up the face of the rise. This side of the hill faced the sunset and in the last light of the day the polished headstone glowed like a crown of light at the heart of the hill.

Many hours had been spent here clearing away weeds and reading the poems of the old language that were engraved on the stones. This evening though, he gave only a passing moment to acknowledge their splendor and continued on his journey.

He strolled through the wheat fields with long lunging steps and crossed the daisy meadows picking several with big sweeps of his hand, always giving them a quick sniff even though he knew they smelt awful. Finally, at the last leg of his trip he squeezed through the broken wooden fence to cut across the local vineyard, always checking the progress of the growing grapes as he passed by the ancient vines.

Finally, Tarl reached the main street of town. The smells of cooking greeted him and a twist of hunger followed. His shoes tapped across the diamond-shaped pavers as he followed the soft glowing streetlights toward his home.

The burning fire sticks at the front entry told him that his father had already arrived. He quickened his pace up to the front courtyard where the cottage garden blooms eagerly fought the ever-consuming weeds that now took over most of the garden.

"Hi dad," he called out as he stuck his head through the wood paneled entry door whilst removing his shoes. Sandalwood incense greeted him. "Dinner won't be long," he continued without waiting for a response. "Sorry I'm a bit late."

"Oh Tarl." His father said trying to sound gruff. "If you're ever early I may die of fright." Reaching out a big hand, he ruffled Tarl's satiny hair.

"Yeah, lost track of time. Sorry dad." Tarl's big green eyes smiled sheepishly.

"Oh don't even try giving me that look." His father cried with mock fear. Shameless, his father thought. But it worked every time.

His father swung a strong brown arm around Tarl's neck and they both laughed as they moved into the cooking room. A wonderful hearty aroma wafted toward him.

"I hope it's not too much of a shock my young man, but I have actually cooked us a big stew tonight."

"Fantastic. How did you manage to have it ready?" Tarl asked with all the enthusiasm he could muster before tearing off toward the stove.

"I decided to finish early today. I thought we might spend the evening catching up."

Tarl was keen to spend time with his father and hoped some of the old stories would come out. He had hardly seen him lately, what with the new project his father was in charge of.

"Smells great dad," he said with a smile of approval.

"Come on I've set up in here." His father pointed to the fire-room.

At the granite table bountiful amounts of thick ragout were scooped into two bowls and loaded with chunky slices of crusty wheat bread.

Tarl ate hungrily. He was surprised that his father had gone to so much trouble without any particular reason. Why then did he feel like something was about to change?

In between mouthfuls he glanced at his father trying to read his face but Tarl had never been able to tell what his father was thinking. They were so different. His father was broad and muscular with skin darkened almost black by the sun. His dark tousled hair and dark-blue hooded eyes made him look striking. It was obvious to everyone that Tarl's looks had come from his mother.

As a Maker, Parvo had become a Master Craftsman of Wind-Ships. His inventive designs had afforded him the respect and admiration of many, but unfortunately had also stirred the spite of a few. As a true Master he never assumed credit but gave it to those who worked beside him. That included the basalt miners who extracted the finest rock for the hulls of the ships - the higher the quality the longer lasting their levitation abilities; and lumber experts who helped craft the masts and booms, and of course the silk weavers who ensured that only cloth of the highest grade was used for the sails. He was known as the most progressive and democratic inventor in the territory.

Parvo had designed and built this very house before Tarl was born. It was made as a tribute to Tarl's mother: A woman, many said, was beyond his honor. The cedar weatherboards had been rubbed with fragrant oils infused with powdered zircon so that they sparkled in the moonlight, and weeks had been spent stenciling ivory constellations across the tops of the walls. He developed paint that changed color with the seasons and sourced fabrics woven with the magic threads of the Wizemen - the most ancient tribe of Keepers, which now hung looped from the ceiling.

When Tarl and his father had eaten as much of the stew as their stomachs would allow, they sank back into their chairs patting their stomachs as if in congratulation. Tarl made two large mugs of hot chocolate and they moved in front of the fire. Tarl couldn't remember the last time the two of them had spent time together. His father usually came home to eat the meal Tarl had prepared and chat briefly before retiring to his work room. But tonight he seemed chatty, as if his voice was a sextant searching for its target on a celestial map.

"How's everything going at work?" Tarl knew any conversation about his job would get his father talking.

"Oh, we're very busy at the moment," his father responded with vigor. "I'm working on an amazing new design."

Tarl smiled to himself. The current design was always 'the most amazing'.

"Have you named it yet?"

"It's named the 'Orbitor'," his father replied without taking a breath, "it will be able to circle the globe non-stop!"

"Wow that's pretty exciting," Tarl couldn't help but be impressed. "How have you managed to maintain levitation over such a long period?"

"Are you sure you're interested?" Parvo was dying to tell his son about the new developments.

"Absolutely," he replied, grinning at his father's eagerness, "tell me everything."

"O.K." His father adjusted his seating position and leaned forward slightly, elbows on knees, palms cupping the air. "Well, you know that the basalt is crystalline and magnetic. You know that for the basalt to create weightlessness we need to make it resonate above the frequency of gravity - this is when we get levitation right?"

"Yep," Tarl nodded. His father's enthusiasm was infectious.

"Well, the only problem has been to maintain this resonation. Even though we built the maximum craft to a full sun-stretch in certain situations it just wasn't satisfactory. Obviously, the aim has always been to increase possible travel distance. I mean, what if the terrain does not allow landing; what if, say, the weather requires alterations in charting your course or you're traveling over the ocean?" He took a moment to swallow, raised his palms toward Tarl as if in offering and went on, "Well I've finally discovered how to maintain this resonation indefinitely."

"How?"

"We needed to pay more attention to the magnetic properties. So, I created a new tuning device. The vehicle is installed with a mechanism similar to a magnetic frequency-compass. When the ship passes over the planet's naturally occurring magnetic points, the device regenerates and the resonation-frequency is restored." His palms slapped down on his thighs.

"That's incredible. I can't believe you haven't told me about this." Tarl was truly astonished. "Wow. Is it a secret? I mean do people know yet?" His mind was full of questions; his thoughts tumbling.

Parvo looked delighted at his son's response. He let out a rich laugh and rocked back in his chair.

"Well my young man, you are the first to know. I have been worried that there are some that are trying to sneak the information from my designers. But they misjudge my crew's loyalty."

Tarl had a strange feeling that there was something that was not being said.

"Did someone try to bribe your designers?" he asked incredulously.

"No one worth their weight," Parvo replied nonchalantly, "Of course, I didn't give any one person all the exact specifications until I was sure it could work." Slowly his smile turned into a smirk and his eyes twinkled with things not yet divulged. Energy was filling the room.

"What's exactly is going on dad?" Tarl returned the look.

Now that the seeds of his secret were out, Parvo was going to take his time. Settling back into his chair, he appeared quite composed. He watched his son calmly hoping he would guess. It would be so much more enjoyable that way.

Tarl sat for a moment trying to comprehend something just beyond his reach. Staring into space he tried to figure it out. Images from his dreams flashed incomprehensibly behind his eyes. Clearing his mind the mental jigsaw-pieces slowly began clicking together. He took a deep breath and looked up to catch his father's expression.

Even though his mind was exploding with possibilities he tried to keep his voice level. How long had he waited for this day? He looked his father square in the eye.

"If it's what I think you mean…I would be honored," Tarl said finally.

His father nodded proudly.

"Then my son, you shall be the first pilot of the 'Orbitor'."

■   ■   ■

They talked long into the night. Strategies and consequences were discussed as were the past and long term desires. They talked of Tarl's mother and of her brother, Rembeu, whom Tarl admitted to missing. But finally, Parvo brought up an unexpected topic.

"One of the reasons I want you to be the navigator of this flight is because there is something else in the cards for you." Parvo's expression became serious.

All night Tarl had felt like there had been something else in the air; something unspoken, something inevitable. He waited, feeling as if he stood at the equator of excitement and fear.

"I'm not quite sure how to tell you." Parvo began to sound somber. Now all that was left was reality. How was he going to tell his only son; his reason for being, that this was really happening?

Alarm buzzed inside Tarl's head. A sense of foreboding had been building within him for a long time now and he guessed he was about to find out why. He thought he might know at least one thing for sure.

"It's alright dad, I think I know what you're going to say anyway." Tarl fought the conflicting emotions. He knew he had to say something before his father was forced to. How would his father feel having to tell his only child that his future did not lay here? It would surely break his heart, again. Tarl could not imagine what his father must have gone through when his mother died and he knew that the only reason his father had wanted to carry on was because he had his son.

It seemed to Tarl that his father felt he had been denied life's freedoms but it was a concern that he would never confess to his son. Eventually his passion for work had given him respite from the long lonely thoughts of the woman he would love forever but Tarl knew how difficult it had been for him to step back into life.

"It's time isn't it? Tarl finally asked. I have felt it for a while now. I am being called aren't I?" The offer to fly the first Orbitor wind-ship across the globe was almost beyond Tarl's grasp. Like the rise and fall of the ocean he knew it would come with both the gifts of the tide and the forfeit of a constant.

"Yes son." Parvo closed his eyes for just a moment.

The wonderful evening had turned. It was so strange. Tarl had somehow always known this day would come and had looked forward to it. There was nothing for him here, except of course, his father. How long had he felt like this without really paying it any attention? His instincts had told him there was something inside him, something that craved more. Yet, all this time he had ignored it. Now, here it was, staring him in the face.

"It's time for you to return to your ancestral roots." Parvo said trying not to show the emotion that was threatening to overwhelm him. "Rembeu has called for you. It feels too early but indeed I have been informed that it is time for you to follow your path." Despite the inevitability of it all, it felt ridiculously unjust but Parvo knew his feelings were not part of the equation.

"Did you make the Orbitor for me because of this?" Tarl asked incredulously.

"I didn't make the offer as a last gesture before you have to go you know son. I would have asked you to pilot this trip either way." Parvo rubbed his hands behind his neck. "You know you are the most precious thing in my life," his sad dark-blue eyes gazed into his son's, "but I also have to allow you to follow your true path." Parvo pursed his lips, perhaps in an effort to restrain the complete truth, "you were only mine until you were called. You must always know though, that you have my faith and trust and I will be here whenever and for whatever reason you may need me." His head nodded slightly with the final word. He had done it. He had spoken those cruel words of finality calmly.

Tarl didn't know what to say. He desperately wanted to spend more time with his uncle: The teacher; the philosopher; the Keeper, but he couldn't leave his father. Tiny beads of water heated his eyes.

Parvo smiled affectionately and moved over to wrap his son in a big comforting hug. He pulled away for just a moment to take a look at the 15 year old boy. He had grown so much yet his face still held reminders of his mother. It was a face holding the memories of the past and reflecting the knowledge of the future. How could he argue with that?

There was so little time now. Soon he would be sending his son off to sail the newest wind-ship around the globe. His final stop would be with Rembeu. And, when his only son stopped there, it would be for a very long time and the circumstances would be, in the very least, challenging.

Finally Parvo walked with Tarl up to his bedroom. He hummed tunes that Tarl's mother had taught him so long ago and after his son had climbed into bed he ruffled his hair like he used to do when he was very young.

"We'll discuss everything tomorrow, O.K?" said Parvo. "So don't worry about any of it tonight. You need to get lots of sleep before your big adventure. And," his father stated with a raised eyebrow, "tomorrow evening, try not to be home too late".

"I promise dad." Suddenly Tarl felt very young again.

Parvo patted his son's glossy black hair and then turned and walked to his own room. He sat at the edge of the large bed, head in hands, wondering how he would cope without his son. There was a world of worry ahead of the boy, a world Parvo did not belong in. He felt exhausted; defenseless and tired with life.

Parvo looked up at the ceiling where the tiled glass allowed him to view the infinity of the sky. There was just darkness. Not even moonlight. He leant his head against his hands. His body seemed so heavy. Without Tarl, life would be really lonely. He had always known the universe and its complications would be his son's future. It was just that their time together had seemed so short. He understood that it was Tarl's destiny, as it had been his wife's destiny, her heart and soul. As a Keeper of Light she was privileged and must pass that right on. How he missed her. She would be so proud of her son. What a fine boy he had turned out to be; smart, compassionate and talented, and luckily he carried the refined good looks of his mother. At least Parvo hadn't passed on the heavy set build of a Maker.

A memory from long ago drifted into his thoughts before a strange feeling began to overcome him. The overwhelming sadness started to lift like a mist evaporating into a sunrise. He lifted his head, chin to the ceiling as the feeling welled. He felt warm, almost serene. For just a moment he could have sworn the room swam in yellow light. Peacefulness ebbed around him like the waters of a heated spring on an icy winter's day. Parvo blinked and beautiful visions flashed behind his eyes. He looked up through the glass-tiles and out to the midnight sky.

"Thank you," he whispered, as his voice dissolved into breath. "Thank you my love."

Tarl had watched his father retreat from his room and wondered what he must be feeling; how he would cope. A picture of his grandfather on his mother's side stared at him from the opposite wall. The great man stood swathed in his flowing ivory robes, eyes twinkling. The man's image stood like a luminous ghost in front of a midnight sky sprinkled with stars. Above his head rose a majestic colored wheel that seemed to move forward when you passed by. Each segment held a different color: Red, orange, yellow, green, blue, indigo and violet and in its center shone a swirl of white. Ever since Tarl was a small child he couldn't help but think of the Ancients' stories of a wizard called 'The Keeper': A man that inspired the very naming of Boundaries. Tarl wondered about his own destiny. Would his uncle know about it? Would he be left to figure it out alone?

Tarl stared up at the sky through the smooth glass-tiles above him. Ursa Major, the Center Sky's heavenly body, twinkled back at him. Lying very still in the dark he wondered what the future held for him? How long would it be before he would see his father again? He looked back toward his father's room. A faint golden glow reached outward across the hallway toward him. Squinting, he wondered if his father had lit a fire stick and then dismissed the idea when not a moment later the light was gone. Tarl shook his head. He was so very tired and there was so much to get used to. His heavy eyes closed. He could do nothing except fall backward into the depths of dreams.

What Tarl did not know was that as he slept he dreamed great dreams: Visions of the past and images of the future. And, while he slumbered, downstairs, the ancient Rainbow Crystal that swam with the secrets of the ancestors, glowed bright and strong with the history and future of the universe.

2

The Preparations

Very early the next morning Tarl woke as the first light of dawn crept across his eyelids. He squinted up at the new day. A high, bleached-blue sky was tinged with the deep oranges of the rising sun. It would be another clear sunny day.

He met his father downstairs with a nod and worked up wakefulness with a steaming cup of lemon-tang tea. Parvo was already seated on one of the crafted baltic chairs, smoking his herb stuffed chillum. The bittersweet aroma rested in the air between him and his son. He watched the sleepy-head boy, with his half closed eyes and his shiny hair swished the wrong way, trying to look alert.

"Do you want some sweet buttered lime jam with your wheat toast?" his father asked trying to sound nonchalant.

"Huh?" Tarl stretched his eyes wide and rubbed his face. "Oh yeah dad, lime jam's my favorite. We haven't had it for so long."

"Mrs. Zuni gave me some yesterday when she saw me come home early." Their eyes met with the reminder of the reason for his early return the night before. His father looked away as he turned to grab the jam jug. "She knows it's your favorite too." He popped open the jug and put it down next to Tarl's toast.

"Does she know I'm going?" His grimace was involuntary.

"No. I wouldn't have told anyone without talking to you first."

"Oh, no of course you wouldn't." Why did conversation feel awkward this morning? He looked down at his breakfast and took a big munch out of the buttery sweet toast. "Oh that's good," he said as he grinned up at his father. Sticky jam and melted butter were spread across his grin.

With his gooey hands and his hair still askew his father was reminded of a time long past. But now, this young man was about to do things he himself could not imagine doing at the twice the age. He was still just a child really; his child; and yet, apparently man enough to follow a destiny that held unbelievable expectations.

"You have quite a few things to do today young man. Perhaps you will have time to come and visit me at work today? I will be at the silk house later this morning. You could help with the finishing touches to the Orbitor. The silks for your sails also need to be chosen." Parvo thought for a moment. "Maybe you would like to emboss something particular on them?"

"Oh that would be great." Tarl's concentration was drawn to his glass of tea, which was slipping from his buttery fingers. He righted his grasp and continued, "Could we go to the basalt caves as well? I haven't been there for a really long time."

"Of course." Parvo said enthusiastically. "Actually, if you wanted to, you could come with me this morning and we could visit the caves first, then go to the silk house and maybe have a bit of lunch together, you know, talk about preparations and things?"

His father was sounding rather cheerful but Tarl knew moods would be undulating quite a bit in the next few suns. Perhaps his father slept well last night. Come to think of it, Tarl decided, last night he had had one of the best night's sleeps he could remember. The flutter of a vision passed across his mind but was gone before he could hold on to it and then a flashback spilled shockingly easily into his mind. It was of his father trying to hug his mother while she was cooking breakfast: She kept laughing and attempting to squirm out of his embrace. His father just hung on tight throwing winks over his shoulder at Tarl while he sat at the table enjoying the joke. He must have been really young, maybe 5 years old? It seemed so real. He shook himself back to reality.

"That sounds like a plan," Tarl said watching his father wiping up the mess.

"Well, come on then, we have to head off shortly." Parvo paused and then with a smirk, pointed to his own head and nodded in Tarl's direction. "You do not exactly resemble the master of global ship sailing."

Tarl brushed down his hair with a sticky hand.

"Oh." he laughed, "I'd better go wash up."

■　　■　　■

The dawn sun was a crest of glorious color that rose around them as they lifted high into the sky. They sailed windward in their small wind-ship toward the Basalt Caves. The ship was one of his father's first designs. Parvo could have had any of the new ships but this one, he said, was special. New is not always better, he would say.

The burning sun dazzled across the golden silk sails as they glided and tacked in the wind. The polished basalt hull of the small rig shimmered with the reflections of golden clouds and sparkling sunlight. The only sound that could be heard in the silence was the soft ringing of the gravity-frequency device resounding within the ship's hull.

They flew across swaying fields of glossy buttercups and over serpentine silver streams that coursed for miles and soared across ancient sites that climbed up towards them in the sky. They even sailed so close to The Towers of Independence that Tarl felt as if he could touch the hundred foot high columns of stone inscribed by the Ancients. On they flew until finally, they reached their destination. Tarl's father let him take control as they tacked into the wind, slowing the ship so as to settle down at one of the many sand-docks.

"Perfect landing son," his father commended him.

"Thanks dad." Tarl was enjoying himself and his father seemed to be too. But somehow, beneath it all, Tarl could feel the slow grind of change churning around them.

The Basalt Caves were incredible structures. Hewn into huge ridged cliffs of hexagonal columns, they sunk deep below the surface. Several of these caverns were believed to lead right down to the magnetic core. Tarl and his father traipsed down one of the black stairwells past the layers of red inter-basaltic beds and wandered into one of the enormous openings. The black walls glistened with star-like specs catching the light of the overhead neon gas-globes.

Parvo was greeted by a few of the Makers before moving off to talk with the Master Miner. The miners were delighted to see Tarl and several surrounded him with welcome.

After catching up with their lives and the goings on of the mines Tarl quizzed them with many questions; anything necessary for his flight. Their enthusiastic answers were invaluable and finally, they steered him toward the cave that was used to create his new flight ship.

Tarl lost count of the steps as he descended into one of the oldest caverns. Shuffling through a small cave-mouth they emerged into an enormous chamber where the air smelled of wet soil. The tall dark, irregular walls were flecked with tiny silver specs and the high roof arched overhead like the gleaming underside of an umbrella. Far below he could hear gushing water, probably an ancient water system. Tarl stepped forward drawn to touch the cool stone surface.

"Careful Tarl," whispered Brin, one of his father's most valued miners. "We are so deep below the planet's surface that this cave can echo sounds at increasing volumes. If the stone is tapped on an apex area, that wall will ring out. Its frequency will penetrate the next wall which in turn reacts from the resonating echo and it just goes on and on." Brin's grimace showed evidence of firsthand experience. Tarl quickly retracted his hand and held it immobile as if it were a snake. Brin refrained from laughing, "You just need to know where to mine from, that's all."

They spent a long time discussing the mining techniques that did not affect the natural frequency of the stone until a voice suddenly interrupted them.

"Come on you lot, can't I get anyone to do some work around here?" Parvo's voice sounded rather bold and Tarl turned in hesitation.

The miners, however, faced Parvo with wide grins. Brin made a grand sweep and bowed low in an ancient gesture.

"The Builder himself, Master Maker, 'Sir Parvo Argus'." The other miners laughed along with the joke.

"Ha ha," Parvo responded drolly as he threw Tarl a quick wink, "you're supposed to show my son how impressed you are by my presence."

"Oh but we are Master Sir." Brin continued, wanting to make the most of his bow. Tarl's father waved a dismissive hand at the lot of them.

"Come on Tarl, I'll show you the hull of the Orbitor. Obviously these men have too much time on their hands." A grin prickled at the corners of his mouth as he threw a raised eyebrow at the amused group. "And then we should make our way over to the silk house, you need to make a choice on a design for your sails." He threw a backhanded wave at the miners. "Gentlemen." He called back in goodbye.

"Bye, Parvo," they chorused behind him. "See ya Tarl. Good luck with the Orbitor".

"Thanks for all your help guys." Tarl waved to the miners as they ascended the stairs back to the surface.

The rising sun was caressing the ground with gentle warmth. Smells of crushed basalt and bitter-herb smoke filled the air as they walked toward the 'keeping place' of the Orbitor.

The specialized hull was kept in an enclosure behind a huge granite door to the west of the caves cleverly camouflaged by surrounding rock. When the huge heavy door was opened Tarl's jaw dropped. The majestic elegance of the vessel's glimmering base was overwhelming. In his awe all he could manage was a strange humming sound.

The craft was much larger than he had imagined and fleetingly, he wondered if he were actually capable of maneuvering such a lofty vehicle. Its hull gleamed with a thousand polishes. The basalt had been cut in such a way that it allowed the sliver flecks within the natural stone to project in various degrees of illumination. The resulting illusion was of a night sky filled with the heavenly bodies of the hemispheres. Parvo looked back and forth from the craft to his son enjoying the astonishment in his son's eyes.

Tarl, finally able to move, stepped slowly around the outside of the ship pointing out the images of the constellations. The winged horse of Pegasus raced upward toward the sails; the chained figure of Andromeda searched for her savior; the river image of Eridanus snaked toward the South Celestial Pole and the sickle shape of Leo's head curved up from the sparkling Regulus. At the front of the ship, looped across the bow, were strings of tiny twinkling fire-globes, which had lit up in the darkened surroundings. The mast was thick and tall made of flexible hewn pine, which would bend rather than snap in the high winds of the capricious sky.

Together, they climbed the great ladder to view the deck. The cabin had been fashioned out of Baltic pine (his father's favorite wood) and embellished with citrine portholes (his mother's beloved crystal) and bordered with thin tiles of deep blue lapis lazuli (Tarl's most favored stone). The cushioned chairs were blushed with the colors of sunrise and the soft bed was sheltered under a sky-light of pure quartz. Tarl climbed back down again to revere the complete ship; his ship.

Parvo followed him as he rounded the bow intent on seeing his next reaction. Tarl stopped again. He brought his hands to his mouth as his throat went dry. Looping silver letters spelled out the name of his mother: Cymbeline. Tarl's eyes stared at the beautiful lettering. His voice was barely a whisper.

"You've named it after mum," he said unable to take his eyes off the the silver curls. He turned to face his ships creator. "It is the singular most beautiful object I have ever seen. Believe it or not, but I am speechless. There aren't any words to explain how incredible this is."

"Wow I don't think I've been guilty of making you speechless before," Parvo stated trying to keep a straight face.

"It's definitely a first; I'll grant you that dad."

"What do you think then, do I qualify for a hug?" His father's eyes had begun to redden but he quickly checked himself before Tarl could notice. Tarl wrapped his arms tightly around him. "This is your craft son, inspiration was not difficult."

■　　■　　■

The silk house was quite a sight from the air. The sterling silver roof billowed with all matter of colored silks. Some soared high from stalks of bamboo and some were slung low on vines. They swam in the sky like the fish of Atlantis, glistening with the light of the mid-morning sun.

Inside the building was a tranquil open arena. Through a low square opening a fountain played its gentle watery sounds into the well-lit area. Several miniature fire-sticks burned gently along a tiled path leading down to a mossy area propped with bonsai trees. The soft strains of birdsong and breeze wafted somewhere above them. A clear-story of open windows ran the full length of the building just below the roofline allowing the suns natural light to flood in. Hugging the walls were hundreds of uneven bolts of shining fabric. In front of the colorful coils several silk-workers stretched their materials across marble benches; each worker swathed in individually designed robes of silk.

Parvo spotted Mr. Tzau the Master Maker Silksman, carefully instructing one of the workers at a back table and pointed him out to Tarl. Parvo then caught the attention of one of the female workers at a table over to their left and waved to her. The girl's lustrous rose silk wrap was embroidered with a design in pale pink, depicting dragonflies maneuvering their way from the base of the cloth up toward the high collar of her throat. Her long black hair swung slightly as she moved toward them, her wrap slightly confining her movements.

"Good morning Mr. Parvo," she chimed as she approached, her head bowed respectfully, "you have come at such a very good time."

"I thought everyone knew my timing was impeccable," Parvo teased.

Tarl said nothing as he watched the beautiful girl exchange pleasantries with his father. He thought he had never seen anyone quite this lovely before. Her pale heart-shaped face was made more so by the blackness of her wavy glossy hair. Her large gray eyes angled upward toward the far edge of her eyebrows making her seem amused and mysterious simultaneously. Her nose was petite and very slightly peeked and her lips were small but full like a question waiting to be asked.

"Tarl, meet Opal." Tarl reached for her delicate hand. "Opal has been working with me to create the style of sail the Orbitor will require."

Opal smiled sweetly and tilted her head toward her toes in greeting. Tarl copied her bow.

"Pleased to meet you," he said in his deepest tone. "I am dying to see what you have come up with. My father has been terribly secretive about this whole thing."

A shy giggle escaped her lips. Her downcast eyes rose to meet his. Tarl felt swallowed up by her fathomless gray stare.

"Also, I am pleased to meet you." Respectfully, her eyes descended. Her tone was gentle but her accent was foreign to him. It didn't sound like the way Mr. Tzau spoke.

Parvo tried not to show his amusement at their exchange. To give his son time to cool his reddened cheeks, he took over for a moment.

"Well, fill me in," Parvo announced, "show me the designs and we will choose one," Parvo said as he gestured toward her table.

"Perhaps one of your favorites," Tarl encouraged her. She bit her lip and giggled again. The sound was like bubbling music to him; a xylophone under water.

The designs were astonishing. Tarl could not fathom the imagination that had created them. There were several to choose from. They varied in size to suit the dimensions of the main sail and the other smaller sails. The first silk sail he saw had a rainbow stretching from the left hand corner and bursting into a flame colored sky. The second appeared to be a sheer sheet of ivory but as he moved away from it, it spun with luminous colors: greens, blues, pinks and violets. The next was a patchwork of orange and greens carefully embroidered with symbols of peace and luck and so it went on. Tarl's father approved of them all but asked Tarl to decide. They were all remarkable. How could he choose just one? He was about to try to make a choice when she quietly interrupted.

"There is just one more," her gray eyes peered up at him through long lashes. She beckoned both of them over to one of the largest tables at the back. As they approached she tugged on some ropes hanging from the high ceiling: A lustrous plane of midnight-blue silk slowly unfurled before them. It was embossed with mother-of-pearl shells representing the silver moons and planets of their universe with hundreds of tiny opals used to replicate the galaxies. In the very top corner was his mother's name in the same looping style of writing shown on the basalt hull. As he looked closer he realized that entwined through the letters was the unmistakable stitching of the family crest: An arch of colored bands.

"As you asked, I have displayed my favorite." Opal gestured to the hoisted sail. Glancing up and down she took fleeting glimpses of their expressions. Momentarily she worried that her boldness may have been impolite but the audience she faced revealed only pleasure and she felt more at ease. "You like this one best, yes?"

Tarl's father broke the silence.

"What an extraordinary piece of work Opal. You have, as usual, outdone yourself." He looked across at Tarl for his approval.

"It's perfect," Tarl declared. "Thank you so very much." He couldn't have imagined a more marvelous silk. "I will think of its creator everyday in flight."

"I am glad you like it," Opal tittered delightedly. Her eyes met his and she sensed she had balanced the requirements nicely. She bowed her head again.

Parvo suggested Tarl help her fold it while he went to talk to Mr. Tzau. As he began to move away he turned his head back towards them and smiled.

"And wrap those others up too please Opal. One we'll use as a spare for the Orbitor and the others I can use on my next designs." The workers all looked in his direction unable to hide their surprise. No one had ever bought all the designs for a single job. "How's that?!" He laughed loudly. "I'm going to design a ship to fit a sail!" Mr. Tzau nearly tripped over a bolt of silk as he hurried over to greet his generous friend the Master Maker Builder.

Opal's creamy cheeks were flushed rosy-red matching her silk wrap. Tarl thought she couldn't have looked more astonishing. He bent his face low to catch her downcast eyes.

"They are the most wonderful sails I have ever seen you know."

"Oh, thank you so very much. I like to create things of the people's mind." A gentle smile rested upon her face as her voice became a whisper. "Sometimes I can see inside." She hoped she had not said too much.

Tarl nodded not really understanding what she meant but for some reason it didn't seem to matter. Strangely, he did not feel the need to reply. It was as if a spoken word would take away from the moment. He had definitely never met anyone like her. His gentle hand on her shoulder urged her toward the sails and they folded, smoothed and folded in silence.

■   ■   ■

Lunch turned into a picnic. Tarl and his father settled their craft on the outskirts of a meadow and spread a patchwork blanket under an apple-tree blooming with late blossoms. Below them trickled a gently flowing stream where, directly to their west, lay The Towers of Independence; their huge columns boldly rising from the hills beyond. The swell of crickets chirping in the warm breezes rose as they settled to eat feeling decidedly happy with themselves. Their experience at the silk factory had simultaneously brought them closer together whilst also motivating the new feelings of independence each would have to deal with very soon.

Parvo had made several sandwiches that morning and had heated a large urn of orange and lime tea before take-off. They sat under the white blossoms in the warm sun and picked and swapped sandwich rounds between them laughing all the while.

"I thought you liked fish sandwiches." Parvo chuckled as Tarl passed another quarter to him.

"I do." Tarl was smiling in reaction to his father's new-found cheer. "But today I like tomato and pickles even more."

Parvo accidentally swallowed and laughed at the same time causing him to cough and choke similtaneously.

"Tea?" Tarl spluttered, just managing to pour a cup after spilling a generous amount on his pants. There was no explanation for their moods, Tarl thought, but for the first time in a long time he was having fun with his dad.

When Parvo had finally composed himself he wrapped a strong arm around Tarl's shoulders and pulled him close.

"I am so proud of you son," he said rubbing Tarl's shoulders before pulling away to look directly into his son's eyes. A brief recollection of Tarl running toward him after after his first day of school flashed in his mind. It seemed like only yesterday that his small child leapt into his arms bursting with news as Cymbeline beamed at the two of them.

"I haven't done anything yet." Tarl eddied. "But I sure am proud of you. The Orbitor is amazing."

"Yeah, it's pretty good isn't it?" Parvo replied with a wink.

"Ha ha. Actually, it's completely incredible. No wonder you've been working so much lately. That ship is undeniably the most incredible wind-ship ever created." Tarl looked for words to explain himself. "It's strong and gentle at the same time." He shook his head unable to explain properly. "You've outdone yourself."

"With a little help from my friends," Parvo nodded.

"Yeah, you've made some good friends, I must admit."

"I take it you liked my favorite silk designer, Opal?" He tossed a grin in Tarl's direction.

Tarl blushed and pinched his lips but he couldn't hold the thought in.

"I've never seen anyone like her before," he tried to correct his gush and cleared his throat before claiming in a much deeper tone, "and of course her craftsmanship is extraordinary".

"Indeed, yes, her *craftsmanship*," Parvo teased mockingly, "nothing to do with her perfect features and creamy skin I suppose?" Parvo was beaming. "I knew you'd like her."

"Dad." Tarl's voice was filled with the embarrassment only a parent could instill.

Parvo sat back again, his voice becoming more somber.

"Opal has had a rather sad life you know. She could do with a friend." He paused and a smirk returned. "Especially such a handsome one."

"Dad!"

"Oh come on now, show us yer stuff."

Tarl rolled his eyes.

"Stop it dad."

"Oh, come on then, let your father have a good look at his growing son."

"There. That good enough?" Tarl flexed his arms to show his sinewy muscles.

"See, you've just got to respect your talents." Parvo said bluntly.

"Ha, ha," Tarl's deadpan face cracked. He flopped back onto the ground next to his father. Parvo started to laugh so hard he began to wheeze. Lying down on the ground Parvo continued making whistling sounds until his breathing eased. The sunshine fell across his face, warm and kind. Tarl rolled beside him wondering what had gotten into his father. He hadn't seen him like this for years.

"How come I have never seen her before?" Tarl finally asked.

"When was the last time you visited the silk factory?" Parvo's raised eyebrows were making a point.

"I'm not sure," Tarl was thinking now. It must have been a long time ago. "A while," he said feeling a little guilty.

"Mmm," Parvo brushed Tarl's embarrassment aside, "she had to study design for a long time before she was allowed to craft the materials. But she has been creating sails for me for a while now."

Tarl nodded but he wasn't really listening. There was another question that was prodding at his mind and it wouldn't go away.

"Dad," he whispered not completely sure he wanted his father to hear, "something's changed."

Parvo turned to face his son. He felt it too but how could he explain something he wasn't sure he understood himself? At least he could start with what had happened the night before. He would leave it at that for now.

"I know son. I cannot quite explain it but I do want to try."

"Something changed last night didn't it?"

"Last night, yes," his father took a moment. He could only tell him what he knew to be the truth. "When I thought you had fallen asleep I left your room and went and sat on my bed. You know how I talk to your mother before I sleep?"

"Yeah," Tarl was nodding picturing his father's regular practice.

"Well, I was thinking about how you were going to leave; knowing you were going to leave. I just felt sad. I mean, of course I'm going to miss you so much, and I felt a bit miserable and lonely, and I just wanted her back just for a moment, to tell me it would be alright..." Parvo shook his head knowing how foolish it sounded.

"I do that too sometimes," Tarl sensed his father's discomfort and turned his eyes away pretending to play with a strand of grass near his thigh.

"You do? I didn't know that. Does it make you feel closer to her?" Parvo asked more confidently, "Like she's still listening?"

Tarl nodded at the grass.

"Anyway," Parvo began feeling like he should have had this talk a long time ago, "I asked her to give me strength. I told her I couldn't do this without her help." He shook his head as he remembered what happened next. "In the most fleeting moment of my life I felt her presence," his voice was a sigh. "Honestly, I can't tell you exactly what happened but I do know she came to me. I thought I might have imagined it, but now I know it was real. The room flooded with her light and then it was like I…" he wished he had his wife's sense of language. His brow furrowed in an attempt to make sense of it. "All I can tell you is, that I know her essence still somehow exists, I felt it. It's like she filled my emptiness with enough love to be able to do this. I won't be alone."

Tarl remembered the flash of light he had seen the night before.

"I saw the light," he said simply.

His father stared wide-eyed at his son feeling an even greater sense of strength.

"You saw it?"

Tarl nodded.

"After you left my room I was looking at the stars wondering how you would be all by yourself and I glanced toward the hallway. A glow flooded passed the door and before I could try to understand what it was I fell asleep. Just like that. I don't know exactly what I dreamed but I have a feeling the dreams were important. Perhaps I'll remember them later." Tarl didn't sound convinced.

Parvo was smiling calmly.

"Your mother sent you destiny. That was always promised." Cymbeline's smiling image spun across Parvo's mind: Auburn flowing hair, green almond-shaped eyes, soft sun-warmed skin, high cheekbones and wide gentle smile. "She always said if anything happened to her she would find a way."

"A way to what?"

"A way to invite your destiny."

"What do you mean, 'my destiny'?" Nothing was making sense now. Words were spiraling around him; unlinked; meaningless.

"Oh son, there are so many things you do not know. Your mother and I discussed how much information we would give you and in what stages of your growth but to be honest, when she passed on, I couldn't summon up the courage to admit that her destiny was your destiny." Realizing what the implication was he quickly added, "Oh, I do not mean anything to do with her passing…I mean the destiny she had to fulfill while she was alive; your destiny now."

Tarl had always known that his heart held something different, but all he had to refer to were memories from a childhood that seemed so long ago he was unsure how distorted the recollections were. Sometimes it seemed as if gaping holes stretched across whole periods of time preventing him from remembering even some basic things. He tried to pull his thoughts together.

"What exact destiny is that?" Tarl had turned to face his father and leant on a bent elbow, intrigue creeping forward.

"Unfortunately, I can't tell you that. Your mother was to hold the truth until you came of age. She could not, out of law you understand, tell me what your future held." Parvo swallowed, "I did know though, that at some point you would have to take over her design and I knew it was very important. Because of your mother's passing, your uncle Rembeu must now complete her task. I was told you would be given knowledge as the situation required. I am wondering if your dreams have something to do with this. Perhaps they are telling you that it is the right time for you to make your journey."

All mirth had dissolved. Tarl's thoughts were swimming. He felt as if someone had cast him into space alone; a black void of loss. And yet, he also felt as if her were part of a much greater whole; part of the blackness that threatened to envelope him. There were secrets he was not being told but he understood that this was the way. There was no point in continuing a conversation that would just go round in circles.

"When am I to leave?" Tarl's voice was matter of fact.

"As soon as we put the finishing touches to your ship and complete preparations for the voyage." Parvo was surprised and grateful the conversation had turned to a subject he could explain: Wind-ships and preparations. He couldn't tell Tarl everything. Not now. Not like this. "I will need to go over maps and plans with you and make sure you're fully versed in every possible problem that could occur during your flight."

"And that would be about…?" Tarl wanted a definite time frame to work with.

Parvo took a deep breath, "About a spell."

"Seven moonspells? That's it?" Tarl sat up in shock. "But there are so many things to do."

His father raised his mug and took a last swig of tea.

"Well then, we had better get a move on hadn't we?"

■   ■   ■

Tarl decided he would not fly back with his father but would take one last afternoon to walk across the stretching terrain of his homeland. Parvo agreed and suggested they attach the new sails the following day and discuss preparations more fully when Tarl returned home. They packed away the picnic remains and gave each other a warm hug. Tarl watched his father's ship slide upward into the wind. He held an arm up in a gesture of farewell until the ship had successfully dissolved into the clear turquoise sky.

The trek would be a long one but Tarl was grateful for the time to collect his thoughts, assess the recent events and ponder what the future may hold. At least, he thought, he could collect the crystals Rembeu had buried at the center of the Stone Circle to purify them. The words his uncle had spoken so long ago echoed clearly in his mind.

'Remember the next time you come to visit you must bring the crystals from within the Stone Circle.' Rembeu had talked of his intentions to collect these for his harmony predictions but Tarl sensed they were a little more important than that. He realized that Rembeu would have known he would be called; that was the providence of Keepers. Tarl couldn't believe no-one had prepared him for this. Whirling fragments of dreams started again to interrupt his thoughts: Bright colors flashing between two mirrors held to face each other. He couldn't make sense of the images.

Tarl blinked them away and tried to think about something else. He would need to find some local nettle weed to wrap the crystals in. With a quick overview of the land he realized he needed to head south-west in the direction of Horseshoe Valley where, after rounding the south wall, he would head towards The Locked Gate of Gold Glen and then course north-west across to Still Hill to say a last farewell to his mother's grave-place. The flashes receded as he pushed them into blackness; into their own void.

The scent of apple blossom followed him as he strolled down an incline toward Shady Rocks River. Looking skyward the bright early afternoon sun allowed him to gauge the time. He crossed over the arched wooden footbridge stopping at its peak to survey the clear running waters of the river.

Once over, he sauntered along the sandy banks of the riverbed finally stopping where the waters spilled into the bottomless lake. Here, he stood and marveled at the large oval shaped crystal of the Moon Gate set at the center of the river: All these centuries it had endured the surging waters without having ever shifted from the river stones. No one understood how the Ancients had managed to implant the 'window' into the smooth water-polished river-stones but all were aware of its power.

Rays of colors blazed from the core of the large pane like a spectral halo. Legend said it symbolized its opposite: A 'house without windows'. It was said that its purpose was as a reminder to keep hearts and minds open, to see change as a positive and to not close the self up to the mysteries of life. These days, however, the most popular reason people made the trek out to this spot was to see the images within the crystal pane. For each it was different.

Tarl took another step. He turned to face the oval pane. The prism of colored light stretched out into the breeze and evaporated leaving the glass so clear it became invisible to the eye. Taking a deep breath, he waited. A vision would come eventually.

A three-dimensional scene began to radiate across and through the glass as if the scene were continuing beyond the Moon Gate's edges. The vision was certainly was not what he expected but apparently his life was going to be very different from anything he had ever anticipated.

It was difficult to make sense of the image, but he knew he had seen enough. How could it be? It seemed impossible. But he knew the Moon Gate could not show untruths. He turned away. The window burst with bright white light and then closed.

Tarl treaded on in a daze. Confusion was a hard task master. How had his father had the Orbitor ready for him just in time to take the journey? Parvo had said he didn't know about this journey while the wind-ship was being built but Tarl didn't believe him. Why would he lie? Then there was the strange pull of his uncle's call and the change in his father. And, of course, there were the dreams and *now* this vision. He felt a sudden and uncharacteristic surge of anger toward his father for keeping all of this from him. How many years had Parvo let him feel like a misfit? At least he would get the truth out of Rembeu. Maybe then things would start making sense.

Tarl was jolted from his abstraction as something caught underfoot. He reached down and plucked a shard of emerald from the sole of his shoe. The sandy skirt of the bottomless lagoon lay beneath his feet. Lately the lagoon was coughing up all matter of gems from deep within the mantle and had strewn them across the sparkling sands. Deep beneath the surface the magnetic forces were reacting with structural changes and heat and the results were an eruption of fractured crystal clusters and fragments of colored stones; destruction and beauty meeting.

Reaching a Y-junction, Tarl followed the finger-posts which led to a path through the pine forest. He treaded across the pine needles, under cover from the sun, smelling their unique tang and kicking their fallen remains across the forest floor until, once again, the light broke through and he walked out onto the valley floor. The ground was studded with lakes that swam like pancakes in the golden glow of afternoon.

Tip-toeing across the terraced landscape toward the highest part of the valley, he stopped at one of his favorite spots where a natural balcony jutted out from the grassy green hillside. He moved over to the ancient stone chair perched solidly at the very edge of the precipice and took a pew, to wait just a moment in his life, to absorb all he was leaving behind, to feel the world rising within him.

Tarl looked up toward the sun and decided it was time to move on. There were many things to do. Its warmth now flooded the ground and Tarl removed his out-shirt to let the sun bath his nut-colored skin.

Thoughts flowed readily as if given access by some higher source. He was reminded of the night before. His father truly believed that his mother had visited. Tarl believed it was entirely possible and tried hard to be glad but a cruel and persistent idea pushed at his thoughts: If his mother had come to visit why had she not visited her son as well? There were a million excuses. Either way it would not help him. Seeing his father without those black circles under his eyes from lack of sleep would have to be good enough.

Taking one last look at the plains surrounding him, he moved gingerly around the edge of the ledge. Once back on solid ground he traversed the long winding path of the upper valley following the length of the river toward the Stone Circle: The most ancient of sites in Calatia. The site was claimed to be over three hundred thousand orbits old.

Tarl had to first walk across several acres of wet lands where he collected the protective nettle weed to wrap the crystals in. The fields and marshes he traversed were reasonably dry due to the lack of rain over the last season-cycle. The weather had changed so much over the last period that people were finding it almost impossible to predict conditions. Even the Tellers could find no basis for it.

The calls of birds resounded across the hills a little too early for feeding time. He followed the grassy-green path and turned left at the rocky outcrop toward the narrow entrance of Horseshoe Valley. Under the steep slope he ducked through the tapered entrance to see the valley open out into a breathtaking vista. He traipsed along the base of towering rock walls, slowly rising up the incline until he could see the ancient rocks jutting vertically from their grassy knoll far ahead.

At the major pass near the chicory mill, Tarl turned toward the sun and headed blindly into the bright light. Many foot lengths ahead of him he could see the sight that amazed him every time. Seven shards of granite broke though the soil charging upward toward the sun; the ring spinning in the oranges of the afternoon.

Slowly and reverently Tarl walked toward the Stone Circle. For a moment he stood outside its granite guards, each representing one of the seven creatures of our souls. With a deep breath he stepped over the exalted pass and stole into the ring. He tried to find the absolute center by looking skyward.

Legend had it that each stone guarded one creature from a time so long ago that it was unremembered by any that lived today. Each of the seven creatures had sacrificed themselves to be preserved within the rock thereby ultimately saving all future souls from becoming extinct.

It was said that when the sun poured into the circle at a very precise moment during the course of a thirty thousand moon-spell cycle the stones held strong their memories and allowed their forms to be released. At this time each creature emerged from its stone and fought its 'opponents' without physical force. A death would destroy all the souls that that creature protected. This process allowed them to reconnect with the planet and renew their pledges.

Unfortunately, each event was lifetimes apart and no person living now had ever seen this occur. But still, the circle was a supreme merge, a heady ultimatum that only the heroic examined.

Tarl took one long deep breath and knelt. After performing the faith-rites according to custom, he bowed his head and placed his palm to the fertile ground trying to sense the vibrations of the buried crystals. Breathing deeply, he prepared. The vibrations were slightly north-west of his position. When he found the spot he began to dig into the mossy soil. One foot-length below the surface he wrenched up seven generator crystals. The bright sun reflected off their cut sides as he brushed away the dirt. He watched delightedly as their crystalline surfaces began to dazzle. Each looked clear and open.

Rembeu would be pleased. As he held them in his hands Tarl's instinct told him that they would be a crucial part of his journey. He would have to learn to trust his instincts now. As he began to wonder why he had suddenly thought of these crystals after such a long time, the stones began to glow. Each breathed with a different color as if filling themselves with fresh air.

Tarl quickly wrapped them with the nettle weed and placed them in a cloth envelope before tucking them into the slope bag around his waist. A strange but comforting vibration hummed inside the bag for before quieting. Emerging from between the stones Tarl exhaled with relief.

A flash of light struck his eyes. Tarl looked over to his left where The Locked Gate of Gold Glen stood rising from its grassy summit, its golden door jazzing with sunlight. Solid gold and lustrous, it held its position; a lone body always locked. It was unknown where the key was held. No one had ever known it to be unlocked but it was said that once opened it performed like a portal to another place, maybe even another time. Tarl guessed the truth would not be found out in his lifetime. Another mystery to tease truths.

Striding the short distance to Still Hill, he climbed the west-facing rise where the late afternoon sun was casting a long shadow, and sat beside the small pane of arched citrine perched at the head of his mother's grave and pondered his father's inscription.

'Dreams of Destiny will Perchance Find us Once Again'.

Tarl placed his hand on the ground and began to talk to his mother. Words flowed easily. There were so many questions. He closed his eyes, silently hoping for a miracle.

The shadows slowly stretched their arms out across the land but nothing happened. Wistfully he smiled and tenderly patted the grassy rise he sat on.

"I guess I have to make my own decisions," he whispered, "I love you," he said as he rose. His eyes circled the sky, "and I know you're there somewhere."

Descending the hill, Tarl made his regular trip past the fields and vineyard; warm smells of wild freesias tangling in the air. He wandered under bird-filled fruit trees listening to their songs until he reached home.

At the front gate he stood still. For a fleeting moment he had to check that this was his house. All the winding weeds in the front garden had been cut and cleared allowing the beauty of the undergrowth to flourish in the late sunshine. The fountain had been cleared of the climbing aspidistra and sprouted a trickling stream for the first time in a very long time.

Tarl strode up the grassy incline feeling quite amazed. Dodging the large pile of cuttings and underbrush along the path he called out to his father.

"Dad?" There was no response. He trod up the back path toward the rear garden. "Daaad, I'm home." Tarl hardly recognized the place. The matted weeds at the back fence had been pulled away revealing bright purple irises. The lawn had been mown and felt lush beneath his feet. The small gazebo they called the Star-glass House had been cleared of straggling ivy, and the glass walls rising up toward a ceiling of carefully shaped curved glass, which magnified the night sky for star gazing, were crystal clean. Long ago, Tarl used to sit there to contemplate the world above. Now he would be able to see out of it.

To the center of the yard a wooden table was dressed and set for eating. Crystal glasses and gold cutlery sat on a green silk table cover waiting to be used.

"Dad?" Tarl called again as he looked for some explanation.

A rustling sound followed and several shaking branches snapped and groaned.

"Tarl!" His father called out. A scratched face emerged from the corner brush. A bright smile and open arms greeted him.

"What do you think?"

"Did you do this all by yourself?" Tarl paused trying to gather his thoughts, "In one afternoon?"

"Oh. Yeah, not bad for an old man is it?!" Parvo's broad face swiveled from left to right perusing his hard work.

"It's incredible!" Tarl could not control the feeling of another time and place. He felt transported back to a world that had left him long ago.

"You should have told me what you had in mind. I would have helped. We could have done it together."

"Well to be honest," Parvo said, "I hadn't planned to do anything this grand. I came home from work early so we could spend some time together: You know, bought some special ingredients for supper, thought we'd share an apple-ale, have a chat," he paused for a moment, "I came home and …well everything looked so messy… I thought your mother would……" he shook his head. "Oh Tarl I just saw this place through your mother's eyes," he looked up to face his son directly. "I let it get in such a mess."

"Not anymore. It looks perfect. Just like mum used to keep it. " Tarl was nodding and smiling delightedly, "It's brilliant."

Parvo proudly scanned the surrounds.

"And in honor of this rather promising moment I have decided that an outdoor meal would be an appropriate way to celebrate the occasion." He gestured toward the table.

Tarl's eyes settled on the cloth and he realized this was a goodbye of sorts. He turned his gaze back to his father. A flush of guilt rose up as he remembered the anger that had felt toward him earlier. Perhaps he could find a way to tell his father how thankful he was tonight.

"Oh this is great dad. We haven't eaten outdoors for so long. What can I do? What do you need help with?"

"Well I could use some help clearing up all these cuttings and weeds and putting them on the compost pile."

"Yeah, of course." Tarl scooped up a heap of debris before looking for the non-existent compost pile. "Ahh, dad?"

"Oh, right, um, what do you think about over there?"

"Compost pile coming up," Tarl stated confidently as he threw his load next to their backyard hut.

Working together, they quickly removed all the refuse. When they had finally completed their work they stood and checked the results both nodding satisfactorily. The light was disappearing so they lit several fire sticks, driving them into the ground around the table. Tarl dribbled a little citronella oil on them to keep away the insects as they burned.

"Wait there," Parvo said as he suddenly disappeared into a dark shadow. Tarl peered into the dark wondering what he was up to. Suddenly, high in the branches of the trees above him, a string of colored gas globes lit up like small balloons. "Hey." Parvo reappeared, "*Now* we can have a party." They both cheered and fought each other all the way to the water-room, to wash, before organizing dinner.

A feast of summer fare was laid out. A layered salmon dish was served on fresh pea pancakes and trickled with the oils of avocado and citrus. Small fillets of chicken were coated in a spicy herb crust and laced with a pomegranate dressing. There were baked baby potatoes, eggplant crisps, and a large salad bowl filled with greens from the garden. They chewed on sour-dough bread and washed it all down with his father's home brewed sparkling apple-ale.

By the time desert came round they were both quite merry. Tarl thought it was one of the most perfect nights he could remember. In the temperate evening they sat talking and nibbling from a platter of mulberries, blueberries and raspberries. The moon had raised high into the cloudless deep blue night and the stars glistened; yellow, blue and white.

Together they discussed sailing and the use of the magnetic frequency compass as well as the use of the many other ship instruments. They talked of map reading and possible dilemmas Tarl may come across during his voyage and sighted the prominent constellations that would guide him at night before beginning an intricate plan of the proposed trip. It was decided that when Tarl finally settled at his uncle's, the vehicle would remain there. Essentially, Tarl was now the proud owner of the first of the Orbitor series. Tarl would send a messenger back to Calatia with the logs of documented information from his journey and forward any changes he felt could be made to improve the wind-ship. Once his father had received the information he could begin to build the specialized Orbitor Series and release them into the market. They laughed about how celebrated his father would become and how Tarl would have to make an appointment to see him.

As the night drew on, the conversation turned toward shared memories and thoughts about life. Tarl began talking about his mother, asking questions a child might ask; wanting reassuring reminders of an ever-fading image.

Tarl's father really was a wonderful storyteller. Words rolled forward like a melody, dancing up and down with images. He had always said that was the reason Cymbeline had fallen in love with him: Perhaps such an imaginative and interesting woman loved having someone to entertain that imagination. Parvo's favorite story was about the day Tarl was born. Cymbeline and Parvo had been picnicking by the jeweled riverbed of Shady Rocks River. It had been a Thursday. 'Thursday's child has far to go,' his mother had always whispered sadly on his birthdays as if preparing him for this very future.

When Cymbeline had a sudden onset of contractions Parvo had initially been terrified and had wanted to run for help. She had begged him to stay and Parvo realized, of course, he couldn't leave her. It was obvious that their son would not wait to enter the world and was finally born in the loving embrace of his parents, just the three of them together in such a wondrous moment. They named him Tarl. It was a reference to the ancient language which roughly translated as 'rising moon' and gave the family a happy new start.

This memory sparked many others and Parvo relayed them with charisma and humor. And, somehow, woven into the discourse and laughter, was a constant reassuring love that bound them both. When they finally retired to bed they slept soundly and without disturbance.

■　■　■

The following morning they rose early again and shared breakfast. Parvo instructed his son to make the most of his time here.

"Go and visit your friends, have some fun," he declared. In turn he would make some finishing touches to the Orbitor and present it the next day for Tarl's approval.

"But we were going to attach the sails together?"

"Oh, that can be done by one of the Makers. Then you can see it finished. Any other changes can be made in the next few suns. Everything else will be ready in five suns." Parvo was surprised at how level his voice sounded as he talked. Inside his head, the word 'five' seemed to crash like a cymbal.

"Five?" Tarl's voice was barely a whisper. It wasn't enough time. He felt the panic rise like a tidal wave.

"Tarl, it's going to be alright," Parvo said trying to sound confident. "I promise." He wished he could take those two words back as soon as they came out. He had only made one promise to Tarl all those years ago and he had had to go to terrible lengths to make it so.

"Yes, you're right, I'll be fine," Tarl lied, "that's plenty of time."

■   ■   ■

The next few suns seemed to drift by as if Tarl were in a daze. He had viewed the finished craft and was unbelievably impressed with its majesty. Seeing the completed vessel with its shining midnight blue sails and its highly polished hull shimmering with sunlight reminded him of those initial feelings of awe. His father had truly outdone himself. Surprisingly for Tarl, even his father had shown uncharacteristic pride.

Together they had spent a great deal of time discussing flight paths and flying techniques but his father had felt it was also important for Tarl to spend time with his friends. Although Tarl was anxious to try to explain why he was leaving he had no idea how to tell them without sounding purposefully secretive. He found a group of his closest friends at Pinpoints Park where they often played spinball.

Beyond the spinball field several other groups were involved in a challenge of pin-pointing. Although there was great skill involved in executing the shooting of a pointer without it shattering, Tarl had not aimed a pointer since his mother's death. In the past he had been known for his excellent technique but now he felt a shudder every time he saw one. No one ever asked him why he had stopped shooting and he was glad of that. Spinball was much more fun anyway and even though he quite enjoyed playing the game, he was just as happy on the sidelines watching the players maneuver the ball as it spun in the air changing colors. Joining his friends on the field, he took a quick pass before affecting a terrific high velocity spin, which brought cheers from everyone.

They were all very curious about his upcoming adventure and quizzed him about the trip. To his relief it seemed his friends were not surprised at all that he was about to leave. Unbeknownst to him, it was generally understood that he was unlike the others in the town and that some day he would have to face challenges because of it. And he certainly wasn't going to be doing that here in Calatia. Hearing this made him feel even more disconnected but their acceptance of his dissimilarity was strangely reassuring.

Their afternoon of spin ball shone with moments of laughter and jokes. Humorous memories of their lives together were spilled and splashed across the playing field like pieces of dreams. The spinball would surge upward into the sky flashing colored rays of light and in the moments it took to fall back down someone would shout: 'Hey, remember when......' and they would all laugh whilst still jostling to catch the ball. Tarl had never felt so much at home. The irony was not beyond him.

As difficult as it had been, they finally said their goodbyes. He promised to send them messages when he could and let them know about any exciting news that he might find out. As the afternoon began to pull the sun toward the horizon, Tarl waved one last time, turned from his friends and without looking back, walked away. Their laughter and chatter grew fainter and fainter until the only noises he could hear were the rustle of wheat stalks and the hum of bees.

During this time he took several walks to his favorite places trying to take mental pictures of the sights so that he would remember them on his long journey. He also spent time making a few slight alterations to the ship and consenting to minor changes on several other matters.

The most enjoyable day was the last day before take-off. Parvo had, without Tarl's knowledge, informed the town that his son would be making his Grand Journey and piloting the new Orbitor on a global mission. The townsfolk had rallied together and chosen to wish him farewell with a huge celebration. It would be a festival to guide him toward fortune.

Several 'Maker' stalls had been erected all across the town-center. The streets were lined with all manner of colored market stalls and were shaded by sheets of rippling fabrics. Striped silks strapped to street poles flapped above his head and colored ribbons twisted and snapped with the rolling breezes. High in the sky a few small wind-ships flew across the clear blue backdrop, their sails shimmering in the sun. The scene was vibrant and exciting.

Banners of painted cloth declared 'Wind-Speed Tarl' and 'Find Luck without Dragon-Wind'.

Traipsing through the streets, he waved to everyone as he passed. He wore his best golden-skin over-shirt that hung loosely over black silk shirker pants: His tanned skin glowing with the reflections of the gold shirt and his green eyes dancing with facets of color in the sunlight.

Street hosts bellowed the values and virtues of the surrounding stall-holders giving a run-down of their goods and wares. Entertainers bounced and bounded along the street encouraging the children to join them. Beautiful dancers swayed and charmed passersby with twirling wrists and long loose flowing garments glinting with jewels.

Tarl strolled past the tables encrusted with hundreds of corals and shells at the 'Pisces Dome'. He inspected the many items of the 'Telescopium' where he found the perfect sky-imager to record his trip and a pocket sized telescope with vast magnification. He smiled and tipped his head toward the Alchemist whose curved glass chests were filled with infused oils, bottled liquids and powders but he refused the summoning Fortune Teller in the small side-arcade. Something was telling him not to ask. Familiar folk lore stories were enthralling a group of children and Tarl stopped momentarily to listen to the Teller of Stories. They made him feel very young again.

Reluctantly, he left the group to find a gift for his father and realized he had no idea where his father was. He had not caught a glimpse of him yet. He rounded the corner of the arcade and strolled onto the street. The next thing he saw caught him completely by surprise.

All thoughts tumbled from his mind as he focused on her incredibly beautiful features. Her slight body was wrapped in a tight fitted lemon silk dress which shone against her creamy skin. Her shiny black hair was looped back into several braids and threaded with fine strands of gold. She was leaning over a tray in the Archery Arena inspecting the bows carefully. Tarl took a deep breath and walked across the street to greet her.

"Well hello there." Tarl was shocked to hear a squeak in his voice. Opal turned to face him, her wide gray eyes meeting his.

"Tarl," Opal's soft accent made his name sound more like an exotic fruit. "I heard there was a farewell for you and thought I must say goodbye." Almost involuntarily her eyes fluttered down again. She liked looking at his face. It was so unusual: High cheekbones and silky tanned skin framed by that shiny straight black shoulder-length hair and those deep green eyes that held such intensity. He looked like the old pictures she had seen of the Wizemen. If she looked deep enough into those eyes she wondered if she would forget everything. It was a strange but compelling feeling.

"Thank you Opal, I am very glad you came." Tarl bent his head a little to try to raise her eyes again. Gray eyes swam up toward him from her heart shaped face. Tarl tried not to stammer but words had never been so hard to get out. "I was going to come to the silk factory to say goodbye but I was worried you may be too busy."

"Oh no, we have been given the afternoon off for the festival," she nodded to the surroundings, "Mr. Tzau said it was a very important day."

Tarl was delighted.

"So you are free for the whole afternoon?"

"Yes, the whole afternoon." She sounded as surprised as he did.

"Wonderful! Would you do me the honor of spending it with me?"

Opal responded with a generous smile and a nod. Tarl was elated. He gestured toward the tray of bows and arrows.

"Are you an Archer?"

"Oh yes." Opal's face lit up with enthusiasm, which quickly became a shake of her head rejecting the implication, "Oh but I only shoot targets." She weighed his interest and continued with a little more confidence. "But it is this display that I wanted to see."

They walked over to a huge display of armory – the ancient art was rarely seen in such an enormous exhibition of wares. Beautifully crafted suits of armor dangled down to meet all matter of weaponry. Although he knew they were only purchased for aesthetic reasons and not for any type of battle Tarl was taken aback.

"You are also an adept swords-woman?" he teased. Some of the swords were nearly twice her size.

"Oh," she looked a little embarrassed, "I was actually wanting to purchase one for you as a parting gift. I worry it could be dangerous for you," Opal said softly, fearing she may have rushed her thoughts. "It is my custom," she sounded almost apologetic.

Tarl felt hypnotized by the soft lilt of her voice.

"It is your custom to worry?" Tarl joked.

"Oh, no," she was shaking her head and smiling feeling both amused and self conscious, "my language is sometimes not correct."

"You speak beautifully," Tarl encouraged her, "I was just teasing."

"Oh, yes, I know." Her cheeks flushed under the gaze of his twinkling sea green eyes and she shifted awkwardly.

"That's very kind of you," Tarl began again, "but I don't want you to spend your savings on me." He caught her disappointed expression and thought his heart might break right there and then. "But I tell you what, if you would like, we could *exchange* parting gifts." Her eyes lifted hopefully toward his. "Perhaps you would allow me to find something for you - to say goodbye also."

"Oh yes, that is a wonderful idea." Her rosebud lips had tipped up into a smile again.

"Did you have a particular piece in mind?" Tarl asked her as he scanned the array of beautifully crafted equipment.

Opal swept her hand across the table, palm down, as if to feel which one was the right one. It stopped above a small intricately carved wooden sword inset with stones of jasper, jet and tourmaline. She picked it up and held it in both hands.

"This is the one." Opal looked at it, her face tilted and serious. "The crafter is from very far away but has given this piece balance." The middle of her right palm ran down the center curve. "See here," her finger pointed to its central point, "it has been inlayed with many protective stones and has been especially made for good luck. I think you will find this a most suitable implement."

"It's really beautiful. Thank you very much." Opal tilted her head in a small bow and handed it to the stall-holder to wrap.

They walked along the street laughing at the goings on and then somehow, they were holding hands. Her skin was incredibly soft and her grasp was delicate but sure. Tarl felt ten feet tall.

"Now it is my turn," he faced her as they ambled along. "What can I buy such a beautiful young lady?"

Opal's face flushed. No one had ever called her beautiful.

"I am in no need of souvenirs," Opal rallied, "I'm afraid I do not need anything." She sounded almost disappointed with herself.

"I know! I know exactly what I want for you." Tarl gasped. He had been struck with an epiphany. "Don't move I'll be back in just a moment."

Opal peered up at him with a smile and raised her eyebrows as she watched him disappear into the crowd. Whatever he had decided, he seemed very happy with the idea. A tingle of excitement sparkled in her stomach.

Opal was enjoying herself more than she had for a very long time. She realized that she had been working so hard for so long that taking a day for herself was almost a forgotten occurrence. Being with Tarl was stirring feelings she could not explain. It had been so long since she had allowed herself to believe in anything good that she felt almost guilty for being so happy. When he had touched her hand an incredible zinging feeling ran up her arm making her heart beat so fast that she thought she may stop breathing. But then he spoke and his words were like sounds she had never heard before. She knew she was imagining it but when she saw him from a distance, like now in the crowd, she thought she could see a glow of white light around him.

The Maker stall holder of Jaded Jewels was a strange looking man. He was guarded and very careful with his words. As he talked he stared right into Tarl's eyes as if he could see a whole world in there. It made Tarl feel extremely uncomfortable. The man would not sell him any item until Tarl had explained exactly who it was for and why. When Tarl had mentioned Opal's name the man seemed curiously pleased. The piece, he said, was going to be very special and it would not be ready until later that day.

Tarl agreed but felt a little disconcerted. This man acted like more of a Seer than a Maker. As soon as Tarl had thought this, the man abruptly told him to go. He felt as if he had just committed to a lot more than a piece of jewelry.

Not long after he headed for the spot he had left Opal and was relieved to find her still there. For a moment he just watched her amazed at the vision. Opal stood chatting with the owner of the Shoppe of Scrolls, her skin luminous in the shaded light and her hair glistening with gold thread. It was as if she was the only person in the milling crowds. She seemed to radiate against a dissolving background.

"I'm glad you're still here. I'm sorry, the stall holder was very talkative," he lied. "I can't pick up the gift until sunset."

"Oh," Opal replied trying to sound mature when really she felt like a little girl on name-day. "That's wonderful." She realized that was a strange thing to say. "I mean..."

"I know what you mean," he said with a gentle smile. The look on her delighted face made him suddenly realize that perhaps she wasn't used to receiving presents. He had an overwhelming feeling of confusion but he tried to focus. "What would you like to do until then?" He asked carefully.

Opal looked around for inspiration.

"There are so many things going on."

It occurred to Tarl that he had not indulged in any of the festive fair.

"Are you hungry?" he asked.

"Mmm, yes, very much." Opal nodded so vigorously Tarl had to stop himself from laughing.

"There's some food stalls over near the green." He nodded in that direction.

"What are the foods of your liking?" Opal asked as they continued their stroll.

"My father would tell you 'absolutely anything'." Tarl made a father-like face. They both laughed. "What do you like?"

"I think perhaps your father may judge my tastes in the same way." She said trying to copy his expression. They laughed again.

They moved around several stalls loading a carved wooden tray with baked rolls, sun-dried vegetables, marinated meats and fresh fruits and then found a small cider stall where they purchased globes of orange cider. They found a quiet table shaded by a stretch of orange cloth and settled.

Opal's appetite impressed Tarl. He thought it was a marvelous contradiction that such a slight and shy girl was able to consume almost the same amount of food as him. This girl was full of contradictions.

Sunset seemed to arrive without warning. Time had flown. A deep red fireball of a sun was settling into the hills behind them. The horizon blazed with oranges and pinks crowned by a deepening blue dome of sky. A Market Host was calling through the streets inviting 'one and all' to join at the riverbank to view the 'imminent' firelights display.

"Firelights!" Opal responded excitedly. "Oh please, can we go and watch them? I adore firelights."

"Absolutely. But first I must pick up your gift. "Wait here. I'll just be a minute." Tarl rushed off in the direction of the Maker Gem-Jeweler.

When he returned he clutched her hand and beckoned for her to follow him. She grabbed his still wrapped sword and let him lead her down toward the river. They joined the crowd by the bank and took a position at the edge of the sparkling moonlit waters to wait for the spectacle. Her lemon silk wrap reflected the ivory moonlight in its threads.

"Your gift," he said as he made the offering.

Opal smiled a sweet immeasurable smile as she opened the small box. Her eyes darted between his face and the present.

Her expression was a gift in itself. And when the smallest of tears formed in the corners of her eyes he knew it was an excellent present.

"It is the most beautiful object I have ever seen," she whispered.

"Then you have neither viewed your own work objectively nor looked in the mirror." This comment encouraged a smile from her but those big gray eyes still swam with sadness.

Opal had never seen anything so perfect. Her name-day had been forgotten long ago and with it a sense of worth. She didn't know how to explain any of this to Tarl and knew how unwise it would be to try, so she concentrated on the piece to stop the emotions overwhelming her.

The chained gold locket was opened by pressing the center. Inside, one half was imbedded with a flawless opal and the other half held a rare small rainbow crystal. She stroked the stones with her fingers.

"They are perfectly aligned," she said with awe.

"It is the meeting of two like-minded souls: A luminous artist and a voyager of the light." Tarl wondered how he had blurted that out. He wasn't really even sure what it had meant.

Opal held the locket to her heart wondering if she had really understood his reference to the 'Light Voyager'. How could it be? There had only been two Voyagers in history. She knew about The Keeper of the Light: The one that Kept Balance, but she had never considered that Tarl's journey had anything to do with that. But no one was really saying what his journey did concern. And then, like a bolt of lightning, she remembered his father's request to include a rainbow motif in her designs – his family's crest was the light spectrum. How could she not have thought of it before? The enormity of the situation unsettled her.

Tarl noticed a stirring of unease in her expression and was about to question her when a familiar voice rang out over the crowd.

"Tarl! Tarl!"

Tarl looked for the source of the voice. The familiar silhouette of his father was approaching.

"I see you two found each other."

Tarl wondered what he was talking about. How had his father known Opal would be at the festival? Suddenly a flood of thoughts swam through his head. His father must have organized for the silk factory workers to have the day off. Everyone knew they were some of the hardest workers in the land. They never took time off. His father was trying to tie all the loose ends before his departure and had not only organized this whole affair but he had thought to make sure Opal made an appearance.

Tarl was grinning. He raised one eyebrow at his father.

"Yes dad, we found each other."

His father returned the same look before turning to Opal and reaching out a hand in welcome.

"Lovely to see you again," he said feigning surprise.

Opal bowed her head in politeness as was her way and offered her hand in greeting.

"Where have you been? I have looked for you all day," Tarl inquired.

His father suppressed a laugh. The notion that his son would be looking for him when he quite obviously had some splendid company right next to him was quite amusing.

"I'm sure you have," he said, sarcasm floating on each word. "I have been helping in the organizing of the firelights display," he paused and checked the skyline. "It's time for the extravaganza." He tousled Tarl's hair.

"Dad." Tarl gave his father a look.

"May I watch them with you two?" Parvo delighted in his son's abashment.

"Of course dad," He said, his eyes implying that it would be, as long as his father didn't do anything else to embarrass him.

"Opal?" Parvo wanted her approval as well.

"Oh yes Mr Argus I would be delighted." She looked directly into his eyes in full confirmation. He caught Tarl's affectionate glance toward her and was drawn to a memory from long ago.

"Wonderful. Let's get comfortable. I brought a blanket." Parvo gestured over to their left.

They moved toward the laid out blanket on which rested a picnic basket filled with delicacies. Tarl peeked inside.

"Hmm," he looked straight into his father's twinkling eyes, "I see you packed an extra plate just in case *someone else* might turn up."

"Hmm?" Parvo wasn't the least flustered. "Well you just never know do you?" He winked at Opal who blushed charmingly.

It was the perfect position to watch the display. They were seated by the edge of the moonlit waters and above them the night sky stretched out waiting to be lit up by burning explosions of light. Crowds were forming in the area around them and the whispering chatter indicated the excitement of the impending display.

Parvo was placing the array of cheeses, pickles, biscuits and cold meats in the center of the trio.

"And now the best bit," his hands were fiddling deep within a silver silk bag. He had their attention. His hand emerged holding an unusually shaped rose-tinted bottle.

It took Tarl a moment to recognize the object. The glass was etched with the arched figure of a woman. In the moonlight the soft glow of color rays curved upward toward the bottle-neck and disappeared at the rounded edge.

"Where did you find that?" Tarl asked in amazement.

"It's the last one."

"The last one?" Opal was intrigued.

Parvo's eyes rested upon hers. Tarl was surprised to see her look at him with such curiosity.

"This, Opal my friend, is the last bottle of what I have lamely labeled as home brew but is what this young man's mother always called wedlock bubble." His convivial words belied his serious expression.

Opal was looking bewildered. Parvo and Tarl laughed out loud.

"Oh stop teasing dad." Tarl was shaking his head. "I think he drank some 'home brew' before he got here."

Parvo, enjoying the joke, lay back laughing while holding the bottle level.

"My mother spent some time trying to perfect a sparkling grape fermentation to celebrate her wedding to..." Tarl looked over at his father and rolled his eyes, "my *father*," he gestured towards Parvo's reclining figure with mock distain. "Anyway, my mother finally made a very nice drop and had it specially bottled with etchings and holograms engraved within the bottles."

"It is incredible." Opal watched the female hologram move as the sun reflected across its surface. Their good-humored repartee made her feel like a part of something special.

"Is this really the last bottle?" Tarl asked.

His father, having now popped it open, had begun filling three glasses. He handed one to Opal.

"Yes son, it's the last one." It sounded so final. He handed one to Tarl. "I guess this is your mother's send off too."

Just as they held the three moonlit glasses up to clink them together, the first spiral of a burning gold firelight burst into the night. It was the prelude to an evening of a spectacular display of twirling colored lights. Tarl reached for Opal's hand and she held it tightly as they delighted in the swirling festoon.

Parvo watched his son under the bursting lights. Already he looked older than he did a few suns before. It was really happening. Destiny had found his son.

3

The Flight

For Tarl, the morning of the flight was filled with such a mixture of excitement and sadness that it was hard to define. His father, however, seemed to know exactly what his son was going through. Tarl was grateful for his tact and assurance.

The conditions for launch were perfect. A slight breeze hummed high above them and except for a few streaks of cloud the sky was blue and clear. Tarl was aboard his new craft before dawn checking and re-checking the instruments for any possible inconsistencies. He ensured that the luggage was safely stored and that his accommodation quarters were not missing anything. His father was also aboard tapping dials and inspecting equipment - Tarl thought, probably for the hundredth time. He guessed it was a way of being near at hand and feeling useful. Finally though, it was decided that all was operational and that it was safe to go ahead with the launch. As the time for take-off was confirmed Tarl caught his father looking rather lost.

"You have built a masterful ship sir," Tarl raised a flattened hand to his forehead copying an ancient salute and attempting to look very serious.

"Thank you Captain," his father copied the gesture, "I am proud to be of service." He inclined his head in a sign of servitude.

"I'll be taking you with me you know," Tarl added.

Parvo raised his head again and smiled at his son.

"You will be taking your mother too." His eyes focused on the looping insignia of 'Cymbeline' on the sail.

Tarl followed his gaze. An image of his mother flashed in his mind and in that instant of memory her eyes smiled at him. He returned the same smile to his father.

"Well, it's time for those not traveling to disembark," Parvo said resolutely. He opened his arms wide. "I love you. You have made us so proud." Parvo's voice caught, "I will miss you son."

"Love you too dad," Tarl whispered as he held his father tightly.

"And," Parvo said as he let go, "don't worry; I'll keep an eye on Opal for you. You know, make sure she is working much too hard to look at any other handsome men."

"Dad." Tarl feigned horror but was actually very pleased that his father was going to look out for her. Even though he had only known her for such a short time he knew she was special and he hated the thought of having to leave her so soon.

Parvo climbed down the netted ladder and jumped the last stretch to the ground. He looked up at his son as Tarl pulled the netting back in. The rising sun of dawn cast an orange halo behind Tarl, blackening his frame into a masterful silhouette. Parvo thought he looked just as a ship's captain should.

The midnight-blue sails were set and Tarl heaved the whole mainsail over to one side.

"Ready when you are dad." He called out with a wave, amazed that his voice was working. "Let her rip."

"Right." Parvo called back trying hard to hold his emotions in check until Tarl had lifted off. "I'll begin levitation."

Parvo had brought a spare levitation-fork as Tarl had decided that he should be the one to commence the ship's first voyage. Parvo tapped the hull, activating the device and a soft ringing sound hummed as the ship gently lifted off the ground.

Tarl's heart was racing. Everything was going as planned but the moment of launch was overwhelming. Emotions came at him from every angle. As he rose his father grew smaller and smaller, but neither stopped waving. It was only when his father appeared as tiny as a spec on the dusty gravel ground that Tarl brought his arm back to his side.

'Right,' he thought as he took a deep breath, 'I must concentrate on the matters at hand.' He checked his compass and made a slight adjustment to the steering. Swinging the wheel to starboard, he sailed into the sun.

Tarl held the helm; sailing fast with all sails set and headed her up into the wind picking up speed and flying quickly over the Calatian Plains. He soared over the local vineyard; the vines so far below they looked like rows of bonsai. The seven stones of the Stone Circle burned with the oranges of dawn looking like shards of blazing glass. For a split second he could have sworn the stones appeared to flash, momentarily transparent and imagined the huge animals growling and circling within their traps. Over Still Hill he sailed as the gleaming grave-plates sparkled their colors toward him and then he turned slightly south in the direction of the silk factory.

A stab of heartfelt sorrow panged in his chest as he soared toward the silk-works where he imagined Opal would be working on one of her beautiful sails. He hoped she would wait for him to return even though he had no idea how long he would be gone. The billowing colored silks on its roof rolled with the breeze. Flying high above the building, he looked down at the roof as he passed.

To his utter amazement and joy he saw a message he could only assume was the collaboration of Opal and his father. An enormous stream of red silk was stretched across the roof of the building rippling against its stone anchors. Emblazoned upon it was a message that read: 'Understanding will smile in this offering of Truth and Light'. It was a good luck message of great importance.

The Light was only offered to beings of a higher understanding; beings worthy of an ultimate sacrifice and it could only ever be offered once. If the Light was offered, that person swore an undying allegiance and would in turn sacrifice themselves if their liege were in need of protection. Filled with wonder that she would make this offering, he waved to the disappearing banner feeling like he was waving goodbye to a part of himself.

Tarl took a deep breath and turned to the front of the ship. He looked ahead toward the rising sun and felt inspired to forge on. As he rose higher the warm smells of the sun-beaten earth slowly subsided and cool fresh salt air filled his nostrils. He pulled on his gloves and a lined jacket and heated himself with hot ginger tea. The Morning was spent sporadically checking the wind direction and enjoying the views.

Over the next few suns he relished climbing out onto the boom where he could sit and watch the dolphins playing in the waters below. The bright skies enabled him to see deep into the ocean. Large turtles coursed without fear and flying fish sprang in arcs across the rippling surface of the turquoise sea. There were many enormous sharks surging through the water with incredible speed and enormous stingrays slapped the surface with such vigor that Tarl almost believed he could hear their splashes high in the air.

Pelicans often circled the ship, their beautiful outstretched wings allowing them to glide with the breeze, and seagulls kept him company when he was close to land. Occasionally he would see old fishing boats sailing on the seas beneath him, some out in the middle of the ocean. Very few of these still existed having been phased out long ago both because of the damage the fuel had caused and the greedy overfishing of the oceans but also because of the dangerous seas. But, every now and then, an antiquities dealer acquired a license and boarded the crafts for whatever reason that drove them to such an unwise task. He admired their bravery against the unpredictable swells but thought their endeavor was much too treacherous.

Fresh winds surged with the ship; all her windward sails pulling. Tarl was glad he was making great speed and able to cover large distances early on in the trip. The jewel-embossed sails sparkled in the sunlight and the sun flecked hull shimmered in the bright blue sky. It all felt quite majestic.

The suns that followed were pleasantly uneventful. He saw only a few small wind-ships in the distance but he never passed close enough to any of them to initiate a greeting. He spent time reviewing his maps and checking and rechecking his instruments. In his free time he lay on deck in the sun reading and thinking. His evenings were spent studying the stars over a warm meal and writing up daily entries in his log and dairy to which he added many sketches of the sights he passed over.

Only sleeping in two-cycle-blocks allowed him to regularly check that his course was consistent. His father's continuous levitation device meant that landing to dock was unnecessary. So, on he flew; the grounds and seas rolling continually behind him.

On the eight sunrise of his journey he found that the morning wind had picked up and was blowing quite strongly. The low-lying cloud was quickly being swept along with him and the higher clouds were growing thick with rising gray. The winds roared across the rolling sands of Sylo and soared and whirled under the Golden Bridge of Antipodes, which jutted from the golden silt; its city having been buried there by countless sand storms. Gales gusted across the Dunes of Dion stirring the grainy dust into tiny tornadoes far below him. Carefully sailing above the huge dunes he managed to barrel across the rolling wind currents.

Tarl began feeling anxious. Beating to windward was putting a huge strain on the beams. He noticed a shift in the wind and decided to change sail. Panic was rising but he would not give in to it. He eased the sheets, dropping both sails as rain began to fall. The wind swirled around the hull and Tarl suddenly found himself wrestling with a tangle of sail wrapped around the mast struts. He was horrified to see the sudden wind shift was causing the mast to bend dangerously. Desperately, he unwrapped the staysail from around the starboard float and soon was given leeway to unbend the mast.

The temperature had dropped dramatically and far ahead he could see dark gray squalls churning across the horizon. The rain was starting to tumble in, blinding him, and the sky had suddenly become menacingly dark. Realizing he had flown straight into a squall of swirling winds he rejected the rising panic. Thunderous clouds crashed and boomed around him and rain sleeted mercilessly. The waves of wind seemed to be trying to pluck the sails from their booms and the rain was pouring over the starboard side making the ship slew around. Tarl trimmed the sails to portside and rode over the waves, rising and falling in swooping motions. Carefully, he maneuvered the ship to counteract them. His control and calm helped him think quickly and adjust constantly.

The flash of a memory almost made him laugh: His father had talked of the romance of sailing the vast skies; the control of a magnificent craft and its graceful lines; the tall mast and strong rigging; the sparkling hull and the billowing silk sails. This was about as far from romantic as Tarl could imagine.

On he sailed, maneuvering across the storms for the rest of the day and into the night. The tempest would occasionally ebb and give him some time to recuperate. By the time he had finally exited the black thundering clouds he was very wet and unbelievably exhausted.

As the skies finally cleared Tarl was surprised to see a full moon smiling down on him in a cloudless dark blue sky. On checking his maps and instruments he was impressed to discover he had not drifted far off course at all. In his living quarters, he changed out of his wet gear and placed a bowl of pumpkin soup in the warmer before returning to the deck. Looking up into that unpredictable sky, he shook his head in awe. He lay the ship ahull, and with all sails set, he glided into the night.

■ ■ ■

In the suns following the storm, Tarl made fast passage across the barren lands of Merit. The only defining feature in this entire desert was the circular formations which curled across the dusty ground. It was only from this height that the many miles of orange crusty dirt became a winding circle, the center of which rose to twice the height of The Towers of Independence. He sat on the bow and viewed the spectacle as he flew across the emptiness wondering if it meant anything, wondering if there was some secret down there.

Finally, one morning, the vast earth below began to show signs of crystallization as Emerald Mountain came into sight. The featureless ground became a carpet of dusty emerald rocks all sizes and shapes. He knew from stories that although it may be beautiful, it was impossible to cross by foot. The ground was very unstable, some said due to the existence of the creatures that stirred below its surface, and with just one wrong move the sharp emeralds could easily cut off a limb. The dark green stones increased in size as he made his way toward Emerald Mountain.

Legend had it that the mountain had been the home of a hermit for hundreds of orbits. Such a tale was great fodder for children but Tarl doubted that adults believed any of it. No one had ever explained either how he had been able to get to the mountain across the emerald covered ground or how he had entered the apparently solid rock-face.

The mountain's glistening transparent walls loomed larger as he approached. The midday sun was shooting rays through its pinnacle and the refractions were firing into the sky burnishing the low thin clouds with shards of bright green. He passed high enough to be safe but low enough to look inside the huge mountain but, unsurprisingly, could see no hermit.

The green-washed sky gradually dissolved into a clear cobalt blue and the rocky terrain below grew thick with ferns and wild flowers, which stayed unchanged for the rest of the day.

At midnight he raised himself from a deep sleep to check the conditions and was delighted to see a huge crystal clear lake shimmying with moonlight below him. By morning he would be passing over Cruit. He was still making good speed. The journey would be quicker than they had originally estimated. Returning to his hammock, he was back in a deep sleep in no time.

The next morning turned out to be quite cool with drizzling soft rain. Tarl rugged up and heated his morning tea. He went out to the helm to study the area below and saw he was flying directly over the red roofs of the Cruit Village. Small fires protected by sheets of bark puffed up smoke as raindrops angled in on them. Their unusual cylindrical homes with their round roofs slick with shine, sat in orderly rows, each surrounded by a circular fence. The Cruit were one of the highest religious orders. No one was allowed to enter the area without express permission. Not a great deal was known about them as they kept to themselves and shunned outside influence. Tarl laughed at the thought of something going wrong right at this moment and having to land in their village.

Far ahead he could see many burning fire-sticks flickering as they were being carried across the hills. The younger pilgrims of the order must have been making a journey somewhere off to the West. Tarl wondered where they could possibly go. He could not see anything in the direction they were heading and his maps certainly did not show anything of significance.

By midday he had out-flown the rains and found strong fresh winds which offered glorious sailing for the next few suns. Except for the quiet anxiety he felt as he navigated one of the magnetic points, which successfully re-ignited the ship's frequency levels, he found this period very enjoyable. Many entries were made in both his log and his diary: He entered thoughts about his father and Opal and his desires for the future, whatever that may hold. Out on the boom, he let the wind rush through his shiny black hair as he watched the world skim by. He read several of the memory-books he had taken for the journey: One on wind sailing, and others on adventurers and pioneers.

On the afternoon of a windy but overcast day he finally pulled out the two tattered books his father insisted he at least browse through. The titles read: 'The Connections between The Light and The Self' and 'Numbers by Color'. They looked rather ancient and certainly well used. He took the first one, wandered out onto the deck and made himself comfortable.

As he opened the cover he gasped as something bright shot out at him. He was horrified to realize that he had inhaled whatever it was. He tried desperately to cough it back out but was completely unsuccessful.

'Oh no,' he thought, 'I've swallowed some kind of ancient bug.' He waited for a moment to see if swallowing ancient bugs could cause illness, pain or possible death, but discovered he felt quite good. He looked at the book and spoke aloud.

"Well, I hope you haven't got any more little surprises like that," and he began to read. Little did he know that as fascinating as the information was, that was not the reason his father had given him the books.

■ ■ ■

The suns following had passed by very pleasantly. Tarl had spent a great deal of time trying to understand the old books but found plenty of opportunities to simply sit and observe his surroundings. The Visce Solais Waterfalls that appeared to flow with ripples of light rather than water especially fascinated him.

Once he had successfully crossed the third and final magnetic point Tarl decided he could sit back and enjoy the remainder of the journey without too much concern until it was time to tack toward his uncle's home.

Only two suns later he became very excited realizing how close he now was. The reality of his destination was finally upon him and the thought of sharing his uncle's life once again, thrilled him.

Tarl stood on the deck wrapped in his waterproof coverall as he approached the Atlas Mountain Ranges. Rain washed the afternoon with a silver luster and a low mist rested on the ground below. Tarl hoped it would clear before having to land. Ahead he could see the Mountain his uncle liked to call home. It rose out of the misty ground like a chieftain.

Tarl's eyes rose to its peak where its grandest feature struck him with wonder every time. It was one of the most sacred phenomenons of the planet: Shooting from the mountain's apex was a spectacular colored beam of light that flew straight up through the sky.

4

Atlas Mountain

As he approached, Tarl realized his uncle had somehow cleared the mist from a flat area of mossy ground at the base of the mountain and laid out strings of lights so that a safe landing could be made.

Trimming the sails tight, he slowly eased the craft toward the ground. Giving himself plenty of time to descend, he sunk lower and lower until he could see his uncle waving madly up at him. Moving gently downwards through the cleared area of sky, he watched the walls of mist rise up beside him.

The craft touched down on a soft covering of ferns and mosses and Tarl threw the anchor lines to his uncle so that they could be tied to the ground pales. He then dropped the sails and inactivated the magnetic frequency compass. Dropping the side ladder, he descended into the arms of his very excited uncle. The misty rain was still falling but neither of them seemed to notice.

"Tarl, my young man. It's so wonderful to see you. I knew you'd be successful at the journey and arrive early so I have kept a vigil to be prepared for your landing."

"Uncle Rembeu! What a marvelous greeting," Tarl paused with a smile and then added, "It's good to be home."

"Ahh." Rembeu threw him a characteristic toothy grin and a wiggle of his head. "You touch an old man's heart."

"What old man, where?" Tarl swished his head from left to right.

"Mmm, and still a terrible sense of humor." They both laughed. He took a good look at his nephew. The boy looked older than their last meeting, but still so young. That was going to change rather quickly. Rembeu suppressed a surge of guilt.

Tarl gazed at his uncle's pale face and bright blue eyes framed by thick straight waist-length chestnut hair, highlighted with ribbons of silver, and knew he belonged. Any concerns he had had about staying here for a long time vanished immediately. Unsurprisingly Rembeu's costume was dazzling with color. He wore several layers of shimmering fine cloth; each wrap imbued with different hues. Their shared colors jazzed, making them appear to move of their own accord.

"How did you manage to disperse the mist for me to land?" Tarl's neck craned upward at the sight.

"Oh, my boy, there is so much to discuss," Rembeu answered as he wrapped an arm around Tarl's shoulders and turned him toward the entrance, "but first of all, I think you are old enough to call me plain old 'Rembeu' – none of this uncle rubbish. Huffedy! Your mother would be horrified if she thought I was making you call me that all the time." He winked as his arm squeezed Tarl's shoulder.

"Well, 'plain old Rembeu', I think she would be more horrified if I starved to death."

"Oh, you've probably been living off stale bread and raindrops for weeks." Rembeu replied mockingly. "Come quickly, before you faint."

Tarl laughed loudly at this but didn't want to confess how hungry he really was. Food just didn't seem to fill him up like it used to.

They moved toward a path that wound through tall ferns and strange looking trees with smooth silver trunks and arching branches of long twisted sea-green leaves. The drizzle made everything wet and gleaming.

"Oh by the way I dug these up from The Stone Circle." Tarl pulled out the bag of crystals from his vest pocket. "I'm not really sure why but it seemed important at the time." Rembeu looked delighted.

"Young man, you are the most wonderful nephew on the planet. Wait till Umbra sees these. Come on let's go find her." Rembeu *was* pleased, deeply pleased. Tarl had passed his first Truth. His nephew was more perceptive than he had hoped.

■   ■   ■

The entrance to the mountain was simple in design but awesome in size. The huge door was perfectly rounded and constructed of teak, so well crafted that the joins in the wood could not be detected. It was highly polished and had no door-handle.

Tarl waited quietly as Rembeu placed a hand on its center and said a few words from the ancient language. These were different every time Tarl had entered and for some reason he had never been able to retain the words his uncle spoke.

Opening soundlessly inward the door dissolved into a pitch-black cavern. Rembeu passed a few words down the corridor and the fire-sticks attached to the walls lit up to guide them. The mountain was mostly limestone and even in this lighting the formations were fascinating.

This passage led to two entries. One was a grand entrance of gold engraved with complicated designs and the other was much less obvious and shaped, not like a door but more like a diagonal shape that appeared to be a fault in the surrounding stone.

Tarl knew never to try the gold entry. He had never been told what would happen if you did try to pass there but it was quite plain that whatever it was, was not good. He was sure that his uncle would do no purposeful harm to anyone but he also knew there was much to protect within these mountain walls.

The entrance of limestone receded on his uncle's command and they climbed through the small space slightly awkwardly. Tarl stood straight again on the other side and the incredible beauty of his uncle's home spread out in front of him and rose up high all around them.

They were standing high upon a ledge on the side wall and had to stride down long wide-stepped stairs to descend to ground level. The floor was polished translucent green and at the center held a sunken area where there was a comfortable living space. Several beautifully woven silk rugs and many large soft colored cushions made the area cozy. A wide, low limestone table that had been carved right out of the mountain's base rose from the middle.

Ferns, several times Tarl's height, stretched up around the high limestone walls and luxurious botanicals and fruit trees like date palms, pomegranate, guava, and mango, all flourished throughout the huge cavern. There were even a few rare birds that flitted and sang amongst the branches.

Tarl could see several of Rembeu's 'smaller' helpers moving around the area. These were the members of the Altai Tribe that his uncle had taken in. Unfortunately this tribe wasn't exactly known for their luck and it seemed there was nothing anyone could do to change it, not even Rembeu, although he had tried many different spells, potions and therapies. They were lovely people, genuine and funny, but notoriously unsafe to have around. Tarl smiled to himself as he heard a plate breaking in the background.

Limestone formations towered around them. In several areas to the sides at the far north and south, the walls fell toward the earth forming cool dark caves and arches. At the mouths of these caves, small sea-boats rested on the tranquil, clear waters in wait for a journey to one of the many grottos, lagoons or estuaries that led to the rest of the mountain's mysteries.

On a small island toward the rear, rose the most fascinating object of all: The Crystal Radiant. The instrument was constructed of several layers of crystal wands which rose like steps up toward the roof of the cave. On close inspection each crystal showed an intricate galaxy held within its transparent heart. Intersecting these layers were tabular crystals which were used to activate the other crystals; like a bridge linking each and every crystal. The instrument stored and transmitted such great amounts of energy that a constant hum was always resonating around it. Tarl had forgotten how incredibly beautiful it was - and how incredibly powerful.

Rembeu caught Tarl's gaze.

"Ah yes, the Crystal Radiant. You know it's probably more important than all our lives put together," he said as he directed Tarl along a narrow path and through a small jungle of palms until they reached the arched bridge which led them over the lagoon and onto the island where the Radiant glowed.

"I forgot how incredible it is."

"Forgot!? My young man, we're certainly going to have to do something about those memory circuits." Rembeu said, too amazed to be disgusted.

Tarl smiled to himself. His uncle's manner took some getting used to.

Rembeu approached the instrument ducking and weaving the many plants as his eyes scanned the section.

"Umbra?! Where on time's behalf are you?" Rembeu cried out.

"Is Umbra close by?" Tarl asked, delighted to meet up with another old friend.

"Well unless she has been using one of my portals again she is." His attempt to sound angry was completely unsuccessful.

A few clinking and pinging sounds followed before a weathered old right hand, firmly clasping a crystal tuning rod, appeared from between two crystals on one of the higher levels of the Radiant.

"Rembeu?" Umbra called out as her rounded, squat figure emerged.

"There you are!" Rembeu could not hide his relief.

"Be careful Umbra, I'll help you," Tarl said as he gently climbed several side stones to reach her.

"That voice?" Umbra stood stock still as her mind pieced together the familiar sounds. Tarl reached out for her hand. The soft wrinkled fingers clasped onto his as she gasped.

"Tarl!" A big smile lit her face. "Keeper Rembeu Cornelious Astraeia! Why didn't you tell me my favorite boy was here?"

Tarl smiled. She had always called him 'her boy', perhaps because she had had no children of her own.

"For goodness sake. He's only just arrived." Again the attempt to sound even slightly grumpy was lost on both of them.

Still standing on the high platform Umbra reached out to hug him, feeling for his form.

"Oh be careful Umbra, perhaps we should step down to the island and then have a proper hug." Tarl suggested. Umbra nodded matter-of-factly and for the briefest moment he could have sworn she had looked directly into his eyes. Of course he knew those lovely cloud-silver eyes could see nothing; had never seen anything. And yet, even without use, they had always seemed to sparkle.

The story Tarl had been told by Rembeu was a cheerless one. Umbra had been born of the Lunescient people; Nomads of time known to travel beyond the limited thoughts of the Caletians. It was unknown how long she had lived but it was longer than Tarl could imagine, even she had stopped counting the passing of time.

Found to be blind at birth, she was denied her Heritage Truth: A place amongst the goddess' table and a lifetime to extol the virtues of her kind. Early on it had been discovered that she had extraordinary abilities; abilities never seen by her kind before. Umbra was both revered and ostracized, many suspicious of her birthright.

Her parents traveled through their many portals trying to find safe refuge for their child. When they found Atlas Mountain they had found what they both desired and feared: The place to which she would be reborn. Tarl's ancestors took her into their home without question. The Light had given life to her mind and as time went by she learned to sense its vibrations. After discovering that the Light energies were diminishing, she worked on re-energizing the mountain before its powers weakened. Crystals from the deep center of the mountain were sourced so that she could build the Crystal Radiant. It was the only way to maintain the Light. The safekeeping of this harmonizer became her life. Umbra was named Protector of the Radiant. Finally, she had found a place to belong.

When Rembeu came to take over his position of Keeper, Umbra had already lost any notion of external time. Rembeu watched her spend her time making sure the Radiant was correctly adjusted and stable. Occasionally she would sit down to caress the crystal 'keys' and Rembeu would listen in amazement as the most indescribable sounds filled the cave. Each crystal pitch flowed into the next, curling through the air like colored ribbons.

It became, of course, one of the most revered abilities of all. If the Crystal Radiant was not in harmony, the balance of the planes was seriously threatened. She may have lost her sight, her Heritage Truth, her family and her extraordinary birthrights, but she found a gift greater than anyone could learn; a gift that continued to save their planet.

Tarl led her carefully down the steps where her soft form encompassed his slight frame with a tight hug.

"Oh Umbra," cried out Rembeu, "Let the poor boy go – you'll suffocate him."

"Mr. Rembeu," Umbra feigned insult as she squeezed 'her boy' a little more. "He hasn't visited us for so long and you say I cannot hug him!" She smiled as she touched the side of Tarl's face and then released him.

"It's good to see you too," Tarl said laughing at the two of them, "I'm glad to see you are still so very charming to each other."

Umbra pursed her lips in a mocking smile and waved a dismissive hand in Rembeu's direction.

"Oh, he is just getting old." At this, even his uncle laughed. Age was indefinable to Umbra.

"Guess what Tarl brought with him?" Rembeu was placing the crystals in Umbra's hands.

"Oh." She looked as if she were about to faint. "Oh you have brought our generator crystals back. This will help me more than you can know. You *are* The Voyager."

Tarl had a strange feeling, as if something dark and heavy were looming behind him. What did Umbra mean by that?

"I need only these three." Umbra was feeling each crystal. You must keep the rest. They are very important Elestial Crystals." She thrust the remaining four into Tarl's hands. "Oh, this is so wonderful," she went on, "and to think you will be working with your uncle on our predicament. Thank goodness." Umbra hugged the crystals to her chest.

Tarl caught the look of concern that Rembeu shot at Umbra. The hairs started to stand up on the back of his neck.

"Oh? And what kind of predicament is that?" Tarl looked directly into his uncle's eyes. When a reply didn't come immediately, he repeated his query, this time a little louder, "*What predicament exactly?*"

Umbra was notably upset.

"You didn't tell him? You didn't tell the boy about this?"

"Now, now, let's not get all huffedy so quickly. My goodness Umbra, Tarl has just arrived, he hasn't even brought his pack in from the ship."

"Oh no uncle." Tarl was shaking his head and waving his arms in front of him, "I'm not going anywhere until you fill me in. I knew something was going on."

"Alright, alright," Rembeu tried a jest, "you have turned into a rather demanding young man, haven't you?"

"Apparently I have." He wasn't backing down.

Rembeu moved back toward the arched bridge and flew a hand past his ear motioning them to follow.

"Come."

Tarl turned and reached out for Umbra's right hand, her left still clasping the crystals. They traipsed behind Rembeu as he continued.

"At least let us sit and discuss all this over some food and drink. We can't have anyone dying of starvation," he said throwing a sideways glance at Tarl. He peered through the thick juicy leaves of some kind of succulent as if looking for something. "Aychu, Aychu!" he yelled, "Where on time's behalf are you?"

The sudden noise must have surprised one of the Altai and the now familiar sound of something crashing to the ground followed. Rembeu, unperturbed, yelled again,

"Aychu? Is that you there?"

"Here Mr. Rembeu, by brook," a small bubbling sing-song voice filtered over to them from the left.

Rembeu swiped a couple of ferns out of the way and searched for the Altai in question.

"There you are." Quite surprisingly his tone suddenly softened. "My goodness me, you people are hard to find when I want you."

"Oh, sorrying Mr. Rembeu," a high pitch gurgle responded, "just watching...er..." Aychu pointed to the water, "fishie..."

"Yes, yes," he cut Aychu off, "no need to apologize," he cleared his throat and his voice returned to its gentle sway. "How are the fishies... er fish looking Aychu?" It was an unnecessary question but it did have the effect of making Aychu a little less agitated.

"Oh, yes, they wonderful, yes, very nice Mr. Rembeu."

"Excellent." Rembeu nodded emphatically, his long chestnut hair swinging forward into his face. He brushed the locks back again. "Now, how is everything going for supper? Did we manage to acquire some more plates?" Rembeu motioned to Tarl to follow on.

Tarl stifled a laugh. He wondered how many plates his uncle must go through with the Altai's in the cooking area.

"Yes, yes, plenty dishes," Aychu stated with obvious relief just as a tiny Altai squeal could be heard over to their right. Rembeu either did not hear it or chose to take no notice of it. Aychu went on, "And I set table for supper. You readying to eat Mr. Rembeu?"

"That sounds wonderful Aychu. Will you sound the bell please?"

"Yes, yes Mr. Rembeu." Aychu sounded delighted.

The three of them finally emerged from the tropical tangle and Rembeu gestured toward the sunken living area. The long limestone table was set with beautiful crystal goblets, gold cutlery and crockery (none of which matched) and was surrounded by a mass of huge colorful cushions.

A tingling sound chimed through the cavern as Aychu tapped the crystal bell and within seconds Altai people appeared from everywhere. At least there would be plenty of company for lunch.

Several Altai brought in the food and placed the dishes along the center of the table. It all looked very good and Tarl wondered if their bad luck stopped at their cooking.

Goblets were filled with sparkling grape juice and plates of food loaded with enticing cuisine were scattered along the table. Once Rembeu started to fill up his plate the Altai followed suit. Tarl raised his eyebrows to his uncle as if to say 'my you are the king of the castle' but Rembeu swept the thought away with a brush of his hand.

"It is an Altai custom - to do with the bad luck thing; nothing to do with my requests," Rembeu stated emphatically.

The Altai started to eat rather daintily and the quiet chatter of their language moved like bursting bubbles along the table.

Tarl found the food truly excellent and wondered if his uncle put up with all their accidents simply for the meals. He could stand the wait no longer.

"Alright uncle, perhaps now you could fill me in on this 'predicament'."

Rembeu swallowed a mouthful of fried peas and put down his fork. He knew this time would come; he just hadn't thought it would be quite this soon or quite this difficult. If he could think of his nephew as he had been taught to and not feel like his protector it would be better for Tarl. After all, he was no longer a child and if they were correct, then he had no choice. This boy would be a boy no longer. An ancient saying came to mind: 'Freedom comes from free minds'. But how many minds were truly free? Tarl would eventually find out if it was true. Rembeu needed to choose his words carefully.

"Well as you know, the Crystal Radiant has been in perfect working order for all our time," he tilted his head toward Umbra who was busily consuming her meal, "thanks to Umbra."

Umbra acknowledged the comment with a nod. For her, the work she had done was a matter of purpose, not pride. They had given her the Boundary of 'Protector' but it had been in her blood long before anyone here had given it a name. She listened attentively to Rembeu's speech and hoped he gave her boy an accurate rendition of the truth. Tarl would find out soon enough. There had been too many secrets for far too long.

"You see," Rembeu went on, "for quite a while now, we have been receiving some kind of interference which is interrupting the energy flow of the Radiant." The regularity with which he spoke gave his words a graveness of which Tarl had never heard before. "Umbra has been working on the problem everyday and often well into the night to keep the crystal's energy balanced but as the interference grows, it becomes more and more difficult to make these changes. I know you do not understand the intricacies of the Radiant but I'm sure you know the seriousness of the outcome if it becomes unstable." Rembeu looked at Tarl for confirmation and saw him wide-eyed and nodding slowly. He doubted Tarl could imagine such devastation but he was not going to go into that right now. His nephew needed to be eased into the gravity of the situation. Shocking him now would only put his lessons in jeopardy. "Do you understand so far?"

"I understand," Tarl lied, wondering if his uncle would be candid with the truth.

"I sent for you immediately when I realized that our mountain's Light-Ray was becoming more and more difficult to access." Rembeu paused to allow some of this to sink in. "I waited as long as I could." He blinked nervously. "As you know the ray is a direct link to all the planes that reflect from this one, so of course that encompasses us also. We are now concerned that if the interference grows greater still, the Radiant will lose the connection with the Light-Ray, thereby dissolving the link which holds the balance..." his voice trailed off as if finishing this sentence would initiate the very thing they were trying to avoid.

Tarl was listening intently to his uncle's words. He had stopped eating and had started to feel ill. His instincts had warned him but he could never have imagined anything this catastrophic. Tarl glanced at Umbra who was eating as casually as if nothing were wrong. Perhaps she had had a lot more time to get used to this.

Rembeu saw Tarl's anxiety. His nephew had never been able to hide anything from him. Cymbeline had been the only one who could ever confuse him. Tonight though, he must try to get as much information out as feasible. He kept his voice level.

"I have consulted our Star Gazer. You remember Melik?" Rembeu asked. Tarl nodded. "Well, he says he has been experiencing storms and electrical interference up there already."

"Is he still up in his balloon?" Tarl interrupted.

"Yes, yes," Rembeu said quite matter-of-factly, "Melik has lived up there for quite a long time actually. He has been studying the star movements and any unusual conditions that may need to be reported straight away."

"Melik lives up there permanently?" Now Tarl was really worried.

"I still talk to him over the Crystal Voicer and I fly up there every now and then on the solar sail to take him supplies but you know, sometimes I think he gets so immersed in his studies he completely forgets to eat. The Altai prepare some good hearty food and I go up and eat with him. You know a bit of conversation for him is good. I tell you though, half the time I simply cannot understand what he's jabbering about."

"Yeah," Tarl tried to inject joviality into his voice but it came out sounding like he was winded. In his mind, however, all he could see was the first time he met Melik.

The 'Star Gazer' had come down to the surface to make some alterations to the skin of his balloon home and Tarl had just returned from an expedition with his uncle. There, outside the front entrance of the mountain was this tall, skinny man with very pale skin, small round spectacles (like the ancients used to wear) and a long brown coat that looked as if it needed a good clean. He was chattering to himself, moving pieces of equipment from one place to another and shaking his brown stringy hair in annoyance. Rembeu introduced them but to Tarl's surprise, instead of the usual pleasantries one would normally engage in at an introduction, Melik went into a long spiel about zero pressure balloons and the pitfalls of a constantly changing altitude.

At the time, Tarl had looked to his uncle for assistance but Rembeu had seemed completely unperturbed by the generous offering of information. So, Tarl just stood there, nodding where it seemed appropriate until his uncle decided that they had listened for an adequate length of time. Then, rather effortlessly, Rembeu whisked Melik inside with Tarl running after them.

Rembeu had popped a few roasted hazelnuts in his mouth and crunched on them loudly for a few teasing minutes. Tarl was anxious to get as much information as was possible before his uncle would inevitable change track.

"Yes...?" encouraged Tarl, "What does Melik say?"

"Well," he swallowed the last crumbs of nut, "he says it is imperative we act immediately. The interference is obviously creating disturbances in the weather and the air waves. That's why I called for you early. You weren't due to attend to your 'education' here for several more season-cycles but this problem may rely entirely on your knowledge."

Tarl's thoughts were a jumble.

"My Knowledge? I don't understand. How can I be of any help?! I don't know *anything*." Fear was now descending on him like heavy gray clouds before a storm. He didn't know about electrical interference or energy transmission.

Rembeu's voice was calm and gentle.

"There is no need to worry Tarl, you will now be able to use your mother's gift."

His mother's gift? What, the baby ring he was graced with after birth? What gift?

"I wasn't given a gift." Tarl couldn't think of a single present his mother had given him that would help in this most serious of situations. He looked around the table as if someone else could offer explanation. How could Umbra and the Altai keep eating?

"Oh nephew, there is so much you will learn here. I have been but a temporary Keeper of the Light. It is a position that was to be held until the True Keeper came of age." Rembeu paused wanting to encourage rather than alarm Tarl. "But a Voyager. Who could have guessed that?"

There was that word again. He had never heard it until just before his journey here and now it was being drummed into his mind like thunder claps.

"Voyager? I am the son of a Keeper and Maker. What is a Voyager?"

"I know it's a little early but your skills and memories will return with the correct stimulus." Rembeu's eyes rested on Tarl's face affectionately.

"But I don't have any knowledge of this sort of thing! Honestly I don't know about any of this stuff." Tarl couldn't think properly. Everything was a blur. He was experiencing pure panic.

"Relax my nephew; there is no need for alarm now. You must trust me and know that everything will pass as it is supposed to." Rembeu raised himself from the table and beckoned to Tarl, "Come." Tarl followed him as if in a trance. One of the Altai was placing a custard dish in front of Umbra who immediately took a delighted mouthful.

His uncle led him north-west toward the limestone entrance of the Dream Grotto and directed him onto one of the boats. When they were both seated Rembeu pushed off into the arching cavern. Tarl was surprised to find his pack already loaded on the boat. Rembeu took out an oar and strode it through the water. Except for the gentle rippling the cave was silent.

Tarl felt like he was in one of his haunting dreams. Everything seemed unreal. He peered into the clear waters lit from below the surface. The movement of the oars caused fluorescent sea bugs to sparkle beside them. Iridescent rainbow eels twisted strangely and florescent sea-weed waved like underwater flames. Fire opals and mother of pearl shells shivered on the sea beds casting rainbow reflections across the cave walls and above them hung purple fluorite crystals which cast unusual shadows around them.

There were many tunnels leading off the main one and Tarl tried to concentrate on exactly which way they were headed. They rounded several bends until Rembeu finally began to talk again. His whispering voice reverberated in the silence.

"You see how the moon lights up the water? It reflects off the bottom of the ocean and spills all the way along these caves. Don't need any fire-sticks."

"It's beautiful," Tarl breathed.

"Watch." Rembeu ran his fingers through the water. The fluorescent bugs swirled in the current and an array of colors flashed across its surface.

As they rounded another corner the arched ceiling opened up into a glorious underground cove; the river opening into a huge round lake. A small waterfall trickled down from the ceiling on the side wall where a single green fire stick jutted to indicate a cove. Further toward the east Tarl could see where the river continued on towards the many other inlets. Rembeu pulled into the shore where several other boats were moored. They alighted onto soft sparkling, silky sand. Tarl reached down to touch it.

"Diamonds. Crushed diamonds." Rembeu said matter-of-factly.

"But it's so soft." Tarl let the diamond dust sprinkle from his fingers.

"*Very* crushed." Rembeu raised an eyebrow and motioned to Tarl to follow him. They trudged up the sandy incline, Rembeu's long robes catching the twinkling sand as he moved.

Ahead, the sandy beach rolled into a lawn of soft grass and flowering moss giving the cove a luxurious, cozy feeling. Several tropical fruit trees rose high toward the cove's apex: Large long benches had been carved from the limestone walls and were cushioned with feather-filled silk mattresses and colored cushions; the walls over to the west were completely lined with books.

"This shall be your room while you attend your education here. Feel free to change the décor. Tomorrow we shall retrieve anything else you need from the wind-ship. You will be very safe here."

Tarl wondered why his uncle would think he was not safe in the central cave. Why wouldn't Rembeu just tell him what was going on? Obviously there was a great deal more he needed to be told.

"Wait, uncle, I will not sleep until you have answered a few questions for me."

Rembeu nodded with a sigh.

"Yes, perhaps we should get a few things out of the way."

Tarl felt both relief and trepidation. He squeezed his fists into balls.

"And how can I be sure of the way back to the central cave anyway?"

Rembeu, happy to start with such an easy question became quite animated.

"Oh, yes, yes, of course, I should have mentioned that straight away." He pointed to the boats moored down by the glistening sand. "I have installed the blue boat with a homing device. When you get in, merely grasp the oars and your fingerprints will activate the boat. You won't even need to row." He smiled at the boat looking very pleased with himself.

"You have my fingerprints stored?" Tarl raised his eyebrows trying to shrug off a feeling of trepidation. He didn't remember anyone taking his fingerprints. "And why are there oars if you don't need them?"

"Hmm? Oh yes, all the family details are stored in the Ancestoral Room. I don't think you've been in there. Remind me to show it to you." Rembeu paused. "And you know I don't like rhetorical questions."

His uncle was doing it again. How did he manage to distract Tarl even when he was determined to get information from him?

"Why do I have to be all the way out here? And why do I have to be 'safe'? I don't understand how I am supposed to be of any help to you? I thought I was coming here to learn about herbs and things, yet I'm told I am already supposed to know everything... which I can guarantee you, I don't!" Now he had blurted it all out, each comment sounding angrier than the next. Why hadn't anybody prepared him for all of this?

"Yes, yes." Rembeu's proud smile had fallen into a grimace. "You have every right to be upset. It is time I explained a few things. I was going to wait until you were a little rested but it is important to discuss these matters now. You may not understand what I am going to tell you but it is imperative you listen to what I say very carefully. These words will come back to you when you need them." He took a deep breath and eyed Tarl intently. Tarl sat completely still as if a single movement may change his uncle's mind.

"Your mother's memories are in your blood. It is because of this you have had to be protected from many sources of possible harm. Before your mother's passing you were taught a great deal about your gifts. But after her passing we had to close this knowledge from your conscious mind or there could have been great danger for you. We had to cease your Teachings immediately. Now you are here again we can open this part of your mind so you will be able to access this information."

"I don't remember any Teachings." It was so strange to be told you had experienced something you had no memory of.

"Well that was the point: To keep you safe. You will however, need to be prepared for the flood of information that will come to you. You cannot be hurt physically by this," Rembeu wasn't entirely sure that was true, "but you may experience emotional pain. We must teach you slowly in the safe environment of this home. You need to know, however, that you are constantly protected by the mountain's aura and that no one can harm you while it protects us. We do have to be prepared though."

His uncle wasn't making sense. He couldn't be hurt, but he could be hurt; he was safe but he wasn't safe. The following flood of nausea was making it hard to concentrate.

"Because of the problems we are encountering with the Crystal Radiant we may not be able to rely on the mountain's aura for long. This cove is almost directly below the apex of the mountain, the strongest point of protection for you." His uncle's blue eyes were heavy with sadness. He took Tarl's hand, his head bowed low.

"Uncle..."

"I am so sorry," Rembeu interrupted, "perhaps it would have been better to tell you this before now but your father and I chose not to risk it. How could I expect him to risk your very precious life after losing our beloved Cymbeline?" He looked up to face Tarl's stare. "Can you understand?"

Tarl did not seem to understand much of anything but pressed a half smile and a nod toward his uncle.

"When can I begin? I want to start now." His voice was purposeful and determined. Rembeu's relief was palpable.

"The first exercise is the hardest, my nephew, perhaps we should wait until tomorrow? You must be exhausted."

Tarl was tired but he knew he wouldn't sleep anyway.

"You must give me this first Teaching. I don't know why it's so important to me but I feel I have to begin now."

Rembeu nodded in resignation. This young boy, too young for what he was about to face, was going to have to grow up much too quickly.

"Alright, but I will not leave you tonight. I will teach you and stay here with you. Let us begin your first lesson."

■　■　■

Tarl felt excited, nervous and unmistakably queasy all at once. Was it really possible he could do this? Rembeu climbed up on one of the benches and using an instrument from his pocket carefully snapped a barrel of the purple rainbow fluorite dipping from the ceiling. He motioned for Tarl to lie on his back on one of the silk mattresses and then took a position behind his head.

"I will not introduce any of these sessions to you. You will have to find the Knowledge within yourself. Do not force it, it will come. Remember, it has been many moons since you have done this so don't try to rush. Feelings and thoughts should flow naturally but don't push it. Your inner self will guide you. Do not be scared of emotion."

Tarl lay still, eyes closed, trying to calm his nervous heartbeat. His uncle laid a calming palm on his nephew's chest and placed the cool fluorite on his brow. Very slowly Tarl's heartbeat eased and he felt his mind begin to fall into darkness.

The darkness became spiked with bright flashes of light. It felt like his head was giving way to the birth of an electrical storm. He could still feel his uncle's calming hand upon his chest. Remembering his words he allowed the sizzling storm to pass through his mind watching it with curiosity rather than fear. The lightening seemed to breathe air into his head. A huge and powerful river followed, washing away the storm. Raging torrents broke dam walls and flattened buildings, taking muck and mud with it. He watched the river cascade across the land until it finally died down and turned into a trickling river surrounded by green grasslands that smelled fresh and sweet. Tarl watched as the river turned into a blue sparkling lake.

It was a perfect summer's day and Tarl could hear the soft buzz of insects and feel the warmth of sunlight on his face. A distant voice called out his name. Tarl turned to see his mother and father seated on a hand-spun cloth under an acorn tree. His heart beat a little faster as he realized what he was looking at. His heartbeat slowed again as his uncle applied a little more pressure to his chest.

Tarl felt his own hand waving to his parents as if he were acting out a dream. He saw his mother laugh and wave back and then he noticed, somewhere deep within him, a voice was speaking. The sounds resonated right through him. He was standing very still, by the lake in this scene, watching his mother and father joke together as he listened carefully to the voice coursing through him.

"Your mother, Cymbeline was highly regarded in her generation of 'Keepers'."

Tarl knew that. The union between his mother and father had been a first. Although mixture of Boundary was unheard of until then, no one had dared confront a 'Keeper' on the choice of their partner. Of course it had not taken long for everyone to adore his father, just as his mother had. Parvo was a hardworking young man, a 'Maker' by birthright, good looking, friendly and infinitely in love with his wife. His excellent craftsmanship and creative skills won over even the most difficult and strict of revelers. Anyone in their company would be unable not to join in their delightful reverie of joy and joke.

"Until the union," the voice went on, "when reforms began." Tarl knew this too. This wasn't a Teaching, it was a Telling. "And soon a child was born."

Tarl was getting annoyed.

"This child was talked of as the delightful outcome of mixing Boundaries and his birth encouraged the townsfolk to make an amendment to the out-dated Systems. The Link System was then introduced whereby members of any Boundary were able to ally or link with another."

"Yes, thanks for that," Tarl thought sarcastically.

"New assemblies brought all the members of the community together at the one time. The new Systems, encouraged by the Link System, began to grow. A chamber of Sway Members emerged and created a united membership, which ultimately allowed all systems to integrate and assimilate. The result was a new thought; a new and resounding wealth of community."

Tarl wondered how he could stop the voice. He tried focusing on the scene ahead of him and tried unsuccessfully to move toward his parents who seemed perfectly happy by themselves.

"This child's birth changed everything, including the course of his parent's lives."

Was this voice trying to blame him for what happened to his mother?

"There were however, certain members of this community that were unable to customize themselves to the new ideas. They felt Cymbeline and her followers did not consider the implications of their new treaties. They believed that it was imperative that the placement of Boundaries remained as it had been: Separate. To them, trying to negate the tradition of their livelihood was irreverent. A new cult was created, their goal being to return the land to its prior traditions. Cymbeline was their retribution."

Right at that moment Tarl realized he was looking at the forgotten memory of the last day of his mother's life. Panic made him forget his annoyance. He wanted desperately to run to her, to scream a warning, but there was no voice, no movement and sickeningly, he was still smiling. He was trapped in a memory he couldn't change.

The vision was so real he wondered how he could have forgotten the details. He had been just ten when he had gone picnicking with his parents at the Lake of Aquila. It had been a wonderful day. His mother had prepared an enormous picnic 'for her two men' and they had enjoyed a beautiful sunny day of feasting and games. His mother talked of making some changes to the garden and his father chatted about some new wind-ships he was building. Tarl remembered his father asking for his mother's advice on some of the tactical arrangements. Tarl left them to be alone.

Now, in his mind, he couldn't believe he was actually turning away from them. He struggled desperately to make his body do what he wanted it to but it was no good. The memory was just going to keep rolling forward; inescapable.

Tarl walked down the slide of the grassy knoll, the smell of the apple blossom riding the air like a coaster, strong and determined. And then that familiar sound struck the air like a roar. The cruel strange cry of his father followed; the sound resounding in Tarl's head like an ache. Running towards the howl, again he saw the devastated look on his father's face; a look he had tried so desperately to forget. For a moment everything went black. Unable to understand what was happening, he tried to fight it; he had to go back! The Teaching couldn't finish like this.

"Take me back!" Tarl screamed.

Light flickered in front of him bringing glimpses of the memory. The scene was shattering. It had turned into stilted moments, flashes in the dark. The last image sent him cold. In the brief moment before her death she remained unconscious, unable to say her goodbyes.

The fragments of that summer's day were now as real as if it had just happened. He had been told that a renegade 'Holder' of the Boundary had pointed his mother and the rest never seemed to really matter; the reason for her death fading into the background of thought. His mother was dead, that was what he had to deal with.

Now, however, it mattered a great deal and amongst the anger and hurt, he felt purpose and its pursuit were important beyond words.

Once again darkness washed over him leaving him feeling stranded in a bottomless void. Soft colors began to glow and he moved toward them grateful for some direction. As he moved closer he could hear the sounds of a rushing waterfall growing gradually louder until at last he opened his eyes again to the cool green surrounds of the cave. He was surprised to see that he was being held in his uncle's arms and that he was trembling and sweating.

"You have done very well," his uncle tried to console him, "excellent for your first and most difficult opening." Tarl tried to wipe the perspiration from his face with a shaky hand but Rembeu took the trembling hand in his. "It's alright Tarl, it has been there for a very long time."

And suddenly Tarl felt tears sting his eyes. Exhaustion was overwhelming him and he let himself sink into an empty slumber.

5

The Teachings

When Tarl eventually woke, it was to the sounds of the sprinkling waterfall and the gentle ebb of the lake. It felt as if he had slept forever. Straining his eyes open, he rolled over onto his side. The feather-stuffed mattress was soft and comforting. For a moment he allowed the memory of the night before to wash over him again. His left arm seized painfully; perhaps he slept on it. Thankfully, the pain subsided as he shook and stretched it.

As he pulled himself up, he looked around to discover he was alone. Rembeu must have left while he slept. His stomach growled with hunger and he plucked several handfuls of juicy cherries before wandering down to the twinkling sand. The water was warm and clear and he could see colored fish flitting back and forth just beyond his toes.

Tarl grabbed several more pieces of fruit but his hunger craved more. Had he overslept? It was impossible to tell what time it was in these labyrinths. Untying the blue boat, he climbed in and grasped the oars as he had been told. Surely enough, the boat whirred and began to move him back the way they had come in. He sat back and let the boat churn slowly back toward the main cave.

Smells of cooking greeted him as he stepped off the boat. There did not appear to be anyone around, not even any of the Altai, and so he began a search for either a person or some food; whichever came first. After entering a small archway near the dining area, he found himself in a room filled with all sorts of goods hanging from the ceiling. There were rows of drying fruit, bunched herbs, dried meats, and bean-seed wheels lined up along the walls. Dodging through the dangling dried sausages, he was unsure who got more of a shock, him or the Altai standing behind a low stove.

"Quiggle!" Cried the tiny Altai in fright.

"Oh, I'm so sorry. I was just looking for some food."

A strange high pitched gurgling noise spilled from the Altai's throat. The facial expression was the only reason Tarl knew it to some sort of laugh.

"Plenty food! What you like?" The sounds were like a combination between bird song and a cry for help.

"Anything would be good, I'm famished."

"No anything," came the confused reply.

Tarl looked around the room and pointed to loops of smoked rashes hanging to the right.

"Yid! Good for you." The words sounded like a yelp. "You go. Table. Sit. I come." The Altai gave Tarl a little shove as if the matter were urgent. Tarl tried not to laugh.

"Well, thank you." Nodding quickly he took a closer look at the Altai. They all looked so similar to him that he felt a little embarrassed he could not tell them apart. Even the males and females appeared to have no defining differences.

He moved toward the dining room and sat at the long dining table. He must have drifted into thought because the next thing he knew the tiny Altai was placing an enormous plate of delicious smelling food in front of him.

"Eat. Good."

And it was. Curls of crisp rashes, soft egg muffins, toast with banana-honey and tropical fruit. He ate the lot quite comfortably and had just sat back when the Altai removed his plate.

"Want more?" The Altai was nodding ferociously.

"No, no, very good thank you." Tarl patted his stomach. The Altai looked very pleased with Tarl.

"You want food, you ask for Coff. Yes?"

"Coff." Tarl grinned widely, "Thank you." He pointed to his chest, "I'm Tarl."

"Yid! Know this. You eat good." And then Coff was gone.

Tarl eased himself from the chair feeling the best he had felt for a long time and went in search of Rembeu. After a quick peek in a few of the rooms to the west, he strolled over toward the southeast to examine the rooms leading from the main eave on that side.

Umbra was off to the east working one of her tuning forks around the Crystal Radiant. Moving confidently around the instrument she appeared to feel the air as the pulsating aura guided her. As she sensed different light refractions she would change direction. Her hands moved gingerly, as if cupping the strange buzzes and hums, altering vibrations with a gesture. Her crystal guide-rod lay unused at the base of the bridge next to the huge open case that held the many tuning forks and other devices she required to keep the Radiant balanced. If Tarl had not known she was blind he would never have believed it.

Tarl wandered, north east toward the Gallery of Time, his uncle's favorite room and rounded the southern wall. Through a small archway he followed a narrow slippery claustrophobic path with a ceiling so low, he had to stoop.

The air grew thicker and more humid as the path descended and he had to stop himself from holding his breath. The path curved back around again to the north and then descended sharply toward a stairwell. Sporadic drips of water from the stalactites fell around him. At the base of the stairs he opened a small wooden door, crouched through the opening and gratefully stretched tall on the other side.

The noise was almost deafening. Clocks spiraled in layers around the center of the room and along the walls, all ticking in syncopated fashion. The fascination in this room was that as well as being the center of the cave it was also the only place on the planet that worked in perfect alignment to the center of the globe. A plunging abyss in the middle of the room, encircled by spiraling clocks, fell straight and fathomless like a void. 'Our sphere's black hole,' Rembeu had joked to Tarl. High above it, a circular opening in the roof allowed light from two points to culminate and feed directly into the magnetic chasm, allowing positive and negative to balance.

Tarl looked around at all the different clocks, each labeled with the realm or planet of which times they were recording. The ones circling the center of the room ticked backwards influenced by the magnetic forces of the core and could be used to predict misalignments.

There were pendulum clocks, grandly standing the test of time; telescopic regulators and even treasured ancient timepieces. Around the walls on the highest shelves were all different sized cycle-glasses. The figure-eight glass 'clocks' held the sands of the ancients. When their sands had sifted through the top section a small tapping device tipped them over to begin again.

Tarl saw a flash of white and moved round the center tower of clocks. His uncle was at his work bench fiddling with the internals of a lovely sea-stone casing checking the mother of pearl pendulum. His ivory robe of moon-thread shone with luminous swirls, like the innards of shells. The front was fastened with Biwa pearls and he wore a twisted silk around his head.

Tarl called out but his uncle did not react. It was quite likely that Rembeu had heard him but was ignoring the distraction until he had followed through with whatever train of thought he was processing. A moment of genius could easily be lost by an interruption. Tarl waited patiently.

"Ahh. Wonderful." Rembeu shouted over the noise as he closed the casing and winked at Tarl. "Another one as good as new." He prodded his nephew on the nose.

"Any other sick ones?" Tarl raised his voice.

"Not yet." He returned, "But we have to keep any eye on these." Rembeu pointed to the clocks circling the center of the room. They are counting down our time."

"Counting down our time to what?" yelled Tarl.

Rembeu brushed the question aside with a wave of his hand.

"Come. I have heard enough ticking for the morning."

They emerged at the entrance to the main cave and Tarl followed the determined strides of Rembeu. Several Altai were moving in and out of the plants injecting them with some type of serum. Tarl was about to ask about this but his uncle broke his train of thought.

"How did you sleep then?"

"Actually, very well. Thank you. You know I think that was the best sleep I've had for a long time."

Rembeu looked remarkably impressed by this.

"Wonderful, just wonderful. You've slept through the afternoon. I expect that your wind-ship journey took quite a bit out of you… let alone your first lesson." Rembeu wrapped an arm around Tarl's shoulders. "I am very proud of the way you coped last night and to be truthful I am also grateful. This bodes well for your future tasks. The balance grows less and less each day."

Tarl couldn't contain his surprise: The uncharacteristic softness in his uncle's voice and the use of words like 'grateful' seemed rather odd. His uncle didn't appear to notice Tarl's concern.

"Did you have some food? You must be hungry." They were heading toward a large entrance on the west wall.

"Oh no, I found Coff before I found you and I don't think I will ever eat again." Tarl exhaled with a contented sigh.

Rembeu found this most amusing.

"That is one thing I never have to worry about. They certainly don't let me forget to eat." They both laughed as they passed through the entrance to the Swords Gallery Room.

The floor was paved with tiles of shimmering moonstone which gave the room a feeling of weightlessness. The walls were encrusted with plaques representing Codes of Arms and long rows of glass cases housed an exhibition of crystal and gemstone swords and shields.

The prize piece in a small case at the back of the room was the Scepter Crystal that had belonged to a protector of Atlantis. It had been found in an excavation many life-times ago by his uncle's great, great, great grandfather to set this lost paradise at peace.

Tarl had only time for a brief look before Rembeu picked something up and disappeared through a small opening in one of the rear corners. Tarl followed him into a dimly lit room. Large indecipherable holograms framed the walls and ceiling. Tarl realized he had never been in here before.

"Geographs," Rembeu announced before Tarl could ask. Rembeu went up and touched one to demonstrate. "They appear perfectly flat but carry a three dimensional moving scape." He pointed to one across the room. "My favorite, that one. A moonscape of Io, one of Jupiter's moons. Look closely, you might see one of its volcanoes erupting."

As Tarl approached, the landscape moved away from him as if it were turning. So precise was the picture, he felt as if he could reach in and touch the silt.

"Now we must discuss your further lessons," Rembeu proceeded. He moved over and sat on a comfortable looking bench covered in glossy red silk. "You did very well last night. Most impressive indeed," Rembeu was smiling proudly, "how do you feel about continuing with your lessons?" The smile was saying one thing but Tarl could have sworn he had heard the vaguest tone of apprehension.

"I am ready," Tarl wanted to sound as confident as possible. "I really do need to send my log books to dad though."

"Yes, yes, I sent a vibrato last night. It's all being taken care of."

"Right then," Tarl took a deep breath, "I guess time is of the essence"

"Ahh," for a brief second Rembeu looked wistful, "if only it were an essence." He then perked up a little, "Imagine that!"

Tarl cleared his throat as politely as possible to bring his uncle back to the case at hand.

"Oh dear me. Yes, sorry about that, but you know, I think I have an idea. We will finish this lesson and then I must do some work. Let us start." Tarl lay down as he had the night before. He tried to relax but this time he felt distinctly uncertain.

"Focus on the geograph on the ceiling above you," came the gentle, reassuring tone of his uncle.

Tarl looked deep into the revolving orange sunscape above him.

"Now breathe deeply." His uncle stroked Tarl's dark glossy hair away from his face and pressed a palm to his forehead. Tarl felt himself falling very gently, as if he were falling inside himself. His body felt as if it were swelling; as if he were becoming the orange sunscape.

Rembeu placed a red aventurine feldspar stone on his abdomen and one on his chest. A flood of warmth permeated Tarl's body. Rembeu then removed a small purse from his pocket and placed it on Tarl's throat. Smells of jasmine, myrrh, sandalwood and ginger wafted around him. A smooth carnelian was then placed upon Tarl's brow and although his eyes were closed he could still clearly see the sun rolling slowly above him.

Distant words began to flow into his mind. This time the voice was soft and reassuring as it guided his memory to a time before this life. The rolling sunscape became different lands; lands he remembered from long, long ago. As the voice brought him forward through time, he felt himself dissolve into the rolling orange landscape only to find himself being born to two very familiar faces. The enchanted smile of his mother cooed at him as he was placed in her arms and the warm hand of his father touched his tiny fingers.

Tarl heard the whispers of his mother's Teachings through the ears of an infant and spun in the arms of his father as they played. The words his mother spoke were strange and unfamiliar; a language he was unable to understand, but her beautiful emerald eyes gazed into his and the words somehow began to make sense. The peace he felt was indescribable; complete in a way he could not have imagined before this.

The voice then slowly drew him away from this precious scene. He did not want to go. He clung desperately to the intangible; arms reaching out, wanting to stay cocooned there, never to leave, but the voice pulled him, ever so gently, back toward the revolving sunscape and finally he opened his eyes.

The reality of the experience was overwhelming and he feared if he moved he may lose the moment forever.

His uncle was removing the stones.

"It was harder to come back this time wasn't it?" Rembeu's face was crinkled with concern and his brow was shining with sweat. "This is not good for you." Bringing Tarl back had taken all his energy. Another Teaching without a substantial break would be very risky. If only they had dealt with this earlier. If only they had not done what they had done.

Rembeu's fear and guilt were intensifying and that wouldn't serve anyone well, especially not Tarl. "I'm afraid we will have to change plans, I cannot do this to you, it is too much too quickly." He watched his nephew's pained face and tried to temper his guilt.

Tarl blinked several times and groggily pulled himself into a seated position.

"No, Uncle! What are you saying?" Rembeu's words had roused fear and confusion in him. "Did I do badly this time?"

"Oh no, nephew, you did very well." Rembeu took Tarl's face in his hands just as his father had done not so long ago. "You have great ability, greater even than I could have hoped, but this is asking too much of you. Teachings should be very slow, very gentle. Progress should be over a long period of time, each lesson only undergone when the previous lesson has fully penetrated." He let go of Tarl's face. "I could tell that you didn't want to waken, in fact it was quite difficult to get you to return to me. That is of greater concern than I can explain."

Tarl again felt the terrible pain of having to leave the company of his mother and father but was determined to forge on. He had no idea where this new found sense of compulsion to take on such a responsibility came from. He didn't even know what kind of responsibility he was supposed to be taking on.

"It's harder when I don't know what I'm going to have to see or feel. And worse when I have to give that up again. I need to learn to detach myself. I need to be able to observe and learn without the emotional involvement. Surely you must be able to create a potion or something to help me."

"Yes of course, but it should not be done," Rembeu said as he rubbed his hands across his brow trying to think how this would be possible. "The Learnings are for all the physical, mental, emotional and causal bodies. If I block one then the balance is lost. That could be incredibly detrimental." His mind churned with the predicament: "Havoc."

"Uncle." Tarl reached out to grab his uncle's hand and his attention. "If what you are telling me and what these Teachings are making clear in my mind is true, my slight unbalancing is a minor concern. I now realize that which you have not made clear to me before." Tarl was frowning with the full weight of what he was about to admit to himself. "If I do not learn these Teachings I cannot help. It seems imperative that I do. I don't claim to understand half of what you're implying but I do understand that if the vibrational pull we are experiencing is not corrected there will be planetary disturbance and instability – I know what dimensional pull is."

Rembeu, half amazed and half relieved, could not believe that Tarl had been able to comprehend this after only two Teachings. He couldn't deceive him any longer.

"That is correct." Rembeu's reply was simple and final.

Tarl stood, twisting on the spot, not knowing how to position himself to absorb this knowledge: One day he was off on a great adventure, flying the blue skies to see his beloved uncle; the next he was dealing with responsibilities beyond his comprehension. Pacing back and forth seemed to help.

"There is no choice Rembeu. You must develop something to help me. When we have everything sorted out you can spend as much time as you want correcting my balance *and* whatever else you think needs fixing."

"I'm sure I'll think of something." Rembeu managed a smile. He knew there was no point in arguing, the boy was absolutely correct. And absolutely brave.

■　■　■

Rembeu's idea of creating time as an essence was put on hold as he worked anxiously on a potion to help Tarl get through his lessons. The potion room was filled with shelves and cases of bottled liquids, several heat distilling beakers, tubes and nearly every type, style and system of crystal and gemstone that existed. The only items under lock and key were all the vials filled the sands of time. They were volatile and dangerous and very rarely even considered for use.

Tarl helped as much as he could, learning about mixing and matching herbs, stones, oils and colors. Even meals were eaten in the potions room. Every combination was tested until finally, they developed a serum powerful enough to perform under such difficult circumstances. Its side effects were limited but still possibly detrimental to both Tarl and the Teaching process.

The exhausted declaration from Rembeu confirmed that the potion was ready.

"Well, we've done it. Measurements are accurately proportioned." His fair skin was looking gray and his eyes were cupped with dark circles. Even the normally bright silver streaks in his dark hair seemed decidedly paler.

"What have we got then?" Tarl asked as he walked over to the beaker his uncle was clutching.

"Well we must remember that all matter is energy," he began, as if this new potion required an introduction, "that energy is the building block of the physical universe. The physical, mental, emotional and causal bodies we exist as could be thought of as a wrapper which our soul wears to protect it from all these energies and vibrations of our multi-dimensional universe," Rembeu's arms were gesticulating as if there was an imaginary opera. "Of course if we take one wrapping away it disturbs the practice of the others," he couldn't help himself; he was just a teacher at heart, "however, if we feed, say, the emotional wrapper with enough to keep it busy it could be working with other influences rather than allowing you to feel the intensity of one particular emotion. For example, the individual experience in a lesson." Rembeu was talking melodically, his shoulders pushed back and his chin raised slightly as if the upper wall was paying avid attention also.

"Right," Tarl said, trying to grasp all that.

"So, we have a potion of ground ruby, to develop your inner fortress, ground frosted quartz to maintain balance, rhondonite, to send out a force like an orbit around the emotional body, purple garnet to develop that warrior within you and develop detachment for which I have also added purple rainbow fluorite all combined with the oils of cinnamon, marjoram and lavender. The final ingredients are combined from these very ancient vessels and will allow the potion to become its own form. And this one has made it digestible. Very important. We have created a new life-energy!" He held the beaker up as if congratulating it for its performance.

"Well should we give it a try? "Tarl was peering into the swirling mass in the raised beaker as if he may see something helpful.

"Perhaps you should get some rest first."

Tarl started to nod when they both felt a chilling change in the air. All around the colored vials began to tremble. They exchanged wide-eyed glances and waited, as if frozen, for whatever it was to end or worsen. It stopped just as suddenly. They both closed their eyes in relief.

"Perhaps we'll rest later," Rembeu said grimacing.

Back in the Room of Geographs, Tarl prepared for his third Teaching. Rembeu measured out a small amount into a vial and handed it to Tarl. Tarl took a deep breath and swallowed the bright swirling liquid. He felt the energy slip down inside him as if he had swallowed light itself.

Lying on his back Tarl looked up at the geograph above him and was amazed to discover it was completely different from the previous Teaching. Instead of the rolling orange sunscape, Tarl watched the bright blue light of Venus expand and contract as the planet slowly rotated. He felt himself relax as his uncle rubbed a little oil into his forehead. He smelled a mixture of cypress, frankincense, melissa and geranium all swimming pleasantly together. Small emerald rondels were placed on Tarl's heart.

As Rembeu placed gems on Tarl's body he ushered soft words like a mantra.

"We must understand detachment to truly love life," A dark green aventurine was nestled amongst the emeralds, "Emerald to locate disharmony and aventurine to metabolize it." An apple-green chrysoprase was placed on his brow and spheres of malachite were secured on his upward turned palms, "find your gifts, fall into your subconscious."

Tarl felt a gentle tingling on his forehead as he watched the strange tundra of Venus rise and fall in its rotating journey. He felt himself falling backward inside the darkness of his mind. This time however, he could see nothing except the overwhelming darkness; Venus had disappeared and he could hear and feel nothing. He thought he should have been terrified, stuck in this emptiness, and yet, the light of curiosity felt bright within him.

A slight breeze lifted his hair and he turned toward its direction. Quickly approaching him was a huge ball of glowing green light. He comprehended the danger of his situation but felt calm and assured. It rushed toward him threatening to roll across him crushing his very existence.

Holding his breath, Tarl felt words inside him emerging from nowhere.

'Just let it be,' he thought, 'I will not run or hide, if it is fear coming toward me I shall acknowledge it for what it is.'

At that very moment the ball surged over him surrounding him in bright green swirling winds and stopped over the top of him, covering his body. Standing at its center, he was quite untouched: He felt no wind, no fire; no fear and was able to watch the scene with interest. Suddenly the bright green ball burst into an enormous display of firelights. All around him small bursts of green sparkles were falling. Each sparkle of light that touched his body helped him relax and then he was falling again, deeper and deeper until he heard the now familiar voice resonating with powerful words.

"The soul has no limitations regarding time; the soul has no limitations regarding space; the soul is freedom from fear and you are not afraid." And on it went with seemingly infinite knowledge.

Tarl's visions this time saw him grow from a babe to a young child but now with hindsight. With the detachment of the potion he was able to move through this, gathering important observations with a mind open to all information. Whispered words from his mother echoed like water rings stretching out into infinity. Images moved and morphed more quickly; information flowed more freely and the words slowly became familiar.

When he was finally brought to consciousness he felt refreshed and relieved. He now understood that the Teachings were returning greater knowledge to him and this in turn gave him a greater sense of self. It was like something had been missing all this time and was now being returned to him; filling him with what should have always been his own. He watched the sphere of Venus still revolving as his uncle removed the stones from his body.

"I see the potion worked?" There was a hint of pride.

"Indeed it did uncle." Tarl sat and faced him. "That was remarkably easier."

"How do you feel? Rembeu peered into his eyes, pulling down his lower lids and feeling around his throat. Rembeu thought Tarl seemed much more aware this time and had definitely come around faster but he sensed his Teaching had not been fully recognized. He wondered if the potion could prevent Tarl from experiencing the full truth. "Can you say anything feels uncomfortable or misaligned?"

Tarl stood and walked in a circle. He made a wobbling movement, clutched his heart and dramatically crumpled to the ground. Rembeu ran over to him horrified. Tarl started to laugh and curled up to clutch his knees.

"Oh how could you! You'd give your old uncle a heart attack for want of a joke?" Rembeu couldn't hide his sense of relief. He was reminded of how young his nephew was and the ebbing guilt returned.

Tarl couldn't control himself, probably influenced by lack of sleep and an intensity of circumstances. He lay back on the floor holding his stomach exhausted.

"Oh, uncle. I'm sorry but your face…" he was off again: Laughter punctuated with attempts at impersonating his uncle's horror.

Tarl's imitation was amusing. The boy needed a bit of humor to get through this. Rembeu joined him on the floor laughing along with him. It was just what they both needed.

Eventually Rembeu suggested some sleep was definitely in order and so, too tired to move from the Geograph Room, Tarl got comfortable on the silk mattress where he had just taken his third lesson. Rembeu patted his nephew's head mumbling something about seeing the Altai before bedding down himself. Tarl was in no state to argue.

"The mountain's aura is still strong. You will be safe here for the time being. I will check on you shortly."

Tarl looked up at the geograph above him. Venus had now disappeared and instead a rolling blue sky streaked with long stretches of white clouds drifted before him. He closed his eyes and imagined the sky as if he were flying in his wind-ship.

■　■　■

The suns that followed were condensed into Teachings, eating and sleeping. Tarl made sure a long letter and all his log books, including many drawings of his trip, were sent back to his father. He missed him terribly and wondered if he and Opal were keeping each other company. How he would like to see her lovely face again. Tarl wondered how long it would be until it would be possible. If he hadn't been so busy, he thought the distance would have made his life impossible. That was not to say his uncle wasn't good company. It was just that going through all this was difficult enough. Without his father to confide in, he felt even more isolated and to be honest, if he had been able to confide in Opal he would have felt completely differently about this whole experience. But he had to be strong in front of Rembeu. There was no way he was going to let Rembeu see how worried he was.

Tarl wondered if his father would have understood any of this; perhaps he would have preferred not to deal with it? Perhaps Opal would have felt the same. He was on his own now and he would just have to do whatever it was that was expected. Somewhere in the back of his mind he had always known it would be like this. How had he been numb for so long?

A memory from his first pin-pointing tournament flashed through his mind. He saw his mother and father's face beaming in the crowd. The weight of responsibility had seemed so great. He would give anything to be there again.

At least Rembeu was comfortable having him around and he seemed happy to teach him. Tarl could sense his uncle's remorse at having to force his mind to open to the Teachings but he seemed to be coping with any negative feelings. Perhaps the urgency of the situation was driving his uncle to alter his standards. That was certainly a first.

Rembeu left the Geographs Room wondering what he was trying to do. The Divine Sources had determined both their lives. How was he supposed to know it was right? It wasn't that he didn't believe in Tarl's abilities but for a young boy to deal with something that was obviously beyond him at this stage of his maturity was, at the least, unwise. And then there was the matter of Tarl's past; what they felt they had to do. How could Tarl possibly understand? He sat down in the quiet surrounds of his bed-cove. He had lost his appetite and all he wanted to do was sleep. His conflict rose from impossibility: He taught Tarl to do what the Divine Sources said he must and risk Tarl's life or, he watched the world die: Something to drift off to sleep with.

■　　■　　■

Small quakes had started to wrack their daily activities and Umbra was having more and more difficulty keeping the Radiant balanced. As far as Tarl could tell she was working around the clock to keep up with the changes. The Altai, alarmed by even the slightest tremor, tried to help her as much as they could but she would shush them away, fearful they might damage one of her instruments. They chose to cope by working harder than ever: Gardening, cleaning and cooking. The latter did not disappoint.

As for Tarl and Rembeu, they ate all their meals on the go, constantly trying to fill their time with all that needed to be done. Every night, however, his uncle would insist, no matter how tired he was, that Tarl must sleep in his little cove on the river. He was adamant that Tarl be safe.

Rembeu felt the time fly by much too quickly. He watched Tarl very carefully trying hard not to make him feel like an experiment in a petri dish. As desperate as Rembeu was to know what Tarl had seen in that first geograph, he had not asked. Rembeu was not sure if he could keep his face expressionless even if Tarl had told him. Only he knew that it was the only geograph in the room that did not have a specific scape held in its configurations. He had always thought it a terrible mistake until he had seen visions in it himself. Every day Tarl seemed to grow visibly stronger. It was disconcerting to watch his nephew mature right before his eyes. Rembeu wondered what was going on in his young mind. Tarl was definitely frightened but the boy would never admit it and that meant Rembeu couldn't ask. He was ashamed to feel relief.

Tarl was getting used to constant change. He no longer felt like a boy. When that had happened he could not tell. The only thing he could be sure off was that he no longer felt like a misfit. His inner strength was increasing and he was changing physically, gaining height and muscle. The Altai were constantly working on adjusting his clothes.

Finally it was time for the last Teaching. The routine was now very familiar. His uncle placed several stones around his body. Tarl recognized the clear quartz crystals and several small diamonds, but there were various other colorless stones that he did not. An unusual bitter smell stretched out toward his nostrils; herbs, that again Tarl did not recognize. Trying to remain calm he did not concern himself with what his uncle was doing.

When Rembeu had completed his preparations he directed Tarl to look into the geograph above. Tarl was surprised by what he saw. A smooth planet-sphere of blue ice glowing so luminously above him that his eyes stung. Against the black of the surrounding sky it looked like a bottomless hole ready to suck in whatever it could; consume it before rippling its skin back to a featureless orb.

Tarl closed his eyes. As usual he could still see the revolving globe but his eyes no longer stung. Amazingly, the sphere began to move toward him, rolling closer and closer as if to engulf him. As it did so, it became darker and darker until it had turned into a twinkling star.

The feeling of falling backwards into his subconscious had become reassuring in its familiarity. Strangely though, this time he was surrounded by pure bright white light. He could see nothing to direct him but could hear the strains of what he assumed to be music.

Tarl wandered toward the off-beat rhythm and discordant notes. A voice wavered in amongst the sounds. It was a new, unknown voice. Tarl stopped walking unsure if this was supposed to be happening.

"You call yourself a human male?! Do you not?!" Pure accusation tempered the words which warbled around the music as if coming from under water.

The strange rhythms moved within his chest beating stronger than his own heart.

"Yes I do," he replied trying too hard to sound confident and controlled.

"And yet you allow fear to rule your logic; to limit your boundaries; to halt discovery." The voice was mocking and cruel.

"I am a human man. I trust my fear to guide me from danger." Tarl's heart was thumping enough to make him feel ill.

The voice was unimpressed.

"You cannot even enter these depths without a cowardly potion to protect your imminently destroyable emotional sheath."

Tarl did not like the sound of this at all. What was this voice? How did it know about the potion? His concentration faltered. The harsh notes were making his teeth grate. He realized he could feel his physical body. The rhythm was jumping in his chest and booming in his ears. His skin felt transparent; his body weak. For a fleeting second he thought that he might not be able to cope and then the words came from his lips.

"I am an infinite being. I am connected with and indistinguishable from, the universe. Time is of no consequence to my soul and you are of no consequence to me." The words rang out: No fear; no doubt.

Suddenly, right in front of him, the ground stirred. A huge pink tornado whipped up, rising high above him. There was no wind even though he stood right at the edge of its swirling vortex. He saw something that looked like a gray shadow being sucked up at the point of the tornado and watched the shadow stretch across the wind tunnel turning it dark and murky.

Deep inside the tunnel he could see unknown symbols flowing in and out unaffected by the wind's force. His lips curled with distaste as the air became permeated with the smell of burning flesh. Again he heard his own commanding voice.

"Why am I here?"

The tornado whipped around and around harder and faster and then, with a jangle of screeching notes, the gray shadow shot upward; spat out; exploding into bombs of bright white light. The tornado blushed pink again and then died down as if it had never been.

Tarl's heart-beat slowly returned to normal as the awful music dissipated. His skin began to prickle and he felt his body separate. His hands and feet dissolved first followed by the rest of his body. He watched with curiosity as his physical body gradually disappeared. There was an explosion of white light inside him and, in that brief moment, he understood infinity: He was all space; all time; all light.

The symbols from the tornado ran through him like a stream of knowledge. Colors and divisions flashed quickly across his mind: War, murder, horror, beauty, peace, love. The vision he saw in the Moon Gate rushed in and out of his mind. Unspoken words caressed him allowing thoughts to form. The thoughts were not his but seemed to be offered as part of his freedom. He listened.

"The human race has many evolutionary streams. The history of your civilization shows that, occasionally the people of these other reality streams have crossed over and met with your people. Each time this has happened, evolution developed."

The voice was deep and authoritarian but not cruel like the one before it. Tarl looked around trying to place its source. The surroundings had settled. It felt as if he were floating without a body. He could only see shades of white but he felt quite composed.

"In this final Teaching you have discovered that you are one of those able to penetrate these dimensions. You need to prepare for many of these crossings. You will see many different parts of human nature. Use Truth and Light in these dealings and remember, they are human, just like you, but have evolved in an alternate environment."

Tarl wanted desperately to ask questions but knew this was neither the time – if indeed this was part of time – nor the place.

"The time paths of all these different dimensions are about to collide and unless their joining is given aid by those that can cross over, there will be unimaginable consequences. Your people will experience a complete change in the structure of everything they have ever known and to some it may well seem like the end of the world."

Tarl couldn't help himself.

"Please, what do you mean the end…"

The voice talked right over the top of his words.

"The final integration of these time paths is your ultimate goal. Remember: Truth and Light."

Then, all too soon, he found himself back in his own body again, standing in the white blazing light. Ahead, the image of a tall ivory pyramid grew from nowhere. The layers of the pyramid were inscribed with the symbols from the tornado. Only now he could understand their meaning.

On the very top of the pyramid was an old man with long gray hair who smiled down at him. The man's voice was kind and gentle and drifted toward him.

"You are a being of truth. Let no boundary secure you; let no reality limit you. You have opened your mind, your heart, your soul. Now you must teach others." The man's green eyes penetrated his own and Tarl realized with a smile that he was looking at himself. "You have finished your Teachings," the old man said sadly as if sorry to have to declare an end to the process. "It is time for you to go."

Tarl wanted to protest, to ask questions but his efforts were in vein. Like millions of tiny particles separating, the image evaporated and he found himself floating in the heart of a glorious colored light ray. Like a ribbon in the breeze it undulated, moving him along the path toward the ice blue sphere of Uranus. Just before he slipped right into that bottomless blue hole he opened his eyes. They didn't sting this time.

■   ■   ■

Rembeu was impressed that Tarl had finished his Teachings so quickly. He was also immensely relieved that he was going to be able to catch up on some sleep, he felt ragged with exhaustion. Tarl on the other hand appeared very healthy and full of energy.

"Oh to be young again," teased Rembeu as he staggered off to get some rest. "Well now, thanks to you my very gifted nephew, we know how to go about fixing this problem." He was disappearing toward the main cave so Tarl ran after him.

"We do? And how do *we* know that?"

Rembeu wasn't allowing interruptions.

"Now," Rembeu began again with a little more zest, "as your uncle…"

"Oh, so now you're my uncle again?" Tarl had been cleverly distracted. "If you order me around you're my uncle, if you want something you're Rembeu."

"Yes, yes, well I am about to order you around, thank you very much." He wagged a rather non-threatening finger at Tarl. "You must go and get some rest. We have a lot of work to do tomorrow. We're going to have a hard enough time getting Melik to work quickly without feeling the need to recite the latest Scientific Digest to us first."

Involuntarily, Tarl laughed.

"But shouldn't we be discussing what exactly…?"

"Now, now, let's not get all grand just because we've completed a few lessons. Huffedy me! We'll talk tomorrow."

And with that Tarl knew there was no reason to continue. If Rembeu wasn't talking, he wasn't talking. He would have to wait until tomorrow. Tarl headed toward his little boat feeling both strangely relieved and yet chaotically busy even though there was nothing to do but sleep.

Rembeu watched him stride away. His young nephew had become a young man. He was now nearly as tall as his own uncle, his muscles had developed, his shoulders had broadened and he radiated a confidence that was quite magnetic. Everything seemed to be going to plan but something did not feel right. He wondered if it was just his guilt talking. They should never have done it. Rembeu knew it was true. He was sure Parvo knew it as well. It was too late now. They would just have to make sure that the consequences of their actions would not be as far reaching as he feared. He shook his head and headed toward his slumber room.

6

Calatian Storm

The first tremors were being felt in Calatia. The community had begun making preparations for what they could only imagine was about to befall them.

A strange heaviness had encompassed the town and the normally friendly, outgoing people had become restrained and reticent. Concern mingled with curiosity creating conflicting feelings. Some people wanted to know as much as they could and others wanted to know only as much as they could process. They passed each other with dark faces nodding mutual apprehension.

Parvo headed a large group of Makers that were able to spend their time building shelters that would withstand the impending disasters. His team, made up of several of his own boat builders was grateful for his enthusiastic attitude. Since the basalt mines had closed due to the earthquakes they at least felt like they were doing something constructive. All the changes were at least fortifying the peoples' concerns but a quiet palpable panic was building.

Parvo, nevertheless, found the long days demanding enough to encourage an exhausted sleep. Each night he would collapse into bed, his only thoughts being about Tarl. It all seemed so impossible. Wracked with guilt he was unable to comprehend that it was his son, such a young and inexperienced boy that was apparently the key to stopping all this havoc.

In overwhelming moments he quarreled with his own reasons for sending his only son off on such an endeavor. If this planet was to be destroyed he was sacrificing the last moments they would spend together. And if not, he was sacrificing Tarl for nothing. Torment and fear consumed him in his sleep. Every morning he tried to clear his mind and would just immerse himself in the frenetic work of construction. Summoning a positive attitude for his men was the only thing that kept him going. He had no idea where it came from but was grateful for that strength.

This day had been especially difficult. Humid heat hung over the Makers from early dawn. The weather was becoming increasingly unpredictable and all Parvo could think about was going home to wash the sweat and grime off his sun-burnt body. When the backbreaking day finally came to an end he bid the men farewell with more vigor than he thought possible. As much as he wanted to go home he really didn't want to be alone but there wasn't anyone to turn to and he wondered whose fault that was. Parvo trekked the road back toward his house knowing there was no food in the cupboards and contemplated how he was going to stave off the stabbing hunger pains.

To his surprise, as he trudged up the incline toward his home, he saw Opal seated on his doorstep hugging a large ceramic pot. Her ankles swam in the folds of her chocolate silk dress delicately embroidered with golden butterflies; the tight bodice revealing her slight frame. Her looped black hair shimmered in evening light and her gray eyes gazed up at him with worry.

"Opal!" He was surprised to hear the energetic enthusiasm in his voice.

"Mr. Parvo, good evening." She stood in greeting, bowing her head slightly.

"What have you got there?" he asked gesturing toward the pot.

"A special dish I have created," she handed it to him, "I have no name for it."

"Well then we shall have to name it tonight, it smells so good! I feel like I haven't eaten for weeks." He motioned to the front door. "Please come in." Parvo was conscious of his sweat covered body.

"Thank you Mr. Parvo." Opal entered the hallway. Memories of this cozy home engulfed her but they were from so long ago that she felt as if they were from a different lifetime.

"Please make yourself comfortable," he gestured to the lounging room, "nothing much has changed in all this time. I'll put on some tea…I think I have some cinnamon tea in the cupboard. Is that still your favorite?"

"Oh yes, thank you." Opal was pleased he remembered. She settled herself on one of the large woven chairs.

"You'll have to excuse me for just a moment. I have got to wash this dirt off. I must look like a mud monster…" his voice trailed off as he disappeared into the water-room.

When he returned he found two cups of tea and a bowl of hot food waiting for him.

"Oh Opal that smells wonderful." he blinked a look of appreciation in her direction before keenly grabbing the bowl and easing himself into the chair opposite her making an exhalation of relief as he reclined. "Now to what do I owe this visit?" He asked as he scooped up a mouthful of food. Chilies, tomatoes and olives struck his palette and memories came flooding back.

Opal smiled. He reminded her of a big bear; one that needed a bit of domestic care.

"Mr. Parvo…"

"Please Opal, you know you can call me Parvo," he nodded encouragingly.

"Of course, Mr.… oh I mean Parvo," she tried to return a confident nod.

"Much better," he smiled, his eyes never leaving the bowl.

"It is a little difficult to explain," Opal hesitated not knowing quite how to go on.

Parvo stopped eating. There was a tone in her voice that worried him immediately. His eyes rose toward hers. Opal tried not to look down in shyness.

"Is there some bad news I need to know about?" he asked keeping his voice level.

"Well, actually I do not know. You see, I knew you would be the only person to really believe me, especially when you realized it was real."

"When I realized *what* was real?" Parvo put his bowl down.

"Oh I am sorry, Mr.... Parvo, I am not making any sense." Her hands moved out and down in a motion that appeared to help her settle her thoughts. Her gray eyes stared up at him with such intensity that all other thoughts disappeared. Parvo waited silently trying to ignore his mounting concern.

"It started several moonspells ago," she shook her head, "actually it started after that really bad tremor destroyed those houses near Rock River."

"Yes, we can't rebuild them until we are sure we have stable ground." Parvo nodded for her to continue. "What started?"

"I have been," she bit her lip before going on, "I have been hearing..." she shook her head knowing how this was going to sound.

"It's alright Opal: 'you have been hearing...'"

"It feels like I am being called." She shifted uncomfortably.

"Being called?" Jigsaw pieces were floating around inside his head; a few tiny shapes glowing with recognition others dull and meaningless. Something was trying to get through.

"It is like," she would just have to come out and say it. "It is like I can hear someone calling me - in my head." Opal frowned. "The voice started to wake me from sleep and now it is quite intense."

Parvo knew enough about this girl to know she wasn't experiencing a reaction to anxiety. But whatever she was experiencing he certainly had no explanation for it. All he could try to do was reassure her and somehow they would have to figure out what was happening.

"It knows about my secrets." Her eyes met Parvo's.

This was the first and only time he would see them turn steely gray.

7

Revelations

Tarl, Rembeu and Umbra met the following morning at breakfast to discuss the day's proceedings.

"Umbra is the most important key to this exercise," Rembeu said shoveling scrambled goose eggs into his mouth. "We will go up on the solar sail after breakfast and inform Melik of the next step. He has been keeping records of all the stellar discrepancies for a long time now. Once he calculates the co-ordinates we require, we will prepare for our first journey. Hopefully we won't have to wait too long. Did you feel that huge tremor last night?"

Tarl nodded resignedly. Umbra just hung her head. Her face held a grimace of inevitability and looked tired and drawn, even her bright silvery eyes appeared faded.

"Well Umbra, your young man here has figured out how we might attempt to stabilize the problem." Rembeu stated with unabashed pride. Umbra's eyes widened. She leant forward as if to extend all available hearing sources.

"The last Teaching gave Tarl an awakening," Rembeu exclaimed. Umbra's mouth opened.

"But…" Tarl tried to interject wondering why Rembeu was bringing this up now when he could have told her at the time of the last Teaching.

"I know, I know." Rembeu continued ignoring Tarl, "An awakening! You don't get one of those every lifetime! Anyway it appears that it is finally time for the time spirals to converge." He was speaking as if Umbra already knew this would happen.

Tarl checked Umbra's reaction. Her head was lifted toward the roof and she had begun to rock slightly.

"It is time already?" she said with quiet resignation. "I fear I am too old for this."

Rembeu spoke as if he hadn't heard her.

"This merging of reality streams apparently is not to result in wars or challenges. Tarl's awakening told him that we can rejoin the time paths using Truth and Light. Tarl sees that it is the link between time dimensions that needs to be balanced in order to bring them into alignment."

To Tarl's surprise Umbra's eyes lit up.

"Our Light Ray!" she cried.

"The primary bridge from the planet's core to the astral energy field," said Rembeu for Tarl's benefit.

Umbra reached out for Tarl's hand.

"That's it! That is the key. I knew it. But it is fading Tarl, our Ray is fading. The Crystal Radiant keeps slipping between energy fields and it has become almost impossible to keep it aligned." She slapped her hand on her heart, "Oh my boy. We knew you could do it. We knew." Umbra seemed to direct her gaze at Rembeu. "But I'm sure we don't have much time."

Tarl was still struggling with the fact that they both obviously knew this problem would eventually arise; knew how catastrophic this problem was and had discussed the possibility of outcomes way before Tarl had any notion of the situation.

"You knew this would happen? Why weren't we working on it earlier?"

Umbra's eyes drifted; unfocused.

"It came to me in a dream long, long ago. At the time I was filled with visions, visions so vivid and cruel that I felt it was difficult to trust them. I became very ill. Your uncle and the Altai took care of me until I grew strong again. If I were to have believed it, it should not have happened for another lifetime. That was what you were to be brought here and trained for, to learn how to prevent this from happening rather than having to correct it. Perhaps there are other reasons this outcome has drawn closer in time." Her eyes rolled upward, distracted.

"Come, come now," Rembeu spoke up, "we are lucky to have had a special one like you here to give us this prediction. And now we have a solution to work on. We must concentrate our energies on that."

Umbra nodded slowly but Tarl didn't think she looked like she thought she was special at all.

They spent some time discussing several possibilities but were not rewarded with anything remotely like a resolution. Rembeu tried to be positive. This problem was not something that would be solved by a simple discussion. If they could only figure out what 'truth and light' meant they might have something to work with. Obviously it had something to do with the Light Ray and obviously Tarl was part of the plan but to what effect he could not gauge.

Just at that moment a thought struck Rembeu.

"I know what we have to do!"

"You do?" Tarl couldn't believe it. "What?"

"Come with me boy, we have some brainstorming to do!" And he was off. Tarl ran after him towards the Potions Room.

"We just have to figure out *how* to do it." Rembeu was mumbling ahead of him. "Melik. We need to discuss this with Melik."

Umbra was glad that at least ideas were turning. She knew Rembeu well enough to know how easily he could go off on a tangent; and hoped that he was on the right track. Umbra returned to the Crystal Radiant. Her job in all this was to keep rebalancing it. It was imperative now that they not lose the Light Ray connection. The Crystal Radiant connected the energy of the magnetic core to the Light Ray. The Light Ray linked this energy to the time paths of the astral world. The time paths in turn, used the Light Ray to connect their energies through the Crystal Radiant back to the planet. In this way everything had been perfectly balanced.

If they were to lose the connection they would lose contact with these other reality streams and this meant the entire planet's energy fields would become irrecoverably unbalanced. The consequences of that were unthinkable. She would have to keep pulling these energies into balance until Tarl and Rembeu could make contact with the connecting paths.

Preparations were made to visit Melik. The Altai prepared provisions and Rembeu collected any instruments that he thought might be helpful. Once ready they made their way to the entrance of the mountain. At the end of the hallway the huge decorative circular door glowed with the reflections of the firelights. Thousands of tiny shining stones glimmered back at them. It reminded Tarl of the ancient kaleidoscope his father had found for him in one of the toy stalls at the markets.

Rembeu placed his hand on the center of the spherical wheel-like door and the colors spun round in a whirl. For a second the door appeared to be transparent before releasing a loud clicking sound and sweeping open. They stepped through it and it closed with a thud behind them. The beautiful exterior of walnut wood shone back at them hiding the intricacy of the inlaid stones on the other side.

It was the first time Tarl had been outside for quite a while. The early morning sun flooded around them making him blink blindly for several seconds. Rembeu had already begun to move off ahead of him, his apricot robes ribboning out behind him. Tarl hurried to catch up to him.

The smells of dew-drenched leaves and mountain soil greeted him. He looked over to the moored wind-ship remembering the freedom of his flight and the wind in his hair and felt a twinge of melancholy deep inside him.

They traipsed through some thick undergrowth and down a damp dirt path which wandered under the moss covered branches of large elm trees. When they came to a rock edge slick with lichen, they stopped.

"Be careful," mumbled Rembeu as he began the descent toward a small creek. "This way," he called again as he swung right and ducked under the lowest branch of a large elm.

When Tarl rose again he faced an amazing view. In front of him stretched a small plateau on which sat what could only be described as a very tall tent. As he moved closer he realized he was staring at some kind of large panel. He followed Rembeu round to its left and, underneath the angled panel, he found a small capsule.

"Come on, give me a hand," Rembeu insisted as he began to retract the segmented panel.

"What is it?" Tarl asked as the top panel slid down.

"It's my solar sail," Rembeu said as if it were obvious. He paused for a moment to admire it. "Made it myself after the last time you left." Rembeu was adjusting some smaller panels. "Figured Melik was not going to come down to visit me that much so I decided to go visit him. You should have seen his face the first time I sailed up there!" Rembeu glanced over at Tarl sporting a mischievous grin.

"How far up there is he?" Tarl was looking up into the clear blue sky.

Rembeu retracted the last panel.

"Too darn far. The crazy man better be exercising up there or his bones will turn into wobble." He busied himself with the capsule door.

"How does it work?"

"Hmm, yes, well, once the capsule reaches a programmed height the eight sails unfurl. I've constructed them from aluminized plastic. Nice and shiny." He was fiddling with a dial on the side of the capsule. "We direct the sails at the sun and particles of light strike the sail and make us accelerate."

"How do we steer?"

"Oh we just have to adjust the direction of the sails; the photons will do the rest." All the bags were loaded and Rembeu stood, hands on hips and eyebrows raised, attempting not to look impatient.

"Is it safe?" Tarl asked tentatively.

"Safe?! Young man I have been up and down in this thing for many season-cycles! Is it safe? Huffedy to that."

Tarl tried to hide the grimace and climbed into the capsule. There was only enough room for the two of them and a few small bags. Tarl controlled his lurking claustrophobic tendencies.

Rembeu punched a few buttons on the panel above his head.

"Just locating Melik's co-ordinates. Even though he stays fairly stationary we have to adjust for the planet's movements."

"Right," Tarl's said trying to sound interested rather than terrified.

"All belted up?" Rembeu was beaming. He obviously enjoyed his solar sail.

"Ready," Tarl tried to sound enthusiastic but belts were for crashing.

"Right then, we're off."

A roaring sound ushered from beneath Tarl's feet and, involuntarily, he gripped his armrests tightly. Rembeu saw this and tried to hide a smirk. There was a slight tremor which dissolved into a jolt followed by complete stillness. Tarl's ears felt strange.

"Why isn't it working?" he asked, relieved.

"Ha!" Rembeu laughed, "Oh but it is. Look." He pointed a finger over to Tarl's left. "You are currently flying toward the atmosphere. Soon we will be flying at millions of foot-lengths per cycle."

Tarl could only manage to move his eyes in the direction his uncle was pointing to. A small window revealed they were shooting up through wispy clouds. He squeezed the armrests a bit tighter.

"Bit more of a thrill than the old wind-ship hey?" Rembeu chuckled. "Won't take long now, just relax." Relax wasn't the word that had entered Tarl's thoughts.

As the sails unfurled they felt a small jolt. Amazed, Tarl watched as they unraveled like giant party tooters. The capsule swung slightly as the sails then stretched out into triangles. His uncle made an alteration on his panel and they turned toward the sun. The sails lit up, blazing with bright orange. It was truly beautiful. Tarl was starting to enjoy himself.

As they soared through the starlit darkness Tarl glimpsed Melik's zero-gravity balloon hovering gently amongst the stars and could make out the radial platform where they were to dock. He was starting to understand why Melik lived up here. It was the most beautiful sight he had ever seen.

Rembeu made another slight adjustment which slowed them down considerably.

"We will need to fly just past the balloon to then bring it back to the docking bay. Remember we have to wait for three full minute-turns before we can exit the capsule and load on to the enclosed docking bay. The pressure must be adjusted to that of Melik's balloon." Rembeu commanded. Tarl just nodded.

■ ■ ■

Melik was delighted to have visitors. He welcomed them on board offering bilberry tea and biscuits and gratefully accepting supplies. Rembeu instructed him on the use of several potions he had brought with him to combat the effects of low gravity living.

The balloon was an enclosed bubble-like capsule and was much larger than Tarl had expected. The interior was as big as his home in Calatia and included quite a few creature comforts. Large soft cushion chairs were snuggled around the room and sleeping bays were shaped into the far right wall. No blankets were needed as the temperature was regulated.

Although it was gravitized there was still a great deal less gravity here than on the planet's surface. This meant the walls and floor could be made of polyester and mylar materials. The result was an opaque surface that yielded very slightly when walked upon: Quite a strange feeling to get used to. The ceiling was of a transparent polyethyele material which allowed undistorted viewing of the universe. The enormous tear-drop shaped sheath rose high above them shimmering with ribbons of color.

There were several telescopes of different sizes set around the upper edges of the enclosure and one very large one was positioned outside in the shadowed area of the radial platform.

Equipment spilled across benches and papers scribbled with various charts and graphs which lay in chaotic piles everywhere, including being spread across the kitchen area and over the exercise equipment. It was obvious Melik didn't care much for keeping fit. He was very skinny and his skin looked slightly pasty under his lifeless fine brown hair which constantly fell across his brow as he talked. He wore the same brown coat Tarl remembered from their last visit and as always appeared jittery and anxious. His round glasses had only been wiped in the very center leaving a grubby rim at the edges.

The three of them sat round a table of air-impressed Perspex and made small talk for a short while before settling into the conversation that had brought them here. Melik listened intently as the plan was explained, his fingers tapping his head and running back and forth across his lips and as he digested it all.

"Hmmm," Melik began, "yes, well I like the plan…hmmm…" His eyes rolled up into his head and his eyelids fluttered. Tarl shot a glance at his uncle in concern but Rembeu twitched his nose in a manner that suggested that this was perfectly normal. "Alright…I just need to confirm…" Melik's eyes returned to his visitors. He raised his hands to head level, pointing both his forefingers like antennae.

"Yes?" Rembeu encouraged him.

"Now to restore the link between our planet and the other reality planes we must correct the balance of the Light Ray. To do that you must travel through these spiraling time paths and correct whatever it is that is causing this influx." Melik's hands were twisting beside his head as if he were trying to wind up his brain. "But, neither you nor Tarl have ever traveled these planes before. I know we can get you to transcend dimensions but to have to cross the seven boundaries without stabilizing. Surely you are aware of the risks."

Tarl slid a look toward Rembeu as if to say: 'Now I find out there are risks?'

Rembeu tried to direct a message to Melik by frowning on the side of his face that Tarl couldn't see. He wasn't successful.

"Melik," Rembeu cleared his throat, "the consequence of taking no risk is 1000 million times greater than the risk."

Melik's hands had become raised stop signs.

"Alright, alright, good then, that's out of the way. Had to be said. Hmm…now what we begin on is calculating the co-ordinates that will enable your entry." He stood and moved over to one of the many benches spread with papers.

"Rembeu…?" Tarl started to ask about the precise details of the risks they were to undergo but small fast shakes of Rembeu's head told Tarl that now was not the time to interrupt Melik's train of thought.

"I have been calculating aspects of the stars in these constellations," Melik was using his forefinger to circle part of a star map that he had thrown on the perspex table. Switching on a light which glowed brightly from underneath, the stars in question became illuminated, "and comparing them to the corresponding times of the stars in the next planes," A large sheet of paper was then tossed on the map that had been worked over several times by Melik's pencil, "I can calculate the time paths from these points." He waved a jittery finger across the sheet. "And then use the Crystal Radiant to trace the appropriate reality stream. Of course you are well versed in the use of the Atlas

Wheel at home, this will be used to transcend." Melik's hands were fighting around the back of his head.

Tarl realized Melik was talking about the wheel-door at the entrance to Atlas Mountain.

"Yes, yes, go on," Rembeu was getting excited.

"The wheel will have to be programmed precisely, and in conjunction with the Crystal Radiant. You and Umbra will have to work together there." Melik stopped, dead-still, realizing something important. "Do you know what you are going to do when you get to each of these streams?"

For the first time Tarl saw his uncle flounder. The awakening had given them the idea of where to begin but the actual solution lay within the experience. The visions had given Tarl abstract images of what they may face but nothing specific. They would have to travel to these alternate planes first and figure on a solution from there.

"They're humans just like us, Melik," Rembeu stated, "they may have had a different evolutionary growth but we will be able to understand their purpose and experience."

"And hopefully their language," Melik's palms patted the top of his head. Rembeu was cross at himself for not thinking of this.

Melik saw Rembeu's expression.

"Oh, oh, just thinking out loud. But you don't need to worry about language." He began rummaging in a perspex draw near some distillation tubes. "I have been sending small probes out to the surrounding systems and I think I have discovered a type of Tektite." He was holding a small black rock out in front of him, gazing at it reverently. "I have put it through several non-gravitational tests and after heating it and combing it with Acidis Nectrim - the rock found on Charon, Pluto's moon- the vapor released forms another solid."

Rembeu, knowing this could go on forever, tried to bring him to the point.

"Does this have something to do with language?"

Melik appeared surprised for a moment as if even he had forgotten where he was going.

"Oh, oh, yes that's right. The solid form is this," he picked up another shiny smooth gray disk about the size of an eye and brought it over. "It stores and transmits energies. It's based on the idea of the Crystal Voicers but much much better." He was smiling and nodding.

"Mmmm," Rembeu nodded trying to encourage a speedy resolve, "and the part about language?"

"Each voice holds a slightly different energy. If you take say, two people and imprint both of their energies onto this stone, each person will hear the energy as their own."

Tarl had no idea what he was talking about. Hoping someone would explain it to him without him having to ask, he waited until he saw his uncle's expression rise with the slow process of understanding.

"Melik! What are you saying? Please just spit it out!"

"It's a voice or language translator." He handed the gray disk to Rembeu. "To open it, press here, speak clearly and say 'open dialogue'. You can speak in any language you like."

Rembeu did as he was told adding a few warbling Altai words. As he spoke the disk jazzed with colors and then turned gray again. Melik took the disk and handed it to Tarl.

"Tarl you do the same but speak the language you want it to translate into." Melik's excitement was causing him to bob on the spot. Tarl did as he was told. Melik then placed it back in Rembeu's hand. Rembeu pressed the disk and Tarl's voice began to speak the strange tones of an Altai.

Amazed, Rembeu handed it back to Tarl. Rembeu's voice rang out:

"Melik needs lessons in summarizing." The joke seemed to go over Melik's head but Tarl and Rembeu broke out in laughter.

"Wonderful." cried Rembeu. "You certainly do keep busy up here don't you?"

Melik's face showed pure happiness.

"I have lots of other discoveries I could show you…"

"And we certainly want to hear all about them but perhaps we should start working on these calculations first." Rembeu was staring at the Voicer astounded. Melik was delighted.

■   ■   ■

It took much longer than they had hoped to calculate the many factors into their first journey. Tarl had begun to enjoy the light weight atmosphere and found a small push from a wall could accelerate his walking speed. He was amazed at how many vitamins and calcium derivatives his uncle insisted he consume in this relatively short time but he did as he was told. He discovered that he loved hearing Melik's stories and listened to him relate tales of star lore and science as they worked.

Melik taught Tarl about red giants; bigger than the sun which blew off their atmosphere leaving a white dwarf behind. He taught him about black holes, the worship of certain stars by the Ancients and even explained his thoughts on the holographic universe. But stars were his great love.

"See that cloudy area there? That's a molecular cloud...inside it, fresh stars are being formed. And see there, that is the Horses Head Nebula ..." and on it went.

Melik spent a great deal of his time checking the telescopes and measuring distances. Prior to their arrival he had sent out several probes that placed mirrors on many of the surrounding moons. These reflected light and gave a point of projection by which he could judge precise distances. His anxiety ticks had all but disappeared now he had so much to keep him busy. Tarl was amazed that he could perform so many complex calculations and recite detailed scientific explanations simultaneously.

Rembeu spent most of his time peering through the external telescope as if searching desperately for something he could not find. They always joined for meals to discuss their progress and exchange their findings.

Finally a breakthrough came. Rembeu's muffled cry from the external telescope alerted the attention of Melik and Tarl. Rembeu was madly pointing to a rich array of stars lying north-west of Orion and south-west of Auriga.

Melik began jolting every available limb.

"Oh, oh, quick telescope three," he was pushing Tarl over to one of the larger indoor telescopes. Melik grabbed it and started to focus in the direction Rembeu was pointing to. When Rembeu saw he was aiming in the right direction he moved toward the entry hatch.

Melik focused on the celestial equator.

"It's Taurus," he said as his hands dropped by his sides, "and it's time."

8

Calatia: Messages Received

A huge crack of thunder roared above Opal's head as she ran from the silk factory to Parvo's House. A darkening sky threatened to hide her forever from the world and she felt as if she were falling in slow motion into some unknown abyss. Heavy rain blinded her and weighed down her golden silk wrap making her steps small and awkward. A flash of lightening instantly pulled Parvo's house toward her before the darkness dragged it away again. She had worked all day without a break - not making silks but sewing crude tarpaulins to help all those who had to endure the loss of roofs and walls. She was nearly bursting with the need to tell Parvo her news.

Parvo, who had been seated on the front porch puffing on his herbal pipe and watching the storm, saw the tiny figure approach in the flashes of lightening.

"Quickly, come, the storms are growing closer," he reached out a strong guiding arm and took her inside. He felt her shiver under his grip. After insisting she dry off and put one of Tarl's threaded shirts on with a pair of his silk pants, Opal did so without dispute. When she walked into the fire room still toweling her hair Parvo couldn't help but smile. Memories were funny things; he never ceased to be amazed by how powerful they were.

Opal saw his expression. Her left brow pulled toward her right in an amused 'don't you dare' look. Parvo tightened his lips in an attempt not to laugh. The sleeves of the shirt hung well below the tips of her fingers and the pants were bunched at the ankles giving her the appearance that she may topple at any moment. As she approached she saw her wrap draped over the clothes-airer near the fire.

"Oh! It's too close to the fire!" She tried to run to the helpless silk wrap but tripped and fell still holding the towel she was using for drying her hair.

"Ooh. Careful little one."

Opal threw a look at him that clearly said: 'You know I do not like that name'. Parvo tried not to laugh as he calmly strolled over to the drier and moved it to the other side of the room and turned to face her with a look of utter satisfaction.

"Feel free to rest there as long as you like," Parvo said as he waltzed out to the cooking room.

Opal laughed softly at her failed rescue attempt. She rested her face in her hands, her wet hair falling around her like a shield and tried to collect her dignity.

"Tea?" Parvo asked in the sweetest possible voice he could muster as he settled in a chair behind her.

Opal raised her head to answer him but just stared into the blazing fire in front of her.

"The messages are coming more frequently. They are quite clear now. There is definitely no dispute about the fact that I am supposed to be receiving them." Her voice seemed somehow still. Noise came out but it didn't feel like it was her that was speaking.

"What's different about them?" Parvo leant forward. This was the moment he had both been waiting for and fearful of. He understood, without knowing why, that this was inevitable.

"The voice has... colors." The fire was curling and twisting in front of her: The shifting shapeless flames allowing thoughts to flow. "The words come to me like a vibration more than a voice. It is like I can feel the words." A slight tremor disobeyed her.

"What do they make you feel?"

"All I know is that I am supposed to go."

"Go where?"

Opal shook her head and lifted herself into a sitting position to face Parvo; the fire blazoned round her like an aura.

"To the place I am meant to go to." The simplicity in her voice revealed her hopelessness and tears welled in her eyes. She shrugged her shoulders.

"Opal, it's alright. You're getting closer. Let's just go over everything you've dreamt."

"The messages are coming when I am awake also." Opal looked almost ashamed.

"Well that's really good." Parvo's enthusiasm surprised them both. She lifted her eyes to meet his.

"It is?"

"Of course." Now we know you can access the messages in different states of consciousness. That's very important." He wondered how he knew that. His mind was churning. This was the key they had been waiting for. "Now we just have to take the information and make some sense of it."

"I've kept a log of everything I have sensed."

"Oh that reminds me," Parvo heaved himself out of the chair trying to ignore the pain that shot through his left calf, "I received Tarl's log books today from his Orbitor journey." He shuffled toward the side table and picked up the cloth bound journals.

"The log books!" Opal was trying to focus a thought.

"Yes, why?" Parvo turned in surprise to see the expression on her face. Surprise turned to fear. His voice became heavy. "What have the log books got to do with this?"

9

Merging Time Paths

Tarl peered through the telescope to see the star-image of the bull; The Lucida Aldebaran showed its red eye and the group of Hyades marked its face. He thought it was lovely but couldn't understand the fuss. And then he saw it. A momentary flash of colors, like sheet lightening, shooting across the bull's head. Another quick flash of colors met the first and they shimmered in a Y-shape and then disappeared completely. He looked up at a shocked Melik as Rembeu entered from the outer chamber.

"What is it?" Tarl asked not sure if he really wanted to know.

"The time paths have begun to merge," Rembeu was looking out toward Taurus.

"Or rather clash," said Melik sounding worried.

"What does that mean?" Tarl's voice disappeared into uncertainty. Silence greeted his question.

Melik's glasses had fogged up and sweat beads were forming on his brow. His hands began to repetitively pat his thighs. His mind was flying in a million different directions.

"Well, now we have your first area of entry. All I need to do is make a final calculation and you can ready yourselves to transcend."

"Right," stated Rembeu boldly, "the journey begins."

"The journey begins?" asked Tarl apprehensively. No one was listening to him. Why should they? He didn't know anything about anything. Did they really expect him to cross planes? Did they think he would know what to do when he got there? This was insane. Everyone was going to die and would be his fault.

Melik was wiping his glasses and shuffling papers at a far desk. He began writing numbers with both his left and right hands. Tarl moved over to Rembeu's side and waited with him.

Tarl stared at his uncle desperately trying to force an explanation from him but the only sounds being made were coming from Melik. Unidentifiable words tumbled from his lips until finally he dropped both his pencils and lifted a large sheet of paper in front of him.

"O.K. Now this is very important," he announced unnecessarily. "I have calculated your first entry as being 27 units from now. We will need to communicate in our regular way with the Crystal Voicers," he turned around and grabbed an extra one.

"This is for you Tarl." Tarl accepted the hexagonal crystal box gratefully. "Now," he went on, "it is imperative you stay in these other reality streams for only as long as I stipulate. Remember, these paths are only open for a certain amount of time. If you miss the re-entry co-ordination you won't be going anywhere for quite a while." The last words sounded heavy and filled with warning. Tarl shivered involuntarily. "And remember we will be able to communicate through any time field with the Voicers. I will keep you fully informed from this end and you can always call on me for scientific help. My calculations will follow from this first opening, so make sure you are always in contact with me in case another system opens up while you're already in one. You may have to jump between them without returning."

"Didn't you say that was dangerous?" Tarl regretted his words as soon as they had been spoken. Of course it was dangerous. He was supposed to be showing everyone how brave he was. Yet even now, he was feeling a heady mix of terror and excitement. Everyone ignored his question, again. But this time he was glad. He could pretend no one had heard it.

Melik sat at the table. He spread out the sheet of calculations and pointed a finger at the clusters of Pleiades and Hyades.

"Your first entry is here. He grabbed another smaller sheet from a desk behind them. "These are the co-ordinates for the Atlas wheel. Tell Umbra the key is G and give her these co-ordinates also." He sat back exhausted. "And *please*, be careful."

■   ■   ■

Tarl was sad to leave Melik. He had felt inspired by his enthusiasm and intellect. When they were to leave, Melik had given Tarl an uncharacteristic hug. His glasses swiftly fogged and he quickly turned away busying himself with several measuring devices and waving a backward hand as they departed.

They watched the colorful balloon diminish in size as they soared off on the solar sail and watched below them the ever increasing size of the place they called home.

It was late evening when they arrived and the air was quite cool. On entering Atlas Mountain, Tarl realized how tired he was. He hadn't been aware that he had been yawning non-stop on the solar sail journey.

Rembeu took a look at his exhausted nephew.

"I'm an uncle again…"

"Let me guess."

"Get some sleep," he ordered.

"Yes uncle," Tarl smiled. It was kind of nice to be told what to do when it was something you wanted to do.

"Go on then, shoo."

"Night," Tarl raised a tired arm and traipsed off to his little boat. He sat mesmerized as it strode through the water; the firelights from the entrance creating glossy rainbows that twisted and twirled like snakes across the rolling satin surface.

The diamond sand felt soft and warm under his feet as he tossed his sandals off and staggered toward the inviting silk bedding. Sleep came immediately. Visions splashed across his mind: very real; very colorful. They reminded him of the images he had seen in the Moon Gate back in Caletia.

When he finally woke he felt as if he had slept for several moons. He staved off a brief moment of panic as he grabbed some fruit and jumped back in the boat.

In the main cave several Altai's were busy planting and weeding over to the south-east.

"Tarl? Is that you?" Umbra's familiar voice called out to him.

"Yes Umbra, good morning."

"Oh my poor boy, it's afternoon. You must have been so tired."

Panic returned. He had overslept. How much time was there now? How many units had he wasted?

"Where's Rembeu?"

Umbra's crystal staff guided her to Tarl.

"Don't worry, you have plenty of time." Her soft face was an all-knowing smile. Tarl noticed though, as she moved closer to him that her eyes were definitely fading. Their vibrant silver was dissolving into a pale, fathomless gray. He reached out to her as she stumbled slightly.

"How are you coping Umbra? Has Rembeu talked to you yet?"

"I am coping just fine." She gripped his hand tightly. "Don't you spend time worrying about an old lady." She rested her hand along the side of his face. "Oh my boy..." was all she could manage before her voice cracked.

A melancholy jingling sound was coming from the Radiant. Umbra closed her eyes as if to gather strength.

"Now you must go and see your uncle. He is waiting for you at the mountain's entrance. He has left the door open so there is plenty of light in the passage. I must work now. Come on, off you go." She tapped his shoulder and wandered back to the Radiant muttering to it as if it were her child: "Don't be naughty now, I'm coming, I'm coming, I just wanted to have a word with my boy, don't be like that."

Tarl followed the light and exited the cave. It was a warm, glowing afternoon. The sun was just dipping from mid height and the smell of apple blossom and elderflowers drifted around him. A soft buzz of bees hummed in the distance and an occasional bird chirped in the background.

He found his uncle dressed in a luminous shell pink robe woven with silver-web thread which spun and glinted in the sunshine. Tarl watched him as he walked in spirals around and around, his eyes closed, his chestnut hair swaying. Quartz channeling-crystals had been laid upon the ground with all their points arrowing in toward the center.

Each individual crystal lit up as Rembeu approached it until he reached the final crystal when he opened his eyes and took a deep breath.

"Tarl, good, you are awake." He rotated his shoulders as if loosening up for something. "Meditation," he stated as he walked over to his nephew. "The spiral of nine. It opens you up to the mysteries; the nature of life and reality," he plonked a hand on Tarl's shoulder, "and hopefully a few time paths." He winked at Tarl as he led him to the herb garden. "I have many dried herbs already packed but we will need to take several fresh ones." He was pointing to plants at the center of the garden.

"I'm sorry I slept so long. How long do we have before we go?" Tarl started to pull out a sprig of eyebright.

"Just under 8 units now. But I want to be ready long before that." Rembeu was digging for a goldenseal root. "I have an ominous feeling that time has begun to shift." He dusted the root free of dirt and popped it into his silk holster.

"Shift?" Tarl looked at him blankly.

"I can't be sure of course. All the clocks are moving in correct syncopation, even the reversal clocks. But I'm afraid I am perceiving the movement of time differently. Only very slightly, mind you, but it does feel as if it's moving fractionally faster than it should."

"Will that upset our entry time co-ordinates?" Tarl was shaking the root of some coltsfoot.

"No, no, I'm not worried about anything like that. I'm more concerned about the planet. You know our historic knowledge has a great deal of gaps in it. I mean we know there has been human civilization here for over 200 million orbits, but we really don't know what happened 360,000 orbits ago. For reasons unknown to us all recorded history during that period has disappeared...or was destroyed. What happened that could have resulted in the loss of so much history? And, if all these records were destroyed, that is even more concerning. The records beginning after this period don't divulge any information about the past. They start anew as if they were recording the beginnings of a new civilization." He shook his head.

Tarl felt like he could see Rembeu's jumble of thoughts rocking from one side to the other.

"Other than the possibility that the human race died out, are there a lot of other theories?" Tarl tried to divert his uncle's negativity.

"Well, we should address that. If the human race did extinguish, it is possible that it could happen again. If we can't fix this, will the same thing happen to the people of this time?" Rembeu was pointing to some herbs in the center of the garden that he couldn't reach.

Tarl stretched his arm out to grab them. He tried to quell the rising panic. Human extinction had been far from his mind until now.

"Well perhaps, if this has happened before we may meet others who have record of it on their paths. Maybe we won't have to fix this alone." Tarl was screwing up his nose at the smell of freshly plucked catnip.

"So simple!" Rembeu stood back enthralled. "You are so right. Why hadn't I thought in those terms before? Oh I'm so glad I have you on this journey. You are with logic and lessons; I am with age and philosophy." They smiled at each other.

"And still I have to do the gardening," Tarl said rolling his eyes.

"And you need more practice – that's a weed."

■　■　■

Lunchtime was finally announced. Several tables had been set so all the Altais could join in. It was a feast fit for the two departing adventurers. Egg chowder was followed by grills of whole stuffed fish, chicken fillets scented with clover-honey and herbed duck in cider sauce. Small plates of sun-dried muscatels and roasted artichoke hearts dribbled with minted butter accompanied by noodle pancakes topped with thinly sliced beef and caramelized onions.

Tarl declared himself too full for dessert until he saw the sticky plum pudding swimming in butterscotch sauce. Custard apple pie also came out with fresh fruits and cheeses.

"I may not make it across to the next time path." Tarl moaned. "You may need extra power to drag me."

"As I feared," Rembeu smirked, "this is to be our last supper."

Tarl was about to groan some more when they both heard voices coming from their pockets. Rembeu pulled out his Crystal Voicer and spoke into it.

"Yes Melik I can hear you, go ahead. Over."

"We have a countdown procedure started. Each turn of the semi-unit will be announced until thirty minute-turns prior to wheel-spin. At ten minute-turns prior to the transfer each minute-turn will be voiced. Please concur. Over." Melik was sounding very professional. Rembeu winked at Tarl.

"He's in his element now. Let's have a bit of fun." He cleared his throat and spoke into the Voicer. "Roger that Star-gazer. We will be standing alert on your call. Over and out." Rembeu was enjoying the part too.

"Roger that. Out."

Tarl was looking at his Voicer.

"That's fantastic!"

"Mmm. Melik is quite the smarty pants," Rembeu said. "Actually, he initially experimented by combining the magnetic qualities of cobalt to store data and found that titanium used as a semi-conductor would process the information. When run through pure quartz crystal, which of course carries, concentrates and amplifies vibrational energy, it becomes a communication device. It also traces vibrational energy," he pointed the face of the Voicer to Tarl, "making these handy little reference points to locate the person using them."

"Who needs science class when I've got you two? How did you learn all this stuff anyway?"

"Ahh, well a lot of it is self taught," Rembeu was looking wistful, "but your mother and I, and you of course, come from a long line of scientists, explorers and inventors." He smiled. "You know your mother and I were taught with very different methods than you have been taught: Books gave us knowledge through light."

"That's incredible," Tarl said remembering the 'ancient bug' he had thought he swallowed whilst on the Orbitor.

"Oh yes" nodded Rembeu. "You know, orbs filled with the planet's history were translated through the palms of rare Knowledge Trees. They dropped seeds which when eaten, breathed the life of flora and medicinal herbs within us. Learning was very different for your mother and I. Of course we had to destroy or hide most of those methods. We were afraid of the consequences of using them. I have kept many of these methods hidden here and when we return you can also learn some of these ways. You must remember we had to protect the Voyager at all costs."

"There's that word again." Tarl was drawn back into the present after letting his mind wander to a place that grew Knowledge Trees. "I keep hearing it but I don't know what it means."

"Yes," Rembeu realized he had stumbled into a discussion he had hoped to save for later, "well now you have heard what is ahead of us and you have done such an incredible job absorbing your Teachings, I guess I must tell you the secret of the Divine Sources."

"You still haven't told me everything? We're leaving practically *now* and you still haven't divulged all your secrets?"

"Come, come, anger isn't the way."

"You have to tell me everything. Now!" Tarl was trying to calm this new found fury. He had never felt quite as angry as this. It didn't feel good but he didn't seem to be able to control it.

"Yes, yes, alright." Rembeu was a little surprised by Tarl's outburst but knew that the Teachings had taken him from one extreme to another. He should have expected this earlier. It was time to fulfill his promise: The promise to his sister, his family, his lore. "Sit down Tarl."

"I don't want to sit down; I just want you to tell me!"

"Of course." Rembeu tried to hide a frown. He took a deep breath and began reciting something he had learned long ago. A vision of his own sweet mother's face flashed into his mind: Her long blonde locks falling in soft curls that framed her creamy soft face; her green eyes, wide and entrancing. The memory of her voice gently rang out toward him and he repeated each word.

"Seven Rights were translated from the Divine Sources a very long time ago. Several have now become apparent. They have been passed down through the Keepers until the child of the seventh generation was born. It is written that this child, the child of the seventh line, will be born for the Greater World in the twist of time. This child will be born of two answers born of two lines." Rembeu's voice was calm and gentle as if he were reading a story to a child that was slowly falling asleep. "You are that child Tarl. You are the child of the seventh generation and born of two lines: A Keeper and a Maker." Tarl shook his head. He had never heard any of this before.

"It is also written that this child will be born under the seventh zodiacal sign, have a name number of seven and birth number of seven. A child of the number seven holds the promise of grand things, you know. He has the ability to inspire, to teach, to lead."

Rembeu waited for the information to form in Tarl's mind.

"You mean?" Tarl was staring at Rembeu as if her were a foreign object.

"The letters of your full name add to seven as does your birth-date." He stared at Tarl as if expecting him to collapse.

"But..." Tarl felt a terrible heat rising toward his skull. He blinked hard several times in an effort to control at least one part of his body.

"It is written that this child shall be coupled with true energies and higher understanding to realign universal law and that when this child's age turns to double numbers, the loss of his care-giver will create a bridge that will span the beginnings of turmoil. You were ten Tarl when your mother..." Rembeu's voice drifted off. He paused for a moment before continuing.

Tarl wanted to think his uncle was joking but Rembeu's serious expression was very real. None of this was making any sense to Tarl. Someone had made a terrible mistake.

"Born of the Source and he of its love, moon and sun shall meet to bear forth the power."

What did that mean? Tarl stood very still, unsure if he would be able to move even if he wanted to. He listened quietly as Rembeu carried on.

"It is written that he will come before the seven colored flames of the throne in the ultimate sacrifice of linking inner light." Rembeu stopped short. His nephew didn't need to hear the last sentence. He had heard quite enough.

Tarl felt ill beyond expression. His hands were shaking and his skin felt slick with sweat. He wanted to yell out that it wasn't him, to protest, but the words stayed trapped in his throat.

Then suddenly another voice interrupted. Tarl realized that the Voicer was still in his hand.

"The sand-glass has turned on the cycle."

"Thank you Melik, we will now start the countdown before wheel-spin. Over."

"Roger that. Over."

Tarl wanted to cry out, to scream, to run. He wanted to get out of this skyless cave, get in his wind-ship and sail through the wind and rain; to just fly through the elements until he was far far away. Why him? He wasn't anything special. He was just some stupid boy that didn't really fit in anywhere. How could they have got it so wrong? And what was going to happen when they found out it wasn't him? He was going to disappoint everyone.

Rembeu put a hand up to stop Tarl from saying the obvious.

"I'm sorry I didn't tell you before but I knew you would be alarmed." He took Tarl's shaking hands in his. "Let's just do the best we can, hey? Let's forget the Rights and just get to the job at hand. We can discuss this later when we have solved this whole problem together. What do you say?"

Tarl felt exhaustion flood over him. He tried to gather strength from somewhere, anywhere, anything. How could he put all of this out of his mind? He squeezed his eyes shut trying to force fear and horror down to somewhere he couldn't find them.

"Another moonspell of sleep wouldn't go astray." He tried to smile for his uncle's sake.

Rembeu ruffled Tarl's silky black hair.

"You're the best nephew in the world...I mean the universe," he teased.

"Apparently." He tried to joke but the words came out sounding forced.

"Should I start bowing now or save it for the public?"

Tarl rolled his eyes.

"I hereby outlaw bowing."

10

Calatia – The Log Books
Sing Their Song

Parvo and Opal spent the evening scanning the log books. Opal had told Parvo that something important would be found within their pages but she had no idea what. Parvo knew better than to dismiss intuition.

In their search they shared all the emotions Tarl had felt. They laughed at some of the more amusing entries and expressed alarm after reading about the treacherous storm he had endured. A confusing mixture of culpability and pride swirled in Parvo's mind.

"He is really amazing. I really don't think I've given him enough credit – or enough opportunities to prove himself," Parvo said quietly.

"You were just trying to protect him," Opal said as she ran her fingers across one of his drawing entries. "He is a very good artist you know." She pointed out the picture to Parvo. He nodded, impressed.

"I miss him," Parvo stated resignedly. I have been socializing more with my workers and I've started to practice the Four Games again but..."

Opal nodded.

"How long will he be gone?"

"I don't know. But quite honestly it feels a bit like the life has been sucked out of me. It takes me back to…" Parvo covered his face with his hands in an effort to hold back the memories.

"Parvo, you have not lost him. I know he is alright; nervous of course, but he is alright, I promise." Opal was torn between trying to be strong and wanting to melt into her own distress. "I miss him also," she said with empathy.

"Of course you do." Parvo was brought back to the present. "Of course you do," he sighed. That reminded him. "Did you see the entry about you in the end of the first log book?"

"No, I am still mulling over this one." Opal's couldn't hide her curiosity. What had he said about her? Was he allowed to do that in a travel log? She tried to hide her urgency.

"Here, this is the one." Parvo handed the log to her pointing to the appropriate section. Her wide gray eyes peered timidly at the writing. Tarl's delicate words spoke directly to her. She felt the voice again. It had something to do with Tarl's entries…something to do with…

"This is it. When you spoke of the log books I felt like I should have known something."

"What should you have known?" Parvo's eyes were wide with the opposing possibilities of risk and chance.

"I do not know exactly yet but it is getting closer." Opal closed her eyes. "The dreams, the voice, I cannot tell you why but it has something to do with Tarl." She looked across at Parvo who did not seem surprised at all.

"Why? Has something happened to him?"

"No, it is not what has happened; it is what is going to happen." Her eyes turned to face his.

"*What* is going to happen?" His voice was almost a whisper.

"I do not know," she shook her head, "I know Tarl and the voice are connected but it is not Tarl calling me." Opal tried to think; make sense of what she was experiencing. "Every night I see a vision of a huge gate; a gate I must find the key to but I do not know where to look." Her hands moved in circles and her eyes gazed mysteriously into the air, "The gate looks familiar."

"Draw it." Parvo searched frantically for a sheet of parchment. "Here, draw what you've seen." Opal sketched the huge shining gate embedded into the soft mossy hillside. The most distinctive part of the drawing was the key hole: it was the same swirling shape of a treble clef. He recognized the image immediately and scratched the side of his chin in confusion.

"That's the Locked Gate of Gold Glen."

"I have heard of that." Opal looked hard at the picture to see if there was something she had forgotten. "What does it lead to?"

"Well, that's the thing. No one knows." He picked up the drawing to study it closer before letting it fall to his side. "And no one knows how to open it either."

"Is there anyone that I could ask?" She inquired tentatively. Parvo looked down at the floor, searching his mind for any kind of connection.

"The only people I can think of are no longer living." He looked meaningfully in her direction.

"Oh."

"Opal, why do you think it's important?" So many thoughts were rummaging through Parvo's mind that he wasn't sure he heard his own voice come out.

"That is where the sound is coming from, but it feels like two voices. One is traveling from a distance, like it cannot pass through the gate and the other is somehow trapped behind the...?" No that sounded like she had lost her mind. "They seem to be trying to reach me through vibration or color." Her frown showed her confusion.

"Then we have to find a way to open the door." Parvo was surprised at how matter of fact that sounded; like he could go to the Locked Gate of Gold Glen, a gate that had, in all the memories of existing generations, never been opened, and just say 'open sesame' and it would miraculously unlock.

"Yes," Opal didn't sound convinced.

"It's really very late," Parvo stifled a yawn. "Tomorrow is your day off isn't it?"

Opal nodded realizing that they had been reading Tarl's log books for most of the night. Now she would have to make the long walk back to the Tzau's home probably waking several of their five children on entry.

"Why don't you stay in Tarl's bed? I'm up early in the morning but you can stay and make yourself comfortable if you like?" Parvo thought having someone else in the house again would be nice.

"Oh Mr. Parvo..."

"Hrrhhmm," Parvo raised an eyebrow at the sudden return to formalities. "P.A.V.O. thank you, and believe me, you'll save me walking you home." He wanted to suggest she stay permanently; while Tarl was gone, but he did not know how to ask and he certainly didn't want her to feel obliged. He was sure she was happy at Mr. Tzau's.

"I... well, I would not want to turn down such a wonderful gesture." Her heart hammered slightly but her eyes just wanted to bow to sleep. Opal realized how wonderful it felt to be back here. She would not ask for more, she would just be grateful for this short time. "I would be honored to stay in your most cherished house."

"I think you have been living under the influence of Mr. Tzau too long," Parvo teased with a genuine smile. Opal inclined her head: A return of Parvo's joke. Parvo's laughter was reassuring.

Perhaps the combination of the evening's discussions and being in the home of the only person whom she felt she could turn to, added to her vibrant dreams. When Opal finally woke up in the early hours of the morning she knew a lot more than she had done the night before.

11

The First Wheel Spin

The final minute-turn call came through their Voicers as they were about to make their way toward the Wheel-Door. They each carried a small pack filled with various contents. Rembeu also carried a golden silk satchel, each small pocket holding several amulets, potion tubes, herbal mixtures, cleansed gems, crafted wands and other such tools.

The Altai had made Tarl a comfortable holster so that he could carry the ornamental sword Opal had given him. He needed all the luck and protection he could get. Rembeu also chose two small crystal swords from The Swords Room and suggested they each place one in the long pockets inside their top shirts.

They made their way past the dining area and over to Umbra.

"So are you ready for the countdown Umbra?" Rembeu called out as they approached.

"I am Mr. Rembeu, I am," she said without hesitation. "Where's my boy?" Her right hand reached out.

"Right here umbra," Tarl replied as he grasped her outstretched hand.

"Now you both must take care of each other, and," she touched her forefingers to Tarl's brow, "remember you don't need eyes to see." For a fleeting moment her soft silver eyes seemed to look directly into his as if in perfect focus.

"Alright then, we must ready ourselves. Thank you Umbra, we shall no doubt see you soon." Rembeu sounded surprisingly confident. Tarl hoped it were true.

"Good luck to you both. We shall hold our trust for you here." Umbra patted her heart with her palm.

"Goodbye," Tarl said as they walked toward the rising stairway that led to the Wheel-Door.

"You haven't told me how we make the cross-over yet," Tarl said, his voice low, as if afraid someone may hear. "I assume you have followed the procedure before?"

"Oh yes, yes. Well, I've completed several portal transferences," Rembeu began.

Tarl felt more relief than he thought he should have.

"However," Rembeu continued as Tarl frowned, "the most recent was for quite a different portal slide. The transference was to check on crystals I've been growing in another area." Of course it was like a fourth dimensional slide so my presence was unnoticed, but it all went rather smoothly," Rembeu stated, sounding very happy with himself. "Nothing to worry about."

Apparently it was as easy as making toast.

"Tell me how it works." Tarl immediately wished he hadn't asked but the words were out there now.

"Well, let's think of these cross-overs as if they enable us to discover another aspect of humanity. Imagine that when all souls were created they first entered into a lower universe to take on a physical body. They then could enter through one of 8 portals. One of these portals is where we are now. If you can imagine each of these portals as being a kind of gate; each having principal differences."

"O.K.?" Tarl was looking at Rembeu as if he were rancid cheese.

"Alright," Rembeu tried again, "let's imagine the very fundamental origin of each portal. Each has a different primary color and vibration and within these, there grows the alternation patterns that create an evolutionary path for that civilization. These aspects then stay with that civilization for the duration of their time in this, shall we say, 'world'.

"Right," Tarl was scratching his head.

"Imagine that within each specific vibration, certain keys are held. If sought for and found these keys will allow the people of each 'world' to return to the original portal through which they first traveled and give them access to the next portal. Each portal holds these 'freedom keys' which ultimately, allow access to the limitless universe and all its factors."

"Right," Tarl tried to sound confident. He wasn't sure what else to say but he hoped if he appeared to understand Rembeu would stop talking. He couldn't concentrate.

"Ten minute-turns starts the countdown to cross-over. Please ready your co-ordinates and confirm." Melik's voice came through strong and clear.

They stood facing the round Wheel-Door. Tarl stared, mesmerized, at the incredible mosaic of polished stones.

"That's a Roger, we are entering the co-ordinates for wheel-spin now. Ten minute-turn countdown to continue as instructed. Over."

"Roger, over."

Rembeu was checking the paper Melik had given him. He then began pressing certain stones around the circle. As Tarl watched closely he could see certain segmented areas depress as Rembeu touched them. The outer part of the circle was divided into 12 perfectly proportioned segments and the inner circle was divided into 8 sections.

"Nine minute-turns. Over."

"There, now the co-ordinates are entered," Rembeu said standing back waiting for the pattern to emerge. The stones began to glow brightly. "Each stone represents a star or planet and each stone I have pressed relates to an aspect of the system we have to cross."

"Eight minute-turns. Over."

Tarl's palms were beginning to sweat. He bit his lip trying to focus.

"As you know our first portal of call," Rembeu chuckled at his pun, "is in the area near the second zodiacal constellation where we saw the time paths beginning to converge. Melik has calculated this star as our focal point." He pointed to a shining stone. "This ruby represents Mars. This has been calculated as the opposite point of entry."

"Right." Tarl's curiosity had been dowsed by anxiety. His uncle was reeling information off like he was instructing a class on the benefits of herbs in the kitchen but Tarl didn't seem to be able to hear clearly any more. The words sounded like they were rising from the depths of the ocean.

"Seven minute-turns. Over."

"Umbra will begin at the five minute-turn mark. Now, remember I mentioned the vibrations being specific to each portal? Well we need to tune our vibrations in with those of the portal we are to transfer to. The notes Umbra uses will access the Light Ray and activate the first portal. We just need to press this stone." Without touching anything he indicated a double-terminated quartz crystal at the center of the wheel.

"Six minutes. Over."

"This will begin the wheel-spin. When the wheel has opened we can enter. We'll be moving across the bridge between our plane and the converging time path. We do our work and come home. Easy as that."

"Right," Tarl felt like an idiot. Why was 'right' the only word that came to mind? Nothing about this felt right.

Rembeu threw a concerned glance at Tarl.

"And then we need to work on your re-balancing. You have got to tell me immediately if any symptoms begin to appear." The look was a no-nonsense order.

Tarl stopped himself from repeating the only word he seemed to be able to articulate. He nodded instead.

"Five minute-turns, initiating vibrational pull. Over."

Umbra began to adjust the Crystal Radiant. A haunting swell of notes rose up around them. It made Tarl feel as if he were falling through water. It was not unpleasant but he found it mildly disturbing as though all his parts existed individually rather than as a whole.

Rembeu saw Tarl, standing taut, eyes closed, fists clenched. He tapped him on the shoulder.

"Four minute-turns. Over."

"You must try to concentrate Tarl. Hold on to the crystal sword in your pocket. Be ready for anything." Tarl nodded trying to open his eyes.

"Three minute-turns and time to initiate wheel-spin. Over."

"Initiating wheel-spin, over."

Rembeu placed his fingertips on the center crystal and pushed. The stone lit up. Rays of bright white light shot out causing Tarl to involuntarily look away. He blinked but his vision was scarred by bursting colors.

"Confirming wheel-spin. That's a go ahead. Over."

"Roger. Two minute-turns. Over."

The wheel was spinning faster and faster. The glowing stones became a blur. The music was rising to a massive crescendo. There was a strong suction starting to pull at him from the wheel. Tarl felt as if he might be torn apart. Water sloshed in his head; his vision blurred in the blinding light before him.

"One minute-turn. Take care and remember I'm watching the universe for you." Melik's voice was anxiously calling out now.

Tarl would have swapped places with anyone at that moment. The wheel was spinning so fast now that all that was discernable was a spiral of flashing color and an arrow of bright lightening light. The suction was strengthening.

"Swords!" Rembeu cried out as he reached for Tarl's hand.

The wheel became a transparent, swirling red vacuum like rushing red jelly. The crescendo was peeking and Tarl felt his left hand trembling on his sword and his right hand trembling in his uncle's grasp.

"Five, four, three, two, one, portal open." And with that Rembeu pulled Tarl into the vortex.

12

Light Ray Red — Shu's Temper

For a moment Tarl couldn't breathe as he moved through a thick viscous skin. He wanted to struggle and scream but before he could try they were free of its heaviness. Relief was short lived. They were standing in the center of a massive dust storm. Fierce winds came at them from every direction. Tarl felt his grip loosen as the winds tumbled around them. He couldn't see anything except red swirls. What were they supposed to do now? His hair was being wiped all around his face, cutting at his eyelids and his skin was burning with the sting of hot wind.

A strong smell of sulphur gagged his throat. He was only just hanging on to his uncle's fingertips. He felt his fingers slip. Their hands separated. It was all going horribly wrong. Desperately he tried to make out his uncle's figure but he could not keep his eyes open in the biting winds.

"Over here, Tarl! Over here!" Tarl fought his way in the direction of Rembeu's voice. A hand reached out for his and yanked hard.

Suddenly everything was still. Tarl carefully opened his eyes and squinted up at his uncle. Rembeu's dark, waist-length hair was an untidy, red tangle and his face and ivory robes were dusted with glittering particles of red dust.

"I have never been so grateful to hear a voice." Tarl stammered as he spat dust out. "I guess I look as ridiculous as you?"

"As a matter of fact, red dust quite suits your complexion." Rembeu's wink caused red dust to flutter from his eyelashes.

"So, nothing to worry about hey?" Tarl recited.

"Umm, yes, well I've never experienced anything like this before in my travels I must admit." He screwed up his nose. They both looked at the surroundings trying to determine what they had walked into.

"It seems we are standing within a bubble," Rembeu pointed out as he gestured around them. Tarl's eyes followed the motion.

"A bubble? In a sand storm?" The same hot winds they had passed through still swirled in front of them but they were trapped behind some kind of protective layer. Rembeu walked up to the barrier and touched it with his finger.

"Hmm. How interesting." Rembeu looked back where they had come from and nodded as if confirming a thought. Tarl watched his changing expressions.

"What?"

"Well it appears we have managed to enter a time bubble," a finger tapped his bottom lip, "excellent for observation of course, but not much good to execute tasks in." He drummed his fingertips across his chin, "you see, we are currently in a time-free zone," he tried a little laugh which came out more like a mumble.

Tarl was expressionless.

"And that means…?"

"Well, as I said, we have exited time as we know it. It is nice to know that Perver's Theory is correct."

"Theory? You mean you didn't even know these were real? Our very first transfer and we find something you didn't even know existed?"

"Well, technically I did know they existed – in theory. You see there are pockets of the universe that are completely separate to all time and space; like little voids. Very rare according to Perver."

Tarl did not appreciate Rembeu making out that time bubbles were cute as kittens.

"If you're trying to tell me that entering this 'time bubble' means we currently don't exist and, due to that, may have never existed, I'm really not sure I want to hear it."

"Well, it's really just while we're in here. Once we enter or rather, re-enter the universal law of time, we shall exist once more. You see?" There was that easy-as-making-toast-tone again.

"I see," Tarl looked around trying to calm his annoyance, "what do we do then?"

"Yes, well, I am assuming that our co-ordinates were not functional at our time. I think the entry was only slightly off mind you. And actually quite lucky really considering." He was pacing around the transparent red bubble looking at the violent storms beyond. "I thought our time was warping slightly on our planet. I do recall mentioning that."

"Yes but you said it wouldn't matter."

" 'Matter'! If only!" Rembeu was smiling with his play on words until he saw Tarl's cheerless expression. "Hhhmm," he cleared his throat and attempted to correct his tone. "Indeed I did. Perhaps we could think of this as a little thinking time?"

The pun was lost on Tarl.

"Thinking is not going to make me feel better. How do we get out?" Tarl's simmering claustrophobia was beginning to surface. It felt worse than it ever had.

"Well, there really are only two possible outcomes." His tone remained relatively cheery. "First, the delay in corresponding time entry and co-ordinates should merge and then, as obviously we do not belong here, the bubble will purge its contents. Then we should re-enter the correct zone." He pointed to the furious burning red winds on the outside of the bubble and his thick eyebrows did a dance. "Or …well, let's just hope it's the first one." Rembeu smiled; all teeth.

Tarl rolled his eyes. How naive he had been when he left Calatia. Even his day dreams of the upcoming adventures with his uncle had been mundane. Oh to be back on that wind-ship, watching the sparkling ocean, reading and sleeping without disturbance or sitting with Opal watching the night sky explode with firelights.

A low rumble trembled below their feet.

"Come here, Tarl, quickly! *Now!*" Tarl moved over to him. "Get ready…"

Tarl didn't know what to get ready for. The rumble came again, louder this time and was followed by a fractured vein of light which skittled around the sphere they were trapped in.

"O.K. Hold on," Rembeu was gripping Tarl's hand tightly and his knees were bent as if he were about to jump into the air.

And then it happened. A burst of light exploded around them and Tarl felt as if he were being shot through a huge sling shot. The force of this movement made his stomach lurch. It had also ripped his hand out of his uncle's grasp. He felt like he had been thrown against a brick wall: A burning brick wall.

Tarl found himself seated, once again with hot winds coursing around him. He was unsure if he had been concussed but he certainly felt very dizzy and quite unconnected from his body. Sheltering his eyes with his hands, he peered into the gusts to look for Rembeu. But it wasn't Rembeu he saw. Definitely not.

He was staring at the front legs of a very large animal. He blinked as his head swam with giddiness. A huge creature, shaped like a red deer, peered down at him.

The only discernable difference was the two long sharp horns that protruded from where its ears should have been. Its big brown eyes were also protected by some kind of shield and its nose and mouth were covered by a mesh guard. Through the dust swirls he noticed that the creature was biting uncomfortably on straps running from its mouth and he realized he wasn't only looking at an animal.

He peered upward at the outline of a strangely dressed, muscular woman leaning down toward him. Her face seemed to be covered with a red gauze-like cloth that formed a hood and her body was draped with a blood-red sheet which was tided loosely at her left shoulder. Her bare, tanned right shoulder and arm revealed a large tattoo of a bird with its wings outstretched. She wore loosely braided jewels around her toes and ankles.

Tarl had never seen anyone ride an animal before. Any kind of enslavement was banned where he came from. What kind of people had they discovered? He jumped to his feet, red dust charging at his body.

"Get off that animal. Leave it be," Tarl cried, but his voice dissolved in the wind currents.

The woman let out a delighted roar which made Tarl stumble backwards. Quickly, he shot a look in either direction for Rembeu but could only make out the image of another of these creatures further off in the distance.

The woman leaned down and spoke to him. Her voice was calm but strong and carried well in the winds.

"Let us dispense of the manners then shall we?" She was smiling and spoke the words as if it were difficult to speak the language; placing accents in the wrong places.

Tarl was still indignant but realizing there was little alternative he decided on a menacing stare. The woman obviously expected him to say something and after waiting with no response, tried again.

"You are obviously lost. Men do not come to these parts." She waited again. "I know you are not from here. You speak a rare hybrid language that only women know how to speak."

Questions were circling in his mind like these damn winds. What should he do? He couldn't see anything except dust. It tasted terrible. Thirst was becoming overwhelming; breathing almost impossible. He nodded and cried out as loud as he could.

"Yes I'm lost."

"Come then," she seemed happy with this result. "I will take you out of Shu's temper." She reached her hand down to grab his and then pulled him up the side of the animal and onto the lower part of its neck in front of her. Her arms were thicker than his legs. Close up he could see that her skin was a smoky black under the red dust, and her black eyes shone deep under the hood of red gauze.

"The ride is not so far," her voice swam around him like the hot gusts. "Hold this." She handed Tarl a strap of leather that pulled at the animal's mouth.

Against his instincts he took the strap and tried to send apologetic thoughts to the animal. He was just going to have to accept certain circumstances if he was going to fulfill this mind boggling task, whatever it really was. His head was light and giddy and although he knew it wasn't true, he felt like he was being ridden around in circles.

The hot wind was making him ill. He could hardly swallow for all the dry dust in his mouth. The corners of his eyes felt as if acid had been dripped into them and his face burned as if it had been sandpapered. The last thing he felt was a strong arm catching him around his chest before falling into unconsciousness.

Tarl woke to the sound of voices: One very familiar one. Inching his eyes open one at a time, he viewed his surroundings. He appeared to be in some kind of underground cavern, quite small, but generously decorated to give it warmth and comfort. Above him, intricately beaded cloths hung in scoops across the ceiling. Some were pictures of battles and bloodshed; others were very different to the world he had seen on his arrival. They showed peaceful scenes of blue-green landscapes similar to those of his world.

Forcing himself up, he groaned involuntarily. It felt as if his body had been in one of those beaded battles. Checking himself for damage, he discovered he was wrapped in a dark red sheet. It was embossed with golden swirls that reminded him of symbols he had seen once very long ago.

"Ah, so you're alive!" Rembeu's voice was a welcome sound. He also wore a dark red sheet like Tarl.

"And so are you," Tarl's voice croaked. His uncle sat at a dark wooden table with four women. The center of the table was lined with plates of food. Rembeu was helping himself to a casserole.

"Stewed deer leg!" Rembeu held a food implement up in the air. "With stewed chestnuts. Delicious."

"Welcome to you Tarl." The woman addressing him sat at the far end of the table. She was completely different from the others. Her delicate, pale skin was framed by long curly ginger tresses and she stared at him with ruby red eyes. She was very slight in build and was dressed in a flowing silver garment tied around her neck. The garment had certainly never seen red dust. She began to speak again. "We are glad of your visit to the Arlou Terrain. Surprisingly, her voice was devoid of accent and rang out, gathering strength as it moved toward him like the growing rings in a lake.

"Thank you." Tarl stood and instinctively and made a small bow. Thoughts of Opal sprang to mind immediately. If she were here ... He stopped his selfish thoughts.

"There is no needs for formalities here," the woman's voice rang out again, "come, sit with us; eat."

Interestingly the chairs were made of wood and yet Tarl did not recall seeing any trees in that swirling mass of heat. He sat in the vacant seat beside his uncle and was passed an empty plate and implement and began helping himself to some food. Several dishes took his interest but he decided against the stew of deer leg.

"My name is Tarna. This is Corsus the Protector." She was directing an upturned palm toward the one that sat opposite Rembeu. It was the woman that had found him in the desert. With her gauze hood removed he saw she had silky dark skin, a perfectly sloped, narrow nose, square jaw and shoulder length dark red hair. Almost black eyes sparkled from beneath her straight claret colored fringe.

"Welcome *again*," Corsus said in her throaty accented voice. Tarl was sure she was teasing him.

Two of the other women were also tall and muscular. They wore the same type of red dress tied at the shoulder and also had tattoos on their right shoulders.

"This is Ambras the Tutor." Ambras sat next to Corsus. She had lighter tanned skin, finer features and blue-black silky hair which made her smiling eyes seem vibrantly blue.

"Welcome." Ambras's greeting was accompanied by an intense stare which Tarl found quite disconcerting.

"And this is Lardia the Carrier." Lardia sat at the other end of the table. She had dark brown skin and soft rounded pretty features. Tarl nodded in greeting as he had with the others but the sweet smile Lardia returned was washed with melancholy.

"Thank you for our welcome. My uncle and I appreciate your hospitality," he took a furtive glance at the one named Corsus; the one who had brought him in. She smiled warmly at him. Rembeu turned toward Tarl.

"We have apparently entered into Solaris. While you were sleeping I explained our reasons for visitation and it seems our help is graciously accepted." Rembeu lowered his head toward Tarna in thanks. "Tarna here finds it unnecessary to add but she is one of what they call an Ardent, which I understand to mean she represents ancient wisdom." He looked around the table for confirmation of this translation.

"Very good," Ambras the Tutor said.

"Tarna is of the origin of our world." Ambras' accent was staccato like. "Tarna's life, knowledge and memories live within us in our collective unconscious. Even though she is very real in both our past and present she is only represented in this form by our minds."

Tarl was completely puzzled.

"Are you saying your minds are projecting a memory?"

"In a way." Ambras frowned in frustration, her silky blue black hair bouncing slightly as she tilted her head from side to side. "Everything about her is stored in our minds, almost like another type of consciousness, but we bring this 'consciousness' into our visible world. However unusual this may seem do not make the mistake of thinking Tarna is simply an apparition or holographic visualization. She continues to exist, storing knowledge, just as we do, and of course this knowledge then becomes part of our knowledge and so on and so forth. Tarna is the respected advisor or Ardent of several Terrains and is joined by only two other Ardents that care for the remaining territories."

"Fascinating!" remarked Rembeu. "The power of the mind is remarkable. We hope to learn a great deal from you."

"And we from you," resounded the voice of Tarna. Both Corsus and Ambras made a nod of acknowledgement. Lardia continued to smile whimsically.

"If it pleases you to follow me, I shall show you our people and our land." Lardia's soft ringing voice rounded their attention again.

Their packs lay at Rembeu's feet. He passed Tarl his and they rose to follow the slender silver clothed lady as she floated toward a barricade on the far side of the cavern. They followed at the back, behind the others. Rembeu looked up as they approached the impasse ahead. Tarna's image dissolved into the thick barrier of rock as Corsus pushed a large round stone along the floor to reveal an open arch. Corsus then took a warrior stance at the entry and waved them through. Apparently she was not going to follow them.

As they walked behind the others Rembeu found a chance to whisper to Tarl.

"It appears that there are only women in these parts." They swapped glances of curiosity. "The whole society here is communal; there are no leaders except for the Ardents. It seems they used to have beautiful landscapes, lush with flora and fauna but a long time ago they experienced what they call the Last Great War. They say that men waged this war over ownership. The women wanted no part of war and so, joined forces against the men sequestering themselves in this

Territory. They discovered that in their moment of desperate need, the stored knowledge of their past materialized into these three Ardents."

"Really?" Tarl was amazed.

"They spent a great deal of time learning from the Ardents before precipitating any action. When the time was right they fought the men with their new found awareness rather than with weapons. They won and banished all men to the eighth land of Octimis where they remain to this day. Unfortunately, the weapons the men used destroyed the planet irrecoverably."

"The whole planet is like this? How do they survive?" Tarl couldn't hide his shock.

"I haven't even figured out how or if they bear children." Rembeu whispered.

A thought struck Tarl as he eyed the powerful bodies of the women.

"You don't think they brought us here to…"

"Oh goodness no!" Rembeu responded a little louder than he meant to. The women turned to look at him. He smiled sweetly and pretended to cough. Tarl was considerably relieved.

The area they had entered was like a huge, ancient auditorium buzzing with the activity of women draped in the same style of clothing.

A soft hum flooded around them like bubbles of music. It was completely enclosed by an ivory dome made of some kind of opaque material obviously strong enough to withstand the seething winds. Bulbous glossy red flowers fell like vines from the ceiling in the large arena like dome: Sofa chairs, small round tables, cabinets and cases and small computer centers were scattered around the area.

Each section was threaded with a thin web of sparkling silver strands. Certain divisions around the edge were graced with sandstone steps which were joined by a full-length pathway around the entire dome that strode down toward the large circular center. Every other panel on the lowest row was perfectly clear and revealed incredible views of the swirling storms outside.

Tarl walked around the sandstone pathway to a clear section and gazed out at the windy havoc outside. Red dust spun low across the ground. Far off in the distance a volcano sporadically belched dark smoke. The late sunlight turned the scene into a glowing wildfire.

Fallen rubble heaped alongside broken stone walls indicated that long ago people did in fact, live outside. But now storms arched and swirled in opposite directions to each other as if they were fighting their own war.

Above the twisting ochre dust, a butterscotch sky stretched wide and still, laced with icy clouds. A large orange moon glowed midway in the sky and large birds swooped high above the solar winds.

"It used to be very beautiful." Lardia was standing beside Tarl looking at the harsh red world outside. Her voice quietly reached out to him; her accent less clipped than Corsus and Ambras; her dark eyes filled with sadness. She gazed out at the stormy landscape. Up close her soft rounded face looked young and her dark brown eyes sparkled with hints of gold. Her brown hair was loose and cut blunt below her ears.

"I saw those beaded pictures in the cavern," he replied.

Lardia nodded, her eyes not leaving the scene she looked out at.

"Each terrain has to deal with this disturbed magnetization." She pointed first at one twister and then another. "You see how they move; this way, that way. Magnetic anomalies scattered across the surface pulling in all directions." Her eyes carried the expression that she understood this feeling all too well.

"Yes, I see."

"The anti-energy tools and laser weapons used in the Last Great War created such terrible disturbances to the original natural currents within the planet's crust that the magnetic forces became unbalanced. Eventually, the electrical currents flowing through the core were disrupted. This ended up affecting everything." Her eyes were focused on the orange moon. "Everything." Lardia repeated softly.

"And you have kept the men banished for all this time?" Tarl couldn't understand how this could help the situation. Lardia nodded once, slowly.

His head told him not to pry but his mouth had already begun without consent.

"Do you agree with this separation?"

"You are perceptive, for a man," she offered a small teasing smile.

"Thank you," he smiled back, "I think." He looked around to see who was in ear shot. Rembeu was hovering over one of the computer stations while Ambras explained its use. There was no one else nearby.

"No I do not agree," Lardia whispered.

"Please tell me why?" Tarl's voice was low as he stared directly into her brown sparkling eyes.

"Why do I not like the separation?" She inquired amazed that anyone would think to ask her.

"Yes, I want to know, please," he offered, trying to encourage her to discuss this apparently forbidden topic.

"I am not supposed to speak of these things," she leaned in a little closer, her eyes quickly checking the surroundings, "but it is true, I do not like the separation. You see, I am a Carrier."

"What is a Carrier, exactly?" Tarl shrugged.

"I am the one responsible for the passing on of directives or messages." She saw he still did not follow. "I am the link between these lands and those of the Outcasts. You see, with all the electrical and magnetic disturbances out there we cannot communicate via any other source." Lardia saw now he was beginning to understand.

"The men?" he asked.

"I have been traveling back and forth for a very long time now," Lardia kept her voice low, "and I have seen how the men of Liagon have changed." The view swirled in front of her.

Tarl had not heard anyone mention this place yet.

"I thought the men were in Octimis."

"That is what the people here are told but the men have created a new land now. They have become good and caring. They have found their own gods and they pray for a united planet; a planet free of these problems." She lifted her forearms, palms up to the scene of the fiery desert. "Why can they not believe me?"

"Who doesn't believe you?"

"I must be very careful Tarl." Lardia's eyes rested on his. "They cannot distrust me or I will lose my position as a Carrier."

Tarl recognized that look.

"You care about someone there don't you?" A memory flashed in his mind of Opal's beautiful gray eyes laughing under the bright firelights.

"I see you understand."

Rembeu's voice brought Tarl back to the present.

"Tarl! Tarl! Quickly, over here! I don't know how much time we've got. I think we can work with this information."

Tarl reluctantly descended the sandstone steps heading toward his uncle. The women he passed spoke in guttural tones; their language sounding harsh and heavy. Lardia followed him.

Rembeu was sitting at a table that was topped with a large tablet of pure red ruby. Ambras sat beside him and Tarna stood to his right.

"Watch," Rembeu declared as he pressed a forefinger to the table's center.

Tarna lifted her chin and her echoing voice spiraled around them.

"This ruby stone holds within it the bloodline of our humanity. It contains the seed of our ancestors and the fires at the core of our world. It holds the memories and knowledge of our past. Akashic... unfold."

Tarl and Rembeu watched as scenes rose from the ruby plate in three dimensional visions. They watched beautiful lush landscapes being torn apart by war. They watched men, fuelled by hatred, destroying each other and spreading the land with bloodshed. Strange devices shook and tore the lands. Buildings of architectural elegance and sturdy stone were flattened before their eyes and rubble eroded in the hot wind blasts.

Magma burst and bubbled from volcanoes, mountains fell into the ground like craters, meadows and fields buckled and broke causing lightening-like scars to rip across the surface. Natural magnetic fields swirled into dangerous magnetic dust storms. Influxes of tiny meteors were drawn into the magnetic pull and the oceans began to vaporize. The vision paused.

"Kinetic energy released," Rembeu muttered.

Ambras filled in the blanks.

"The women saved the last remaining animals and plants, protecting them until they could make proper enclosures. Those pioneer women created and built this enclosure, enduring unimaginable heat... and without any men to help. When the war was won the men were sent to Octimis. They fought between themselves and nearly wiped out the whole male population. The few who were left began to work together and built a retreat."

"Trishic... close." The visions fell like dust with Tarna's command.

Lardia became agitated and gave Tarl a knowing look. He did wonder why the vision had stopped amid all the destruction. Unaware of the exchanging glances Rembeu began thoughts of resolution.

"It is obvious your magnetic fields are distorted. It's a wonder you've been able to remain revolving and rotating! What have your experiments shown so far?" Rembeu was certain: It was this place that was causing the imbalances across all the reality paths. He was confident if they could figure out a way to correct these distortions they would be on their way home; back to a world of safety.

As Rembeu turned toward Ambras he caught sight of Tarl and Lardia and sensed a connection had been made. Perhaps a trust had been swapped. That was good; it could prove to be a valuable affiliation.

"We have tried to send out signals on varying degrees of low and high frequency electromagnetic waves to balance the forces but there was no discernable effect." Ambras replied.

Tarna turned and moved toward a table behind them where another woman worked. They exchanged looks but not words. The woman then effortlessly picked up a large carved wooden box, placed it in front of them and began to unload spherical rocks.

"This is Indigna. She has spent all her time experimenting with excavated stones." Tarna nodded toward Indigna. "Go ahead Indigna."

"At the time of the Last War," Indigna said, her voice very deep and her accent tossing the words straight at them, "The molten metal from the core was expelled creating these spheres of rock. The steam escaping from the magna in the fissures below the crust allowed space for minerals to crystallize within them. I have discovered in some of these that magnetite crystals have been made by bacteria within the rock.

"Should have met her first," Rembeu whispered as he nudged Tarl. Tarl simultaneously nodded and shrugged.

"It appears the bacteria have used them for orientation within the magnetic fields. They must have formed at around 800 heat-points and there seems to be some kind of lattice defect in their makeup, as if it were confused by the different magnetic forces."

Indigna's black eyes were flashing. She held up a large rock that had been sliced in half and pointed to the whisker-like crystals of magnetite at its center.

"I have been experimenting with them to see if I could change their formations. I was curious to find out if we could alter their basic construct. Then we may come up with a solution to alter the magnetic currents out there."

Rembeu was thinking furiously.

"This is definitely where we should begin. What possibilities have you come up with?" he asked.

"I discovered just one thing and that was by accident. I was washing one of these smaller rocks while studying a magnetic representation on the ruby stone and this combination seemed to affect the magnetic forces on the simulated poles."

"Of course." Rembeu enthused.

Tarl suddenly realized the implication and they both spoke simultaneously.

"A magnet!"

Tarl understood.

"If these stones hold some kind of magnetic force they will draw currents toward them," as the words came out, his enthusiasm waned, "but it would have to be an incredibly powerful magnetic field."

Rembeu was not going to give up on this possibility.

"How do you run things here? I mean what do you use to generate power?"

"We have an energy capsule sunk deep within the crust," said Indigna, "it picks up the electrical currents and stores them. We then can transform it into energy."

"Hmm," that was not what Rembeu wanted to hear, "so your energy comes from the very currents which are destroying your planet?"

"How else are we to collect energy in this kind of terrain?" Indigna sounded defensive.

Tarl caught a strange glance from Lardia and it gave him a thought.

"Are there other terrains that source different energies?"

The women looked as if someone had reached out and slapped them simultaneously.

"There is." Lardia spoke out for the first time knowing that Tarl had given her an opportunity, but the resulting stares made her incline her head in apprehension.

"It's in Liagon isn't it?" Tarl pushed on.

"How do you know about Liagon?" Tarna's ringing voice expanded toward him. "Ambras?! You have discussed matters that are of no importance to these newcomers, these men! You have taken a position of peril." Tarna was clearly going to punish her, mistakenly. Ambras was shaking her head in short defensive movements.

"Please," Rembeu raised a hand upward, "we are here to help you in any way we can. It is most important we are offered all available information. We need an energy source that we can use to, let's say, re-program your terrains. Redirecting the source you already use will not give us the strongest energy available. And, we will need lots of it. If there is another source in Liagon you must allow us to investigate it."

"It is not I who you will have to ask." Tarna regained control.

"Then who do we need to ask?" Tarl flicked a look at Lardia before facing Tarna.

"Magnaten, Third Ardent of the Fourth land of Dion, the Fifth land of Liagon and the Sixth land of Tentus," she inclined her head in respect. "Please inform me of your proposal." She raised her head again to face Rembeu, her red eyes flashing.

"If we can devise a way of redirecting the current magnetic forces we have a chance of correcting the anomalies. I will need to do further work with Indigna." Rembeu's shoulders were squeezed tight in anticipation.

Tarna stood perfectly still as if she were a hologram on pause. Everyone sat silent until at last she spoke.

"I will agree to this," she said finally. "However, I insist on certain conditions. Once you have made contact with Ardent Magnaten and have visited upon the men of his terrains you will be unable to return here." Tarna's voice chimed out across the dome unswerving in its finality.

Rembeu relaxed his shoulders but his expression remained unchanged. If she wanted to banish them for doing nothing except trying to help, so be it. He nodded.

Tarl tried not to show his panic.

"But the entry point is here." His voice was too high and he tried clearing his throat. "Rembeu…," he said, this time with warning, "the *entry point is here.*"

Rembeu frowned at Tarl, his expression dismissive.

"That is fine," he replied. He saw Tarl's concern but nodded politely anyway.

"Also," the rings of Tarna's voice rang out again swallowing the bubbling tones of the background music, "I will only allow the Carrier Lardia to travel with you." She smiled without warmth. "Our gravity pods will suffice for this exercise."

Exercise? This wasn't a sightseeing tour. Tarl was beginning to find this particular Ardent rather unlikable.

"If you succeed you must remove Ardent Magnaten and take his rule."

Tarl now couldn't hide his panic. What was Rembeu supposed to do with the existing Ardent? What did 'remove' mean anyhow? Rembeu couldn't stay here and rule a strange terrain in this mixed up world. They had other reality streams to justify; other evolutionary paths to smooth. How long would all this take anyway? What was happening in his world? It may have already been too long. Melik hadn't made contact with them. Perhaps he couldn't reach them through all this magnetic turbulence. They didn't know the effects of being stranded in a time bubble. And now, they weren't allowed back to the area they needed to use as an exit point. What could they do? Tarl looked desperately at Rembeu and caught several of the horrified expressions of the women around him. That made his panic swell even further. He felt his face flush and his heart beat harder. His pounding heart made his left arm ache horribly.

Rembeu's blue eyes hadn't flinched. Although he bit his bottom lip he seemed to be pondering this last condition as if he were about to make and unusual chess move. He had no choice.

"I agree and I certainly hope there are no more conditions."

"There are not." Tarna looked pleased, gallant.

Just as Tarl was about to protest, her image jolted like a series of frames that had lost continuity. Something strange was happening to her visual representation. The women didn't seem to notice, so either this was not unusual, or they simply didn't perceive it. Was something changing already? Or, was time running out?

"We will begin work right away. When will we be able to travel?" Rembeu was turning back to the spherical stones.

"I can prepare the vehicle immediately," Lardia answered.

"Excellent."

■   ■   ■

Indigna, Rembeu and Tarl worked well together testing ideas on the ruby stone simulator. After checking and double checking the instruments, Lardia loaded the vehicle and brought it round to the docking bay. By the time she had returned, she found the three of her companions seated around the ruby stone eating from large bowls of stew and gazing abstractedly at a simulation of the old terrains of Arlou; before the wars and destruction; before the tidal waves of magnetic energy whipped their world into desert storms.

Lardia sat down beside Tarl and gazed into the beautiful scene of rolling hills and silver leafed trees, trickling streams and grazing animals.

"You have brought up the simulation of the way our planet used to be," Lardia whispered. Tarl shook his head.

"No. That's not before, that's after. The simulator has produced this scene as a result of our last experiment."

"You've found a solution already?"

"Apparently so." Rembeu said showing no pleasure in the achievement.

Tarl swallowed as though his food had no taste.

"Do you believe the simulator is showing a correct representation?" Lardia asked.

"I cannot see why it would not," Indigna contemplated. "All the stored information regarding the planet is supposed to be correct."

"*Supposed* to be correct?" Tarl challenged.

"It is possible that there have been changes on the other side of the planet, after all, the settings have not been adjusted for a very long time and the planet is obviously altering.... I suppose the basic principle is the same."

Rembeu frowned resigning himself to the reality that there were no more facts available. He looked at Tarl and clapped his palms across his thighs.

"What do you say Tarl? Go or no?"

Tarl wished he could see that easy-as-toast expression again. There were just too many factors involved and so little time.

"Go," he said as he shook his head and shrugged his shoulders, "definitely go".

13

Calatia - Where Destruction and Vision Meet

Opal dozed in and out of a fretful sleep tossing and turning in Tarl's bed as the heat of the early morning sun swarmed upon her skin. Suddenly her eyes opened wide with fright as an incredible cracking sound boomed above her. She clambered over the bed and into the closest corner of the room as a shudder ran through the floor beneath her. The cracking sound was followed by a hideous groaning that reminded her of a wounded lion. As the shuddering grew stronger Opal tried unsuccessfully to grasp the rungs of the bed but it shuddered away from her. The whole house felt as if it were being thrust across rolling gravel.

Opal reached out her arms to try to grasp at anything semi-stationary, but everything was moving. Her body slid forward toward the escaping bed and her heart thumped sickeningly as another thunderous clap resounded above her. Holding her breath she felt ready to accept the worst until suddenly, the world was silent again.

For a moment she sat unmoving, staring at the wall behind the bed. The silk pants that Parvo had given her the night before, now had a large rip at the thigh which she fumbled at, bewildered. Her eyes were wide with panic. It was certainly another quake and they were definitely getting closer. Scrambling to her feet Opal ran into Parvo's room to see if he was alright but he had already gone.

Through his window she noticed the height of the sun. It was late morning. Opal ran downstairs frantically calling Parvo's name in the vein hope that he might still be home. Downstairs was a mess of fallen debris and Parvo was nowhere to be found. She had to find him.

The dreams from the night before were not just some imaginary inventions of the mind. Opal was dreaming the truth.

■   ■   ■

Visions spread before her all jumbling for attention. Where was Parvo? Grabbing her fire-scorched silk wrap she ran from the house in the direction of the silk factory. The sky was strangely dark for such a hot day. Frantically she ran joining the hoards of people that were also hurrying along the streets. Women were hugging each other and children were running past her, screaming indecipherably and a group of lone children were standing motionless, howling and desperate.

Suddenly she saw what she was running through. Houses had toppled; people were bloodied. Slowing to a walk, she scooped several of the howling children into a circle and finally got the attention of the eldest boy.

"Do you know Mr. Kelvi?" Opal directed her voice at him in such a way that his eyebrows quivered and he managed to look at her unswervingly.

"Yes." He nodded.

"Good. Go to Mr. Kelvi's house. It will be safe there. You are in charge now. Take all these children with you. I will send help very soon. Do you understand?"

"Yes." The boy's fear had been taken over by direction. "My mother is trapped. I could not lift it off her…"

"We will get to your mother," Opal tried to hide her horror knowing full well that there were simply not enough people available to help the so very many hurt, "you must do as I ask first though."

"Yes. I'll take the children to Mr. Kelvi's house." The boy looked up at Opal, his eyes brimming with fear.

"That is very good. I promise I will have Mr. Tzau send help." She hoped that was not a lie. "Alright?"

"Yes."

"Then go! Hurry!" Opal was shocked at her own forcefulness but she felt there was little else she could do. On she ran, hoping the boy would do as she asked.

Even from the distance, she could see that the silk factory was only slightly damaged. Relief was mixed with a strange sense of disappointment.

Inside, several tables had been smashed and part of the west facing wall had been damaged. Many of the bolts of silk were covered in debris and numerous windows had been broken but nothing major had been destroyed. Mr. Tzau was surrounded by some of the silk workers, all trying to console each other.

Opal began shouting out to Mr. Tzau. He heard the alarm in her voice, and there was something else. Somehow, he had suspected this was coming and now he realized what he was going to have to do. Surprisingly, he felt some sense of relief. This had been a long time coming. Now finally, after so very long, explanations were going to have to be made.

Mr. Tzau dismissed the silk workers telling them to go home to their families. He asked to be informed if any of them needed help – in any way at all. The terrified workers drifted past Opal wishing her luck, too involved with their own fears to notice anything unusual.

"Mr. Tzau," Opal bowed her head respectfully in greeting, "I must attend Mr. Parvo. Immediately." Her emotional state denied her grace.

"Mr. Parvo is not here," Mr. Tzau said apologetically. "He left here before the quake. I believe he was heading toward the mines."

"But the mines are too dangerous!" Opal was shaking her head in horror.

"He was worried about his men," Mr. Tzau said simply. I told him of the terrible quakes in Amania last night and the floods that followed and he decided to go and make sure the mine was properly closed. Several men were still in there trying to excavate stone for building shelters. Parvo was worried because Amania lies along the same fault line as the one that runs near the mine." Mr. Tzau eyes were telling her more than she wanted to know.

"You think the mine was damaged by today's quake?" Opal squirmed at the demanding tone of her voice but Mr. Tzau did not seem to notice.

"Perhaps. There has been a lot of widespread damage." His eyes implored her to accept the possibility that Parvo may have been in the mine when the quake hit. Opal shook her head.

"I have to go and find him."

"Opal, please, look at me," he said imploringly, "you cannot go out to the mines. There are huge cracks in the ground; we are still feeling tremors underfoot; you must wait for Mr. Parvo to return."

"What if he is hurt?" Her gray eyes were swimming with disbelief.

"There are emergency services attending to all the areas struck. They will be able to help Mr. Parvo better than you."

"Yes," Opal's voice whispered without her heart's approval, "but I have to ask him something."

"Perhaps I can be of assistance. I know you do not make a point of coming to me for help but surely... the situation..."

"Yes," came her whisper. Opal looked up into Mr. Tzau's face. The man had been her guardian for a very long time but she had learned never to rely on anyone other than herself. Now she may have no choice.

"Come, sit." Mr. Tzau reached for a stool from beneath one of the undamaged benches. Opal sat upon the red silk cushion. He pulled another out to sit close to her.

"Last night I dreamed of a world where searing winds swirled; where people were filled with anger and where forgiveness was lost," she hesitated, "I saw Tarl, Mr. Parvo's son."

"Yes, yes, you saw Mr. Parvo's son. Go on."

Opal could see concern wrinkling his brow but he didn't look at her like she had lost her mind. Turning her eyes away from his, she forced herself to continue.

"He needs help." Her apologetic tone was not lost on Mr. Tzau.

"There is no need to be ashamed of what you dreamed. You dreamed this when? Last night?" His tone was kind and compassionate. Opal was curiously surprised. Her eyes rose to meet his.

"Yes," she tried to feel confident, "but there is more." She took a deep breath. "I hear a voice calling me. I know I am supposed to go to it; to help it. I think it has something to do with the Locked Gate of Gold Glen...and Tarl."

"Much sooner than I thought," Mr. Tzau sighed, "but I suppose due to the circumstances..." he was thinking out loud as memories clouded his vision.

"What did you say?" Opal was confused.

"Oh I am sorry," he brought himself back to the present. "Yes, The Locked Gate of Gold Glen."

"Yes The Locked Gate of Gold Glen," she repeated her eyes widening with indignation. "Do you know something about it?"

"Well, only the legends that have been passed on, but there is something very important that relates you to The Gate." Mr. Tzau suddenly looked very old. "I thought that perhaps I should wait until you were... well...." He was shaking his head. How could he explain that he had never wanted to tell her, that he had just wanted to protect her?

"You have to tell me Mr. Tzau," Opal could see he was debating how much to divulge. "You have to tell me everything." Her hand reached out to his and rested gently on the old man's skin. His eyes lit up with her touch. Had she really been so remote toward him to make him delight in a simple touch?

Mr. Tzau nodded, a tiny glimmer of appreciation in his eyes.

"No one knew why you would have it and no one knew how to make it work anyway. I was just worried that they would try to take it from you."

"Take what from me?" Opal tried to keep the edge from her voice. How could she have anything to do with The Locked Gate of Gold Glen when apparently there was no one alive that knew more than its legend?

"Well, you see, legend says that the holder of the key is the only one that will have access to it. It certainly did not work when the Keeper Council tried to use it. Everyone just assumed it was some kind of copy; nothing more than a jeweled imitation of what the key may have looked like. But I thought differently." Mr. Tzau was nodding at that long ago assumption.

"The key?" Opal's cheeks had inched up in confusion. Mr. Tzau's circuitous words were beginning to form an impression - an impression that both incited a thrill of curiosity and wakened some lost dark fear.

"Wait, I will go and get it." Mr. Tzau eased himself into a standing position. Years of hard work had nearly crippled his small body. He tottered off toward the family's accommodations at the side of the silk factory.

Opal sat stunned and silent unable even to demand that Mr. Tzau not go wandering off before he had explained whatever it was that he was supposed to explain.

"Wait!" she finally called and ran after him.

■ ■ ■

When Mr. Tzau finally placed the object he had been searching for in Opal's hands she gasped in awe. A flawless emerald had been carved into the shape of a treble clef; its features glistening even in the dull light. It rested comfortably in her palm and was surprisingly light. Something about it felt familiar. At the very end of the clef's tail were two deep impressions. She ran her finger over them. It felt as if something was missing, as if the cavities should have held something within them.

"Hold it up to the light." Mr. Tzau was smiling as if he had just shown her a lovely trinket that he had bought for her birthday. When she held it up she could see movement inside the emerald stone.

"What is it?" She asked in amazement.

"Some kind of fluid," he said, his voice filled with the pleasure of being able to finally present it to her. "Maybe just water?" Mr. Tzau suggested unconvincingly.

"It is truly incredible but what is it and why are you showing it to me?" Opal was still gazing into the heart of the stone.

"It is yours, or at least you were wearing it when I adopted you." He remembered the day he took her home to meet his five children and his wife. "You were so scared you did not talk for many sun-stretches."

The memory of that awful day returned to her. She had not wanted to go to into Mr. Tzau's house with all those other children. They just reminded her of... Suddenly her train of thought was broken. The truth was blaring at her. The voice called to her again.

"This is the key to The Locked Gate of Gold Glen... and it is mine. I have the key. Mr. Tzau, I have the key!" Quite uncharacteristically, she jumped in the air holding the key tightly.

"Yes. I know." Mr. Tzau was delighted by her reaction. In all these years he had never seen her so animated. Of course she had had good reason to hide inside herself; he just never knew how to get through to her. "Perhaps I should have given it to you a long time ago." Regret tinged his words.

"Now is perfect timing," she cried out with joy. Opal hugged her arms around him careful not to loosen her grip on the key.

Mr. Tzau's face lit up and he hugged her back. He had waited for this for a very long time.

"Now we have to figure out how it works." Mr Tzau squeezed the words out as she continued to clutch him.

14

Red Pledge

The gravity craft was roomy enough. Lardia sat in the front section and proved to be a very capable driver. Tarl was surprised to see how confidently she took this role. Obviously Lardia was quite self-assured. Rembeu and Tarl sat in the lounge area behind her, constructing a plan of action and preparing the magnetite.

The wild wind currents blurred the red horizon outside their vehicle but they felt neither force nor high temperatures. They caught sight of a few of the strange desert animals but generally along the journey, the terrain did not appear to differ.

The vehicle with its magnetized base was cleverly designed to work with the magnetic pull of the terrain. It churned through the hot sands, dragged by the forces beneath them, so stored energy was not required. Their maps were not of roads and rivers but of the lines of magnetic pull which coursed around and under them.

Tarl handed a tray of the carefully extracted magnetite to Rembeu.

"You know there are a couple of things we need to discuss," Tarl stated. Rembeu hummed ascent. "And shouldn't we have heard from Melik by now?"

"Yes, I'm afraid that is undoubtedly due to the electrical and magnetic forces interfering with our signals. I have been thinking about it though and I am quite unconcerned about the length of time we need to spend here."

"But the calculations? If we overstay here, how do we return without the correct co-ordinates of the portal?"

"Yes, that is what I have been considering. You see, according to our calculations the next portal will be opening in seven moonspells – our time."

"*Our* time? There's a different time passing here?" Tarl accidentally stabbed a magnetite crystal into his forefinger. He looked accusingly at Rembeu.

"Look, let me explain before you start thought-jumping." Rembeu ignored his nephew's indignation. "Right. Settled?" Rembeu couldn't allow Tarl to start acting like a child. For better or worse, this was the situation and they had to deal with it."

"Yes," was the curt reply.

"So, I know Melik pretty well, I can just see him in genius-panic-mode, but he'll know exactly what to do. I guarantee he will have already contacted Umbra and she will have enlisted the help of the Altai. Melik has all our co-ordinates which he can pass on to Umbra – she can show the Altai how to use the Wheel-Door.

"O.K. that's a point," Tarl felt a little foolish.

"Now our only problem is that: A): We need to figure out how this time-shifting is affecting *our* planet's related time and, B): How do we cross from here over to the next reality stream." He smiled serenely.

"Oh is that all?" Tarl felt the tension swell again.

"Now, now, that time bubble we merged with when we first entered is our key."

"You mean the one that nearly entered us into non existence?" Tarl was lost as to how that was going to help.

"Yes, that one." Rembeu gave Tarl a cautionary stare.

"Just confirming," Tarl tried to keep his voice even but the fact that Rembeu was getting irritated with him wasn't helping his composure.

"Now, I know we can't return to Arloun which is where that time bubble existed but I expect there will be another on the opposite pole. You see any opening must have a closing, even if it is the absence of something. You know, like time."

Tarl was starting to think his uncle was just trying to be difficult. None of this was making any sense.

"When we entered that time bubble," Rembeu went on, "we should have stayed until we were pulled through its time tunnel. We would have entered this planet on the other side – the side of the men!" He slid a sheet of paper in front of Tarl and began to draw. "Now, you remember the simulation when the magnetic currents were finally redirected toward the North and South poles" he formed a squiggle with his pencil, "and there was an outpouring of electromagnetic energy as all the forces met," he was outlining the area of the final blast, "that is exactly where the exit time bubble should be." He made a large cross on that spot.

"Then what?"

"If we are in that time bubble when the explosion occurs it will effectively create a time-storm. The rest of the planet will not experience anything except a loud blast that will shoot from the planet's surface into the atmosphere, like you saw on the simulation. But, for us, it will be like accelerating the quantum particles – we will be exposing time and opening the doorway to another realm. If Melik has done as I think, he will be looking out for an opening which can be linked to his co-ordinates. We will be sucked back into the wheel-spin and spat out at our next address."

Tarl felt ill. The gravity craft was making several lurching movements in an attempt to grate through a burnt-red sand dune. His arms were covered with hundreds of shards from the magnetite crystals and they itched terribly. Not only were they not going back to Atlas Mountain between paths but he was about to meet with a terrain of people that had destroyed their own planet. Then they were going to have to take over their ruler; enter into non existence, again, and blow themselves up in the hope of being sucked into a whirlpool and spat out at: 'destination unknown' all on the proviso that his uncle's hunch was correct.

"I don't suppose Perver theorized any of that?" Tarl pushed an unenthusiastic smile toward Rembeu.

"Now, now, let's take one thing at a time, I'll finish up here. Go and rinse your arms and have a chat with Lardia. I'm sure she could use some company up there, and don't worry, everything will be fine, you'll see."

Tarl did as he was told. The seat next to Lardia was surrounded by dials and levers and he wrapped his arms round his middle so as not to accidentally touch any of them.

"How is everything going?" he asked at last.

Lardia dodged a deep ditch and zigzagged to her left.

"The drive is not so bad. The sand does seem to be moving quickly though. The changes are rapid and constant."

"Are you going to have a rest? Maybe stop and eat something?"

From the corner of her eye, she threw him a look.

"That is a good way to get caught in a sandshift." She replied as she concentrated on a difficult swing to the right.

"A what?"

"If we stop for too long the sand will churn around the vehicle, sucking out the sand below us and building up around us," her eyes flashed gold sparkles at him as she swung the steering wheel down to her left, "good way to get buried alive."

Tarl had come to 'chat'; forget about concerns for a few moments. This wasn't helping. She laughed at his expression.

"Right."

"Don't worry; I have been doing this for a long time. I have no intention of having a sand-burial thank you."

"That's the first good news I've had all day." Tarl huffed out a laugh in an attempt to feel confident. Lardia smiled silently.

If the scenery hadn't been so dangerous it would have been quite spectacular. The ochre desert sands spun and swirled like spirit-dancers. The rising ridges of the sand dunes swam with wafting sheets of dust. Huge canyons fell away below them; the dry river beds and craters forming ancient designs across their walls.

They passed what Tarl thought was a shimmering lake but was told it was the 'Prismatic Springs': A sulphur filled crater surrounded by the pigmented Cyanobacteria which created the effect of a shimmering ghostly mirage.

In the distance a volcano broke through the dry ground dribbling luminous red plasma from its peak, and all the while, not a tree to be seen.

"So tell me about the source of energy the men use in Liagon?"

"Well it is, unfortunately, the same they used to create their anti-energy tools and light weapons," she said as she wrenched the steering wheel to her right. "They store energy from the sun and the solar winds. It is a source completely free of electromagnetic currents, unlike ours. It's a much wiser way." Her accent made the whole thing sound ingenious.

"But, how can they…" Tarl never got to ask the question. Lardia forged on as though no one had spoken.

"They also are able to harness many times more energy than we can." She took a split second to look at Tarl. "That is why the women of Argou are worried."

■   ■   ■

The journey took a lot longer than any of them had expected. The drive had been grueling for Lardia who had expertly coursed the unpredictable terrain. Finally Tarl saw a change in the landscape up ahead. In the blood red sky a large land mass rose like a high red rock plateau stretching across the desert.

Atop was a low level rectangular structure, obviously some kind of living space. Red dust covered the material it was built from and formed small sand dunes at its sides. It looked as if it were deserted: There was no discernable lighting, no sign of life at all. Tarl shot a look of concern at Lardia.

"I know, it looks like an ancient relic, devoid of population and left to stand against time itself, doesn't it?" She appeared to be amused. "That is also what I thought when I first came here. Do not worry; there is plenty of life in there." Tarl's mouth lifted into a smile but he didn't feel like smiling. He wished people would stop telling him not to worry. They might as well be telling him to jump off a cliff.

They prepared to exit the vehicle as the craft pulled in under the docking shelter. Although the area was enclosed they all felt a surge of heat wrap them in a suffocating swathe.

"Come quickly." Lardia was beckoning to them. She approached a large gray wall and began pressing several buttons until it lurched open. It was as thick as Tarl's body was wide and made a heavy scraping noise as it opened. Lardia climbed over the high step as sand sifted at its base and directed for everyone to follow. Their movement caused many tiny pinpricks of light to flicker on above them. They were standing in a dull, featureless gray corridor.

Lardia walked toward the wall at the end of this hall and again pressed a series of buttons. Tarl and Rembeu jumped with surprise as a booming voice echoed all around them: Neither Tarl nor Rembeu understood a word of the guttural sounds.

"Please identify language as Hybrid, Anglo-Norm." Lardia stated.

A pause and then: "Who does the caller identify as?"

"The caller identifies as Lardia Arness, Carrier of Arlourn and servant of Tarna, first Ardent of the lands Arloun, Tespra and Fargon."

After a pause the voice boomed out again.

"You carry others also."

"I carry the visitors Tarl and Rembeu who have come a great distance to ease the temper of Shu. I have confirmation from Ardent Tarna." She slid a tiny square stone into a side panel. Silence followed. Tarl could have sworn he saw a flicker of uncertainty in Lardia's eyes.

"Acceptance is given," the voice echoed down the corridor.

The wall opened by folding into thick segments, scraping as it retracted. They followed Lardia inside. They were greeted by three men, each tall and muscular with dark hair and deep coffee-colored skin. Each wore a silver sleeveless top marked only by a red globe at the center and a red triangle of cloth tied at the waist which draped across black open-weaved pants that fell loosely to their calves. Their appearance was undeniably imposing.

"Lardia," came a deep throaty voice from the man just left of the center as they exchanged a three fingered welcome. He moved toward her and took hold of her shoulder to guide her ahead.

"Welcome visitors," another voice declared and Tarl and Rembeu found themselves surrounded.

They were shuffled into a room of black walls and basic design and were seated in a circle of deerskin lounge chairs where introductions were made. The structure apparently was made of many rooms branching from this one. Tarl could hear noises echoing from the other rooms and was curious to see how different this structure was from the one in Arlourn.

Rudhira, dark and burly with black wavy hair and penetrating blue eyes, was the most talkative of the group and led the conversation.

"So, you two men-folk have come to save our planet?" He looked at the two rather small visitors. "Let us hope it does not require too much brawn!" The men laughed loudly and Lardia flushed with embarrassment.

"Please Rudhira, show your manners. These men have traveled a great distance to help us. Imagine a planet of life again. We must work together now." Lardia's voice was pleading and urgent. Tarl wondered just how this was going to work.

Rudhira roared with laughter again and Lardia inclined her head shaking it in dismay. Her sad smile had returned but Rudhira was still laughing as he addressed Lardia. The words were unfamiliar but held an abrasive tone that both Tarl and Rembeu were becoming accustomed to. He then faced his two slightly anxious guests.

"Please my foreign visitors allow me forgiveness." His large palms were turned upward and were gesturing toward them.

"Not at all," was the calm reply of Rembeu. "It's nice to hear a bit of laughter again."

Tarl could always rely on his uncle to put that buoyant twist on things. He tried to look affable.

"You will have questions, I'm sure," began the man called Lionus, "we have conducted several experiments ourselves." He was reclining in the deerskin chair like a king that had just eaten his fill. Ruddy cheeks and twinkling eyes gave the impression of good humor and he seemed to enjoy shaking his head so that his large curls bounced around his wide face. "But first, I am sure Lardia wants to go and find her man." He tipped an amused smile toward her. "The luckiest man in Liagon. Literally." Huge guffaws sprang from his throat.

Lardia was not going to wait for a second offer. She glanced at Tarl and Rembeu. Both nodded assent and Rembeu tried to hide his surprise. Leaping out of her chair a little too quickly, she headed out of the room and off to her left.

"This is good news indeed. Who might be in charge of these experiments?" Rembeu asked apparently undaunted.

"That would be Sorsun. I will take you to him shortly but I'm sure you have further questions before running off to play with beakers?" Lionus led the laughter this time.

Tarl found it interesting that the men seemed more comfortable communicating in this language than the women. He remembered being told the men did not speak this language by Tarna. How much other information had they received that was false?

"My question will surely drive you all mad." Rembeu made an attempt at self depreciating humor: An attempt to let the men think their attitudes were well taken. The men looked back blankly. Rembeu's almost imperceptible hesitation was only noticed by Tarl. "I would like to know about Ardent Magnaten. Does he reside here?"

Tarl tried to hide the shock from his face. He wasn't really going to 'do' anything to the Ardent, was he?

Rudhira spoke again, his voice accusing.

"You wish to call upon the past? And what has our silent friend here to say?" He pointed a blunt finger at Tarl.

Tarl cleared his throat, hoping he would sound every bit as confident as his uncle.

"I believe a discussion with this Magnaten would be helpful. We understand that Ardents are represented visually as a manifestation of your collective knowledge of the past, but don't they also continually collect information to represent a true reflection of the coherent nature of this world?" Tarl let his voice lift at the end of the sentence to leave an opening for any additional information.

Rembeu didn't bother to hide his satisfaction. Tarl had spoken decisively.

Lionus held up a hand to silence Rudhira's impending retort.

"You have understood well. However, the Ardent can only accumulate new information if he or *she*," he put a slightly demeaning lilt to the word 'she', "has been given agreement." If we collectively choose not to configure our Ardent, he will exist only as knowledge."

"I see," Rembeu uttered.

So there was no Ardent Magnaten: Ruler of men. There was just a vessel of thoughts and memories, a historical record to review, a truthful record of the destruction.

Ardent Tarna may or may not have known. Rembeu wanted to give her the benefit of the doubt but it all seemed very convenient. He knew his lie about agreeing to 'remove' the Ardent lay uncomfortably with him but how else could he have approached the situation? If he told them the truth he may be placing their lives in jeopardy. On the other hand if they knew he had lied to Ardent Tarna they may not fair much better. At least in this terrain, the Ardents were less revered; used only as a reference to history. That's what he would have to work on. Rembeu's mind was working furiously and from the uncomfortable grimace on Tarl's face, Rembeu thought he was probably doing the same.

"So I assume then, that you men are the leaders of this terrain?" Rembeu was hoping to massage their egos. It didn't work.

"I sense your discomfort regarding the keeping of our Ardent and I can assure you our motives are valid." The third man, named Dusilu, who had seemed rather disinterested with the whole conversation, finally spoke. His dark thick hair ran like a river down his back and across his shoulders. His near-black eyes were a secretive place where unsolved mysteries had settled.

"Our Ardent resides in a protected area," Lionus added. "You must realize you are the first people to be informed of this outside Magnaten's supposed areas. Not even Lardia knows. We had little choice but to place him in the memory stalls if we wished to continue our community here."

"You see," Rudhira started, his blue eyes focusing on Rembeu, "when we were banished here and finally comprehended the extent of our destruction, we called together the men of these terrains. Most wanted to cease fighting. Ardent Magnaten's existence was picking up on the more demonstrative males. Of course that meant he sided with those wanting to continue to fight. This could not be so."

Dusilu's face was composed but the frustration in his eyes betrayed him.

"How could he have not seen the truth? We called on the help of both Ardent Tarna and Ardent Obique but Ardent Tarna would not communicate with us. Ardent Obique was most respectful and assisted us in returning Ardent Magnaten to the memory stalls and that is where he remains today."

"Very well protected," Rudhira added with gravity.

Tarl's relief was palpable. The job had already been done. Rembeu however, did not look so pleased. Tarl wondered what was going on in his head.

Rudhira began laughing.

"We have made sure there is no one here to fear. If you are here to help us, which I am sure we all believe is the truth," he looked between the two men beside him, "then we support you're contributions."

"Where does this Ardent Obique reside?" Tarl turned to Dusilu with his inquiry. Dusilu raised an eyebrow.

"You two are curious aren't you? Oblique holds the terrains of the East. His followers have turned toward their beliefs in Sidin. They believe this 'God' has the ability to reunite planet and sky to its former glory."

"They'll be waiting a long time!" Lionus bellowed and then slapped his huge leg.

Dusilu continued as if Lionus had not spoken.

"These followers are harmless. They are a mixed group of men and women and spend their time praying and singing waiting for Sidin's return. Where did you think our population comes from? A portion of the children born there are sent to either one of the separated terrains: Females that way, males this way. They firmly believe they will see their children again when we are reunited. Of course," he added with an air of resentment, "how they will know which of us is their child remains a mystery."

Rembeu's final question was pushing at him. He had to do it. He had to ask.

"On the Acceptance Stone that Lardia gave you when we arrived, did Ardent Tarna tell you of her conditions?"

"She did indeed," Redhira declared, "and we did think her conditions were, shall we say, hopeful." All the men bawled with laughter at this.

"Thought it might be fun to see who our new 'leader' was going to be, though!" Lionus hollered between staggered laughs.

"Might have to grow a bit first," Redhira choked amid grunts of laughter.

Tarl knew it was funny from their perspective but that didn't stop him from feeling annoyed.

"Oh no, we've made the little one angry. Seriously unintentional!"

Redhira tried to calm himself.

"We have a lot to work on. I think it is time you met Sorsun."

Sorsun slept, ate and worked in a warren of rooms at the furthest end of the building. His laboratory was cluttered with jars of liquid; unusual forms suspended in glass frames, and draws full of land samples. Small machines beeped and buzzed, heated and cooled, vibrated and exploded all matter of bits and pieces. He was burly and tall and wore a simple shift of worn red cloth. He was friendly but revealed none of the gregarious humor of the other men. Rembeu explained the detailed plan and asked Sorsun for his input on the energy transformers. For the next few days they worked long hours until finally falling asleep at their tables.

■　　■　　■

On the morning Rembeu dubbed 'exit-fire-wheel day', Tarl and Sorsun woke bleary-eyed to the bright face of Rembeu. They all shared a warm breakfast with several of the Liagon men and Lardia who sat next to the man she introduced as Treel, a good looking young man whom she constantly swapped sweet smiles with.

"Now let us go over the plan once more," announced Lionus after they had eaten. He gestured toward Rembeu.

"Right," Rembeu cleared his throat. "Firstly, Sorsun has our main energy stored in several cases. It is very important to stipulate how dangerous these cases are. We have used the condensed helium drops from the helium rain falls in Tentus. We have also siphoned sulphur from your Prismatic Springs to make batteries which have been used to make hydrogen from your water stores. The cases contain a mixture of these and will be used in the final stage of our plan. He took a deep breath to settle his thoughts. "Now theses will be used to start your energy tools…"

"No." Lionus interrupted.

We have not used those tools since the Last War. I don't want anyone to believe…"

"No one will know that these instruments are being used for this," Rembeu promised. "We have already suggested to Ardent Oblique that they should protect themselves. We have told them we predict a quake and not to fear or retaliate in any way." He smiled and added, "They believe that they have predicted a visitation by Sidin in this same period and are spending their time praying for forgiveness." The men slapped each other's shoulders.

"What excellent timing this Sidin has!" roared Rudhira.

"Alright," Rembeu moved on, "we are to use these tools to fire the magnetite crystal into the molten layer of the planet. And, then," he looked furtively at Tarl, "we will use these energy cases to ignite them."

"This will cause the grand explosion," Sorsun said as he adjusted his seating, "but it is the only way we can achieve what we need to do. Tarl and Rembeu will ignite this charge which will send an enormous surge through the planet altering the convection currents of the molten layer. This will create a chain effect pushing the electricity and magnetic forces in the one direction and dragging the twisted magnetic fields of the surface with it. Once these forces are realigned, the planet should settle again and eventually return to its former state. The planet will cool; rain will come; we will be able to sow plants and traverse the lands. Rembeu has given me plans to build orbital sun shades which will allow us to go outside sooner than I'd hoped."

"Well done," roared Rudhira enthusiastically. "What do *we* do?"

Rembeu gave each of the men their directions. Each seemed satisfied with their inclusion. Just as they were about to rise to set things in motion Tarl waved an arm to stop them. He needed to say something, something he had wanted to say since Lardia had made her confession.

"There is one more thing we will need you to do. I'm afraid I too will have to add a condition." Tarl stated. Rembeu looked surprised and the men looked amused. "If we accomplish what we are setting out to do Rembeu and I wish you to attempt reconciliation with the women of Argou."

Lardia's face shone with anticipation. Treel swung a hopeful glance at Lionus. The men were unable to conceal their shock. "But we cannot!" Rudhira boomed. "It is they who should reconcile with us!"

"They are afraid, even though they would never admit it, to take the first step." Tarl faced them with all the strength he could muster. "They fear it would undermine their position. If you could show them you've changed: Destroy the weapons and offer the remnants back to the women; send messages of peace; show them what you have learned here." He looked for the words that would appeal to them. "Imagine sharing your knowledge; sharing your *needs*." The last words made an impact.

Rembeu stood behind Tarl, placed a hand on his nephew's shoulder and continued in support.

"I agree. It is a condition. If you choose our help you will need to concede to this stipulation. Do you want a planet that you can safely walk across, that you can nurture and cultivate? Do you want to keep receiving children from strangers or do you want to raise your own? If so, this is what you must do in return." In reality he and Tarl just needed to realign the planet's energies but he trusted Tarl and he needed Tarl to trust himself.

The men looked at each other trying to gauge opinions without statements. Dusilu imagined the people in Ardent Obique's terrain praying for an event that was to be achieved, not by a God, but by these two strangers who asked nothing for themselves. Perhaps they were the gods. It was time to heal the fears of the past.

Lionus gave a short nod in Rudhira's direction.

"It appears your condition has been accepted."

"Right then," Rembeu stated simply, "let's begin."

■　■　■

Everything was going according to plan, which was nice for a change. The energy cases had fired up the tools from the Last War and the gravity craft had traversed the hot sandy desert to their required destination.

The energy tools, loaded with magnetite, successfully shot their contents deep below the surface into the molten layer along the lines of magnetic force. Their power was quite awesome; their rays capable of minute adjustments. Tarl tried not to envision destruction with every shot.

Rembeu had located the time bubble to the south, his initial estimate not far out at all. The group spent a long day, their faces covered in gauze masks, traipsing in and out of the winds, following the dry river bed and pumping the ground with magnetite. When at last they had finally reached the end of the intended trail it was time for Tarl and Rembeu to leave the group.

They unloaded the carefully packed energy cases of helium and hydrogen and began uncurling the enormous coils of rope. They then collected their own packs ready for their departure.

"Remember what we've asked of you." Rembeu spoke loudly over the swirling winds.

"We remember, and you are right, it is time for reconciliation." Lionus' voice carried easily over the noise. "Are you sure we cannot help you with this last stage?"

"No, this is our exit I'm afraid, but thank you." Rembeu was finally looking tired.

"We must make a move now," Tarl said.

Lardia ran from the gravity vehicle towards Tarl and wrapped her muscular arms around him.

"Thank you. You both have our deepest respect. We will honor you always." She moved her mouth close to his ear, "I have decided to stay here on Liagon. I will make one more trip back with the weapons and tools of the men and initiate the first stage of resolution and then I have been invited to return here for good. Believe it or not but Rudhira made the suggestion." She pulled her head away, her soft warm smile gazing down at him. She mouthed the words again, 'Thank you'.

The men raised a three fingered salute. Tarl and Rembeu copied the movement.

"I really hope this works."

"So do I Tarl, so do I."

Tarl smiled at the impossibility of their situation. What else could he do? It was quite possible that all they were about to do was blow a big hole in this planet's surface and blow themselves up in the effort. He slung his pack over his shoulder, grabbed two of the energy cases and coils of rope. Rembeu followed suit. They watched the gravity craft turn and disappear into the dust storms.

At the end of the trail they carefully lowered the cases into the narrow holes until the rope had almost run out. They then gingerly moved toward the time bubble. An opalescent glimmer was only just discernable in the hurling dust.

"Right now we must not let go of the ropes until a split second before we jump into the bubble. O.K.?" Rembeu said. Tarl nodded.

"Will the others be at a safe distance yet?"

"Oh they will be well over the fault line now." Rembeu's eyes followed the tracks of the unseen vehicle. He took a deep breath.

"We'll jump on three. Ready?"

"Ready. Count it down." Tarl's arms felt like someone was stabbing him with pins and his hands were shaking. The weight of the cases and the instability of the dusty ground were taking their toll. He wondered how his uncle coped so well.

"One..." Rembeu had begun the count. Tarl held his breath.

"Two... Three."

They both jumped simultaneously, dropping their ropes and leaping sideways into the bubble. The energy cases fell the rest of the way down until they crashed and exploded, blasting their way through the planet. They both lifted themselves from their landing positions and found that they were enveloped in complete silence; no winds; no roaring explosion. Through the transparent wall of the bubble they watched the land around them tremble with the impact. It felt strangely remote and yet they were watching the area that they had stood on just moments ago.

"Fascinating," was Rembeu's predictable observation.

"What now?" Tarl's voice was unsteady and his body trembled.

"Watch and wait," Rembeu replied simply. "We should see the blast as it follows the path around the planet until it returns to this point." Rembeu was standing strong, hands on hips, very impressed. "That was a mighty big blast." He turned his amazed expression to Tarl. "You know one of the possible results of this 'exercise'," Rembeu thought his pun at Ardent Tarna's expense very clever, "is that we could have blasted the planet right out of its orbit." He was looking at the blazing light ahead of them. "Lucky our little trick did the job."

Tarl moved very slowly in his uncle's direction. Was he angry or just plain horrified?

"We could have destroyed the entire planet?"

"Oh huffedy yes." His eyes were scanning for signs. "But we didn't, look."

Tarl hadn't finished with his uncle yet but his eyes followed. He forgot whatever it was he was about to say. The ground below them was quivering as the explosion coursed toward them from the opposite side to meet the point of ignition…to collide underneath them.

"We're going to die," Tarl said rather resignedly as he watched the ground rumble toward him.

"Look," cried Rembeu, "it's working!"

"Well for Sidin's sake," Tarl said astonished. Maybe there was a visitation from the Eastern god after all.

The winds were being drawn in one direction; the many different whirlpools of dust were slowly curving, being caressed toward the flow of the blast deep below them.

"The winds will rush in one direction before settling. The magnetite is carrying the magnetic forces like we hoped…the explosion will have resolved the core heat…"

The heaving ground was coming closer.

"Hold on," Rembeu reached for Tarl.

A huge blast of light exploded under them. Like a dying star, it swelled; bursting with red light around the outside of their bubble. It was incredible, blasting flames and bright white light rising up and being sucked into the atmosphere.

In the instant of the flash, they both witnessed an extraordinary sight. In a fraction of a second they saw several streams of transparent color like abstract elevators of light. Each rose, perfectly parallel, without meeting. It was too quick to grasp but Tarl could have sworn that he was being observed.

"I can hear it. I knew Melik was a genius."

"Hear what?" Tarl was still trying to comprehend what he had seen.

"The Crystal Radiant! Umbra's range is circling 'C'."

Just as Tarl recognized the haunting sounds of the Radiant he also sensed a loss of sight. His eyes could focus on nothing. It felt as if he were swimming in liquid diamonds. Facets of light pierced the corners of his eyes: Blue, green, violet, and orange. He closed his eyes to shut out the light but the shards of color still struck his vision. He cried out to Rembeu.

Rembeu said something back but his voice was distant. Tarl could not make the words out. He reached out for his uncle unable to see, unable to hear, unable to feel. It was as if he were being stretched across the space-time continuum.

"Over soon… hold on…bit longer." Rembeu shouted as he grabbed hold of his nephew.

They were spinning like wheels, around and around. Tarl was clenching every muscle in his body in an attempt to stop himself from being torn apart. Then, suddenly, he was being sucked backwards: Much too quickly.

They both burst out of the spinning cycle and into still clean air, finally landing side by side and flat on their backs. Looking up into the smoky orange sky, they could see a few wisps of white cloud hovering near the horizon. There was a buzzing coming from their Voicers. Melik had made contact. They could only catch every other word but it sounded like he was explaining some phenomenon he had just seen in the universe.

"Looks like we made it to the next part of our journey." Tarl said lying as still as was possible to counteract the effects of the washing machine he had just exited. "Don't think I'll be moving anywhere too soon, thank you." Rembeu made an effort to huff out laughter. Words were quite beyond him at this stage. They remained motionless making no effort to move whatsoever.

15

Calatia - True Dreams

Opal relayed her dreams to Mr. Tzau over and over again to no avail. The voice was still calling her and since she had held the key it had grown stronger and more urgent. Nothing they had discussed gave them a clue as to how to make the key work.

Mr. Tzau had told her the many facets of the legendary stories that he had collected ever since finding the key attached to the thread around her neck but nothing gave her any further insight. He told her the strange stories he had heard about the Key Holder but the disturbing tales only worked to make her feel even further from the truth. Apparently the Key Holder was both innocent and formidable. If confronted or threatened the Holder could employ horribly destructive forces. It did not sound like her. How could she be the Key Holder anyway? Too many clues were missing?

Opal decided to leave Mr. Tzau's house, much to his dismay, and go over Tarl's log books once more at Parvo's house. She gathered only a few of her possessions and headed back into the chaos outside. The air had become increasingly thick. Breathing was becoming difficult and several of the older people could not cope. The declining numbers in their small town were becoming alarming.

Parvo had not returned and when she found out that the mine had been completely destroyed she could not deny her worst fears.

Emergency crews had worked round the clock but had not found anyone yet. Of course, the rubble was so thick they may never be able to get down to the deepest shafts. Opal tried to be strong. No news was good news she decided. The sooner she worked out how this key worked the sooner she would be of some use. Of exactly what use that was she had no idea.

Opal tried to focus. She read the log books over and over again until she could read no more. Clutching the key tightly, she curled her torso around the scattered log books. Her eyes closed and she sank into slumber as if being sucked into quicksand with no way out.

A voice was calling her. It embraced her so fully she felt it was like a part of her very being. Its reassuring tones enticed her to wake from the darkness. Her eyes opened. Everything was pitch-black except for a small spot of light ahead of her. She walked toward it. The log books were spread open and she was curled around them asleep. Opal was looking at herself sleeping. But she felt wide awake. Walking around the small figure she studied the scene. There was a large rip on the leg of the pants Parvo had loaned her. This felt very strange. The implications of looking down at her own body were teasing her concentration. Obviously there was something she had missed. And then she saw it. A flash of light shot out from one of the log books. Squinting, she peered down to see a paragraph of writing glowing from the page as if it were illuminated.

The passage described the experience of purchasing her locket at the fair: One side with a shining opal and the other with a rainbow crystal. Tarl described the Holder of the jewelry stall as a strange and guarded man: A man that seemed to delve into the secrets of the buyer without any effort at all. He wrote that the overly curious man had insisted on knowing all the details of the person receiving the locket and when Tarl had mentioned Opal's name the man had reacted with a calm satisfaction that could have even been relief. It was as if he had been searching every customer for a very long time for this information.

Suddenly Opal was immersed in what she assumed was a forgotten memory: Back there, reliving fragments of the worst day of her life. Tree branches slapped her face as she ran madly through the forest overwhelmed by terror and horror. Someone fiercely grabbed her arm. A man stared down at her; his piercing pale blue eyes, desperate.

"Take this!" he demanded frantically, "I am the Holder! You must take the key. Protect it with your life." He had squeezed her arm so tightly that at the time her fear had blocked out his next words. But this time she heard them. "You must find the Keeper, you must make the union of Truth and Light." He let go of her arm and quickly placed something around her neck. "Go quickly, they are getting closer." He pushed her forcefully further into the forest and she ran on, fear screaming in every part of her body. She must have still been wearing it when Mr. Tzau finally adopted her.

How was the key related to the locket? Was the Holder that had grabbed her in the forest the jeweler that had made her the necklace? Ideas were clashing in her head like lightening. And then one solid thought opened up like a ray of light. The cavities in the treble clef.

Before she had time to consider this further she found herself lying on the floor surrounded by the log books again. Blinking her eyes open, she tried to sit up. It was very dark now, deep into the night. Her body felt like lead. Looking down at her thigh she saw the rip in the black silk pants. Reaching around her neck Opal found the locket and opened it. Carefully she pried the stones from their sockets and then looked apprehensively at the emerald key. She pressed the opal into the impression at the end of the clef tail. It clicked in making an empty echoing sound. She felt the next hollow on the slanting line of the tail and pressed the rainbow crystal into it. A shot of light spilled upwards inside the crystal and then the emerald began to glow. Terrified of what might happen next she tried to remove the stones again but they would not budge. Unsure what to do she just sat there, stunned.

Suddenly another tremor shook the ground. Now she had no choice. It was time to move quickly. Clasping the glowing key Opal strung the empty locket around her neck again and ran upstairs to change. Grabbing her midnight blue high necked caftan she changed without letting go of the glowing key.

Opal took a deep breath and ran out into the darkness of the night.

16

Light Ray Orange - Riddles and Rings

Melik was still talking when they both noticed the shadow blocking the sun overhead. They squinted up into the dark shapes floating in front of them trying to discern what they were. The needling in Tarl's arms had turned into prodding pains; jabbing twinges that smarted rather than prickled.

Sounds of gaggling ducks drifted away from them and sounds of laughter floated toward them. When Tarl could finally focus, he saw several people peering down into his face. They were pointing at him, jabbing him with their fingers.

The figures wore shapeless cloths in various shades of tan, saffron, ochre, green and rust. The material fluttered around their bodies like butterflies wings. Tarl thought he might have been surrounded by some kind of angels – except that he sensed these creatures were far removed from the kind of angels that their ancient books had described. He felt no comfort from these beings at all.

He looked around to see Rembeu also experiencing the same kind of jostling. Although irritated, he seemed incapable of retaliation.

"Ahh, give this one the green light." A clipped voice came from the crowd. The owner was peering down at Rembeu.

"Ey, this one's jumped on the bandwagon." A woman's voice retorted in the same short twanging accent.

"Come on then, get a leg up. We thought you two were out to lunch."

Tarl tried to sit up and found himself quite unbalanced. He reached for the ground to steady himself but found he was upside down, looking at the ground several feet below him. Laughter rose around him. It took a moment to comprehend that he, and for that matter all the people around him, were actually floating in midair.

In the middle of the sniggering and tittering a voice rose up.

"Hold your horses there lad," a tall thin man with pale ginger hair breast-stroked through the air toward him. "Here, set your sights on that," he lifted Tarl by the shoulders, uprighting him again. Tarl followed the man's gesture as he pointed toward the horizon. That definitely helped. He nodded to his prostrate uncle to do the same.

"Ahh, that's the spirit, give it a whirl then," the same man was encouraging Rembeu.

Rembeu checked the horizon and carefully stretched his body into a standing position. He grinned widely.

"Oh, yes, got it, thank you."

"See, there you go. You've hit the ground running." The man looked down past his feet to the ground far below him and laughed at his joke. "Well as a matter of speaking that is."

Rembeu was trying to comprehend what was going on. He looked down to the ground below to see his feet dangling in the air, in the process losing his balance and ending up with his face looking at the orange soil below, his toes aimed at the sky above. Peals of laughter jangled around them again.

"Alright now," cried the same man, "it's a bit hit and miss". He wasn't hiding his disappointment. "Come on you lot, give 'em a leg up, for goodness sakes."

One of the older women glided over to Rembeu and gripped his arm.

"Cannot 'ave you out on a limb, so to speak, can we?" She smiled and winked.

Rembeu managed to stay in a 'standing' position by leveling his eyes on the horizon. It felt strange without some kind of solid reference point to use for balance but he was beginning to find it quite comfortable. The air felt soft around him like a cushion that gently supported the outer curves of his body. His dusty red stained silver over-shirt that the men of Liagon had given him fluttered around him like dancing veils. He was glad they had also issued him with a pair of loose black pants.

Tarl was settling into this new experience too. It felt like he was floating in silky warm water. If only he could understand the gobbledygook these people were speaking. The words were familiar but their usage made them redundant. He looked across at Rembeu who seemed to be enjoying himself.

The sky was warmed with apricot tones and icy white wisps of cloud lay low near the horizon. Both the sun, high in the sky, and moon, below it shone a bleached light onto the surface.

For the first time he noticed how lovely this place, wherever it was, appeared to be. The canyon-like depression they floated over was covered with patches of dark mossy growth. Bright orange soil spread out in rings across the floor of the canyon as if someone had deliberately burned circles into the dark green ground cover. Plateau's rose up at its sides where the rings continued across the top of the flat land. Some of the circles intersected and some lay separate. There seemed no discernable pattern in the great expanse. Several strange pieces of apparatus disfigured the skyline, but at this distance, it was impossible to make out what they were.

The tall thin man that had directed Rembeu was now making hand signs to a man much further ahead who was hovering about a peculiar device that consisted of a very long pole and some other levers. He could see the man was pulling on several handles. Some of the crowd then moved over to Tarl and Rembeu and grasped their forearms.

"Now, don't be worrying, this is just par for the course. It's as easy as falling off a log." He laughed to himself at the irony, "Aye, but we haven't fallen off anything since we borrowed time." Ignoring Rembeu's curious expression, he went on, "Aye, but you'd be having a tin ear for that stuff."

Just as Rembeu was about to reply, they heard a loud clatter before a whirring noise rose in the distance rose followed quickly by a disturbance in the air. Tarl and Rembeu exchanged curious glances.

"Time to make tracks," the man said jovially. The rest of the crowd had already started to move ahead in the direction of the noise.

A tepid wind was encircling them and Rembeu's robes began to whip at his sides. They felt a slight pulling motion as if they were being dragged forward – but not by the people holding on to them. These people just kept trying to reposition their new guests to keep them upright. They happily chatted between themselves as if two strangers turning up in the middle of nowhere was nothing unusual.

Rembeu and Tarl were floating quite close together now and Tarl took the opportunity to try and get a grasp on things.

"Well we have definitely moved on to a different path. Just be honest with me, am I hallucinating? Have I died and gone to some bizarre afterworld? Have you died and come with me?" He was shaking his head; an expression of astonishment directed at Rembeu. "I can't understand what these people are saying."

"Hmmm," Rembeu contemplated, "well, you're right about the first point: This is definitely somewhere new. But no, I don't think we are dead." He displayed a satisfied smile.

Tarl stopped himself from rolling his eyes. Instead he took a deep breath and mentally counted to ten.

"Yes, and…?"

"Well regarding the language, don't try to decipher every word literally. I think we are lucky that we have arrived at a part of this planet that speaks a strain of our language. It's just that they have created a kind of slang, a bit like a regional dialect. Try to get the general idea; the essence of what they're saying. Get a feeling for their phrases rather than dissecting them word by word."

They were moving faster now. Rembeu's auburn hair was flowing behind him in streams. His stained silver shirt shone in the sunlight, fluttering at his sides like wings. He was really enjoying this feeling.

"And as for where we are, I have absolutely no idea," Rembeu stated delightedly.

"Right, good then. Well I'm glad we got that sorted out." Tarl's attempt at sarcasm eluded his jovial uncle.

"My I feel good." Rembeu was lolling his head this way and that looking at the 'sights'.

Tarl decided to try and do the same. It wasn't like he had a choice at this stage.

"Where are we going?" Tarl addressed the woman holding his right arm, interrupting her non-stop chatter with one of the crowd.

"Off to home-sweet-home, my lad." She answered. Tarl thought if she hadn't been missing her front teeth she almost might have been attractive. Her long red spiral locks bounced around her creamy fair skin as they flew and her large hazel eyes twinkled with humor.

Tarl was starting to enjoy the gently lulling scenery. Now that he had given in to whatever his fate was to be, his mind began to feel as buoyant as his body.

"How are we moving like this?"

"You enjoy bein' as light as a feather, ey? Well that's the order of the day."

Tarl nodded at her. He understood part of what she was saying but he was pretty sure she didn't answer his question. For some reason though, it didn't really seem to matter.

As they flew over a cliff edge Tarl caught sight of a creature coming toward them. The animal had a rich brown coat and huge wings that stretched slowly up and down. It didn't look like any bird Tarl had ever seen but seated atop its back sat a woman, her sandy hair flowing behind her like a veil. He wanted her to move closer but she turned off to the west. His eyes followed her as she disappeared into the distance.

On returning his focus to the direction they were headed, he almost couldn't comprehend what he was seeing. An enormous circular device sprouting several looping carriageways began to take shape on the horizon. It looked like fragments of some crazy roller coaster ride but the loops didn't seem to lead anywhere. Each one arched and twisted differently and ended in a dead end scoop. Rembeu appeared to be muttering to himself but their speed had increased so much that Tarl couldn't hear much over the whistling winds.

"On the home stretch now." The tall thin man had moved beside Tarl's group and was smiling broadly.

They flew high and to the east of the strange sight and finally the reason for their wind drawn movement became apparent. A huge machine like a giant fan whirred and whirled ahead of them. And below this massive fan, a village expanded across a vast expanse. The entire village was covered in a tan mesh supported by tubular poles which arched across its center.

They flew on as the sun began to fall toward the horizon glossing the sky with liquid gold. As they closed in on the area, they could hear music filtering up toward them and the smells of cooking filled their nostrils and awakened their hungry stomachs.

Another clacking noise revealed that the fan was being slowed and they gently wafted closer to the ground. The fan then clicked a few times and slowed to a stop. They drifted right to the edge of the village, now just a short distance off the ground.

Several members of their support group were leaving their new apprentices and swimming toward a tall transparent door. Tarl and Rembeu followed them into a foyer area where, after entering the main doors, people walked normally and objects were safely bound by gravity. The woman who had helped Tarl laughed at their surprise.

"Suits us down to the ground."

Inside they felt the full weight of gravity and stretched uncomfortably with the pressure. Tarl felt like someone had strapped rocks to his feet. He took a few strained steps forward. The entire city was housed under the arching gauze enclosure. Although barely visible it enhanced the lion-colored light of the sunset sky outside like some glorious colored filter.

The streets were lined with small homes interspersed with spectacular flowering flame trees. A trickling stream over to his right widened as it ran down toward a small lake to the north. Herb gardens jostled at the sides of houses and carefully tended gardens flourished with bright flowers. The piping calls of small birds zigzagged across the tree tops toward them and butterflies bobbed high above them. The crowd that had greeted them had dispersed amongst the streets and no one else seemed to pay them much attention.

"It's incredible," Tarl gaped.

"It certainly is," Rembeu responded, his face lit with pleasure despite his struggle to drag his leaden feet.

"Aye, take it in your stride gentlemen, there's plenty more where that came from." The tall thin man had come up behind them.

"I'm terribly sorry," began Rembeu, "we haven't thanked you for your hospitality, and in fact, we haven't even introduced ourselves."

The man looked delighted.

"Meself is Carny an' this be Eby." The man named Carny rolled an expressive wrist over to the woman who had helped Tarl. She smiled a toothless grin as her red ringlets bounced in elation.

"Aye, but I won't blow me own horn, we wouldn't have left ya high and dry." He gave a practiced wink. "We saw ya comin'you know."

Tarl wondered what he meant. He should have been glad that these people were so friendly but was unable to resist his suspicions. This was all very strange and very different to their dealings on the last path. Even though he was beginning to understand the gist of their conversation, something was niggling at him. They seemed to be talking in riddles, never really saying anything concrete.

Apparently his notions of alternate planes left a lot to be desired. So far these reality streams were nothing like where he came from. But then perhaps that's why they were here. Tarl nodded as his uncle introduced them.

"Come on you two, you must be hungry enough to eat a horse." Carny scooped his arm over his head gesturing for them to follow. Tarl held an expressionless face but he wasn't about to eat a horse for anyone, he didn't care if it looked rude.

The man was walking off to the right toward the river. They were led to a house that was much larger than any of the others. It had two large gabled doors which he threw open without effort. Incredible smells greeted them.

A long heavy wooden table stretched out in front of them laden with all manner of food. Tarl wondered which one was the horse. Several of the townsfolk were already seated and looked up as they entered. Tarl had a strange feeling these people had been waiting for them. They all looked so prepared.

Carny stood at the end of the table and made an announcement. "It be our newest on the block, Tarl and Remeu, the ones that sailed a little too close to the wind!"

A huge cheer rose from those seated around the table. Large goblets were raised and then clanged together before the contents were washed down in one mouthful. Tarl wondered if this was how they greeted all their 'block people' or whatever it was that Carny had introduced them as. This world was getting stranger by the minute and worst of all his uncle didn't seem to be perturbed by any of it. Yes, his uncle had always had strong tendencies toward optimism but this was different.

They sat at the center of the table and the people began to load their plates with food. Tarl looked suspiciously at the courses. He waited for Rembeu to choose a dish and then helped himself to the same meal. The dish turned out to be beef sausages in spicy mushroom gravy with soft mashed potatoes. It was so delicious Tarl helped himself to another serving and added some fried vegetables. He washed it all down with zesty ginger ale. He was starting to feel good, really good.

Rembeu struck up a conversation with those seated close to him, and surprisingly, was even starting to sound like them. Tarl couldn't eat another bite and sat back feeling full and sleepy. The others continued to indulge and he wondered how they all stayed so slim.

Tarl thought he may fall asleep right there at the table if he didn't try to get up and have a walk around. Rembeu was enjoying his conversation and did not relish the idea of lugging his cement feet around so he suggested Tarl go alone. Tarl surprised himself by asking Carny for permission.

"Aye, lad, go follow yer nose, no shuffle here to get lost in." It sounded like a yes so he nodded and thanked Carny for the wonderful meal. No one paid much attention as he left.

The sun had slipped below the horizon and through the gauze he could see a fading apricot corona ebbing at the sky line. The air was warm and comforting. The gentle flicker of iron streetlights bathed the lanes in an inviting yellow glow. He breathed deeply.

A moment to be quiet and calm was exactly what Tarl needed. He hadn't felt well since arriving in the last plane but had no intention of telling Rembeu. No one needed to think he was incapable, especially not his uncle. But he knew that all this anxiety was having an effect on his body. His left hand had been twitching uncomfortably, nothing that was visible; just an irritating trembling that wouldn't go away. A slight but constant headache was also bothering him. It swelled behind his forehead making his earlier feelings of euphoria considerably duller.

As he wandered, a vision of the strange curling spires he had seen on the horizon hovered in his mind like an apparition. Curiosity was being overwhelmed by concern. He would have to ask Rembeu what they might be and wondered if his uncle was acting up the pleasantries a bit. Although, he did look genuinely jubilant.

People milled about ahead but no one seemed to take much notice of him. He was intending to walk north along the river toward the lake but for some reason his body rounded the next corner turning him right and into a dimly lit side alley. Perhaps it was the beckoning smells of patchouli and wormwood that enticed him. His attention was caught by a group of people gathered together further ahead who were immersed in some sort of game and so he approached and watched.

A young woman clothed in a long sleeved, deep green dress which matched her sparkling eyes, sat at a table opposite an older man. Her dark blonde hair was looped in plaits at the back of her head.

For some reason a vision of Opal flashed in his mind. It was so real he experienced a sense of loss when the image dissolved and then suddenly, he felt like he was being stabbed in the chest as a wave of dizziness swung over him. Attempting to pull himself together, another horrible and intense feeling overtook him. 'Calm down,' he told himself, 'try to concentrate'.

The woman with the plaits shook a delicate left hand and threw out two cubes of carved carnelian across a shiny orange table cloth. She scooped them up again, closed her eyes, whispered the words, 'third time lucky' and spun them from her palms across the table again. The man's eyes turned cold. He began to protest but she dismissed him with a wave of her hand and the avowal: 'There's no smoke without fire'.

The mood here was very different to the cheerful smiles and greetings he had experienced earlier. A woman with light brown hair wearing a shiny rust shift replaced the man. Settling herself into the seat, she shook her long locks and locked her soft gold eyes hesitantly on the woman opposite her. She was told to ask three questions.

"Will I meet mine in the fullness of time?" The first question made no sense to Tarl.

After the question the woman with the green eyes spun the cubes and pronounced an answer. Her voice was quiet and Tarl had to strain to hear. The answer was illusive, indefinable.

"All periods are not equal; you cannot find it in time prequel."

The second question was asked a little more hesitantly.

"Will my journey be found in time's absent bounds?" The cubes were tossed again.

"A journey is seen, wrapped in a dream, when something buried and burning, bridges time's sleeve."

The woman asking the questions had become obviously fretful. Her voice wavered as she asked the final question.

"Will the secreted maximum spin or be spun?"

The woman with the green eyes looked upon her patron sadly.

"The time is still spring and yet to be spun, the House of the Dragon holds time yet to come."

The woman seemed terribly unhappy with this result but made no protests. She inclined her head in a gesture of respect before vacating the much sought after seat. A young man quickly took her place.

Tarl started to realize there was a lot more going on in this place than he had first thought. Moving around the crowd, he pressed on further into the alley where there were many more tables similar to this one. Smooth white pebbles with strange engravings on them were being spread at a table over a gold cloth; another table used rounded disks with beautifully inscribed pictures to form certain meaningful patterns; and then there was the man with eyes so pale that he looked almost blind, whose tales fascinated a young girl.

When a cool chill danced at the back of his neck Tarl made his way to the end of the alley and turned left into another softly lit street. There was more activity here but thankfully it was of a more cheerful mood. Except for the orange sliver of moon kicking its toes up at the horizon, the sky was now very dark.

He passed a few men juggling oranges while others sat on the grass watching and teasing as they drank large terracotta mugs of mead. They waved to Tarl as they jested with the jugglers. Someone had finally noticed him.

Ahead he saw a small undercover stand which tempted the buyer with brightly colored bottles of liquor and where large taps poured freshly brewed mead. Several of the customers sat at wooden tables chatting. The mood was jovial indeed.

The jugglers were amazing. One of the performers managed to spin an orange so it hung in the air as if stopped in time. It was an amazing feat but there was nothing here he could make any sense of.

Noticing a slight tremor in his left hand, he grabbed hold of it with his right to steady the twitch. Deciding to move on he suddenly wondered how to get back. Somehow, he had lost all sense of direction. If he could locate the lake he would know which way to go.

When he found himself in a very quiet street lined with small wooden houses he realized it had been a while since he had seen anyone. Golden plaques hung from every door and each plaque held a different name. He read them as he walked: The House of Position; The House of Distance; The House of Movement; The House of Separation; The House of Triangles; The House of Spirals; The House of Divine Proportion and on it went.

An uncanny significance tapped at his memory but he could not place the thought. He laughed at himself as the words, 'on the tip of my tongue' flicked through his mind. This place certainly did 'rub off on you'. Oh, he had done it again. Turning left at the end of the street, he heard a woman's voice call out to him.

"Stranger Tarl! You tryin' to scare the livin' daylights outta me?" It was Eby, the same toothless woman who had helped him when he arrived. "You're not so easy to find lad, come on then, don't drag your feet."

Tarl looked down at his feet.

Eby looked back at where Tarl had come from.

"Ay, yer got a few ales under your belt then?" She grinned a toothless grin.

"Oh, no..." he started to protest but she grabbed his hand and pulled him in the opposite direction.

"It's time to call it a day. There's forty winks holding bay right over there." She led him to a small house that displayed a plaque reading 'The House of Dreams'. She opened the door and gave him a push inside.

"Well don't let the bed bugs bite. The morning'll come soon enough." And with that she was gone.

The small two roomed house was neat and tidy. It was lit by a large candle in the center of the room and a sweet smell of lavender permeated the air. His pack had been brought here and laid next to one of two huge cane chairs. The thought of a shower was almost too good to imagine. A large bed billowing with pillows and a soft luxurious quilt beckoned to him but he resisted. He wanted to find his uncle before slipping into the dream world. His senses were telling him that something was missing; something important. The shower could wait.

Turning back to open the entry door, he realized there was no inner handle. The panic that rushed through his body was enough to make the dull ache in his head scream across his forehead and pierce his eyes with pain. Just as he was about to wrap his fists on the door it was wedged open by an external force.

The face of Rembeu was a welcome sight. His pack was slung over his shoulder as if he were making a midnight escape run. His auburn hair glossed in the street lights and he wore fresh robes of shimmering burnt orange. Tarl suddenly felt extra dirty. He was still wearing the red dusty silver robes and black pants of those from Liagon.

Tarl was about to blurt out his growing panic but his uncle put a palm over Tarl's mouth before stepping inside and shuting the door tight behind him.

"There's no handle!" cried Tarl in a frantic whisper.

"That's the least of our worries." Rembeu was waving a dismissive hand.

"There is something very weird going on here and I don't think we are part of the plan." Tarl's whispers were rising toward voice level. He was trying not to appear as frantic as he felt but he did notice at least, that his uncle's behavior was less vague than before.

"Shhh," Rembeu placed a vertical forefinger up to his lips, "I think you're quite right on the first count but I'm afraid, very wrong on the second." He ushered Tarl away from the door.

"What have you found out? Nothing they say really means anything." Tarl said, managing a whisper.

"I think that's the point. They talk in riddles and I don't think it's just to put us off discovering the truth." He scratched his head. "After dinner all the people dispersed into groups; some left the building. Those that stayed carried on with their 'happy-go-lucky' attitude."

"They what?"

"Oh sorry, it's quite catchy you know. I think some of these people are portraying a character that is not real. In fact, some of them act like they're hypnotized. I could feel it happening to me but for some reason

I was able to still have a sense of our reality. Anyway, a while after you left, Eby left too. Did she follow you?"

"No. Well I don't think so. She didn't find me until just before she showed me here." Tarl looked exasperated.

"Yes I saw that." Rembeu's mind was turning quickly. "There was a group of people that kept giving me strange glances. When they left I carefully snuck out and followed them. They saw me following and pointed to a place ahead that I hadn't seen earlier. It was quite dark and there were a few others there to meet them. When I got there they ushered me into one of the houses and told me there wasn't much time. They asked me to return later with you. There is something very important they want to inform us of."

"Can we trust them?"

"I don't think we really have a choice."

"I guess you're right. What happened after that?" Tarl asked, his mind churning.

"Well, I snuck back into the dining hall and entered into their riddle talk until I was taken to a house just like this one. I have been waiting for your return since. Had a lovely long shower though." He closed his eyes with the memory of it.

"Yes, I noticed," Tarl wasn't at all impressed with this fact.

"Anyway after this incident I realized I needed to make a herbal potion to counteract this lackadaisical attitude. I've made extra for you but you don't seem to be affected. I don't quite know how that's possible.

"Perhaps something to do with my Teachings?"

"Quite possibly. Better take some anyway." He searched his bag and then handed Tarl a vial.

Tarl knew why he wasn't affected and it was nothing to do with any Teachings but he wasn't about to confess to a headache and twitching hand…not yet anyway.

"I think I'll wait. I don't feel like that potion would do me any good." Tarl chose not to look directly at his uncle and continued speaking to deflect from the topic. "There are others you know."

"Others? What do you mean?"

"I mean others that aren't affected. I saw several groups trying to see a way out of their situation and I don't think they are happy about the conclusions. They seem to want to move past all this… whatever *this* is."

"I fear *this* is going to be a bit more difficult than I'd hoped. Come on we must go." Rembeu moved toward the door.

Tarl was about to bring up the lack of door handle when Rembeu made an unusual gesture with his hand. Rembeu then smeared a dark slimy substance on the opening side of the entryway. With his eyes closed, he moved his hands around the door's edges. Tarl had no idea what he was doing. Rembeu then grabbed the candle from the middle of the room and placed the flame on the dark paste. A small fizzing noise followed and then a hole appeared exactly where the flame had been. Rembeu reached through the hole and used the outside door handle to open it. The door jutted open. Tarl was astounded.

"Nice trick. Remember to teach me that one."

"Of course," Rembeu said smiling. They stole into the darkness. The street lights had all been extinguished. "Ooh, we're out past curfew." Rembeu whispered mischievously.

Tarl frowned at him. This wasn't in the least bit funny.

"There is plenty of potion left in this vial if you need it," Tarl threatened, holding up his unused container.

Rembeu just prodded a wink in Tarl's direction and then pulled out a satchel from inside his robe. Plucking a tiger's eye stone from the contents, he gripped it tightly and when he opened his fist, the stone glowed. The light was just enough to stop them from tripping over their own feet.

Arriving at the spot where they were supposed to return to, they scanned the area but could see no one in the vicinity. After waiting for a few moments a cool hand clasped Rembeu's arm. The tiger's eye shone upon a pale skinned young girl who was looking around furtively for any signs of discovery.

"Meinda!" whispered Rembeu in recognition.

Her sandy hair was cropped short which made her pale green eyes seem very large. A dusting of freckles fell across the bridge of her nose.

"Quickly!" She scuttled away and they quickly followed.

They were pushed inside a house and three candlelit faces stared up at them from around a basic wooden table. Their pale skin looked almost ghostly in this light.

"This be them," Meinda said softly.

"Aye," offered a slim man, "lay yer hat down". He gestured to two empty chairs. "Please be welcomed."

"I be Rembeu and this be Tarl." Rembeu smiled in a slightly regal manner.

Tarl looked at his uncle as if he had suddenly turned a nasty shade of green. Joining in this conversation was going to be difficult. Rembeu caught Tarl's expression and reacted with a kind of eyebrow scrunch that indicated he would try to work the conversation both ways.

"I'm Meinda," she was addressing Tarl, "and this be Fiana," who was a very thin woman with dark brown eyes and frizzy strawberry blonde hair, "this be Peater," a slight man with light blue eyes and bright orange hair, "and this be Breight." Meinda's glance indicated that he was her partner. He was of stocky build and had an amazing head of long curly ginger locks. Tarl wondered if that was why her hair was so short. How could you compete with hair like that? Involuntarily Tarl patted his dark straight locks still covered with red dust.

"Guess we'll be burnin' the midnight oil tonight." Peater tried a humorous approach but was slapped on the knee by Fiana.

"Please let's cut to the chase," Rembeu offered, "I take it we can talk freely?" Everyone nodded.

"I won't beat around the bush." Meinda saw Tarl grimace. Rembeu had explained earlier that Tarl was having difficulty with their phraseology. "Oh I be sorry Tarl, I will try to speak straight to the point... Oh sorry..." She took a moment to compose her thoughts. "There be much to explain." She nodded satisfactorily at this attempt. "We have certainly seen better days." She hesitated again at her slip. Breight smiled encouragingly at her. She continued, "Much time ago, our Leading Light was Magel. Magel was very suddenly absorbed." The staccato sounds of her speech showed how much she was trying to make herself understood. "Very mysteriously gone. After this Carny put down roots as an Over-Rider. Course, we be suspecting a plan all along."

Peater sniffed with annoyance. His light blue eyes piercing the air.

"Plain as day, it was. Carny wanted his place in the sun and I be damned if he didn't make Magel walk the plank." His pale face appeared quite lined in the candlelight and Tarl suddenly realized he had not seen any old people. In fact, Peater was the oldest person he had seen and he didn't appear to be older than Rembeu.

"Die," Meinda said bluntly.

"Yeah." Tarl nodded. That was the only thing that didn't need explaining.

"Then he put somethin' in the airwaves. Everyone started thinking everythin' was funny. Everyone's cares went out the window. Well, we didn't like it - we didn't like it at all. So several of us got together and managed to invent a carry-on device. It reflects his suggestions. We have given these to many of the people that disagree with Carny but we don't rightly know what else ta do."

So that was how it was done. Tarl wondered if that had anything to do with his headaches.

Rembeu was curious.

"Explain this 'absorption'."

"Oh, best we start at the beginning." Meinda concentrated again. "Well, Carny claimed to 'ave 'reinvented the wheel'. That's what he called it. The basics of it be, that he was time borrowing."

"Time borrowing?" Tarl piped. "That's what I heard him say when we first arrived here."

Meinda was delighted that he had entered the conversation. He must have been able to understand her.

Fiana thought she would give it a try also.

"Well he be stealing time from the past and impregnating it into the future. He sold the idea like hotcakes, like it be the best thing since sliced bread. The people fell hook line and sinker, couldn't see past the end of their noses, I say." Her frizzy blonde hair was catching flickers of candlelight.

"I see," said Rembeu. Tarl didn't' but Meinda pressed on.

"He be telling 'em all, that it bring longer life, less aging, more productivity, scientific discovery and the like." Her face showed disgust. "They 'ad no idea."

"He's brought us to rack and ruin." Breight shook his head.

Tarl tried to hide his confusion. Rembeu tried to hide his horror. He could only imagine the long term consequences of such a foolish premise.

"Aye," Meinda picked up the trail, "but that's how we saw the Passings," she said.

"The Passings?" interjected Rembeu.

"Aye, the Passings. We be seeing visions of time in the past and future," Breight said, "like a toss of the dice, splashes of life, fully formed in the sphere. We be seeing you both an' all."

Rembeu and Tarl swapped glances.

"Where have you seen us?" Tarl was completely lost.

"Oh you been in the sphere." Peater answered and Fiana slipped an indignant stare at him. He sat back immediately and let her explain.

"Carny be theorizing about findin' a fixed point: A point that would correspond to the southerly limit of our moon's monthly motions at different points in the stretch of a cycle. When aligned with certain other elements there be a major standstill point. Of course he refused to divulge the other elements - in case they got into 'the wrong hands.'" She added an insolent huff.

"This 'fixed point' would it have anything to do with that monstrosity of a sculpture out on the horizon?" Rembeu asked candidly.

"Aye. The standstill point. It be like the meeting point of all time: Past, present and future. That's where Carny began building the Timesolve: Them the rings that you talk about that rise from the north plateau. That's where we be seeing you both."

"How exactly did you see us?" Rembeu asked, curiously.

"When it be activated," Meinda said, "the forces combine to extract certain points of time. When that 'appens a huge revolving sphere displays visions. A lot of the time we can't understand what we be seeing, but we understood what we saw you two doin'."

"What were we doing?" Tarl asked a little too loudly.

"Shh, Tarl, let Meinda finish," Rembeu said not taking his eyes of her.

"Carny be securing an area so he could suck these time pockets back down to the surface via the rings. That be when all those concentric circles began to appear across the ground."

"And weightlessness began to be effectin' us," Fiana put in.

"Ey, crops were good as gone; territories were kaput; people walking the plank all over the place." Breight was looking worn.

"Then the circles spread and now cover the planet's surface," Meinda added.

Rembeu was feeling more and more overwhelmed. This information went against all the scientific laws he had been taught.

"What happens exactly?" Rembeu directed his question to Meinda. He thought she was doing a bang up job. He was thinking like them now.

"They start by creatin' whole cylinders of missing land an' then every other expanding ring just becomes empty ground. The ground is literally fallin' away! The past now be contained in the future: It become interwoven in the cosmos." Her expression was of pure disgust.

"We feel great fear for our future," Peata added unnecessarily.

"The ground is falling away?" Tarl's voice rose above the whispers. Rembeu threw him a warning glance. Tarl tipped his head self-consciously.

"Magel tried to destroy the device but the people rose up and attacked him. Carny invited Magel to the Timesolve to prove its benefits but be tricking Magel into the carriageway. He shut it and shot him up into the time sphere. He disappeared. Just like that. All the people were laughing and cheering. It be so horrible."

"Where did he go?" Tarl's abashment didn't last long.

"If the points are aligned," Rembeu thought out loud, "there could be a slipstream of past lines, but if they are not, it would be like a mish-mash of time lines. He could be lost in an unimaginable abyss."

"Ey," Meinda agreed.

Whatever that meant it did not sound good. Tarl had heard enough. He really wanted a shower, and sleep, lots of it. He tried not to frown when Meinda started up again.

"On top of all this we be experiencing time slips – something to do with the time borrowing we imagine. Sometimes it feels like we are going backwards in time and sometimes it's like we've slipped forward."

"We be havin'a saying: 'Missing time, fragments the mind, extra time, makes continuity die,'" said Fiana. "It be like no one can keep to the point of the subject."

"Like slippin' on a banana peel." Again Peater was slapped across the knee by Fiana.

Rembeu started to postulate.

"The removal of time in a constantly expanding universe would create holes in the fabric of time."

"Would that have anything to do with the time bubbles in the last plane?" Tarl asked, hoping his suggestion wasn't stupid.

"Could be Tarl, well done," Rembeu was nodding slowly. "So when you saw us coming, what did you see us do?" Rembeu surprised himself by crossing his fingers. He tried to restrain his amusement at the thought that such ancient superstitions were terribly 'old hat'.

"Ey, that is why you are in so much danger." Meinda jumped in again. "It be seen that Carny..." she stopped suddenly realizing what she was about to say.

"What's been seen?" Rembeu remained calm and encouraging.

"Ey, well..."

"We seen you being killed by Carny," Breight blurted out.

"Right, more good news," Tarl rubbed his forehead.

"We have to find a way to get you out of here." Fiana exclaimed. Peater placed a reassuring hand on her shoulder.

Rembeu's thoughts were spinning like the wheel in Atlas Mountain. He didn't disbelieve this last report but somehow it didn't feel right. He consoled himself with the fact that even all the science in the world couldn't dispute the fact that instinct was fundamental in life.

Rembeu was about to ask exactly what they had seen in their vision of death when the door swung open. They were faced with a bright light shining in their eyes. It was hard to make out how many there were but the silhouette at the front had a familiar voice.

"So, who have we here then? Four weak-links and a couple of Johnny-come-lately's." It was Carny.

"Take it in good part ey, Carny. Join the party then," Peater said quickly.

"Not trying to do a number on 'ol Carny now is ya?" The 'weak-links' all shook their heads.

Rembeu knew they were in trouble now but he could see no point in fighting it. Best to go along for the moment. A renewed feeling of impending opportunity was rising. Perhaps his counteractive potion was wearing off.

"We're playing a different ball game now I'm afraid," Carny's eyes glinted with pleasure. "Shall ya be friend or foe?" He was the one playing the game. "I've heard that curiosity killed the cat you know." Carny was enjoying himself immensely. He waved an arm to the faceless bodies behind him. They moved forward, each grabbing one of the four trembling occupants. Tarl and Rembeu were left untouched.

Their four helpers were removed and Carny took a seat on one of the empty chairs. There was just the three of them.

"I see you're an easy catch. Lovely." Carny moved his chair closer for effect. "They haven't been bendin' yer ear 'ave they?" He was shining the torch-light in their eyes.

Neither of them made any attempt to reply. Tarl didn't care if he went blind he wasn't about to turn away.

"Right then, if that's the way yer want it," Carny clapped his hands twice. Two more silhouettes approached and pulled them out of their chairs and out of the house. They each felt warm hands cupping their mouths. Their last conscious sensation was the pungent smell of some kind of sleeping drug.

■　■　■

Tarl woke first to find himself in what appeared to be a solid metal room with a hard shiny, metal floor. A transparent ceiling high above him allowed enough light in to observe his surroundings: They were basic. He squinted up into the bleached apricot light of early morning and looked for Rembeu. Several bowls of dried food and two large tankards of water implied they were going to be here for a while. There was only one of their packs in the cell. It was Rembeu's. Tarl squeezed his eyes shut. He had lost his pack. Quickly he felt for the sword Opal had given him, thankfully it still rested in its holster at his side.

His head throbbed and his eyes felt like someone had pierced them with needles. Lifting his heavy right arm he rested it over his fidgeting left arm which now seemed to have a life all of its own.

Rembeu was crumpled in the corner. His orange robes were rumpled about his body as if he had been thrown in. Tarl managed to crawl over to him as he made an awful sounding moan. Tarl ripped part of his silver shirt to wipe his uncle's brow. Rembeu blinked his eyes open, squinting at their new surroundings.

"Bet this one doesn't have a door handle either," he croaked.

"Actually, here you don't really need one." Tarl helped him sit up.

"Mmm?" He tried to focus his eyes.

"It doesn't seem to have a door."

That got Rembeu to his feet. He wobbled slightly and moved around the solid room looking for any indication of an opening.

"How did they put us in here?" Rembeu asked.

Tarl pointed up to the high ceiling. Rembeu's eyes followed.

"Looks like the floor is some kind of lift." Rembeu said as his thoughts settled.

"Mmm hmm," Tarl nodded waiting for his uncle to make the connection.

"...Must move up and down...but why on time's behalf would they..." Rembeu stopped and looked directly at Tarl. "Oh." So much for that momentary feeling of optimism he had felt the night before.

Tarl returned a lop-sided smile.

"Looks like we're going time traveling again."

"Oh dear. Yes it does, doesn't it?" Rembeu sank back down to the metal floor and began removing his top robe so as to unload the satchel that was strapped underneath it. He breathed deeply with the release of weight.

"You hid that under your robe?" Tarl was astonished that his uncle had the foresight to do so. "And you didn't mention that I might want to save a few things?"

Rembeu handed Tarl the large satchel. Tarl opened it and saw that the majority of the contents were from his pack. As he was about to apologize, Rembeu interrupted.

"We must be harbored at the base of one of those carriageways..." Rembeu muttered trying to get a fix on their situation. He pointed to the ceiling. "I dare say that's some kind of access point...or exit point depending on which way one might look at it. They'll have to load us in it somehow..." Rembeu looked around the floor of their cell. "The floor can be raised and lowered... so they'll raise us up and somehow load us in… but we don't know how…we don't know when." He was gazing abstractedly at his outstretched toes.

"Perhaps Melik…" Tarl began.

"Your crystal Voicer, where's the crystal Voicers!?" Rembeu cried as they both frantically searched their pockets. Simultaneously they were produced and held outstretched like trophies.

Rembeu pressed the center.

"Melik please respond." Rembeu tried to keep the urgency out of his voice. "I fear we've found ourselves in 'a spot of bother'."

Tarl looked at his uncle with a purposeful blink.

"Er," Rembeu tried again, "rather we're in a somewhat dire position, please respond immediately. Over." He shrugged his shoulders. "Well it is catchy you know."

An indecipherable voice crackled back at them.

"Melik, please repeat transmission, over."

"I thought…w…lost…" The scratchy voice replied.

Tarl and Rembeu smiled at each other.

"We're not lost, Melik, we're trapped. Over."

Words came spilling through the Voicer.

"You have no idea how worried we've all been. Umbra is frantic. Please confirm health specifications. Over."

They couldn't contain a chuckle.

"We're O.K. Melik. Tell Umbra we're O.K. We need help A.S.A.P. though. Over."

"I'm ready and waiting. What's your most immediate need? Over."

"Is everything all right at your end?" Rembeu wasn't sure if he wanted to hear the answer. These reality streams were a lot worse than he could have imagined.

"It's definitely getting worse, but we're holding our ground. Umbra is amazing. I don't think she sleeps. But let us worry about things here. What's your problem there? Over."

Tarl was desperate to ask about his father and Opal. Her image had been haunting him. Trying to stop himself from blurting questions out, he vowed if they got out of this situation they would be the first things he would ask Melik.

Rembeu considered the situation trying to decide where to begin and again looked up at the ceiling as if the answers were written in the sky.

"That could be an idea."

"What?" Tarl followed his gaze. He didn't see anything different.

Rembeu held his Voicer up and briefly explained their situation to Melik leaving Tarl in the dark as to what the idea was.

"Remember," reminded Melik, "you have the Elestial crystals that Tarl brought from the Stone Circle. Over."

"Good point Melik".

"O.K." Melik said. "Let's think about the arrows of time here." His voice was fading in and out. He was obviously walking and talking as he thought. Tarl and Rembeu stayed quiet trying to pick up everything he said. Tarl envisioned him, his hands fluttering as he spoke. "Right. Reactions amongst particles are different between time flowing forward and backward. If we replace anything here we must have the correct particles. O.K. Also, we have to think of the universe as producing a definite cosmological direction of time. Of course so does the memory of the mind. Yes. Good. Now, we can see dimensional reality but not dimensional time so how are they seeing the events in this sphere?" Melik stopped suddenly. "Have you seen this sphere yourselves? Over."

"No we have not but we have no reason to dispute its existence. Over." Rembeu was looking up at the ceiling. Tarl was looking expectantly at Rembeu's Voicer as if it were about to produce a miracle. Rembeu moved the Voicer away from his mouth nodding at Tarl.

"Melik is about to produce a thought stream." He said looking hopeful.

"It's interesting that the gravitational field has been affected. Is it possible that the planets acceleration has been altered?" Melik asked. "Over."

"It's possible. Over." Rembeu was starting to understand where Melik was going.

"Holes in the quantum tunnel of time would cause an increase in disorder and perhaps..." Melik's voice faded away entirely.

Rembeu thought they had lost contact again but he realized the line was still open at Melik's end. The look he gave his nephew was a look Tarl would never forget. They waited as a few lengthy minutes passed by and then finally Melik began to shout.

"Wait!" The clatter of instruments dropping followed. Melik was obviously onto something. It was going to be a while before he made any sense.

"You know," Rembeu addressed his nephew, "I feel very confident that we will solve this problem. I know what we were told about our 'outcome' but something about that just doesn't feel right."

"I know. I have the same feeling." Tarl paced over to the far wall and placed his palm on the cold metal. "And yet, I believe that they have seen the images of our death. I can't understand it."

"No, I know what you mean."

"How long do you think they'll have us holed up here for?" Tarl asked as he turned his head back over his shoulder to face his uncle.

"Honestly, I don't know. Judging by the food supplies, a good while. If we're still here tonight and we can see the stars we may be able to get a bearing to give Melik."

Night time seemed an awfully long way away.

"At least they didn't take away Opal's sword." Tarl pulled out his silver shirt, still stained with red dust and showed Rembeu the holster.

Rembeu wrapped a consoling arm around Tarl's shoulders.

"Tell me about her, tell me everything," Rembeu said hoping this would be an excellent distraction.

"Well…" Tarl was surprised that his uncle was asking him that now.

"It's not like we've got a whole lot of other things to do," Rembeu said wryly.

"As usual you're right." Tarl revealed an exhausted smile. "Are you ever wrong?" He quickly held up a hand. "No, wait. I don't want an answer to that."

"No. I'm never wrong." Rembeu's teasing smile made his nephew laugh. "Talk to me."

Tarl's words spilled out like he had just discovered speech. He told Rembeu of his visions of her, the incredible sails she had created for his Orbitor, the afternoon they had spent together and the message she had left for him on the roof of the Silk House. He was just about to ask

Rembeu what he thought the effects of all this would be in their world when Melik's voice warbled from the Voicer.

"You know the ancient Hawaiian Kahunas believed that the future is fluid and it is in the process of crystallizing...."

"Melik!" they both cried out in their thrill to hear from him.

"I have a few thoughts on the situation. Over." Melik finished.

Rembeu remained calm.

"Please go ahead, any information is good. Over."

"Right. Well I'll try and make it simple then. Firstly, I'm glad you have your Elestial crystals with you. They are what I would like to base this proposal on," he paused as if he were some great story teller, "now, think of the past like an infinite library of perfectly treasured books. If you remove one, you leave a gap that can only be filled by another book; a book of the same type of information; a book that fits this space; a book that is sequentially correct. Imagine if many of these books were removed. The remaining books would fall down, lying in a jumble on the shelves. If you tried to put the books back in their original slots you could not because the slots would no longer exist. Are you receiving? Over."

"I hate his book analogies," Rembeu whispered to Tarl before returning word to Melik. He held up the Voicer, "Yes Melik. Library, holes, got it. Over."

"Essentially what we have to do is reconfigure the collapsing time fabric and basically plug the holes with the perfectly matching puzzle pieces."

Both Rembeu and Tarl looked at the Voicer as if it had just told them their names were Boris and Bawdly. Melik kept going.

"I know it sounds impossible but I have an idea. You know, if time collapsed like this, it could cause induced states of hallucinatory visions. The EM fields could definitely affect the temporal lobe of the brain - not only visions but it could make you feel disoriented: Like a double hologram with one image mirroring the opposite of the other and moving simultaneously..."

Rembeu was wondering if Melik had made another device which allowed him to talk non-stop without the need for breathing.

"...Except you are the double hologram. Very weird that would be. Anyway, onto the difficult stuff. And Tarl, you're up for this one I'm afraid." Tarl faked delight. "…You'll have to call on your Teachings for this one. Rembeu you'll have to perform your magic to put him in the access zone. Still receiving? Over."

"We're 'all ears'… er, I mean, we're listening. Is it possible the visions could have been seen by these people; perhaps even visions of us before we arrived? Over."

"Yes, quite possible. The collapse of time pockets could easily have reflected images of you from the past and accidentally combined them with images of your current present. It's all a bit of a learning curve really."

Tarl leant over to Rembeu.

"Yeah, if you actually learn something that is." They both smiled but Melik grabbed their attention again.

"But if I explain the flow of time as a product of a constant series of unfoldings and enfoldings, perhaps you can envision how the present enfolds and becomes part of the past. You see, the past does not disappear once it has passed but rather, it lies within the storehouse of cosmic time still active in the present. Right? Over."

"Yes, Melik, go on. Over."

"Right then. Now I've got to be blunt." Melik stated.

Rembeu turned to Tarl feigning shock.

"Is that possible?" Tarl whispered to Rembeu whilst stifling a snigger.

"Well it's always nice to be a part of history," Rembeu murmured to Tarl.

"I don't believe this sphere shows all time. I think it's like a jumble of books. Over." Melik said in summation.

Rembeu smiled at Tarl with a look that said: 'You're right, it's not possible'.

"Try to think of it," Melik had started up again, "like a whole lot of holographic entities floating and converging in timeless and spaceless waters. This sphere is like seeing fragments in an abstract situation. What I'm thinking is; it's like a portal. Perhaps with the correct corresponding co-ordinates we could use it to transfer you, but I think without these, the sphere itself is of no consequence at all. Following? Over."

"Melik perhaps we could fast forward a bit. Tell us your idea. We need to know what to be prepared for. Over."

"Yes, yes sorry. Right. The second of the Elestial Crystals will hold the right vibrations for you there. We will need to work its storehouse. O.K.? Over."

"One moment Melik please. Over." Rembeu wanted to explain. "Tarl these stones were originally buried at the Stone Circle by the Light Guild and were passed on through the generations until they were passed on to your mother and me. Sporadically they have been returned to the Stone Circle to be replenished. They capture the time, memories and wisdom of a lost period. These crystals hold the knowledge of the creatures that protect the circle; memories before humankind existed. There are no other stones like these that we know of. I cannot stress how incredibly important and powerful they are. Umbra kept the first, fourth and fifth crystals to power the greatest weaknesses in the Radiant. We have the second, third, sixth and seventh. They must be treated with the utmost respect." He waited for Tarl's slow nod of comprehension.

"I understand."

"Right Melik, go ahead. Over."

"Right, well we need to use this stone to amplify time back into their system and, if we're lucky, maybe a bit of wisdom as well." They were both surprised at his attempt at humor. "We must amplify the correct waves – all time has an equal and matching opposite. That is what you must find. How are we going? Over."

"Roger. Over."

Rembeu appeared to understand what Melik was trying to say. Tarl wanted to interrupt, scream out that it was all meaningless to him, that he had no idea how to find the past inside a crystal that he just found out was one of the most powerful in his world. He bit the inside of his lip in frustration and felt his teeth pierce the skin.

"Good. Right. First you need to access the past within the stone. To do this you will need to shift the focus of your consciousness. Rembeu you can explain it better. You will have an enormous job leading Tarl into the trance. Your experience is invaluable here to keep the focus controlled.

Tarl, once you're in the access zone, you will need to locate the crystal's past. Remember the stone will be protected. You will have to work your way through these barriers to get to the storehouse at its heart. Be Careful. These protective devices will try to deceive you. If you are true to yourself and honest at all turns you will be fine. Remember: 'Truth and light'. I have complete faith in you. Over."

Tarl wished he had faith in himself. There were no 'protective devices' in his Teachings and they had proved difficult enough. Feeling his left hand trembling again, he moved it out of his uncle's field of vision.

"How will I know which of the time pockets to select?"

"Right. Yes." Rembeu suddenly realized what he was going to have to do. "Now that is the difficult part. You see you will have to actually be in the sphere to correlate the time veins. So, you will have to have already located the heart just before we both enter the sphere."

Tarl's eyes were wide. He shook his head at Rembeu.

"You mean I have to be unconscious in the sphere?"

"It appears so. We must find out when the sphere will be active."

Melik began talking again.

"As you travel through the crystal you will sense resonations around each time vein. It will become apparent which vibrations match those of the sphere. You can then activate the heart which will allow those veins to be released. Once the experience is over the crystal will need to be closed and protected. It can then be returned to the Stone Circle to reabsorb. A bit like giving the crystal a good clean. Over."

A good clean? What was he? A big duster?

"Back to you shortly. Over." Rembeu put the Voicer down and faced Tarl. "Tarl this is your call. I'll only accept it if you agree. Who knows, we could think of another way."

Tarl sank his back against the wall. Visiting the past was terrifying. But somewhere deep inside him he felt a bright flicker telling him it was the right thing to do. Trying to reject it wasn't an option, it was there, burning quietly, waiting for him to recognize it. He had no idea how he was going to do this but he had to try. An amazing calmness came over him for the first time since his Revelation.

"If instinct is to be trusted I think this is the way we should follow." Somehow, suddenly it just seemed that simple.

"All systems here are 'go' Melik." Rembeu nodded confirmation to the invisible speaker. "What I do want to try to figure out first, is a time frame for this whole process. We need to find out when the sphere opens. We'll have to wait for nightfall to give you our location. Over."

"I have several proposals that I was working on earlier. There is a >.05 probability I could miscalculate your location gauged from your last entry point. What I don't know is what time you're experiencing there. Your night sky information will give me that. Unfortunately, my current estimate is between two to four moonspells before the sphere is active. Over."

"We'll need some rest anyway. Over." Rembeu stated calmly. "Shame we can't do a bit of sightseeing," he added for Tarl's benefit only.

"I think we've done quite enough sightseeing, thank you uncle."

"What? Are you telling me you're sick of volcanoes, burning winds, ground that looks like it has been cut by a giant cookie cutter, handle-less doors, door-less cells, death predictions...?"

Tarl pushed out a laugh. It was all too ridiculous to be real. A sick feeling was turning his stomach and his head felt like it was floating somewhere up near the glass ceiling. The lunacy of this whole situation was overwhelming him and waves of heaving laughter began to roll from his chest. Bent forward like a rubber doll, the tension was being forced from him. He thought he might not be able to stop. Tears were streaming down his face and his stomach muscles panged with the spasms.

Rembeu was initially alarmed by his nephew's reaction but the laughter was infectious. Against his will he started to laugh too. It was all turning out to be quite a bizarre experience. The irony of laughing whilst trapped in this prison of unfathomable consequences was not lost on Rembeu.

By the time they had stopped, they were laying on the floor of their prison, worn out. In perfect silence they escaped into a sleep that only exhaustion can induce. But even in that deep dark place Tarl dreamed vividly.

Opal's face stared at him without expression. Her gray eyes regarded him emptily. She ignored him when he reached out to her.

Flowing toward her, he was getting smaller and smaller as he approached. He was flying fast now toward her growing face and then he was falling; falling into her gray dead eyes. Engulfed in a sea of thick gray water, he floated, directionless, lost. When he tried to call out her name, no sound came. All he could hear was an echo: The same words repeated over and over: 'You don't need eyes to see'. He was drowning; it was all over. He was lost and unable to save himself.

17

Beyond Borders

After stumbling through the dark for what seemed like an eternity Opal was nearly ready to give up. The tremors had been growing stronger and stronger and she feared she may slip into one of the many crevices that divided the land. She could disappear forever and no one would have a clue. Hesitation and fear circled each other and she stopped dead.

Hot winds were rising from the ground like furious lions. Her grip on the key around her neck tightened turning her fingers white like translucent silk. She turned to go back. But behind her the land raged with blackness and more danger. Opal steeled herself: This was what she needed to do; what she would have to do. It could not be much further, she convinced herself. Her legs turned her around again and on she ploughed.

When she finally saw the moonlight glimmer on the huge golden door embedded in the grassy summit, she ran frantically toward it as if she were being pulled by unseen forces. If there really were a tunnel inside, she realized, it could only go down. She stared up at it, awe and fear swelling in her like an ocean undecided on its tide. She breathed deeply, the hot air stinging her throat, and then held her breath. Her lips shed their color as anxiety ran through her like ice.

Opal held out the key. It glowed ominously in the black night. She moved closer. The key illuminated the perfect swirl of the treble clef key hole. Slowly she moved forward placing the emerald twined stone over the knot. Suddenly she wondered how she was supposed to place the key inside the hole without her fingers getting in the way but she didn't have to wonder long.

Colors shot from the key hole like rays from the sun. Instinctively, she pressed her thumb across the opal and rainbow crystal as if they were her talismans, as if they would protect her. An incredible humming sound began to rise from the key. The movement must have initiated the resonance. The key began to vibrate as the hum grew in intensity. Shocked, she momentarily released the key. The key began to fall. She plunged her hands toward the ground before realizing that the key had been pulled upward and into the key hole.

The huge golden door dissolved in a flash of light. The blaze was so bright that her eyes flinched closed in reaction. In that instant she was amazed to see, lit like lightening across the back of her eyelids, was the impression of a map. She recognized the Stone Circle at the beginning of the map and a huge mountain at its end before an explosion of color burst again and she felt herself being pulled through the invisible door.

At once, she was blanketed in solid blackness. The illumination from the key was gone and panic rose within her like a blaze. A strange irritation tingled on her chest and she swatted at it. Her locket fell into the blackness.

"Oh no please, I know my locket no longer holds stones but please, if anyone is listening..." Pleading with the darkness was irrational but the locket was more important than she could ever have explained, especially now. "Please, help me."

A voice resounded around her. It was strong and clear.

"Fear is the voice of folly. You have no need of this." It said calmly.

Her blind eyes were wide with surprise but it didn't stop her from frantically scratching the dirt below her feet trying to find the locket. As her fingers touched the opened locket, she gratefully scooped it up and gasped as she felt its surface. How could the stones have returned to her locket? Hugging it to her chest she wondered how she would be able to get out of here without the key. She ran toward where she thought the door was but felt only solid surface everywhere. How was she supposed to know what to do? Opal swallowed her fear. She would just have to move forward. Perhaps she could feel her way along the wall? Perhaps she could just ask?

"But I am not afraid," she lied, "just impatient. Although I can hear you clearly I do not know where you are coming from. I cannot see anything. I do not know where to go or how to reach you."

"You must listen to me carefully. There is not much time. I am tired beyond borders and I cannot pursue help and complete my tasks here." The voice sounded frighteningly drained.

"Please, I have entered the Gate but I cannot move forward. It feels like I am in some kind of void. I do not feel weight or warmth. I have no direction." Opal tried to hide her growing confusion.

"You are expecting to be guided and yet you have already led. There is no place for fear here. Perhaps I assumed you to be stronger."

The voice anchored in her heart. It was true. Opal felt blinded by fear. There had been so many worse things she had dealt with. Why was she so afraid? Forcing her shallow breathing to even out, she swallowed and pressed her eyes shut.

"Fear may very well be the voice of folly," Opal repeated, "but I have no time for such indulgences. I wish to follow the map that leads me to the mountain." She nodded as her throat ran dry. Opal opened her eyes only to find herself still surrounded by the power of blackness.

"Good. You have destination in mind. That is where you are needed. Try not to let fear interrupt the aim. If you do, your destination may be drawn by the wrong mapper." The voice was growing weaker. "I have called and you are the only one who answers. You are strong and you are needed." The voice began to fade. "The world you know is not the one you belong in. They have tried to protect you. They should not have. It is time f... y... to fulfill ... tasks." The voice was faltering.

"Please do not go. Please just give me something so that I can seek the destination."

"It is not I who should be giving. It i... time f... you ... harness..." The voice dissolved into nothingness.

Opal closed her eyes. She had no time to waste here in the darkness. Trying to allay her fears, she visualized the map that had scurried across her eyelids. The Mountain. Bubbles of thought rose as she tried to focus: Parvo under a mass of rubble; Mr. Tzau's face as she left; Tarl's log entries about her.

There was a rush of cold wind. She grabbed at her locket as the force pulled her backward. Her hair stung her face as she soared uncontrollably; horrible thoughts filling her mind. The voice began to whinny like a dying horse. She could see Tarl. He looked like he was floating; floating in thick muddy air. The vision gave her the impression he was no longer alive. Opal called out to him but he did not appear to hear her.

When she called out his name the second time his dead eyes shot open. He was surrounded by an eerie light and she reeled back in horror. The next thing she knew she was flying backward again. It felt as if she were being wrenched against her will. Fighting it was hopeless. Finally she stopped and jolted forward only to feel the cool edge of translucent stone in front of her. Dazed, she opened her eyes.

This was not where she had envisioned she would turn up. Yes, she was inside a mountain, but this was not the mountain her journey was destined for.

18

Hall of Visions

"Tarl! Tarl!"

From somewhere deep within the shifting tides of gray ocean a voice called to him. He swam toward the surface, every muscle in his body straining to get there. Sparkles swayed just above him. He could make it.

"Tarl wake up!"

His grainy eyes fluttered open. Rembeu was seated in the center of the room. One hand was madly scribbling down calculations while the other was fumbling with a telescopia that he was intermittently aiming at the ceiling. Tarl's eyes followed the tiny telescope. Above him a black sweep of sky glittered with tiny points of light.

"Get the Voicer."

Tarl forced himself into full consciousness and scrambled to get the device. He handed it to Rembeu.

"Melik, there she is. I see the moon. Directly overhead now. She has an orbital inclination of 11 degrees. One degree high. It's three quarter. I can see the southern highlands and Mare Imbrium. Respond, over."

Melik reacted immediately.

"I knew it. That's excellent for my calculations. Just give me a moment to finalize my computations. Well done. Over."

Rembeu released the Voicer. He moved the telescopia to the east, obviously looking for more references.

"More waiting I guess," yawned Tarl. He moved over to sit next to his uncle.

"It seems so."

"How long do you think it will take for the message to get back to dad? Although I guess he wouldn't have any idea of what we've got ourselves into."

Rembeu was surprised by Tarl's question. His nephew had hardly talked of Parvo since arriving at Atlas Mountain. It could have been a sign his nephew wasn't coping. Rembeu knew it would do no good to ask. Tarl would never admit to feeling cowardly. If he performed any kind of tests on Tarl he worried that he may undermine his nephew's confidence. Tarl would have to let him know of his own accord.

"Actually, I think your father was only too aware. He may have never had the insights of our clan but he certainly has experienced the results of his involvement." Rembeu gazed at Tarl, sadness descending, "Your mother was a true soul, you know. Many men were enamored with her but it was your father who saw all her truth. Coming from a 'Maker' family it really was an unusual pairing. When your mother saw him, her world soared with reason. Even when the Holder of Armories made it quite clear she was assigned to another suitor she unashamedly went ahead with the relationship. It was simple to her: Parvo was her path and she would not release herself to any other man no matter how inappropriate everyone thought their partnership was."

"It's strange thinking of him being on the outer, I mean considering the way things worked out."

"Yes," Rembeu paused, holding on to the memories. "You know, he was so in love with her, yet he asked her to reconsider her decision."

"Really? No one ever told me that."

"Oh yes," Rembeu released a little snuff of air from his nose. "Brave man. Cymbeline told me that this request was what made it impossible for her not to choose him. She used to visit me often you know, before you were born. I remember she told me that whatever happened in her life, I was not to worry; she had found it, the one thing we all look for, and the one thing most difficult to find: She had found true love." Rembeu focused on his nephew. How unfair it had all been. How he wished he could change it: An impossible thing, a wish, such a waste of emotion.

"Tell me more." Tarl liked this conversation. Somehow he needed to hear these stories from his uncle. Imagining the long ago scenes of his mother and father happy together again made him feel safe.

"When you came along, so perfect and tiny, your mother told me that 'if she lived for another hundred moonspells she could never be this happy'. It was like your arrival proved their worth together." His voice was quiet with reverence. "I really miss her."

Tarl swallowed down swelling tears. His throat hurt as if it were being slowly crushed. Rembeu's eyes were glossed with unabashed sorrow.

"I hope dad's O.K." Tarl whispered.

"So do I." He reached over and squeezed Tarl's hand. "What is taking Melik so long?" Rembeu longed for the distraction. He couldn't fight it any longer; he was losing his fight against tiredness. On the cold, unforgiving floor, he lay down placing the Voicer under his ear and quietly slid into slumber.

As tired as Tarl was, he couldn't sleep. So many thoughts were coursing through his mind. That was the trap - his mind. The four walled prison cell was just a room. They could possibly escape that. His mind on the other hand, well that was not so easy to leave behind. Pacing the small block, he tried to deflect unnecessary thoughts and concentrate on the important ones. He had to prepare himself. There were preparations that needed to be made if he was to enter into the recesses of that very prison. And this time there would be no teacher. No one was going to guide him. It was quite likely, even though no one had said it out loud, that he could take a wrong turn, make the wrong decision and be caught, twisted amongst the ancient time passages of the Elestial Crystal.

Looking up at the black sheet above him, he wondered where Melik was. Why was this taking so long? Every minute ticked by louder and louder. His tired legs finally sank to the floor. He curled up next to his uncle, closed his eyes and imagined what it would be like to fall into the blackness of sleep, no dreams just rest. But, in the in-between world of consciousness and unconsciousness, visions inevitably floated.

■　■　■

Tarl could see Opal calling him urgently; her words dissolving as soon as they left her mouth. She was ensnared in a room made of translucent green walls: Trapped inside like the color-rays were trapped inside the rainbow crystal he had given her. Unsuccessfully he tried to figure out how to get inside. Why couldn't he save her? Looking around he saw his mother and father laughing together in the hot winds of Shu's world; a beautiful child with large gray eyes crying in the arms of a stranger; and a young, still blind Umbra, twirling and dancing as crystal notes rose and crashed around her before shattering into beautiful harmonies.

A shrill and insistent noise began to nudge at him from a distance. Something was jerking his body.

'Dad?' Unconsciousness was draining from him and his eyes rolled back slightly as his eyelids momentarily flickered open. The bright light was searing.

"Tarl, wake up boy!"

Tarl pulled his eyebrows up in an effort to force his eyelids to stay open.

"He's coming round Melik, over."

"Good. Right. Explain the situation and return to me. Over."

"What's going on?" Tarl's voice croaked out of a dry throat. He felt as if someone had strapped basalt bricks to his head.

"My assumption," Rembeu sounded anxious, "about possible time anomalies was correct. We are experiencing different expediential time zones on each of these paths. The low gravity is causing time to pass more quickly here. So, even though we are experiencing artificial gravity in this 'tube', Melik has still had to calculate probabilities for the world outside. That's why it's taken so long."

"Right." Tarl's eyes were finally open. A huge yawn was building. It was one of those things you can't fight. His voice made a skipping sound as the yawn finished and he blinked his eyes widely.

"Estimated countdown is six sandglass turns for us." Rembeu was looking expectantly at Tarl.

"So we're experiencing a different time frame to those outside our steel well?" He tried unsuccessfully to stifle another yawn.

"Yes. Six turns is good."

"O.K. so what do we do?" Tarl was reaching for one of the water flasks.

Rembeu nodded in the direction of the bowls of dried food. "Eat up. I've planned for your interaction with the crystal in about two sandglass turns."

"You mean I won't be conscious for over four turns?"

"Well I'm already assuming it will take some time to induct your thought processes toward a state compliant to the crystal's vibrations."

Tarl was trying to nibble at a bit of dried meat. He was ravenously hungry but having to chew and swallow felt like he was being forced to eat sand. Having done that in the last plane he knew it wasn't much fun. He felt like a child that eats in protest with their tongue thrusting out between chews. Tarl handed a piece to Rembeu.

"How do you feel?" His uncle was looking at the piece of dried meat as if it were a crystal ball.

"Are you trying to make a pass at that particular piece of meat or are you just trying to eliminate the uninteresting ones?"

Rembeu blinked up at his nephew.

"Well it does look lovely but I've heard it's what's 'on the *inside* that counts'".

"Ha ha." Tarl had successfully eluded the question of his health. "You've really got to stop the riddle language – it's becoming offensive."

"'Offensive is as offensive does'." Rembeu was enjoying himself.

Tarl had no offensive or defensive, he still couldn't speak 'riddle'. There was only one solution. He planted a big kiss on the the piece of meat he was holding. "How do *you* feel?" Tarl said affectionately to the wrinkled jerky. Under the circumstances it seemed as inappropriate as could be. His uncle burst out laughing. He laughed so hard his own revered meat product ended its life on the hard steel floor.

The frivolity ended with just one word.

"Correction!" Melik was screaming into the Voicer. "Tarl, Rembeu. Immediate action is required. Over."

"Go ahead Melik." Rembeu was sober in an instant. "Oh, over."

"Sorry, sorry, my calculations were correct but I've just discovered that the increased tilt of the moon creates a 17 percent increase in the incident of time between your holding cell and your outside world. Over."

"And?"

"Time has been reduced to 3.8 sandglass turns. You should initiate inducement now. Over."

Just as Tarl and Rembeu began to comprehend the implication a huge jolt rattled their holding cell. The floor had slowly begun to lurch them upward. They looked up at the ceiling to see the wavy beginnings of the emerging sphere: Their imminent destination. By the time they got up there the sphere would be fully formed and they would follow the same fate as Magel. They had to hurry.

Tarl dared a look in Rembeu's direction. The horror on his uncle's face was enough to make him turn away quickly. He told himself to prepare, be calm, be positive. What had he been told? Melik had said: 'Truth and Light': The words of his final Teaching – whatever *they* really meant. What else had seemed important? Umbra had told him that apparently 'you don't need eyes to see.' Where else had he heard that? He couldn't remember but it wasn't helping anyway. There must be something to help him concentrate. And then, like a vision, he remembered the message on the roof of the Silk House: 'Understanding will smile in this offering of Truth and Light'. A calming warmth rose inside him. Opal had faith in him. Perhaps a lot of people were counting on him. His heart-beat slowed and his mind felt strong and focused.

"I'm ready," he said somberly. Rembeu's chest rose with a deep breath. He indicated where Tarl should lay down. He stroked his nephew's dark glossy hair.

"I want you to know how proud I am of you."

Tarl couldn't look at him. He hadn't done anything yet. This would be his defining moment. No pressure then. He took a deep breath.

'I can do this,' he thought, 'because I have to see my father again… and I have to tell Opal something'.

19

Emerald Eye

Opal's fear strode in bounds as her palms moved silently across the solid emerald walls. She had heard of this place. But how had she ended up inside the top of Emerald Mountain? This was a place legend had maintained was the shell of a very ancient stone which had supposedly been 'planted' and had miraculously grown as tall as a mountain. It was made of pure crystal; no windows and no doors. So how did she get in here? Her palms followed the walls hoping to find an unlikely exit.

"What you are doing here?" A frightened voice whinnied behind her. His words were fragmented, as if speaking was difficult.

Opal reeled around to face a thin hunched old man staring at her with sad watery eyes. White wisps of hair floated about his head as if they were buoyed by a thick breeze. His skin was pale, almost translucent. It reminded her of rice paper. The beige robe he was swathed in swam at his bare feet.

Pressing her back against the wall, she remembered that behind her, past the perfect sea-green stone, the world fell away far below. Staring speechlessly at him Opal realized she was facing the hermit: Another part of the legend. But that was impossible. Suddenly a thought sprang into her mind: If someone lives here there must be an exit. 'Be careful,' she told herself, 'and you just may get out of here.' Of course Opal had no idea where to go after she got out, but she had to deal with one thing at a time. The urgency of a world she could not find was already weighing upon her.

"I am so sorry," she bowed her head in the manner of politeness she had been taught, "I appear to have arrived here unwittingly."

"It seems so." His voice had become stronger as if he were becoming more used to speech. "A surprise I had not expected."

"Again I do apologize, but I must be blunt, I feel I have little time." Opal tried to keep her voice steady.

"Hmm. A lady who decides to burst into my home and then chooses to make demands. How interesting." The words would have chilled her but his sallow face hinted at amusement. He seemed almost as surprised as she did. "Well now, I do believe this conversation is going to be rather fascinating. I admit it has been a while."

Opal was glad that he appeared accommodating but he did not seem to understand the immediacy of her problem.

"Yes sir, I am Opal. May I ask your name?"

"A name is what you are known by. Names are only great if the person given the name has made it worthy. If the name has been great but then abused of its guarantee it can no longer be used. Please do not ask me further."

She nodded in acquiescence even though this just made her more confused.

"I am afraid I have taken a… wrong turn… I…"

"Indeed you have," he interrupted, "and which turn were you supposed to take?" His eyes were tightening suspiciously.

"Well, actually, I am not sure," she said feeling rather useless. "But I really have to leave. You must tell me where the exit is," she swallowed and then added, "please."

"Ahh, but there is no exit from this Mountain." The hermit looked quite satisfied with his answer.

"But there must be," Opal blurted, "you got in here! And you must be able to get out. How do you breathe? How do you eat?"

"There are some things in life that have no explanation and then of course there are some things that have an explanation but cannot be explained." He nodded listlessly.

"That does not make any sense." Opal was showing her frustration. She turned back around to feel her way around the wall. Looking down through the stippled crystal she saw a world that fell so far below her that she could make out nothing except plateaus and plains. The panic was rising again.

"How did you get here child? Through a door?" What sounded like sarcasm to Opal was completely unintended. The hermit thought he was merely stating an obvious point. "You will be staying. Now perhaps we can familiarize ourselves. Although, as I said, there is no need for names."

Opal covered her eyes with a palm. How did she get here? The Locked Gate of Gold Glen? But that did not lead her here. She did that. Why was *she* being called? None of this was working the way it was meant to. How long had it taken her already to leave Calatia? Too long. And now, here she was, trapped in a mountain with no doors, with a hermit that made no sense, and that was obviously quite happy to have her stay here for the rest of her existence. Weren't hermits supposed to shun company? Cringing, she thumped her rolled fists against the glistening walls.

"There is no need for that." He reprimanded her.

Opal sank to her knees, her palms sliding down the pane. All she could think about was Tarl. Unexplainably, she imagined him calling her name. It reminded her of the strange words of the hermit. Rubbing her eyes with the balls of her palms, she tried to pull herself together.

"You are right. I did not get here through a door as such, well not a door in this mountain. I came in from the Locked Gate of Gold Glen and followed the map that lit up inside my mind." It sounded ridiculous but who better to sound ridiculous to.

"Ahh. A journey of the Light." The hermit nodded contentedly as if he expected as much.

"The light?" She said before realizing this would probably lead to another perplexing explanation.

"Someone was calling you. Oh yes. I can see it now. You know it has been a long time since I have talked to one so... dimensional." He seemed pleased with this choice of words. "Yes you have them."

Opal rubbed her forehead in frustration. How did he know someone was calling her? What did 'dimensional' mean? Was that even a word? And what was 'them'?

"I do not know how to go forward," she said resignedly. Surprisingly this appeared to make him very sad.

"It is, in itself, a dilemma that I have chosen to relinquish spirit against." The hermit sounded hopelessly defeatist.

"Well I am not resigning myself to the confines of this …place!" Opal was not about to surrender *her* spirit. Maybe the voice had stopped calling her, and she may not have the treble clef key any longer, but the stones were still in her locket and if she could just bring back the image of the map she might have a chance: If she could figure out how to get out of here.

The hermit turned away from her and nodded to himself. He was right. He knew it from the moment he saw her. This child was born of the Light. Finally, after all these years of waiting, she had arrived.

"A mist must pass
Before the will can grow bold,
After the green eye of envy
Has taken its hold,
For I am the fear within:
That which is unresolved,
And I will give up such life
Until it is told."

Opal had no idea what his poem meant. Deciding to ignore him she tried to concentrate on the map inside her head but all she could visualize was Tarl drowning.

The hermit traipsed off to the center of the room and began fiddling with something. When he returned he held something out toward her. It sparkled even though there was no direct light.

"You must take this ring," he announced. "It will guide you to the place you cannot find with sight. The past must meet the future to dissolve all spite."

"Thank you but I do not want your ring," Opal replied as she stole a glance at the beautiful object the hermit offered her. The stone was remarkable. It was a completely flawless emerald that twinkled with internal light as if small firelights were exploding within it.

"You must take this ring. It will help you converge. You have only come half way. You must no longer allow your emotions to draw you. You can use this as a medium key – just as you used the clef key."

How did he know about the key anyway? Opal was sure she had not mentioned it. Everything was turning out to be a complete mess. How could she have thought *she* was needed? This could have been one of the worst decisions she had ever made and she had made some considerable ones.

"It will give you your journey but it must be returned to its rightful place."

"But I do not care about the ring's 'rightful place'."

"You are letting emotion carry you again." The hermit pressed the ring into her palm and sighed. "My use for it has expired."

"But I do not even know where it belongs."

"Then you will have to work a little harder this time. Place the ring on your finger, here." He pointed to her right forefinger. "Give him back to life."

"What does that mean?"

"You will know when you take the next step."

"Do not give me riddles! Tell me the truth. How will I know where the ring belongs?"

"The truth is exactly where you are headed. And stop believing you need eyes to see." He looked intently into her gray stare and then down at the ring again before ambling over to an angled wall behind her. There was something very familiar about that saying but she could not place its origin. Perhaps she was becoming so confused that she had never really heard it at all. Opal desperately wanted to get out of here. Her head was buzzing with uncertainty and frustration. She would have to try something.

"What does the ring do, exactly?"

"Ahh," he said emphatically as he turned to face her, "this should help you." On his raised palms he balanced a golden sword so perfect it looked as if it had just been drawn from a vat of molten liquid. "A golden sword to cut the 'umbilical' cord between this world and the next. Understand though that this is just a physical tool to assist your cerebral ability. You have a greater capacity than you can imagine. Perhaps even greater than I can imagine. You got here didn't you? Disbelief is your worst enemy." He laid the sword down in front of her.

Opal stared at the smooth glistening blade. For just a moment it appeared to be invisible before a swirl of colors surged across it making it look as if it held a depth that she may fall through if she kept looking at it.

"Now you must go." He pronounced as he wandered off toward the east side of the mountain.

"But," her eyes moved from the blade to his retreating back, "I do not know what to do!" He disappeared through an emerald corridor with a brief flick of his raised hand. Running after him wasn't going to help. He had given all he was going to give. She sat staring hopelessly from the blade to the ring shaking her head in confusion. How was she supposed to know what to do?

20

Images to Last a Lifetime

Tarl lay with his back on the cold floor. His head rested on a makeshift pillow of Rembeu's pack buffered by the silks of one of Rembeu's robes. He closed his eyes and tried to relax. The floor was vibrating ever so slightly reminding him of the consequences of his failure. His uncle was placing gem stones around his body. The Elestial crystal weighed on his brow; his third eye, but it felt strangely comforting.

Rembeu then placed a polished clear quartz wand on the floor above his head to amplify energy and set several star quartz cabochons on his chest and in his uplifted palms. Trigonal carnelians were positioned around Tarl's naval with a corresponding one at the top of his head. A staurolite crystal formation was finally placed on his abdomen. The twin crystal, forming the shape of a cross, was the inspiration for many legendary stories. In fact, Rembeu knew only too well, the cross was a powerful tool which most effectively focused energy and thought, amplified it, transmitted it and transformed it.

Tarl began to breathe deeply and started the difficult process of clearing his mind. He listened to Rembeu's soft, reassuring tones and felt himself drifting inward, deeper and deeper into darkness. Rembeu's words stretched through the dark toward him.

"Visualize a cascade of pure white light showering across your body; bathing you from your head to your toes. Visualize this white light entering the surrounding crystals. Ask for protection and guidance." Rembeu took a deep breath. "Find a sacred space within the light and follow your instincts toward that sacred trust."

Sweat was trickling down Tarl's face. Rembeu could only imagine the sheer energy involved in this task. He continued calmly trying to gauge the state of Tarl's mind. Venturing into the white light of the Elestial crystal would feel like entering infinity unless Tarl focused; focused hard.

"You need to find the entrance. When you do, reach in and grasp its energy."

The last words Rembeu spoke were spiraling away into the distance of the unfathomable darkness in which Tarl now found himself. This place was overwhelming him with numbness. He needed to find something, anything in the emptiness. Rembeu's voice had died away, drawn into a black hole of loss. Tarl was completely alone.

Trying to concentrate on the center of his body, he squeezed every unfeeling muscle. A slight tingle began to turn within him. It grew into a burning, bright orange swirl of stars that spun from his stomach into a dazzling galaxy, reaching outward into the blackness.

Finally able to focus, Tarl discovered he was floating in a dimensionless whorl. The vortex of sparkling orange light was coiling outward from the center of his body and twisting into the darkness. The spiral became a spinning wheel of white light whipping around faster and faster. He floated with calm curiosity at the thing he had 'created' until it suddenly burst into seven perfect segmented rays of color. Each colored ray then separated, wrapping themselves into seven wheels of color. They flew inward, smashing into each other and finally creating an explosion that nearly blinded him.

Tarl struggled desperately to see past the iridescent slashes which burned his field of vision. When his eyes finally focused again, he was standing on a rainbow bridge which rolled ahead toward a single point of light. The bridge began to undulate behind him, pushing him forward, transporting him toward the spinning white light. Tarl wasted no time. Reaching in, he grasped but felt the pull too late. It was as though his body was being crushed. He was merging with the spinning white disc: No longer did he have a human body, and then, he felt himself shatter and scatter into the infinite starry skies.

Then he saw it: A burning orange five pointed star. Tarl was being drawn into its center where five huge ochre stone doors surrounded him. One would have to be chosen or he would be trapped. The only solution was to transform. His star body contracted and he fell toward the featureless floor, landing on strong legs – four of them. Raising a large padded paw, the paw of a lion, he ran furiously toward one of the doors thrusting his massive form upon in it.

An involuntary roar escaped from his thick throat. The door opened and a new scene spread before him. Everything was on fire. Images of burning creatures twisted in the ribboning flames. His father's face howled in agony. Even though he was horrified, Tarl's instincts were primed. His heavy but agile body moved forward.

The desperate cries of Tarl's mother sliced right through him as if his very heart were burning. He roared with pain. This was a trap. At the moment of comprehension the scene dissolved and he found himself crouching on an orange cylinder; the world around him a cavernous blackness dropping below him. The cylinder began to rise upward. Far below circles of burnt grass began to appear. One by one they were crisping up like burnt leaves. He had to get back to the exit. The cylinder he had been crouching on was moving farther and farther away. With no time to think, he sprang; his muscled hind legs thrusting him toward the aperture, which now stood like a window surrounded by emptiness. He didn't want to think what would have happened had he not jumped when he did.

As he moved through the opening, his human form returned momentarily before transforming again into a sleek silver horse. This was taking too much time. He would have to move more swiftly. Rising onto his hind legs, he pushed another door open.

Silvery-blue glaciers slid like snakes amongst high ice-white mountains. Rotating tiny crystal balls hung in the air like stars in the cold daylight. Visually, there was nothing to make him believe this was a trap. Relying on his instincts, he sniffed the air but felt only the burning cold. There was no balance here. He stepped back. As he did he felt his human form return to him once more. This time it remained.

Facing the other three doors, he saw that they all looked the same except for one door. High above Tarl's head, at the center of the door he spotted a small circle cut through it that hadn't been there before. Without understanding why, Tarl knew that this was the door. How was he going to access that hole? He needed to be small and he needed to be able to fly.

Immediately his body began to shrink; smaller and smaller. Wings like kites stretched out from his soft worm-like body. Moving them up and down, he bobbed uncomfortably, until he felt himself rise upwards. Tarl hoped his butterfly wings would fit through the hole, which was now so far up that it had disappeared from his view.

Finally, he found the opening. The space beyond the hole was mesmerizing. There appeared to be no walls or floor inside this door and, at its approximate center, revolved a translucent crystal ball glowing with opalescent light. It captured a light show of galaxies moving within its sphere as if the lights were being conducted like an orchestra. He had found it: The opening to the heart of the crystal. Now came the difficult part; entering it and making the necessary time alterations.

Tarl concentrated on inducing the recent events that had taken place. The revolving sphere started to become cloudy. The panic inside him was rising. Was he losing alignment with its energy? The clouds sifted outward around the sphere's edges. Within its center, images expanded and sounds grew like sonic holograms from a cosmic past that both inspired and destroyed.

Careful to remain disconnected from the outpourings, he still felt like they were taking too much energy, too much control. He realized, so very late, that the butterfly was a mistake. His butterfly body was too flimsy. It would be ripped to shreds by the energy. How could he gain strength but retain the freedom of flight and the need to be a fighter? And then he remembered a long ago tale of a bird that could retrieve thunder bolts hurled by the great sky god.

The claws of an eagle pushed him from the small circular entrance and launched him toward the sphere. Memories were being plucked from his mind and converted into holograms revolving within the crystal. Plunging thru its jelly-like skin, he soared inward toward its heart. It was like being inside a bottle: Weightless; soundless; empty.

Tarl fought the paranoia that overwhelmed him: He did not exist; had never existed; he was of no consequence. His head screamed with a desperate cry for validation. "I do exist, I am here!"

The soundless bubble stopped spinning and the images around him dissipated as if they had been given permission to leave. Human form had returned to him and he now stood inside the middle of the crystal and in front of him a stood a cylindrical tunnel lined with mirrors. Tarl stepped in.

Every tile held a moving reflection of moments in his life but not only was the display non-sequential – it was a complete jumble. A mirror displaying him playing spinball with his friends just months ago, sat next to a reflection of him as a baby being nursed by his mother.

The tiled cylinder appeared to go on forever. Shocked, Tarl realized this must be how he could access the crystal's heart. 'Very clever', he thought; 'making a human confront the very thing they reject: The absolute truth about every living moment - including the very last one'. And there lay his task: To correct the time frames. He was going to have to put his entire life in order. It was physically impossible and anyway he had lost all perception of time and he still had to locate the correct vibrations to match the ones that were missing.

Feelings of defeat and failure were rising like a tide. Clenching his fists, he steeled himself against the negative flood of emotions and raised his arms above his head, teeth gritted, muscles gripped. He sucked in enough air to fill his lungs and then released his roaring voice into the echoing tunnel.

Until he heard his own voice echoing back he had not realized what he had called out.

"I am a being of truth and light. The consequence of my life is not *my* importance. Images and memories need only to remain as they are. My indulgences are beyond these borders."

The image of his older self faced him again. It wore robes of silken gold. His hair was still shoulder length but streaked with silver; his face was lined but his eyes sparkled back at him.

The reflection smiled gently at Tarl and reached a palm outwards toward his younger self. Tarl pushed out an opposing palm and rested it upon the opposite palm. This act produced a wink from his observer before a surge of lightening-rod-light ripped through the tunnel of mirrors amending their sequence from birth to death.

"Think of the mirrors as books," the voice said calmly.

It took a moment for the words to make sense. He remembered Melik's library analogy. The mirrors represented missing time: Clever if not a little too personal.

Tarl looked again and saw the same images he had seen in the Moon Gate in Calatia. As the last shocking image flickered into place a blinding light burst behind his eyes. The mirror tunnel was exploding. Several shards struck his hands as he tried to protect himself. Their vibrations charged up his arms and out of his head. He felt himself being pulled into a doorway of light and then into oblivion.

21

The Golden Link

Rembeu was rocking his nephew back and forth. His arms were gripped tightly around Tarl's unmoving body. They were trapped inside the sphere.

"You did it," he was whispering. "I don't know how, but you did it." Rembeu had tried to administer a potion to Tarl but he was not coming around. His near lifeless body hung in his uncle's arms.

Images whirled about them as time quickly began to be replaced. Incredible changes were occurring. The ground circles below him were starting to heal but as they did he saw a rebellious group of people throw Carny into one of the crevices just before it closed up. People were celebrating and many had started to move out from the enclosure. Many figures were looking up at the sphere waving their arms and cheering. 'Good for them,' he thought, 'but I wish you could do something for my nephew'.

"Melik?! Melik?!" There had not been a single utterance from the stargazer. Rembeu squeezed Tarl a little tighter. He had no idea what would happen next and certainly no control over it.

Tarl was trembling now in Rembeu's arms. His limp body felt cold and clammy. Melik needed to get them out of there. Now! They seemed to be moving within the sphere, twisting and turning away from this world.

Rembeu kept rocking Tarl back and forth watching the scenes outside. The terrain was changing yet again.

"Melik! Answer. Please!" He waited. There was no answer.

Rembeu suddenly realized: It wasn't he and Tarl that were moving, it was the sphere itself. The sphere was being pushed away by the repletion of time. It was going back to where it came from.

Rembeu's stomach lurched as the sphere dropped slightly. Instinctively, he clenched his stomach muscles for the ascent and held Tarl as tightly as he could. He wanted to tell him that everything would be alright but he couldn't get any words out. It felt as if he were being divided into several realities, each of them simultaneously active.

Clenching his jaw, Rembeu forced his eyes to stay at least minutely open. It felt as if they were being shot through a cannon. Images struck him like face slaps. He saw what Tarl had just been through. Tears squeezed from his eyes.

"…em…co…o…r".

"Me…lik!" Rembeu's voice shuddered in the vibrations. "Me…lik come in. O…er."

"Hol… on…over."

"Me…lik. Sph…re return…ing to origin!"

"Hold on. I've g..ot it. Over."

If only it were over Rembeu thought. He pressed his eyes shut and held on to Tarl.

Suddenly he felt as he had been dropped into nothingness. They were completely weightless. Everything fell silent and any movement felt like slow motion.

Still in the hovering sphere, Rembeu dared to peer out about him. Several friendly looking people milled ahead in the distance. There was a woman wearing a beautiful rainbow colored sari with an exquisite looking bird, much like a toucan, perched on her shoulder. He saw a lovely looking dark skinned older man with a jeweled headpiece that sparkled in the afternoon sun. Huge golden embossed tents glowed with warmth and promise. Several sandstone buildings topped with coiled roofs glinted with the streams of gold and silver thread flying in the wind. The people all had varying features; all different races happily mingling.

Rembeu felt a strong vibration coming from the pocket inside his robe. One of the Elestial crystals was opening. They were not meant to do that by themselves. He felt for the satchel strapped to his side. It must be the third crystal. That would make sense. They were teetering on the edge of the third Light Ray.

"Rembeu? Do you copy? Over."

"Yes! Oh Melik Tarl's in a bad way!"

"Right. O.K. Well I'm working as fast as I can. I guess you've figured out what's going on? Over."

"The sphere has returned to where it was sucked from but why is it still here? Why hasn't it been absorbed?"

"Yes. Well," Melik didn't want to break the news to Rembeu but he figured honesty must prevail, "I'm holding it back. Over." He waited for Rembeu's response.

"Oh. Oh dear. You mean if it's absorbed so are we? Over."

"Yes Rembeu. But I've got several pieces of good news. I've immobilized the sphere for the present. I've just got to hold it in this position for a little longer. Your next co-ordinates need to be accessed fairly shortly. I've been checking the environment this sphere came from – you're in the locality now. It probably has the most positively motivated calculations of any place I've ever encountered. Over."

"I can see it. I can see this place. It is incredibly beautiful. The people look... well, wonderful." Rembeu lifted Tarl's chin to check his face. "Melik, Tarl is not responding to treatment. He's unconscious, cold and clammy. What's the plan? And seriously Melik, make this quick. Over"

"Yes. Quick. Right. The evolutionary path you're currently residing over has no anomalies except for their missing time. When you and Tarl reversed the effects of excess time in your last reality path you essentially 'cured' the only problems the people in this current path were dealing with. It appears to me that their 'positive building energies' have counteracted most of the detrimental effects of the extracted time but I can tell they were experiencing more and more difficulty. After all my calculations I believe that it makes perfect sense. Once the sphere is absorbed their planet will return to the supreme world it was before. If I am correct you will move to the subsequent path after accessing the next co-ordinates. Over."

"Can't we get Tarl back home first? He needs proper treatment. I can't do that here. Over."

"Due to the immediacy of co-ordinate emergence it will be necessary to transfer you to your subsequent arrival point on the next path. Once you're on that path I can access a new transfer point and bring you home. I will try to be as quick as possible. Standby for countdown. Over."

That apparently, was it. More waiting. He grabbed his pack with his left hand while still holding Tarl tightly with his right. One-handed he began to mix a potion. His aim was to decrease anxiety and build immunity against the demons Tarl was obviously still trying to fight somewhere in the recesses of his mind. He also tried to treat his physical symptoms, careful not to challenge the first treatment. Afterward, he held Tarl close, trying to keep him warm. All he could do now was wait.

■　■　■

The world beyond this weightless observation bowl was lovely to watch. Men and woman greeted each other with smiles of love and compassion. Colorful seamless saris glistened in the saffron-yellow sunlight. There were no visible markets, just people with baskets exchanging goods with each other. People moved in and out of shimmering tents that stretched across the sandy paths, waving and laughing to passersby. Encircling the settlement were several large citrine carvings of dancers. The glowing figures included men, women and children posing gracefully in flowing garments. Smooth sandstone buildings climbed up the cream cliffs as if they were reaching for the lemon dipped sky.

"O.K. Prepare for transfer. Over."

Rembeu wondered exactly what it was he would have to prepare for. The Third Elestial Crystal was still vibrating at his side. He had no time to examine it. He looped his satchel around his left arm and held on to Tarl firmly.

"And counting down…three…two…one…"

Rembeu felt the familiar tug. The weightlessness of the sphere was lifting away from them. A shrill sound caused his head to pulse. The E sharp note screamed in his ears. Umbra was having trouble accessing the divide between paths. The note gradually ebbed and fell around him like a loose blanket. He felt as if he were falling into a tunnel of luring winds, both pulling him away and pushing him toward something simultaneously.

Rembeu felt his satchel loosen. Its weight was pulling his arm away from Tarl. He tried desperately to heave it back down; back to his side, but the contents were too heavy. He let go of Tarl just long enough to untangle his arm. His potions, stones and light-ebbers disappeared above him. The Second Elestial Crystal of his ancestry now belonged to lost time. He hoped he would not need it to help revive Tarl. Managing to keep hold of the straps, he squeezed his eyes shut against the pressure and tried to rehearse affirmations in his head.

22

The Umbical Sword

Opal took a deep breath. She sat cross-legged in front of the sword allowing the tips of her toes to touch its edges. Gripping her ring-free hand over her emerald clad finger, she squeezed her eyes shut. The hermit obviously believed she could do this. Pushing the images of Tarl out of her head, she forced herself to concentrate.

The ring began to heat up in her palm. The heat distracted her but she strained her concentration even harder. To her amazement she could see bright green rays of light shooting from the ring even though her eyes were closed. The rays expanded, brighter and more vibrant than anything she had experienced. The map burst into rivers of light behind her eyes as if her very nerves were pulsing with illumination. Summoning every degree of energy possible, she bent down over her feet and squeezed herself into a tight ball to focus on the pulsing vision of the map.

Slowly a wall rose up in front of her: The sword had levitated up to the height of her head. The discovery of knowing things were happening without actually seeing them was, in the least, unsettling. An area of the map began to pulse more strongly. She concentrated on that part and it suddenly zoomed in to show her details of the area. The same thing happened and again the map zoomed in to show her more and more detail.

Then, unexpectedly, the map dissolved behind a murky wash and she was plunged into darkness. The more she squeezed her eyes, the muddier her surroundings became, until finally, an image of Tarl floated up from the gloom.

Tarl was not moving but he looked both lost and trapped at the same time. The hermit had said, 'a golden sword to cut the umbilical cord between this world and the next'. Perhaps this was a way she could communicate with him. A cold wind from the gold sword chilled her skin as it slashed past her face. It had swung downwards in front of her body like an axe. With all her might she heaved the vision to Tarl. As she did so, she felt the ring's energy surge and then she felt herself drop.

"Tarl!" Her voice screamed out without intention. She could see neither Tarl's image nor the map. She was falling, rushing down; faster and faster. The air was being ripped from her lungs and was being replaced by thick stagnant air. It was becoming harder and harder to breath. Viscous liquid was washing up against her body. Again she tried to call out but her mouth was full of liquid. She couldn't breathe.

'I am not going to make it,' she thought desperately as all the air disappeared, 'I am going to die.'

23

Three is company

The force below them was now stronger than the force above. Rembeu and Tarl were being sucked into the next plane and the surge was affecting Tarl's condition.

Tarl was able to recognize that he was not conscious but he was unable to force himself to stir. He was trapped.

Fighting to bring himself out of this uncomfortable slumber he tried desperately to open his eyes but his subconscious wouldn't let him go. And something murky was growing at his feet. He couldn't move and now green liquid was rising around his body threatening to engulf him. There were shapes but nothing he could recognize. Where was this place? What was this place? Surely this was not inside him? Wherever it was, it was grave and dangerous.

Suddenly, he saw his arm lash out in front of him swinging a golden sword. Apparently he was fighting a battle he couldn't even see; a battle, until now, he didn't know existed. The blade swung back and forth but hit only thick green liquid. His were movements slow and useless; his intentions ineffective in this mire.

Aware his consciousness was calling to him from far away, he could do nothing to garner it. It seemed impalpable, illusive. He tried to clear his thoughts and focus on whatever the shapes were lurking around him. Something ahead was becoming clearer. It was turning into the form of a human. What he saw didn't make any sense at all.

Opal's silhouette appeared in the green fluid ahead of him. Her arms were raised in front of her; her palms facing outward as if she were pounding on a wall. She was screaming. The shock jolted his entire body. He desperately wanted to get to her, help her, but he couldn't move.

At that moment he also realized he couldn't breathe.

Tarl took a last look at Opal, his eyes sad with defeat. He couldn't tell her how sorry he was, he couldn't even tell her the one thing he needed to tell her before he was gone. His eyes rolled closed and he sank deeper into the viscous green liquid.

■　■　■

"No! Tarl. No." Opal was screaming as she stood over Tarl; her delicate accent smoothing out the letters of his name. "No! I can't be too late. I can't be too late."

Opal was watching Tarl in the viscous muck as he slashed the golden sword aimlessly, incompetently. And then, suddenly she was standing over him in a different place altogether. Tarl lay still and unmoving at her feet and another man lay unconscious further away. She began shaking Tarl unsure of what else to do. Why had she decided to give him a weapon? How stupid of her to listen to a hermit; a complete stranger. Tarl obviously did not understand its meaning. How was he supposed to know that it was symbolic?

Rembeu's eyes began to flutter open with sounds of fear echoing around him. He couldn't believe what he was seeing. A young girl was shaking Tarl and calling out his name. He felt a strange lack of continuity as if he had been split into different people, different times, and different places.

Blinking again did not change the vision in front of him. The girl wore a deep blue, high-necked silk caftan with golden butterflies embroidered across it in swirls. Her black silky hair was tangled with glistening midnight blue thread and swinging wildly in the wind. 'How lovely,' Rembeu thought.

Suddenly remembering their situation, Rembeu sat up in a daze and struggled toward his nephew. They had been separated in the transfer. He assumed he must have been knocked out on landing. The strong wind was pushing at him and his flapping robes were hindering his movements. Rembeu knelt beside Tarl and checked his vitals. The girl was crying now and sobbing out Tarl's name in waves of emotion.

"He's sick." Rembeu managed as he reached for Tarl's brow.

The girl appeared to be surprised by this interruption but she wasn't giving up on the fact that shaking him may help.

"Tarl!" she screamed again frantically. "The golden sword was a symbol. It wasn't meant for battle use. Tarl. Listen to me. It's Opal. You must listen."

Rembeu took another look at this surprising girl. Opal? How on time's behalf did she get here? He was sure he was conscious. It took him a moment to comprehend the circumstances. And then he realized the seriousness of the situation.

"Melik? Melik we've arrived. Some kind of pasture. It's very windy. Tarl needs to return to Atlas Mountain. Do you copy? Over." There was no response. He tried to collect his thoughts.

Opal looked desperately at the stranger who was talking to someone that did not exist. Was this man his uncle? She turned back toward Tarl. His lovely tanned skin had dissolved into a pasty gray. The life was literally draining out of him.

"We must help him!" Opal wailed as she tried to think. What did the hermit say? What were the last two lines of that stupid poem? It must be important she just knew it.

'And I am fear within that which is unresolved, And I will give up my life until it is told.' Opal repeated the words slowly trying to make sense of them.

"Those lines sound familiar," said Rembeu, his brain feeling as if it were in a high speed blender.

"What was he doing when this happened?" Opal cried out to Rembeu.

Rembeu's was so surprised by her forceful attitude that his answer just came out without thought of how it would sound to a stranger.

"He entered the heart of the Elestial Crystal." The words seemed to take the last fragments of his energy. Suddenly he was overwhelmed by weakness. He held on to consciousness as if it were a raft on a swelling ocean.

"What happened?" Opal begged.

"Well, I saw what he saw…close to the end." Rembeu was pouring more of the potion into Tarl's numb mouth.

"What? Please what did you see?" she pleaded.

"I saw… well," he pulled his thoughts together; "it was his whole life; every image, every thought, every loss."

"His mother?"

"Yes, and you," Rembeu said, grimacing immediately after realizing what he had just told her.

Her eyes shot open. She looked back down at Tarl.

"Tarl. You must understand. You fought with the sword out of fear. You do not need to be afraid. You lashed out at the nothingness you were faced with." She placed a delicate hand just above Tarl's stomach. Her emerald ring shone brightly. Two rays of light stretched from its apex like reaching arms. Opal just kept talking. "There is everything out here for you. You cannot give up your life. You are needed so much by so many people. Tarl Please. I am here right beside you. Your uncle is here. We need you."

Tarl's mouth opened very slightly. Rembeu and Opal swapped amazed glances. They both cried out Tarl's name. He moved his mouth again but no sound came out. They called out his name again and Opal wrapped her two hands around the hand closest to her. Rembeu did the same. This time he appeared to be mouthing the word 'Opal'. Tears began streaming from her eyes. He squeezed her hand slightly before falling into unconsciousness again.

"Rembeu, I have accessed the co-ordinates of your path shift. Do you copy? Over."

Opal jumped slightly; her eyes wide with surprise: An invisible man was talking. She clung to Tarl's hand and looked incomprehensibly at Rembeu.

Rembeu saw her flinch and held up the Voicer to show her how to press its center first. She appeared to be fleetingly amused and then remembered where she was. Her beautiful gray eyes were pleading with the thoughts that Rembeu himself was feeling.

"Melik. Tarl is gravely ill. You need to return us to Atlas Mountain. Now. Over."

"I strongly advise you to hold your positions at current location. The access co-ordinates are proving difficult to constrain. I cannot confirm re-entry."

Rembeu was surprised at himself for feeling any hesitation.

"Melik get us home NOW!"

Melik got the message.

"Co-ordinating units now. Over."

"Melik. Confirming: Three people are being transferred. Over."

Melik didn't have time to ask questions.

"Confirmed. Three units for path slide. Prepare for countdown. Over."

Opal heard the countdown and wondered what this transition would be like. She hoped no one was going to get trapped. Then the pull of an unknown force tugged at her dragging her body across the continuum.

Rembeu was grateful that this transference was an easy crossing. It felt like home was calling them: As if they were just slipping back to the place they were meant to exist, not forcing their way into someone else's world.

The transference was reasonably easy and they arrived at the Wheel-Door without a hindrance. The only hint that something was wrong was the fact that Atlas Mountain felt cold: Extraordinarily cold.

24

Life-force Green

In the Healing Room Tarl received proper medicinal mixtures to try to ease him back to consciousness. Even though there was no physical evidence, the readings indicated he was having serious heart problems.

Rembeu was constantly trying new blends to revive his nephew until he finally realized that potions were not going to bring Tarl back. For the first time in many years he had to face the fact that he could not fix something. On this most difficult day, a day he accepted that not even his Teachings could help him heal his nephew, he took many things into stock. Finally, he had come across the thing he most feared; incapability. If it were not for Opal he may have given up.

Opal's dedication was impressive and honorable. She had barely taken time to think of herself. Opal never left Tarl's side. She refused food from Umbra insisting that Rembeu had given her an herbal infusion that would suffice. She only left to quickly wash and change into the cream cotton wraps that Umbra had supplied her with. They hung so loosely that she almost disappeared inside them.

Sleep was never far from her thoughts but she feared that if she slept he may wake. Whatever she did or said, her efforts seemed, to her, to be futile.

Rembeu watched her curiously. The connection between Opal and Tarl was obvious. He wondered what Parvo must have felt when he saw them together. Rembeu's heart beat a little faster as he remembered the words of the Divine Sources. Perhaps Tarl's strength was greater than Rembeu had given him credit for. Too much time had passed. It was time to approach Opal. He hoped the correct words would come to him. Turning to Opal, Rembeu made his first ever request for help.

"Give him back to life," he said as calmly as he could. "You may be the only one who can."

Opal looked up at Rembeu. They had barely spoken since their return. It had not seemed important but the words he spoke were familiar. Where had she heard them? Were they the same words the hermit had spoken? Rembeu had quoted the words of the hermit. Or was it the other way around? Either way, there was a link and she must figure out what it was. Maybe she *was* the only one who could help him?

"I will try with everything I am made of. I promise," Opal said quietly as she looked into the Rembeu's sad eyes. "I promise," she whispered looking back to Tarl.

It seemed such a long time ago now that she had dedicated herself to him with her message on the roof of the silk house. Now she must do whatever she could to prove it.

Opal tried to imagine the place Tarl must have withdrawn to; what he might be going through. Finding him was the only way she could think of to bring him back. How had she found him the first time? She did not have a clue. If she could help him she would have to try something, anything. An image of the golden sword came into her thoughts. How and what could she replace it with? Thinking hard she suddenly remembered the ornamental sword she had given him as a parting gift. Sorting through the small pile of Tarl's personal items that the Altai had left after removing his dusty clothes for cleaning, she found the perfectly crafted wooden sword sparkling with gems. Perhaps this time a sword would protect him. But she must make sure that he knew it was not a weapon.

Placing the sword above Tarl's head and holding his left hand with hers, she then placed her right hand with its sparkling emerald ring over the middle of his chest. The same words were repeated over and over again until she could no longer stay awake. As her head sank toward his shoulder, she drifted into semi-consciousness.

Something began to pull at her. She did not want to give in to it, to be swallowed up by the feeling but it became impossible to resist it. It was not her life she particularly cared about, it was Tarl's. She knew now how important he was: Not just to her, not just to his father or uncle, but for the balance of the cosmos; something too big for her to imagine.

Opal's eyelids fluttered as she tried to resist the drag of unconsciousness. It felt as if she were floating in an ocean, her body undulating with the currents. Reality was dissolving behind her. The silent slip into her subconscious was effortless and when she opened her eyes and saw she was under water and surrounded by swaying seaweed and colorful fish she did not feel at all surprised.

The initial spike of panic she felt melted as she observed the beautiful surroundings. She was able to breathe easily and her sight did not seem to be affected. Her cream wrap floated around her ankles and her hair swam around her face like fingers of anemone. Her arms drifted out in front of her and she was glad to see her emerald ring fixed to her forefinger. She must try to wake herself up. If she were asleep Tarl would never wake up.

A strange moaning sound echoed through the liquid. Opal swished her head from one side to the other trying to figure out where the noise was coming from and tried to swim toward it.

The fear only began to rise when she saw that the closer she swam to the moans the more disturbing the surroundings became. The sea was becoming darker, the fish had disappeared and it was much harder to see. Ahead, she could just make out several thick columns of black coral which rose high up above her and broke through the surface of the water. Black muck swam around these pillars like smoke, sifting out to camouflage some kind of entrance. The closer she swam toward the wispy effluent, the harder it was to breathe. Now she was really beginning to worry. If she was asleep, why had she turned this into a nightmare? Thinking positive thoughts, she told herself to wake up, but her body was rolling on the currents moving closer and closer toward the dark mess ahead.

Opal rubbed the emerald on her ring finger with her thumb and thought of Tarl. As she glared at it hopefully, she tried to settle herself. A slight glow emanated from it like arms of light reaching out around her. Everything suddenly became very clear.

This was no dream.

■　■　■

Rembeu had checked with Melik and Umbra so often they actually had told him to go and get some sleep. But he couldn't rest. Not now. Not with his nephew lying lifelessly in the Healing Room. He closed his eyes, trying to hold in the fear he was feeling. The longer Tarl stayed in this state, the more likely it was that he would not waken.

Thank goodness Opal had found them. He still didn't understand how that had happened. Rembeu could tell there was a lot more to her story but right now he didn't feel it was important. The girl held secrets. That was obvious. Secrets, he guessed, even she may not know about. And then there was Umbra. The blind woman had taken to Opal as if she was her own daughter. There was no way Umbra could have known about her. Perhaps she had understood how important Opal was to Tarl, or perhaps, she felt something else? He would have to wait to find out. There was too much work to be done right now.

Umbra informed Rembeu of the continuing destruction and devastation across the planet: Quakes had ripped cities in two; tornado-like winds had whipped up dust creating wind-storms that had destroyed beautiful landscapes; tidal waves had surged into coastal townships and drowned many; and volcanoes, previously dormant, had now erupted across the lands causing massive destruction. So far, it did not seem as if their work had done any good at all.

"Melik have you any news yet? Over."

"Rembeu, there are serious anomalies here. Each computation is changing. It is though I am working with practicalities that appear to be fixed but are not. As fast as I make adjustments, the calculative result has changed again." He sounded defeated. "If I can't fix the calculations then I cannot find a fix on the point of entry. I literally can't keep up. Over."

Even in the cooling air, Rembeu felt a trickle of sweat slip down the side of his face. He tried to think. There must be something. A thousand irrelevant thoughts flicked through his mind. What was wrong with him? Why couldn't he think straight?

"Melik, I'm sorry, but you have no choice. You have to keep trying. Without a re-entry point I will lose track of the access point to the next anomalous path. If I miss that, I've lost all the following ones as well. Over."

"Yes, Rembeu." He sounded frazzled. "I do understand the situation. Over."

"Of course you do Melik. Again, I'm sorry. I don't seem to be able to think productively. Over."

"I thought that might happen. Over."

"Thought what might happen, Melik? Over?"

"There appears to be surges in electromagnetic currents all around the area of Atlas Mountain. I bet if you visited your Clock Room, you'd find it a little more than worrying. Over."

Rembeu sighed. That meant there were significant time discrepancies here too. He didn't need to see the Clock Room. He didn't want to see it.

"Melik, it's going to be O.K." Rembeu managed a little more conviction than he felt. "Just keep trying. Over."

"Of course. How is Tarl? And your lovely new assistant?" Melik tried to be light-hearted. "Over."

"I'm just about to go and check on them. She's been doing incredibly well under the circumstances. Standby for report. Over."

■   ■   ■

Opal was heading closer and closer to the black pillars and darker and darker waters. She could barely breathe. In vain, she tried to remain calm. There must be something she could do? Her only choice seemed to be to swim with the current. Wherever she was headed she at least wanted to get there quickly.

Pushing her arms through the thickening liquid, she found herself surrounded by black muck and debris. Just when she thought she was about to take her very last breath she felt her long hair swirling strangely around her head. A feint gray light hovered above her. Ripples rang out around it. The surface! Her mouth rose from the dirty water and she inhaled desperately, trying to fill her empty lungs. The air was thick and tasted like smoke but she could breathe in and out. When she had finally taken in enough air to accommodate thought she looked around and saw she was treading water in gray-green sludge. Several of the black coral columns rose above the water's surface standing like protectors in front of the smooth silt shore. The land ahead rose to a steep mound where an incredible building spread its arms out across the gray sandy slopes. The sky was dark as if filled with rain yet to fall. Black clouds hung heavy and low and very still. A chill ran through her body. She realized how cold she was.

Opal pushed her way through the dark slimy mess trying not to think about what she was moving through. She swam between the black pillars almost expecting them to shoot her with lightening but nothing happened. There was a strange feeling here, a lethargy that weighed her down, physically and mentally. It took all her effort to focus her eyes. They stung terribly. By the time she had reached the shore she wondered why she had bothered. She was too tired to do anything else and too tired to care. Her body was covered with fine gray mud and her wet hair hung in a sopping tangle around her face.

Limping out of the water, feeling as heavy as lead, she saw a dark shape over to her left. Her eyes would not focus properly. It looked like a man: A dead man. He was lying motionless on the gray silty sand.

Crawling slowly, she made her way toward him; not sure she really wanted to see a dead man right now; and wondering if she may be joining him soon.

Slowly, slowly she crept closer.

Horror wakened her energy. The cotton shirt looked just like...

"Tarl!" Opal screamed out his name as she staggered over to his side; the water-soaked cream cotton wrap restricting her steps.

"Tarl?" She shook him as she had done in the Healing Room in Atlas Mountain. It had the same effect: Nothing.

Opal looked about frantically for help. All she could see was the black skeletons of trees harboring the shore and a deserted beach save the curious building far off, elevated on the mount.

"Tarl." she cried again as she raised her hand to his forehead. The emerald ring glowed dimly on her finger. All she could think to do was to press her hand onto his chest - as she was doing in their other reality, if in fact any of this was reality. Gripping his left hand with hers, she mimicked the same position.

A shot of green light shivered up from the ring. It rose up high before dipping back toward her head. The moment the light shard made contact with her it burst into a prismatic arc and blew colors out over the two of them. Except for Opal's big gray eyes following the spectacle she didn't move at all. And then she heard Tarl gasp.

"Tarl? Tarl it's all right. It's me Opal. You're going to be alright." The bow of colors still arched above them and she tried to suppress a shiver.

Tarl's voice was just a hoarse whisper.

"Opal?" He attempted to open his eyes.

"Yes Tarl it is me. You have to wake up. Please, try to open your eyes." Desperation was pouring from her words.

His eyelids fluttered again before he managed to focus. Tarl couldn't believe what he was seeing.

"Opal?" His voice was getting stronger but he was still feeling quite dazed. A green sky rose above him and a girl with long black wet hair and a mud streaked face was looking down at him. He was looking up into two of the most beautiful, and most frightened, gray eyes he had ever seen. He jolted with recognition.

"Opal?" He tried to sit up.

"That is good. Yes Tarl, please sit up." Opal kept holding the ring to his chest, her eyes gazing into his for any worrying signs.

The effort of sitting up forced a groan from Tarl's throat. His muscles felt as if they had been pummeled and his head felt like it had been hit with a rock. He held up his right hand as a sign that he was alright.

"Oh Tarl, I'm so glad you are awake." Opal waited until he appeared to be fully aware and then began to remove her hand from his chest. The rainbow arch dissolved.

Tarl cried out. It felt as if a sword was being pulled out of him. He had to force himself to stay awake and not to fall back into the oblivion he had come from. Trying to remember what had happened, a vision of the mirror tunnel struck him. It had exploded in a blaze of light and pieces had come flying at him from every direction; so much for putting them all in order. Checking his body, he could see he was no longer covered in the broken shards. The piece that had shot out of the mirror tunnel and struck him through the heart had cruelly shown him a vision of Opal laughing before it sliced into him. For a moment he had been amazed at how easily it had pierced his vest and skin and then he saw blood flowing from his chest like water. Tarl felt the spot that the shard had pierced but there was no blood. His energy was disappearing again. His last thoughts melted within him like wax flakes.

"Tarl. Please stay with me. Please."

Tarl stopped himself from drifting. He forced his eyes to open and squinted up at Opal. Smiling, he raised a hand to touch her face, to make sure she was really there, wherever 'there' was.

"Opal, how did you get here?" Tarl asked still fighting the pull downward.

"That story will have to wait. For now we should figure out where we are and try to get back home."

"Calatia?" he asked. Opal's smile made his heart beat a little too quickly. Shaking his head, he struggled to concentrate.

"No, not Calatia; Atlas Mountain. Our bodies are in Atlas Mountain but we are somehow here." How could she explain this?

Tarl didn't know how his body got back to Atlas Mountain or how Opal had arrived in this strange place but he knew he hadn't completely left the the last experience. Somehow he had been caught in the elestial crystal. Perhaps this was some other subconscious trap. He hadn't returned to his body he knew that. If Opal was a figment of this manifestation, well, what a nice figment to have to put up with. Great he was going to spend some time with an imaginary Opal. Why not? This was going to be a lot more pleasant than anything he had gone through so far.

Taking a moment to absorb her image, Tarl smiled a peaceful kind of smile that made him realize how wonderful her presence was; real or not.

"I like being with you. You make me feel better," he said feeling groggy and a little nonchalant.

Opal could not help but smile back coyly.

"I like to be with you also." She stopped herself from continuing. Getting side-tracked was a waste of valuable time. It was going to take a while for Tarl to adjust.

"Tarl, I know you are still weak but we need to focus on this situation." Opal nodded in the direction of the castle.

"Oh, yes," he tried to collect his thoughts. "Do you know where we are?"

Opal shook her head and then looked up at him with a thought.

"It has something to do with this ring."

"It's extraordinary. Where did you get it?" Tarl's eyes focused momentarily on the green stone.

"From the hermit in Emerald Mountain," she said cautiously.

"Oh that sounds nice."

"Tarl, please you have got to concentrate. We are in danger. You have to help us get back. We are not supposed to be here." The urgency in Opal's voice forced him to concentrate.

"Where's Rembeu?" He stretched his eyes and blinked widely as if to try to clear the sand from his mind.

"Rembeu is in Atlas Mountain – with our bodies." She emphasized the last part of the sentence.

"Right, yes, our bodies."

Opal thought the only way he was going to make sense of her being here was to briefly explain her journey. She relayed the hermit's riddle in the hope it may help but Tarl remained unaffected by the words

"So you're really here? I'm really seeing you?" He wanted to wrap his arms around her; tell her everything he had been thinking through all these trials but he gritted his teeth. 'Time and place,' he thought.

"I'm really here." Opal nodded patiently with only the inference of a frown fluttering across her forehead.

"Dad!? Is my father alright?" There were so many questions.

"Yes," she hated not telling him the truth but she could not have him distracted now. Time felt like it was dissolving; as if every minute here was taking a good deal more out of their lives. "When we figure out how to get back to Atlas Mountain I will fill you in on all the details." A growing urgency in her voice was thickening her accent.

"Yes, you're absolutely correct." Taking her lovely delicate fingers in his hand he looked closely at the ring. "Do you know why it glows?"

"It only glows when I am near you or I think of you. I think it is connected with the hermit's riddle and with this place but I do not understand how. It also seems to help you. It is as if everything is related in some way."

"Do you feel any different wearing it?"

"Well," she thought for a moment, "no but I feel I can sense something...something indefinable from it."

"Indefinable, how?"

"It will sound strange..." She looked down shyly.

"Don't worry about how it will sound. Believe me if I had tried to explain to you what I've been through you could not possibly think anything you said would sound strange."

Opal nodded and returned her gaze to his.

"It feels like a door has been opened. I thought it was because I had traveled along different reality paths but it is something more." She hesitated, "I think when I was trapped in Emerald Mountain that ... I was actually in a different stream, perhaps one related to the one we are in now."

"Really?" Tarl thought hard. It all made sense except for his inclusion in this reality stream. "Well at least we have a basis for why we might be here." He looked up the hill at the castle and for the first time, quite ashamedly, he realized he hadn't asked Opal how she was.

"You're shivering," he looked around but had nothing to offer her.

Opal caught his expression and realized she knew exactly what he was thinking.

"I am all right Tarl. Honestly." She shone a small grin at him. "I found *you*, remember?"

A laugh escaped him causing an agonizing pain in chest. Involuntary he cried out. Panic rose inside Opal but she managed to keep calm. There was no need for Tarl to worry about her. There was no time to waste on emotion right now. The image of his comatose body in Atlas Mountain encouraged her to remain strong.

"Tarl..."

"It's OK. I'm fine." He interrupted. "Right then let's find out where 'this' is." Tarl took a deep breath as Opal helped him rise. Taking a look at her cumbersome mud stained wrap hanging loosely around her tiny frame, he tried to suppress a smile. "Nice outfit by the way," he said wryly, trying to cover up his pain.

"Umbra lent it to me." Opal looked down at the filthy cloth and smiled at his jest, "I thought it was rather fetching actually." She tried to keep lightness in her voice but the way Tarl was gripping her hand gave her even more cause to worry.

They began dragging their heavy bodies toward the steep incline.

"There is definitely a dispirited feeling here." Tarl was looking at the low dark clouds.

"It's quite oppressive isn't it?" Opal replied not taking her eyes of the uneven ground.

Tarl looked across at her; she was obviously struggling. A pang of concern so great struck him that it caused his chest to burn and made him double over with pain. He wanted to scoop her up in his arms and carry her up the incline but he could barely manage to make it himself.

Opal did not want to tell Tarl the reason for her urgency. She could feel her energy draining away. How long she would be able to continue was uncertain. Every time she had used the ring to help Tarl, the loss of energy became greater. If she could just make it up the mount; just get into the castle then maybe they could sort this out quickly. Tarl would figure out what to do. It did not matter what happened to her but Tarl must pursue his quest.

"Can you make it?" he asked anxiously.

"Oh yes," she summoned all her strength, "absolutely." She threw him a glance, "perhaps next time, though, we might take a walk in the Calatian Forest instead?"

"Sounds good to me." Tarl smiled warmly at her knowing she was trying hard to sound strong. It was a nice thought though.

The humidity was rising with every step and the last ridge took so much energy that they both had to lie still for a while before continuing. Opal's hair had nearly dried and she made an effort to loop it back behind the nape of her neck. Tarl saw her struggle and moved over to help. Holding her fine glossy locks in his hands, he gently tried to pick out any bits of debris that had been collected in the murky waters. Following the movements she had been making, he twisted the three divided sections into a type of messy plait. He could sit here forever.

Opal sat, gratefully accepting assistance. She could have sat there, just like that, endlessly. Thankfully, some energy began to return to her. When he finished plaiting her hair he patted the long strip he had created.

"Not bad for a first try," he said, reluctantly admitting he had finished.

"Thank you," she replied as they unenthusiastically began the walk toward the imposing entrance of the castle.

"Not exactly how I imagined we'd spend our second date." Tarl grinned surprised at himself for saying something so bold.

"Nor I. But it is good to be different. Who needs a wonderful dinner by candle-light when you can have a swim in black sludgy waters, emerge covered in mud to find your date unconscious; and then walk exhausted, up a hill to enter a strange building without any idea of where you are." Opal's voice petered away.

"How true." Tarl said keenly trying to distract Opal from her exhaustion. "Why we must recommend this to others." It was funny but neither of them could muster a laugh.

The entrance looked less impressive up close. The large engraved slab that had appeared to be a huge door was in fact just a decorative area around a much smaller stone entry. Seeing the door slightly ajar gave rise to their doubts.

"Perhaps we're expected?" Tarl tried to make a joke but it fell flat.

The air was even thicker up here and a gray-green haze hung like fog around them. The humid air smelt fetid and the threatening clouds seemed to close in upon them. Tarl had to fight off his ever present claustrophobia. Telling Opal to stand to one side, he pushed the heavy door open. The following pain that seared through his chest made him wince involuntarily. He tried to cover it with a cough.

Darkness hung like a blanket in front of them. Tarl stopped still, unsure of his next move. Opal held up her left hand. Green arms of light stretched from the emerald ring as if guiding them forward. They advanced quietly.

The castle consisted of many arching tunnels. Every ridged archway was sliced with other tunnel entrances. It was impossible to know where they were going or where they had come from.

They followed the arms of the emerald light and hoped they were heading in the right direction. They had no choice but to keep going. Tarl paced slightly ahead of Opal trying not the get in the way of the striding light, but hoping to be able to protect her if anything came at them.

It was getting hotter and hotter and Tarl's claustrophobia was wrapping around him like a deadly snake. Opal sensed the strain he was feeling but also wondered how long she could keep going. Her energy must have been dwindling again because the emerald ring seemed to be getting heavier and heavier. She removed it from her finger and held it in cupped palms. The light glowed more strongly. A strange tingling feeling began to needle her hands and a feeling of foreboding sparkled in her stomach. Opal looked down at the emerald.

"Tarl," her steady voice held an element of alarm.

The tone made Tarl stop still. He turned slowly around. His eyes grew wide when he looked at the emerald.

"I think we better hurry."

■   ■   ■

Rembeu moved through the doorway of the Healing Room to find an extraordinary sight. Lying her head neatly on Tarl's arm, Opal had finally given in to sleep; her left hand, fitted with the emerald ring, rested upon his chest.

The extraordinary part was, that arching from the ring and falling back down toward the crown of Opal's head, was a vibrantly colored light arc. The colors stretched out like rivers, each ray isolated and yet shared at the same time.

Rembeu didn't move for fear of disturbing whatever was going on. He held up his Voicer and whispered as loudly as he could.

"Melik, come in, over."

"Rembeu? You're not coming through very well. Over."

"Melik," he whispered again, "I'm in the Healing Room with Tarl and Opal. Something is happening here. Over."

"Why? What's going on?" Rembeu waited for 'over' but before it came, Melik started up again. "Oh wait a minute Rembeu. Just hold on please. Over."

Rembeu heaved a sigh and lowered the Voicer. The sight was amazing. He wanted to check their vital signs; see if he could administer anything to assist them but he wasn't about to disrupt whatever was going on. Rembeu smiled to himself. Tarl certainly could pick them: No ordinary girl this one.

"Rembeu, are you there? Over."

"Yes Melik, I'm right here, go ahead." Rembeu resisted the urge for sarcasm. Where did Melik think he went?

"You are in the same room as Tarl and Opal? Over."

"Yes Melik. Over."

"Something is happening. Over."

"Yes Melik, I have an incredible situation here. Over."

"Me too. Got to test something. Could you please place your Voicer close to Tarl? Over."

"O.K. Over." Rembeu was becoming even more intrigued. He followed orders.

"Yes! That's it. Rembeu, the variances have slowed right down. My calculations are finally catching up with the irregularities. I don't understand... how is this possible?"

Something truly incredible must be happening for Melik to forget his Voicer protocol. Rembeu waited until he could hear Melik's Voicer switch over.

"Melik. Listen to me please. Some kind of energy is being emitted between Tarl and Opal. They are experiencing a connection but they are both unconscious. Over."

"Yes," the vagueness in Melik's voice was rising toward comprehension, "That's it! Over."

Rembeu rolled his eyes. Now Melik decides to be succinct. "That's what? Over." Rembeu's voice had returned to normal pitch.

"The connection point to the next plane is being passed through now. Oh wow! I don't know how this can be but it appears Tarl must be accessing the plane...now! Over."

Rembeu was stunned. Tarl was accessing the next plane? But he was right here. His body was right here... but his mind...

"Melik, is that possible? Over."

"Yes, of course. Anything is possible. The mind is an indivisible continuum. There is no real fixed physicality on what the mind is capable of. It makes sense. Tarl ended his time on the last path whilst under the power of the crystal. His conscious mind has taken a back step to allow his subconscious to control his perception. The subconscious is a very powerful tool and bears no grudge on the conscious sensitivity of three dimensional forms. Over."

"I assume Opal is with him… I mean her essence or whatever? Over."

"That is what the connection of energy taking place indicates. Over."

"So what now, Melik? Over."

"Well, now that the aberrations have slowed I can continue my calculations for the passing of the next opening. You'll still be able to access the following path. I just have to calculate in those factors. However, I am assuming you may have to go on your own. Over."

Rembeu wasn't worried about that.

"But what about Tarl? Opal? I can't just leave them here like this. What if they can't access the portal to return to this path? Over." He felt strange saying that whilst he watched them lying in front of him.

"Perhaps we should just wait and see. I'll let you know as soon as my calculations begin to look promising. Keep one of the Voicers next to Tarl. Over."

There was nothing Rembeu could do but wait. He swore that after all this was over he would do anything to avoid waiting.

■　■　■

The ghostly green glow shimmered around Opal. Tarl moved over to her to inspect the ring more closely.

"It's growing," he stated obviously. The emerald ring was crystallizing. The hole at its center was disappearing; it was turning back into its original gem stone form.

"And look," Opal whispered as she held her cupped hands straight out in front of her. Several elongated arms of light reached out much further ahead than before. The offshoots of light seemed to grope about in the dark as if searching frantically for something.

A look of distaste curled across Tarl's face. He tried to stifle the expression but Opal had already seen it.

"Something more to add to our dating notebook?" She quipped.

"Indeed." Tarl claimed. If she was frightened she was hiding it very well. "A delightful addition I believe." They both attempted a smile.

"We're definitely being led somewhere," Opal said.

"I guess we better hurry up and follow then." He replied. "Is it heavy? Would you like me to carry it?"

Opal would have liked nothing better but she was afraid if she let it go the light might die. She could not explain to Tarl that it felt as if the stone carried life within it and the longer she had possession of it the more it felt alive.

"Thank you, but it is not so heavy. I will let you know if it becomes so." Opal nodded toward the guiding light and they followed the groping arms.

"Alright."

"We're almost there I can feel it," she whispered after several more turns. The emerald had doubled in size again. Now it really was growing heavy. Her arms ached and her head felt so light she thought if they did not get where they were supposed to very quickly, her head might float right away from her body. She had surprised herself by coming this far.

Up ahead the rays of green light suddenly rose upward and outward to look like the spokes of a wheel. Panic welled up as they both realized they had come to a dead end.

"It can't be." Tarl walked up to feel the solid stone in front of him. It was cold and smooth. He swept his hand around the outer edge of the green circle trying to figure out what to do next.

Suddenly there was a lurching noise. The wall in front of them was rolling to one side. The green spokes of light narrowed into one bright beam shooting straight through the middle of the opening. Their eyes followed the beam.

They found themselves looking into a huge room. The place appeared to be deserted. Enormous stone pillars supported an arching roof. Long mesh curtains, torn and stained, hung across the pillars and dust covered the gray marble floors. They moved tentatively through the opening into more thick, humid air.

A huge motionless pendulum hung from the center of the room over a dusty but translucent green stone hexagonal enclosure. The stream of light from the emerald Opal carried swung around the room before zeroing in. It pierced the stone seed of the pendulum and shot down vertically into the depths of the enclosure beneath it. They approached cautiously. The stone cavity was filled with stagnant green water and smelled foul.

Opal placed the emerald on the ground. It was much too heavy to keep carrying and until they found out where they were it seemed useless to waste energy. She tried to keep up her concentration but her thoughts had started to scatter and her body felt as heavy as stone. The humidity was not helping. A trickle of perspiration ran down the side of her face.

Tarl moved over to the curtained area to look for some kind of clue as to what to do. The next thing he saw made his limp body jolt. Instinctively he reached his arms out wide as if to protect Opal who stood behind him. He was staring at an oversized throne and seated on that throne was an impressively sized man, who they had apparently woken from slumber. His long white hair and beard flowed down over his fleshy white arms and protruding stomach. The man wore a tattered bottle-green robe and his light hazel eyes stared widely at them from his flushed face. Tarl wasn't sure who looked more shocked.

The man seemed incapable of speech. Tarl had no reason to be rude. After all they were the ones encroaching upon his territory.

"Hello," Tarl said hoping this man would understand him.

"Hello!?" The man looked astonished. "You address us with hello!?" His voice was deep but its volume seemed to be swallowed up in the layers of fat.

Tarl realized his mistake. He was a stranger entering a residence without permission, and the owner could quite possibly have been a very important person – he was after all seated on a throne - of sorts.

Opal stepped forward.

"Oh forgive my friend's informality my lord. We are but unaccustomed to such noble company." She curtsied. Tarl followed her movements wondering how Opal knew of these customs. Their actions made the pasty looking man bellow out an enormous laugh. Tarl quickly stood straight again wondering what was so funny. He had read of royalty in fairy tales but surely such an archaic ideal could not really exist?

"You curtsy to us? Like a girl?" he bawled at Tarl, before a roll of laughter echoed out around them.

Tarl threw a sideways glance at Opal. She checked his glance and made a bowing movement for him to follow. He copied this movement and the man laughed again; his mirth interrupted by hacking coughs.

"Better," he wheezed, "needs practice though." There was no humor in his leaden voice. He slapped his knee with a thick pudgy hand. "What is your business here?"

Neither of them knew how to answer. They looked at one another hoping the other would have a satisfactory response and then looked back at the man in silence. The man looked perplexed.

"How did you find your way in here?"

Opal turned to point at the emerald stone. It had now grown to the size of a small table. The beam was still steadily focused on the dangling stone of the pendulum; its light still shooting down into the murky water below it.

The man looked confused. He looked from the stone to the projection of green light and back at the stone again. Fury enveloped his face.

"How did you get this stone?" he boomed. "What mischief are you two up to?"

They shook their heads vigorously. Opal felt a wave of giddiness roll across the top of her skull but tried to remain stable. Something was wrong with her. Something was very wrong.

Tarl took a small step forward to defend their actions.

"Please. We do not mean to offend you in any way. We believe there is a reason this stone has led us here. We hoped you may have an answer as to why the stone has directed us to this place." Taking a step backward, he bowed again as Opal had shown him.

The man obviously wanted to get up to look at the stone but seemed quite incapable without help.

"I repeat: Where did you get this stone!?"

"My lord," Opal began, "I was given this stone as a finger ring by the hermit of Emerald Mountain. He said it would 'guide me to the place I could not find with sight, and that it would dissolve all spite'."

The resulting expression was mingled with wonder and horror. Opal wondered what terrible admission she had made. They both waited for his outburst but couldn't have been more shocked at what happened next. Tears began to stream from the man's eyes.

Opal ran toward him. Tarl was too late to stop her.

"Oh please my lord. What have I said? Please forgive my rudeness." She knelt down at his throne.

"Oh child," the man began, his voice fighting for dignity, "you have brought us back our life force." His magnified manner had diminished entirely. He attempted to wipe the tears from his face with his massive hands.

"Your life force?" Tarl said as he approached the two of them.

"You say you were given this by a hermit?" The man had not taken his eyes off Opal.

"Yes my lord."

"What was his name?"

"He said he was not worthy of a name my lord and requested I not ask him further."

"What did he look like my child?"

"He was rather old my lord and he…" Opal's mind began reeling. How could she have not seen it before? She looked up into the man's eyes. "My lord, his face looked a lot like yours."

"My brother." More tears streamed over his pasty cheeks. "My twin brother."

Opal and Tarl eyed each other, sharing their confusion. Opal could not understand how this was possible. How could this man, so obviously different in physique, be the hermit's twin brother? And how could this man's twin brother exist on another plane? If her arrival at Emerald Mountain was a mistake maybe this was one too. Maybe she had not found Tarl at all but created some other bizarre hallucination. Maybe it was all an illusion? None of this was making sense.

"Please," Tarl tried to follow the conversation, "what do you mean 'life force'?"

The man finally raised his eyes and looked into Tarl's.

"We have been waiting a lifetime for the return of this stone." The man tried to adjust his sitting position. "Well *I* have been waiting."

"Please we would like to help." Tarl needed answers and quickly. Every glance at Opal revealed her waning energy. Her skin was glistening with perspiration and her face had paled so much that he didn't know how she stayed conscious.

"You see, when I was a young boy, this Kingdom was filled with wonders." His eyes glazed over with the memories. "My brother and I grew up here - in this very building. We were the sons of King Hydruse and had all the tidings we could ask for. There were several other sovereignties then but we were the ruling family. Life was prosperous and not just for us. We believed that good thoughts brought about good deeds and we encouraged our folk to wish for the same." A whimsical smile emerged before quickly disappearing again.

"What happened?" Tarl couldn't believe he was talking about the same place they had found themselves in.

"Our race was evidently at the pinnacle of our world's life-span. Then our father died. He was very old and it was his time but he was mourned greatly. Of course, the ruling declared that his eldest son must take over the reign." He nodded in a way that suggested some kind of irony.

"But you were..." Opal started feeling rather confused.

"Yes," he said knowing what she was thinking, "as we were twin brothers we thought we should rule together. But it was deemed by the people that one King only should be in control. The idea was to stop any possible dissention evolving." A sarcastic smirk curled his lips. "How wrong they were. You see, although my brother Erise and I were twins, I was very slightly older and so deemed the next ruler. I could not dispute what the people wanted although I would have nominated him before myself. He would have been a much better ruler." The fleshy man looked around at the dusty ruins he sat amongst.

"Was he upset?" Opal asked realizing how understated her question must sound.

"Upset!?" The dull boom of his voice hung heavy in the air. "My brother was horrified that this could happen to him. We always thought we would rule together. I told him we would do so anyway even if they called me the leader but he was inconsolable. To him it meant our relationship was a farce; that I had no place for him in my heart, which of course, was very untrue.

"But how did he end up in Emerald Mountain?" Opal just wished he would hurry up. Her vision was fragmenting and she was experiencing flashes of black and white light. It was becoming almost impossible to stay balanced.

"One night as the people slept, my brother carved out a shard from the life-force of our kingdom." The man pointed a hand over to the hexagonal wall encircling the fetid water. "He must have decided to start a kingdom of his own. Obviously he didn't realize the devastating effects this act would have. I'm sure, if he had known..." His face crumpled into sadness. "I never saw him again. I assumed he had made a success of himself somewhere else but it certainly wasn't here. Our kingdom couldn't survive the loss."

"The loss?" Tarl still didn't have an answer to his life-force question.

Waiting for a reply, he kept a visual check on Opal. Her appearance was becoming really worrying. Her skin had become almost translucent and she looked as if she were about to pass out. Even though he had discovered that Opal was a lot stronger than he could have imagined, he could tell she was struggling hard to stay alert. The quicker he understood what was going on, the quicker he would be able to figure out how to get them back to Atlas Mountain.

"This Kingdom was run on the energy of our life-force." The man said pointing at the hexagonal pool again. "This holds the balance of nature; the arms of nurture. This life-force is, or rather was, like our heart. It was the origin of life. It housed the mind and guided our spirits. Without it we could not function." After taking a furtive look at his surroundings he continued, "We had prospered with it as long as it was held as a whole, but when part of it was excised, the life-force was drained to such an extent that it could not recover. Believe me we tried everything. Disease spread and slowly most of the people became sick. They started dying and I could do nothing to stop it. It was as if the people's immune systems just couldn't combat any disease. Infection spread; negativity took the place of joy, and soon anger, melancholy and grief reached out to annihilate. The destruction was triumphant."

Opal could understand how these people felt. The humid air was stifling. She wondered if it were still possible to be struck by these maladies.

"How is it that you are still alive?" She inquired trying to hold back the exhausted tears wanting to escape her ever weakening body.

"The life-force is only strong enough to protect the ruler. More irony: A ruler of what?"

"But the hermit, sorry, Erise, is trapped inside the mountain. Why would he have been trapped?" Just as the words spilled from Opal's mouth it suddenly all made sense. She must try to put it into words before passing out. As she was about to speak she glanced back toward the emerald behind her.

"Tarl, I understand."

He moved to her side and grabbed her hand.

"Opal what is it?"

"Tarl, the stone," she said weakly, "It is how the hermit was trapped in Emerald Mountain. I understand now. The part of the life-force that he stole tried to rebuild itself; not here, but in the time path he took to appease himself of shame. There was enough energy in the piece he cut off to maintain just one life force – his. However, I think the stone was trying to protect the hermit from....himself."

"But why was he trapped?" Tarl felt cruel forcing her to go on but he had no choice.

"The stone took the dishonor he felt and held it captive – with the hermit. It is trying to rebuild itself again. That is why he gave it to me. That is why we are here: to return it to its rightful place."

"It makes sense." Tarl gently placed a palm across her shoulder. "I know what we have to do." Placing his forefinger under her chin, he lifted her pale face. "Everything is going to be alright. I promise." His words were warm and caring, just what she needed to hear.

Tarl checked the beam of light shooting onto the motionless pendulum and down into the center of the watery enclosure. It was perfectly steady.

"What is down there?" Tarl demanded.

"That is where our life-force used to reside; deep deep down. He made an immense effort to lift himself from the throne. His weighty body stood unsteadily and he grasped an arm-rest for support."

"Is that where your brother removed the segment?" Tarl asked anxiously. The emerald was quickly becoming larger and Opal was quickly becoming paler. He knew the answer. "Stand back."

Tarl moved over to the stone and heaved it up into his cradled arms. He staggered closer to the fetid pond. The beam of light grew stronger as if gaining power. The stone on the end of the pendulum was glowing bright and hot. Lifting it over the edge of the hexagonal wall, he dropped it into the sludgy water.

A burst of light exploded out around them. It was so bright they had to shield their eyes. Then a blast of wind shot up beneath the pendulum causing stagnant stinking water to erupt across the entire area. Tarl was blown back toward the circular door and the King was slammed back onto his throne.

By the time the wind died down enough for Tarl to open his eyes it was too late.

■　　■　　■

Rembeu had sat watching Tarl and Opal for a very long time. He would have lost track if he had not been constantly reminded by Melik. So far their vital signs had remained constant, which was was certainly better than any disintegration. There had been occasional murmurs from Tarl but he was no closer to consciousness. The colored bow still arched above them glowing intensely. Rembeu wondered how it was formed. He theorized that it could be some kind of protective measure or perhaps even the bridge that led them into the next path.

The time-slips were still disturbing him. For a while time seemed to drag; quite possibly because he had spent so much of it waiting. And he knew from experience that waiting for the bad to turn into the good always takes a lot longer than it's opposite. But then moments slipped by just like the escaping memory of a dream.

The quakes were also getting stronger. If the limestone walls, the most protected place on their world, were feeling the shivers of breaking ground what must it be like in the townships? He sent good thoughts out to Parvo.

"Rembeu, come in, over."

"Yes Melik, come in. Over." Rembeu was jolted from abstraction.

"Rembeu, my calculations have indicated an access point for the next path will be available in approximately two moonspells. Over."

Rembeu placed a cupped palm over his mouth wondering how to react. "Right Melik. Well that's good. I'll be ready to transfer on your call. Over."

"Yes but that's not all. Over"

"O.K. What else Melik? Over." Rembeu squeezed his eyes trying to shut out an influx of thoughts.

"Well," Melik hesitated, "there is more interference with one of my co-ordinates. I hold it for a moment and then I lose contact again. Over."

Rembeu realized he had not been concentrating on Tarl and Opal. He shot a look up at them. Alarm bells rang in his head. The prismatic arc had disappeared.

" Melik the arc over Tarl and Opal has gone! Over." He ran over to them to check their signs.

"Rembeu. Listen to me. We have to figure out how to bring them back. If we lose their connection we lose the co-ordinates entirely. Over."

The co-ordinates? Rembeu thought in shock. He didn't care about the co-ordinates.

"We've got to bring them back to *have* them back! Melik give me your readings."

∎ ∎ ∎

The emerald stone had forced all the filthy sludge from the well-like enclosure. The marble floor was swimming in slippery muck and the King's face was immobile with shock. The bright white light pulsed like a heartbeat and Tarl had to squint to focus. He looked around to see where the wind had pushed Opal. He screamed out her name when he saw what was happening. Opal was being sucked in toward the light. She tried to mouth words to him but her weak body held little resistance.

Fighting the still swirling winds, Tarl pushed himself toward the well. Opal was disappearing into the pendulum's bright white light. And something else was happening. Bright green light was arching up from the hole. The emerald stone, now the size of a huge boulder, was thrusting up from the center. Long sharp green arms reached out like an opening eggshell.

"No!" screamed Tarl as he realized what was about to happen.

The arms closed around Opal encasing her within it. Opal's palms ran down the transparent walls of her prison as she collapsed. Above her the pendulum began to swing.

"It's working," yelled the King over the noise of the wind. "But why has it taken the girl?"

Tarl was looking at Opal through the stone. He called out to her but she remained unmoving; slumped at its base. The transparent green wall was now growing hexagonally around the egg and the top of the stone kept rising higher and higher. Tarl kept his palms resting against the growing stone wall. He feared if he let go Opal might disappear forever.

"How high is it going to go?" Tarl shouted.

The King pointed to the high ceiling.

"To the life-wheel."

Tarl looked up at a large hexagonal shaped hole. The opening had inscriptions carved around its edge.

"What do they mean?" he cried out anxiously.

"They are the seven circle carvings of our spiritual representations."

That didn't help Tarl. Frustration was seething inside him. He moved around the stone trying to decipher the inscriptions whilst never letting his hands leave the emerald surface. When he saw two familiar figures carved next to each other he stopped still. One was a male brandishing a small sword and the other was a woman holding some kind of arc over her head.

"Why would the stone want her?" Tarl demanded of the King.

"Only my brother would know. I am sorry."

The emerald moved up into and through the hexagonal hole and ground to a stop. The wind died down and the bright white light diminished to a feint green glow. Inside, the pendulum swung smoothly over Opal's motionless body.

Tarl noticed the air cooling down. The oppressive humidity was dwindling quickly. Even the King's pallid skin began to look a little flushed. Tarl took a deep breath and let the cool air flow into his lungs.

"Opal needs this air!" He screamed desperately at the King, "Please, you've got to help me."

"I cannot." The King looked down sadly at this strange boy that had come out of nowhere to save his dying planet. "I am so very sorry." He looked at the lovely female girl lying inside the emerald. "But I do not believe this can be undone. Although the life-force has been put back into place and has reformed, it has not initiated yet. Without initiation the life-force cannot be accessed. Without life-force I cannot find the power to release her. If only my brother were here."

Tarl was furious.

"I will not let her die in there. Your brother is not here so you will have to work this out by yourself. Whether you like it or not you are still the King. Do something or I will find a way to undo all of this. I don't care if your world dies. You'd given up anyway. You didn't even try to stop her being drawn in."

The King was taken aback. Realizing he had forgotten his duties, he tried pull himself together. It had been so long since he had wielded any power.

"You are quite correct. It has been a long time since I have served the people. Please forgive me. Give me a moment to think."

Just as the King put his head into his hands to trigger an idea, bubbling green light began to surge upward inside the emerald spire. They both turned to face the emerald.

"It's beginning," cried the King in delight.

The emerald was turning. The hexagonal shape was moving around to the left. When it had moved just as far as the next point, a white light shot up from the center of the stone toward the sky. When the light reached the apex a burst of color exploded above them throwing Tarl's head back onto the hard marble floor knocking him unconscious.

He didn't even get a last vision of Opal.

■　■　■

"Tarl. Tarl. Come on boy, wake up."

Tarl could hear strange noises in the dark. Someone was calling him.

"Tarl. Tarl listen to me it's very important that you wake up."

Tarl felt a searing bright light burning his retinas. His fluttering eyelids squinted until he could take in the light.

"Well thank time's behalf for that." Rembeu lifted his Voicer. "He is awake, Melik! Tarl is finally with us again!" He leant over his bleary nephew. "I must say I probably will never experience such worry again in my long life."

Tarl suddenly remembered where he had come from. Pushing himself into a sitting position caused a sharp intake of breath. Looking around for Opal, he discovered she wasn't there. He wanted to feel relieved but the realization that he must have imagined the whole thing fell upon him like a weight.

Rembeu wanted Tarl to stabilize before he said anything about Opal. Her immune system had collapsed once the arc had dissipated. Within a very short time her health had disintegrated so badly Rembeu wondered if she would live through it. He had placed her in one of the protective bays where he could keep her properly shielded and where he could keep her life-stream in a constant continuum. He still had no idea what the two of them had experienced, or even if Tarl had any clue she was here.

Tarl's chest hurt terribly; as if his body had been sliced open yet he could see no injury. The tremors in his arm were quivering again and he glanced at it briefly hoping Rembeu wouldn't notice but it didn't appear to be shaking at all.

"Tarl, look at me nephew."

Tarl looked up at his uncle still slightly dazed.

"Tarl, it is important that you focus."

"Yes Rembeu," Tarl nodded as a hoarse whisper came from his lips, "I am listening."

"You need to tell me what happened in the last path. You need to tell me what happened to Opal."

"Opal?" Tarl's eyes shot open. "You mean she really was there? No." He had been too quick to disbelieve. "But she's not here? And I am." Tarl's face was desperately looking to Rembeu for answers. He was overwhelmed with guilt and failure, fear and confusion. Tarl clutched Rembeu's arms. "We've got to hurry!"

"She *is* here Tarl. Please you must remain calm. She needs our help. You need to tell me what has happened to her."

Tarl swallowed and tried to calm his shaking body. He quickly explained what had happened. Rembeu listened carefully trying to pull any relevant information that would assist Opal's recovery.

"Is Opal still wearing the ring?" Tarl asked anxiously. "She told me she was wearing the ring in this plane."

"Yes she still has it on." Curiosity was building in Rembeu's voice. "Of course," he said, his eyes smiling with a million thoughts, "that is what has been helping you… but draining Opal. The ring must be the connection." Rembeu's smile didn't last long. "You're going to have to find a way to make contact with her."

"Anything," Tarl was nodding, "I'll do anything you can think of."

"That's a good man." Rembeu held out a supportive arm, "Lean on me, we will have to go to her. She is in the protective bays."

Tarl looked at Opal's peaceful face behind the protective covering as he lay on the bay beside her. Silently he begged her to help him find her. Lifting the covering, he removed the ring from her slight finger and held it in his left palm. Reaching under the covering, he placed her right palm on top of his and then lay back and closed his eyes trying to feel the life-force of the emerald.

When he opened his eyes again he found himself inside a beautifully carved transparent green room. A voice behind him made him turn around. The man who addressed him looked familiar, no, more than that, he looked like a thin version of the King. He also had long white hair and a long white beard. His watery hazel eyes blinked cheerlessly back at Tarl from almost translucent skin. Tarl suddenly saw what lay at the man's feet.

"Opal!" He ran toward her and knelt at her side but she lay unmoving. Now they were both trapped in Emerald Mountain. He looked desperately up at the King's brother, the hermit.

"I hoped she would bring the ring back with her," the hermit announced, shame filling his eyes. "I didn't realize the force would be so strong. I didn't think it would affect her so badly…I had forgotten its power."

"You trapped her on purpose?" Tarl couldn't conceal his shock.

"I trapped her in the life-force so I could pull her back here. The return of the ring would have allowed me to return to my brother's world; back to the world I belong in. I have misunderstood the life-force again." The hermit crouched down beside Tarl, his sad eyes passing over Opal as if she had just died. His look made Tarl panic even more.

"She is still alive...?" his statement rang out like a question. Her peaceful face lay as still as it was in Atlas Mountain. Tarl looked at the hermit in desperation. "Your brother said you would know what to do. He acts as if he is only half a person. Without you he seems incapable of affirmative action. You're the only one who can tell me how to fix this. Please, you must be able to help us."

"But without the ring..."

"The ring may not be here but it still exists in another plane. She wears it in my plane." Tarl wondered how that was possible but he had no time to worry about that now. "Obviously it needs to be with the King - in *his* world." The implication was clear.

The hermit placed a forefinger on Opal's brow.

"The girl must learn. She has a power beyond her knowledge you know."

Tarl didn't know and he wished the hermit would stop talking and do something. The hermit traced a circle on Opal's forehead.

"When she first traveled the pathways I felt her presence and pulled her in. I could sense our purposes were linked, although I'm sure she didn't know it."

"So you pulled her into your pathway when she was trying to access mine?"

"Yes, I still have limited abilities trapped in here. I sensed her clarity when she arrived and knew she was the one who could transport the ring to the correct path. Of course I did not tell her the complete truth and for that I am deeply apologetic. Perhaps if she had known..." he shook his head in defeat, "But it is too late to realize my terrible error."

"Error? What error?" More panic. Why wasn't he helping her?

"Once the life-force was returned and initiated, the stone should have separated and the ring should have been returned here, ultimately destroying this creation before returning to its rightful place."

"Of course, the poem you recited. What was it? 'A mist must pass before the will can grow bold'?"

"Yes, she told you?" The hermit seemed surprised.

"Yes." Strangely the words seemed emblazoned in his mind. " 'After the green eye of envy has taken its hold, For I am the fear within: That which is unresolved, And I will give up such life until it is told'."

"You have a good memory." The hermit looked wistfully toward Opal again.

"You needed the ring to destroy this place... and yourself?"

"Only if the ring was returned. It should not have healed completely while I still remained trapped in its external forces." The hermit's forefinger traced a star on each of Opal's cheeks. It looked to Tarl as if he were preparing her for some ritualistic death. "But she does not have it. I cannot save any of us. And now that we are connected to my brother's path, when the life-force completes initiation we shall all be disconnected."

Tarl didn't like that final word at all. Somehow he would have to bring it here. And then he remembered he was holding it in Atlas Mountain. He shut his eyes tight as if wishing would make it so. He spoke to Opal in his mind, telling her what she she had to do. When he opened his eyes again and uncurled his left hand the emerald ring lay dull in his palm.

"The ring!" cried the hermit. "Why did you not tell me you had the ring?" He looked uncharacteristically delighted.

"Now please help her! Please." Tarl cried, shaking his head in bewilderment.

"You are also one of clarity. Your purpose is also true. I will be returned to my world to make peace with my lands, my brother and my soul. You have freed us all."

The hermit removed the emerald from Tarl's palm. He placed the stone band in the center of the transparent green floor on top of a glistening golden sword. A flash of memory swooped across Tarl's thoughts. He imagined himself swinging the sword aimlessly without understanding why but shook the reflection from his thoughts.

"Come. We shall all be returned to our rightful planes."

Tarl picked up Opal. Her lightness told him there was still plenty of life in her. His hopes began to soar. The hermit directed Tarl to lay Opal down on one side of the ring and to stretch her left hand out to the side. He asked Tarl to lie above her at an angle and to do the same with his left hand. He then lay at a corresponding angle to them creating a triangle. Their hands joined at the center of the angle.

"Ready?" the hermit asked unnecessarily.

Tarl wanted to be holding Opal tightly; to make sure he couldn't lose her this time. He tried to hold on to her with his thoughts. The hermit then placed the emerald on top of their hands.

Tarl felt as if he were lifting off the floor. He quickly glanced at Opal who had risen also, apparently as weightless as he was. They began to wind round, slowly spinning around the ring in a motion that was not unpleasant. The emerald stone floated above their clasped hands glowing like a bright green moon.

The faster they spun the brighter the emerald became until at last it burst like an exploding star. Tarl felt like he was being crushed by forces of an unbelievable nature. Colors swirled around him until he could look no longer. He felt Opal's hand slip from his just before a bright white light slapped him into oblivion.

"Tarl, it's alright, you're alright."

The strange dreams of floating on tranquil waters ebbed away as Tarl rose into consciousness. He spoke before his eyes had opened properly.

"Is she alright?" he murmured hoarsely.

"Yes Tarl," Rembeu whispered gratefully, "you saved her."

"…must tell her something…" This time Tarl allowed himself to swim in relief.

"It's alright Tarl, there's time for that. Opal is still recovering in the bay. She needs to rest. Tarl listen to me. I have to go on to the next path."

Tarl struggled to wake himself fully. He forced his eyes open when really all they wanted to do was to roll back into his head and drift into the forgotten bliss of sleep.

"Wait. Please, just wait a minute."

"It's alright Tarl. Just rest. You'll follow me later," Rembeu said knowing this was not possible.

"No!" his insistence roused him further. His body strained into a seated position.

"I'm coming with you." Tarl raised his heavy head and looked directly into his uncle's eyes.

"Tarl you must give yourself credit for accomplishing such a feat. It is extraordinary that you have found your core so quickly and easily. I have been unable to correct any of your prior weaknesses – which I have inflicted upon you from the beginning - insisting you have your Teachings. Tarl if you do not rest now we all may suffer later."

"There will not be any more suffering. That is why we are doing this." Tarl swung his legs from down to the floor and gently rested his body weight on them. He wanted to prove himself but he was terrified his legs would give way underneath him.

Rembeu watched his nephew stand. He hated himself for hoping that Tarl would insist on transferring but he knew his nephew's capabilities were far beyond his own. Ultimately, Tarl was the key.

"Please Tarl, listen to me... I..."

"No," Tarl held up a firm hand to stop his uncle. "Rembeu, *you* must listen to me."

His uncle tried to constrain both surprise and pride. He nodded and let Tarl continue.

"I am coming with you and that is all that is to be said." Tarl knew the only way Rembeu was going to allow him to continue was if he gave him no choice.

Rembeu cleared his throat. Maybe he wouldn't ever forgive himself but he would allow Tarl to persist. He had done worse things. Rembeu took a deep breath.

"We leave in a little less than two sandglass turns."

"Good. That's settled."

"Tarl?"

"Yes?"

"Now could you please rest?"

"Yes uncle." A defeated smile lifted Tarl's determined expression. He was grateful for permission to rest now that he knew his uncle wouldn't change his mind. But before he rested there were things that needed to be cleared up. "I need to know so many things: what happened in the crystal heart; how did we get back here; why do I feel like I've slipped through time? I feel like there are memories but I can't hold on to them. And Opal how did she...?"

"Tarl," Rembeu interrupted him, "we have some time. Please lay back down and I will fill you in after I ask the Altai to make you some of your favorite soup." Rembeu rang a small bell which echoed through the mountain.

Soup sounded more wonderful than Tarl could have imagined. When was the last time he had eaten? All these paths: reality in so many facets! He certainly could not tell his uncle that he was finding it more and more difficult to determine which physical reality was his. His left hand felt as if it was trembling so greatly that he was amazed the tremors couldn't been seen externally. Trying to concentrate, he focused on his uncle. If he had the strength he would have walked straight to Opal. He needed to talk to her but as usual, he would have to wait.

"Only you can tell me what happened inside the Elestial Crystal," Rembeu began.

Tarl had a sudden flash back to the shattering mirrors. He grimaced and held his chest as he recalled the pain.

"I saw it. I saw everything..." Tarl's voice petered out.

"Go on." Rembeu knew this was not going to be nice to hear.

"I felt my death."

"It's alright Tarl. I saw those mirrors too."

"Yes, they were the mirrors of my existence. They shattered... I don't know why. The final image pierced my heart."

"Yes," Rembeu listened trying not to show how upset he was, "I thought you had experienced a trauma to the heart. Your vital signs indicated as much, but I could find no physical damage."

"Opal somehow pulled the shard from me with the ring."

Rembeu nodded. He wasn't entirely sure he understood but nothing in this venture was unremarkable. He thought he might know why the images had shattered but how could he divulge this to Tarl now? Perhaps the knowledge would have even greater negative effects on Tarl. They shouldn't have kept these secrets for so long. However, Tarl did seem to be coping without too much duress. So, for now, he would just have to wait and see. A satisfactory explanation would still have to be made and Rembeu thought quickly.

"Maybe removing time from the Elestial Crystal had an adverse effect on our world. It's possible that our time disturbances were the result. I don't claim to understand, but it's possible that this had something to do your progression to this other path."

"So I didn't just imagine it?"

"Oh definitely not." Rembeu decided that it was important for Tarl to move on. The less he delved at this stage, the better. "You know you did miss something incredible."

"Really? What?" Tarl asked almost glad to have the subject changed. Something in that hall of mirrors was haunting him but the memory was slipping from his grasp, like a fistful of water.

Rembeu went on to tell Tarl about the world he had seen after he fell unconscious; the beauty of the place and the kindness of the peoples' faces. Tarl was fascinated.

"Where's that soup?" Tarl finally enquired. The bed was too comfortable. Resisting sleep was getting harder and harder. He moved to get up.

"You know the Altai. Everything must be perfect. You'll appreciate it when it comes." Rembeu tried to stop Tarl getting off the bed.

"I need to say goodbye to Opal."

"All in good time…"

"And," a timid female voice came to them from the entrance of the Healing Room, "when exactly is a good time?" Opal stood at the doorway dressed in one of the linen wraps that Rembeu used for healing. Her long hair fell behind her shoulders in glossy waves and her gray eyes peered serenely from her pale heart shaped face.

Tarl's face was beaming. Rembeu caught the look.

"Well that's how we get the young man some energy, why haven't I taken that into consideration?" he joked. Tarl threw him a look of embarrassment. Rembeu went over to her to check that she was alright. "Opal, you should be resting."

"I couldn't rest without knowing what had happened." She looked directly at Tarl any coyness overtaken by concern.

"Opal," Tarl tried to keep his voice steady, "you're alright."

The statement was obvious but she seemed to enjoy it all the same. Her head tilted downwards in her customary way.

"Perhaps the third date should be the decider?" She was surprised at her own frankness. Her eyes lifted upward to check Tarl's response.

"Well I don't doubt it will be an interesting one," he replied with a large grin.

An Altai shuffled past her with a tray holding a large bowl of soup and some thick slices of hot buttered bread and placed it on Tarl's bed.

Rembeu couldn't believe it. Opal appeared to be perfectly well. He could find no ill effects whatsoever. Her strength had been seriously underestimated. Who was this girl? Where had she come from? He knew how dangerous it was to risk trust on a stranger. And yet, there was something about her that encouraged him to do so. He would be guarded but he needn't say anything to Tarl.

"Chingle, please could you bring another bowl of soup for the young lady." Rembeu smiled at the Altai and beckoned for Opal to sit down.

"Wok surl mi laster." The Altai looked delighted.

"Now I must consult with Melik. Opal I will see you before we leave. Thank you for your help, my respect is unfathomable." Rembeu thought they should spend a bit of time alone before the imminent transfer.

"Leave?" Distress made her voice leap an octave. She looked at Tarl not knowing how to react. "You're leaving?"

Suddenly he realized that was exactly what he was going to have to do: Leave her again – and soon.

"Opal, I thought you were still unconscious in the bays. I've only just woken myself. I was coming to speak to you but Rembeu said you needed rest." The tray of hot soup and bread didn't seem so interesting any more.

"Oh." Although she tried, her face couldn't conceal her disappointment.

"Opal I don't have a choice I have to go."

"I know, I know this." She wanted to say more but couldn't form the words.

"Opal I need to tell you something."

Opal tried not to hold on to the fear that was now flooding her body. She forced herself to be strong. Unsure of what she wanted to hear from him she waited. Just as Tarl was about to confide in her, Rembeu came striding into the room.

"Tarl, Melik has confirmed the co-ordinates. We have only a little time. We need to wait at the Wheel-Door to be ready. I have packed us some new bags to take. They will be waiting."

Opal was shaking her head at Tarl.

Tarl was nodding at his uncle. Tiredness was crawling back into his body, its claws ripping away at his strength.

"No!" Opal cried out. She wasn't the only one who was surprised at her outburst.

Both Tarl and Rembeu stared at her not knowing what to say. Tarl looked at Rembeu as if to ask what to do but Rembeu appeared not to know.

"I do not understand myself, but I must come with you," she said, the coyness returning to her voice as her cheeks reddened.

Tarl couldn't allow this to happen; he couldn't put her in such danger again.

"Opal we'll be alright, I promise. We have to fix this."

"Tarl we really need to go to the Wheel-Door." Rembeu's face was insistent.

Tarl couldn't hide a grimace. All he wanted was a proper goodbye. And then another voice rose above the anguish.

"The radiant is awake." Umbra's words broke the tension.

"Umbra? What on time's behalf are you doing out here?" Rembeu's surprise was obvious.

"Oh, Mr. Rembeu I can actually survive for a few moments away from my Radiant." Her jest caused one of Rembeu's eyebrows to rise.

"Indeed, but can it survive without you?"

"Oh, Mr. Rembeu, I think you underestimate the weight of my influence." Umbra's cloud-silver eyes were gazing in Rembeu's direction but her arm was feeling out toward Opal.

"Well I would prefer not to test it. Tarl and I were just making our way to the Wheel-Door." Rembeu was directing an urgent look at Tarl.

"Just you and Tarl?" Umbra asked with gravity.

Tarl closed his eyes as if this could help him pass thoughts to Umbra. He needn't have worried.

"Yes just *us*." Rembeu was becoming impatient.

"You know you will need Opal don't you?" Umbra asked with candor.

Opal was as surprised as the others. She knew she needed to go with them but she had no idea why.

Rembeu was astonished by Umbra's statement.

"You think we should take her with us?"

"Not should. Must."

"Umbra, I know you think..."

"Mr. Rembeu, you have trusted me on many things. One of those things is assisting you in upholding the guidance system in our universe. You must trust me with this. She is the one I have sought. Opal is the force of equilibrium. Her control will help us stabilize unseen powers."

"The what?" Tarl couldn't understand. A thousand questions were charging through his mind. He looked at Opal accusingly as if she had been hiding this from him the whole time. Opal shook her head at him in disbelief.

"Rembeu," Umbra's tone was conclusive, "read the Divine Sources again and you will understand."

How could Umbra of all people be saying this to him? Rembeu's heritage was being challenged. The Divine Sources were being challenged. And the challenger was the one of the most trusted people in his life – a trust that had been built from a lifetime of proof. His mind was spinning.

"Initializing countdown, over." Melik was counting down time already.

Umbra placed a protective arm around Opal and whispered into her ear.

"Remember child, you don't need eyes to see. You know what you are made of; you just have to learn to see it." She handed Opal a folded garment. "The Altai made this for you. I have placed another in Tarl's pack so you can change." Opal gripped Umbra's hands in appreciation. Umbra felt the vibration. She realized this child didn't even know what she was capable of. No matter, she would learn quickly. Umbra tried to direct her eyes toward Rembeu. Tarl's eyes followed.

"Uncle, we don't have much time." Tarl took a deep breath and focused his eyes on Opal. "And I believe, in *this* reality stream, majority still rules."

25

Earth-bound Blues

After a swirling harmony of 'A' notes, the Wheel-Door finally spat the three of them out at their destination. This time the pull felt pleasant. Either this path was more easily accessible or Melik was getting better at transferring them.

Melik insisted he be contacted immediately on their arrival. He had steadied the unstable co-ordinate but he could not judge whether the relationship between the magnitudes would vary once they began to shift. He compensated by amplifying their land destination points; aiming for one of the larger continents of the planet instead of allowing them to arrive at the point of the greatest anomalous characteristics as he had done previously. He hoped they would still be able to find the origin of the abnormalities.

They were greeted with a confusing chaos of people and colors. Tarl instinctively stood closer to Opal as hoards of people swept past them. Many of the inhabitants had similar features: black straight hair, lightly colored skin and small lean bodies. While the older people wore more conservative tunics the younger people were dressed in all manner of hideous outfits that Rembeu could not even begin to guess what kind of fabrics they were made from. They were certainly not made from natural fibers.

The gray-blue sky hung heavy around them as if threatening to storm and the air was hot and humid. Unusual smells swelled and swirled around them. Tarl wished the tremor inside his arm would stop, even if it were just for a while. It was becoming very uncomfortable and had started to distract his thoughts. Strangely enough, it had not bothered him in the last path.

Tarl looked at Opal to see how she was fairing. She didn't seem to be affected by the heat at all. Her face was calm and curious and he had to admit to himself that he was ecstatic that Umbra had overruled his uncle. He would never have believed it if he had not seen it himself.

The Altai had made Opal an extraordinary dress. Flowing sashes of shimmering blues and greens fell from a tight bodice and swam around her ankles. As she moved, carefully stitched filaments caught the light and, for the briefest of moments, colors would flame in-between the folds. Her long black hair was laced with bright blue silk thread and looped into several circles cascading down her back. Tarl was mesmerized.

"Melik, we've landed safely over." Rembeu had to speak loudly to be heard over the clamor of the traffic. Hundreds of different vehicles were fighting for space on the road and blowing out great puffs of gray smoke. The hot afternoon sun made his yellow robes glint with refracting light. Tarl hoped his uncle had a change of clothes lest he blind someone. Personally, he was glad to be back in his nice clean white over-shirt and black silk pants.

"I've got you on monitor Rembeu, thanks for the call. What have you found? Over."

"Well," Rembeu wasn't quite sure how to answer, "We have arrived in a very busy area that is surging with people. There are places of purchase everywhere and they use an ancient style of transport that is spewing effluvium into the air. We don't appear to have woken the interest of anyone. I haven't heard a familiar language yet either. Any ideas? Over." Rembeu was right. As surprising as it was, no one seemed to take any notice of them.

"Shame the language decipliers were lost with your bags. That reminds me I'll have to make new ones... Where did I put that file?"

Rembeu and Tarl swapped smiles.

"He's still got his finger on the activator. He might be a while. Perhaps we should just look around for now." Rembeu's eyes were scanning the shops for a clue as to what to do.

"How awful," Tarl said as he pointed to a shop where all manner of dead animals hung in the window. A huge vehicle soared past and released a huge plume of smoke and Tarl started coughing.

"Yes, I think that shop could be contributing to this smell." Rembeu made a grand gesture that encompassed the area.

"Oh look," Opal moved over to a shop window displaying rows of shining bronze coins dangling from the ceiling tied by red ribbons. On plates below them, beautifully polished stones of aquamarine, turquoise and blue lace agate lay in piles.

"Come on," Rembeu beckoned. There was no time to go shopping.

They moved along the street jostling amongst the crowds. Everywhere they looked hordes of people swarmed. Crumbling gray buildings rose up above them in the haze, their balconies draped with drying clothes.

"I hope we do not have to cross the road," Opal's terrified face scanned the chaos.

"Let's just stay close together." Rembeu wasn't impressed with that possibility either.

In most of the alleyways they passed they saw groups of old men and women seated on rusted or broken plastic chairs crouching over thick cigarettes.

Suddenly Opal stopped walking. When they saw what she was looking at they stopped too. Across the road an adult and two children climbed out of a large cardboard box. Tarl wondered how they could look so clean, living in such conditions.

"I cannot believe what I am seeing. Is this how people live here?" Her sad eyes drifted over to one of the shops. Moving closer, she tried to see if she could make out what was happening inside.

Tarl followed after her. The entire window displayed screens of visual images. He tried to find an image that wasn't in some way offensive to his senses. In shock he looked over toward Opal but she was standing completely still, staring at the terrible images while tears streamed down her face.

The horrible representations of death and destruction were arousing Opal's own memories; memories she had tried so hard to forget. The pain was surging inside her swelling from her stomach to her heart to her throat. How long she had held herself together, keeping all that hurt boxed up inside? She had never talked about it to anyone and it suddenly felt impossible to hold on to it any longer. All she wanted to do was to let go of the pain, but if she confided in Tarl she was sure it would destroy their friendship.

Rembeu walked toward them to see what they were so interested in.

"Well, look at that they're just like our old vision screens. Before your time Tarl. Before mine too believe it or not." He jabbed Tarl in the ribs with his elbow. "People didn't want to get rid of them, you know. There was a huge upheaval. But when we realized how badly they interfered with our planet's natural vibrational fields we had no choice. Electromagnetic radiation emissions: Terribly destructive, you see; can completely destroy the ozone not to mention our natural body rhythms." He smiled. "Sometimes what we think of as technological progress is really just taking a step further away from our true selves. Important lesson to learn that one."

Rembeu didn't get a reaction from either of them. He turned toward the screens to see what held their attention. Looking from one screen to the next he stood silent. He didn't need to understand the language to comprehend what was being depicted. One news story showed children climbing rocky mountainsides wearing torn clothing and holding large weapons. Another scene showed many people running from an explosion; all of them covered in blood. One half of a split screen showed an attractive older woman's face while the other half showed the same woman but her skin had been drawn back to pull away all her lovely smile lines. A fight between a man and a bull ended when the man pierced the bull's stomach. Some kind of patrol, wearing full body suits, bashed people with batons and one of the screens flashed pictures of wares so insistently that Rembeu had to blink quickly to erase the burning images. It went on and on.

"Images of hostility everywhere," he murmured to himself.

"They pay for water?" Tarl asked in confusion.

"This is not good," Rembeu stated quietly.

"What are we going to do?" Tarl looked over to his uncle trying not to show how desperate he felt.

"This world is already destroyed. We can't fix this." Rembeu was staring absently at a vision of a woman holding her dead child.

"What would happen if the planet destroyed itself?" Tarl turned back toward the images. Terrible storms raged across one of the screens. He thought of home.

"Perhaps that's what needs to be done?" Rembeu couldn't believe what he was saying.

"No. No." Something else besides her own pain was now stirring inside Opal. The pain of these people was overwhelming her. She could not let this happen to them. "We can't leave them here like this. You... *we* have to help."

"Yes, we have to try," Tarl said wanting to believe it was possible.

"There is something else," Opal murmured, her eyes closed trying to see what it was that she was feeling. "I cannot explain it properly but inside me it feels like the light is splintered."

"Yes," Rembeu sighed. "I've been sensing that too." Rembeu's eyes arrowed up toward the sky. "Can you see that?" Opal and Tarl turned their faces up into the polluted blue sky.

Melik's voice broke their shocked silence.

"Sorry Rembeu, I forgot to turn my Voicer off. Are you there? Over."

"Yes Melik we are receiving you." Rembeu's voice was somber. "We have a slight problem here. Over."

"Go ahead Rembeu maybe I can help?"

"I'm afraid I doubt it Melik. I am detecting light fractures; fragmented blue color-rays expanding across their atmosphere. The sky is terribly clouded by smog and it is difficult to make out but I'm afraid it is conclusive. We have all sensed them. The people probably aren't even aware of the problem. They have obviously lost their ability to sense any of the natural energies of their planet. Over."

"Oh. Fractured light, you say. That's definitely not good. That could mean one of two things. Either you are not wholly existing in that plane, or and believe me I know this first one doesn't sound good but I prefer it to the second, and that is, that the path you are on is losing contact with the white light stream. Essentially the world is so badly fractured that the white light can't be held at a constant." He paused not wanting to say what he was going to have to say. "We may be too late. That world may be too far gone. Over."

"We have definitely entered this plane so I'm afraid it is the second option Melik. Over."

Opal spoke up. "How long do we have?"

"Melik, can you tell us how long we have here? Over."

"You've got at least two moonspells before I can start calculating the logarithms to assess the measured energy required. I can give a closer estimate with some further analysis. Over."

"Thank you Melik. Also, when you can, can you calculate when these light fractures first began? And anything else you might think is helpful. Over."

"Absolutely. I'll inform you as soon as I can. My main concern is to get you out of there before a possible collapse. Over."

"Thank you Melik. Over." Rembeu looked across to his companions. "Any ideas?"

Tarl had no idea what a 'collapse' meant but he wasn't going to ask in front of Opal. He looked up at the fractured light but nothing came to him.

"There has to be some hope?" Opal looked from one the other.

"Perhaps we need to find some." Tarl tried to smile. That seemed to cheer Rembeu up.

"Indeed you are utterly correct. We have found good in each terrible place we have come across. We will find it here too. Let's have a look."

Each shop housed an unusual assortment of wares. Rembeu tried to stop several passing people to communicate with them but they just looked at the trio strangely and hurried on. Finally, as they passed a dirty side alley, a wrinkled old woman ran up to Rembeu and began tugging on his arm. He looked at her with surprise but allowed her to pull him into the alley. She talked insistently and rapidly to him in an unfamiliar language.

Opal and Tarl hurried after them as they disappeared into a very messy little shop. They squeezed through the small door and pushed their way passed the jumble. Open boxes spilled unknown dried objects onto tables and into bowls. All manner of fresh and dried herbs wobbled on aging stands. Vials of liquids sat in neat rows inside glass cabinets along the back wall and several hanging sachets and nets were swollen with gemstones and minerals.

The woman was jabbering at Rembeu and showing him sheets of fine paper that showed drawings of different types of wheels. She motioned to a chair covered with more papers indicating he have a seat and then spread the papers out across the cabinet top frantically pointing to the one in the center. Taking out three bronze coins, she tossed them onto the picture. They twirled before dropping flat. She held her hands up to her mouth as if afraid. Her eyes then rose towards Rembeu's as if to say 'I told you so'. Rembeu could not piece together what she was trying to tell him but he was fascinated. Perhaps if he just let her continue something would make sense.

Tarl watched the proceedings. He didn't have a clue what was going on but he had great faith in his uncle. Opal appeared to be studying a large pale root of some kind at the far end of the crowded shop so he went over to see what was so captivating.

"Yum," Tarl joked, but Opal's eyes didn't move from the herb. At least he could see a hint of a smile.

"I can feel it you know?" Her smile disappeared with her quiet words.

Tarl was getting used to feeling confused.

"Feel what?" he asked.

"I can feel the tremor in your arm." Opal put the root down and looked up into his eyes.

Tarl couldn't hide his shock. He took a quick glance at his arm to see if the shaking was visible. It was not.

"I don't understand what you mean," he tried to bluff.

"Tarl I can feel it." Her delicate fingers reached out for his left hand. A shot of warmth rose up from his wrist with her touch and his heart began to beat more rapidly. Involuntarily he bit his lip.

Opal blushed and released his hand. She felt his intensity. His lovely green eyes were reaching out to her and rejecting her at the same time. Timidly her gaze fell to just below his face, accidentally resting on the smooth tanned skin at the opening of his over-shirt. Flinching from embarrassment, she diverted her eyes.

Tarl didn't know what to do. He didn't want her to let go of his hand but he didn't want her to know about his tremors. The way she had looked at him he thought… but then she had pulled away. Maybe he was imagining it. Maybe he had misunderstood everything. The combination of anxiety and humidity was making him feel dizzy. Why wasn't Opal perspiring? The old lady in the background continued nattering away to Rembeu; her words as incomprehensible as before. Confused, Tarl turned away from Opal and pretended to search through one of the baskets.

"Tarl, it is alright." She followed and stood behind him. "I will not tell Rembeu. But I think you should." Her gentle accent rested in the air.

"Opal, there is something I need to tell you…" He had no intention of divulging the tremor to Rembeu, but now Opal knew, perhaps he could confide in her.

"Tarl, it is alright. I know what you want to tell me. It is not true."

He looked ashamed.

"But it is true. I'm a fraud."

"Your hand is shaking because you are fighting something. You must just let it be."

"But I cannot let it be. I'm not supposed to be doing this. How, out of all the people on our planet am I the one to be responsible for this? I don't feel it. I don't know how to feel it."

"Then we will learn together. I am developing abilities that I did not know I had until recently. I am learning too. But I don't want to fight the fear, I want to embrace it, let it help me to grow."

"The force of equilibrium…" he remembered Umbra's words.

"All I know is that I am changing too Tarl, and as much as I long for the safety of the past I must move forward into whatever this is. Perhaps, eventually, the future might be even better than the past." If she were honest with herself, she would be happily rid of what had gone before.

Tarl realized he had been wishing that someone would come and take him away from all of this; to say he didn't have to do it anymore; to send him back to his father and his home. Yet when he was home he had hoped for the reverse. He now saw how naïve he had been. Opal was right: The past was gone; and possibly, so was everything he knew.

He couldn't think about that possibility and shook the horrors from his mind.

"Opal?" Tarl wanted to tell her how he felt about her; let the words roll out of him; embrace his fear, but he couldn't, not yet.

"Yes Tarl?"

"I'm glad you came."

"So am I."

Tarl was about to reach for her hand when the sudden noise of the woman screaming made them hurry over to Rembeu. Rembeu was looking as shocked as them.

"Time to go," he declared as he rapidly moved toward the door. They didn't take any convincing and quickly followed him out.

"What was that about?" Tarl asked as they moved back amongst the throngs of people. The sun had begun to set and the murky skyline shone with hazy orange light. The humidity had not diminished and Tarl's stomach surged with the surrounding smells.

"If I understood correctly I believe she was telling me she had seen our coming." He winked at Tarl with the memory of the time sphere, "seems to be a popular theme at this stage."

"Maybe they help draw us in?" Tarl was thinking out loud.

"I think she was trying to explain the dichotomy of this path." Rembeu shuffled them over to a less trafficked area. "It seems there is some kind of shift taking place. Her wheel pictures apparently indicate the combating of a 'good against evil' type of situation. The era of violence, oppression and hatred is being slowly dispelled with a new age of self actualization and the development of inner harmony; relying on oneself to pursue a good life rather than the powers that be."

"You got all that from her?" Tarl asked with a twist of his top lip.

"No need for sarcasm, thank you. You'd be surprised how much can be understood from expressions and drawings."

"So we did find hope?" Opal was smiling at their banter.

"Why did she scream?" Tarl interrupted Rembeu's next thought.

"It seemed that she saw something in her readings that frightened her."

"Oh wow, I never would have guessed that."

"Tarl."

"Sorry," Tarl replied, "so what did she see?"

"I can't be sure but the coins appeared to fall on a section of the wheel indicating an uprising of violence: Destruction that ultimately could end the human race on this reality stream."

"Perhaps we could go back to the 'hope finding' part?" Opal tried to divert the increasing negativity.

"Well, I don't believe that this is as bad as we initially thought," Rembeu responded.

"Rembeu?" Opal timidly interjected. "Did you not tell me that there has only been one path you have passed so far that did not hold any anomalies?" The comment started Rembeu's thought processes churning.

"Yes Opal that's right. What made you think of that?"

"I am not really sure. I can feel a thought hovering but I cannot focus on anything yet."

"We really need to find some shelter for the night." Tarl was looking at the cardboard boxes hoping there was an alternative.

"Quite correct Tarl. Perhaps I can trade some goods in our packs for accommodation."

"Wait here for me while I try a couple of places over there." Rembeu said as he shuffled off. He was starting to struggle in the heat. Perhaps if he could find them accommodation, that with all this technology they may be lucky enough to have a cooling device included. The smells were a wonderful mix of herbs and cooking, dirty streets and culture. He sniffed it all in as he scampered up the street.

Opal and Tarl did as they were told. They stood together pretending to look at the closest shop window which displayed buckets of what Tarl assumed was food. One of the female customers was purchasing something from one of the larger buckets. Taking a closer look Tarl eyed a mass of black fat worm-like creatures which squirmed frantically as the assistant scooped out a handful. Quickly, he looked away. He desperately wanted to get Opal's attention; say something clever; make her laugh. But nothing came to mind.

Opal wanted to stand a little closer to Tarl. She wondered what it would feel like if he put his arm around her but she didn't move. Instead, she pretended to be interested in the surroundings. If Tarl was not going admit the truth to her this was going to be more difficult than she had hoped.

Rembeu finally returned with a sure smile and led them to a decrepit building. They entered through a damaged wooden door and passed a dusty stone front desk into a corridor of doors.

"This one." Rembeu moved a key into the lock and twisted it.

They entered the room. It felt like the humidity had been boxed in here waiting to be let out: The heat hit them like a wall. Four grimy walls stared back at them. A tiny window, too high to open, butted up against the ceiling. Three mattresses covered the floor and a tap and sink were the only amenities.

"Well it's...umm...compact," Tarl looked up at the ceiling fan, "and we have wind."

"Indeed we do." Rembeu moved over to the switch and flicked it on. The machine churned into action. He passed out bottled water and dried fruit from his satchel. They were gratefully accepted.

"So, perhaps we should nut out this little problem of ours." Rembeu began as they seated themselves on the grubby mattresses. "I think Opal was on the right track before when she mentioned the reality stream I viewed when you were unconscious. That plane somehow resisted the pull of the anomalous one but I can't see the connection yet." He gnawed at a piece of dried mango. "Oh I nearly forgot," he began again, "before that woman started screaming she gave me these two stones. Rembeu held out his palm so they could each take one. "She wanted this one, the turquoise, to be given to Opal and the amazonite to be given to you Tarl."

The stones were incredible. For a moment they all just stared at them. The turquoise was blue-green and veined with a dark matrix. It shone out to Opal as she reached for it. The amazonite shimmered with the colors of the sky and ocean. Tarl thought he saw a shape shift within it.

The very moment each of them touched the stones, the same thought charged through their minds simultaneously. Wide-eyed, they froze as the thoughts cumulated. Opal was the first to speak.

"Did you feel that?" she asked already knowing the answer. She looked down at the stone in her hand. Tarl was doing the same.

"You both felt that too? Very interesting." Rembeu was wondering what to make of it all. "Well, now some of the things she was showing me make sense."

Opal and Tarl looked at each other astounded. Tarl was shaking his head in disbelief.

"We are supposed to…" Opal could not even verbalize the rest of the thought.

"But how do we accomplish such a task?" A frown crumpled Tarl's face.

"Well," Rembeu's excitement was building, "obviously the three of us are supposed to work that out." He smiled at Opal feeling an unexpected twang of guilt for assuming she should not make the path transfer.

Opal smiled back. Now she just had to understand the strange thoughts she had just shared with her two companions.

■　■　■

They stayed up late into the night discussing options with Melik, who was in fact, very helpful at inspiring ideas. They had decided to retire to sleep after the inkling of a solution had churned its way into the conversation

Opal couldn't sleep. Rembeu was snoring lightly and she turned toward Tarl and whispered just loud enough to see if he was still awake.

"Tarl?"

"Yes?" Sleep hadn't been forthcoming for him either.

"I need to tell you something also."

"You can tell me anything," he stated, hoping it was what he wanted to hear.

"It is hard to explain," she responded half knowing he would say that.

"I'm not going anywhere. Just take your time."

"Well I'm not really from Calatia. You see…" her voice had almost disappeared.

"Opal, you don't need to tell me this if you don't want to. Honestly it doesn't matter to me." Tarl remembered his father telling him that she had a very sad past.

"It matters to me, especially now." Her chin was tilted down and her lovely gray eyes swam up to him.

"Now?" His heart was pumping so hard it was filling his head with noise.

"Yes...now that I am discovering these new abilities."

Tarl couldn't help feeling disappointed. He was hoping that she would say something about him. It was stupid and selfish but his brain was screaming at him from a million different directions.

"Of course. But you don't need to explain yourself to me. I know who you are. I don't need to know where you came from to give me reason to like you."

"I think you need to know."

"Alright, if it's important to you."

She nodded and took a deep breath.

"I was orphaned when I was very young. My whole family was killed in an act of vengeance."

Tarl's eyes grew wide with horror. His father should have told him.

"I'm so sorry Opal. I didn't know."

Opal shook her head to halt his words. There was a lot worse to come. She had lived with this for so long that it suddenly seemed impossible to keep inside her any longer. The closer she was to Tarl the stronger these feelings became.

Tarl realized how difficult this must be for her. He nodded encouragingly to her.

"My family was a traveling family. We had to. We were unwanted in almost every place and so we moved often. My memories of my parents have faded a little but I remember them as being good people with .... well, special abilities. We were quite poor but I remember being happy. They would have done anything for my brothers and sisters. I have been told why they were murdered and I know I must learn to accept it but I still cannot believe that they could have done what it has been said they did." Wrapping her arms around her middle to stop herself from trembling, she blinked away a welling tear. Now she could not stop herself. If only she had let Parvo tell him. Desperately, she hoped Tarl would not judge her.

"The reason they were murdered is because they were said to have murdered someone else. I was told they were to be paid very well to carry out this act and I can only assume that was the reason they might have done it." Another tear welled. "The person they say they killed was…" She could not breathe. Perspiration dotted her brow. She had started; she had to finish. If she wanted the truth from Tarl she had to give it to him also. "The person was Cymbeline Argus." She raised her hands to cover her face.

Tarl couldn't understand what she had just said. He wanted to ask her to repeat herself but he didn't want to hear it again. It was impossible to process the information and have it make sense.

"No. No. It can't be true. She was pointed by renegades," he mumbled.

The shock on Tarl's face was enough to destroy Opal right there and then. He was frowning and shaking his head. It looked as if he was seeing the whole incident occurring right before his eyes: He looked like he had been stabbed.

"Why do you think your father felt responsible for me? Parvo organized the adoption with Mr. Tzau. He always looked out for me; made sure I was safe."

Tarl's head was spinning. That's why his father had taken a special interest in her. It had nothing to do with her craft; nothing to do with a hope that she and Tarl may like each other. She was the daughter of the people that murdered his mother? He needed time to think. He needed rest. Nothing had made sense for a long time. Perhaps his brain was incapable of taking in any new information. This was shocking yet for some reason he couldn't react to it.

Opal watched him turn sheet white. As soon as the words had come out of her mouth she knew it was a mistake. Why could she not have waited? Wanting to rid herself of guilt, she had just loaded it all onto Tarl. Everything was ruined. The one friendship she had made to keep and what had she done? She had ruined it.

Tarl turned away from her and curled up on his mattress. He felt so tired. He thought that if he could manage to sleep now he might never wake up. That sounded good. He wished he could remove the information from his mind. Perhaps he could black it out; all of it. But there was another side of the story he couldn't wash away: Opal was also the orphan of a slaughtered family. What a horrible time she must have endured. Feeling sick, he clutched his stomach, shut his eyes, and without another word, gratefully slipped into the depth of dreams.

Opal curled up on her bedding and tried to shut the image of Tarl's horrified expression from her mind. Silent tears flowed down her face and onto the hard mattress. She honestly had hoped that it would not matter to him. He had said as much and she believed him. How stupid she was; how very stupid.

Rembeu lay as quietly as possible. He had heard everything and he couldn't imagine how either of them felt. This girl was the daughter of the people that had killed his wonderful sister; Tarl's mother; Parvo's wife. Parvo had never said a thing. Perhaps he wanted to protect this girl from the very prejudice that had killed Cymbeline and ultimately, Opal's whole family. Well, if Parvo could be so selfless, so could he. He would have to help Tarl to understand that this girl's parents were not her.

Tarl woke early the next morning. His head ached terribly and his body was slick with sweat. Images from the night's dreams fluttered through his mind. He remembered dreaming he was back there; back at the scene of his mother's death; hearing his father cry out. The harder he tried to run toward them, the further away they appeared. Tarl tried to shake the images from his mind and pushed himself off the mattress before quietly leaving the humid room.

Tarl stood at the entrance watching the already busy streets humming with life. What could he say to Opal? Why did she tell him? Why did she think he had needed to know that her family was responsible for his mother's death? It wasn't her fault or his. He hated thinking of her being orphaned in such terrible circumstances. It was hard enough to lose one parent but to lose both of her parents; her whole family. That was undeniably unbearable. A terrible pain shot up through his left arm and through his throat. He clutched at the ache. It felt like a sword had sliced into his neck. He couldn't even cry out.

When Rembeu rose, he saw Tarl was gone and quietly left the room so as not to wake Opal. As he walked toward the entrance, the bright hot light of the morning sun struck his eyes. When he had managed to focus he saw Tarl crouching just outside the door clutching his throat. Something was very wrong.

"Tarl? Tarl, tell me what's wrong?"

Tarl's squinted up at Rembeu. All he could manage to do was shake his head. No words would come out.

"Quickly," Rembeu demanded, "come with me."

Tarl followed Rembeu back to the room trying not to pass out with the pain. He lay on the mattress unable to straighten himself.

Opal woke with the noise. Tarl lay in front of her curled up in agony.

"What has happened?" she asked.

Rembeu was rummaging in his pack plucking out vials of geranium, tea tree, sandalwood, bergamot and marigold oils to make a compress. He had to pry Tarl's hands away from his throat to apply it.

"Opal, please, hold that in place." Rembeu commanded.

She did as she was told. The moment Opal touched him she sensed his pain and cried out as if she were suddenly burnt.

Tarl began writhing in anguish and his eyes were rolling back in his head. Opal could not understand how this had happened. Rembeu was pouring a very tiny vial of clear liquid into Tarl's mouth trying to get it past his clenched teeth.

Rembeu had seen Opal's reaction as she touched Tarl's throat. Umbra was right: Opal was a Lightworker. How could he have not seen it before? He spoke softly to guide her through the process.

"Opal, focus on experiencing the sensation rather than the pain."

She looked up at Rembeu in surprise. What was happening to her?

"I do not know how to do this!?"

"It's alright, just stay calm."

"It hurts so much."

"That is because you're absorbing the pain. Try to pass your own energy flow through your hands and try not to use your conscious mind to focus. You should find you'll be able to deflect the pain. Try to sense any shifts in the flow of energy. You're a vessel now. You can release the pain I know you can do it."

As Opal closed her eyes her mother's face swam toward her. She was reaching out her hands showing something to Opal. It was beautiful. Opal reached out to grasp the glowing ball of light in the outstretched hand but the object was whisked away so quickly that she could not touch it. Her mother's words rang out to her.

"You cannot just take it; it is not yours to have. You must learn to work the light, for possession is not our fate. Learn to carry it inside." Her mother's warm smile shone down at her before dissolving again.

Opal imagined Tarl's pain like a ball of light. She imagined wrapping her hands around the ball and lifting it from Tarl's throat. Immediately Tarl's movements calmed down beneath her hands. Opal opened her eyes as Tarl lay gasping for breath. Without words, he looked up at her in gratitude before succumbing to the sedative Rembeu had administered.

Rembeu looked upon her, his kind eyes making her feel like she had done well.

"So you're a Lightworker then?"

"A Lightworker?"

"Let me guess," Rembeu was nodding affectionately, "you can sense the pain of others and perhaps even their feelings? And, unbeknown to you, you can heal them." He shook his head in amazement. "You know I've heard of Lightworkers but I have never met one."

"But I can only sense Tarl's pain; no one else's," she offered, "and I certainly cannot sense anyone's feelings." This last comment was tinged with disappointment.

"You are just learning Opal. You must take one step at a time. You will learn to harness the life-force of energy that naturally circulates the body. Ultimately you will learn to help others. There is obviously a special connection between the two of you."

This last comment reminded her of the conversation with Tarl the night before. The pain on her face reminded Rembeu too.

Rembeu wanted to comfort her but he dared not reveal that he had heard the conversation. He was there if she needed to confide in him.

"You know what?" he asked her, his face lifting into a grin.

"What?" Opal felt infected by his smile.

"I think we better get in contact with Melik. I think I know how we can leave this place and I think we can leave it with some of that hope you were talking about." He moved over to retrieve the Voicer. With his back turned he ushered the words, "I certainly am glad you came along." Opal couldn't hide her gratitude.

While Rembeu held a lengthy conversation with Melik, Opal stayed beside Tarl placing cool cloths on his forehead and checking the compress on his throat. When Rembeu and Melik had concluded their discussions Rembeu announced he was going to see if he could barter something for a proper meal.

"Oh you're not leaving are you?" Opal asked desperately. She did not want to be left here alone with Tarl. What if he woke up? What would she say to him? Would he even want to talk to her?

"I promise I won't be gone long," Rembeu promised, "Tarl should come round soon anyway. I should try to find him some sustenance."

"Oh yes of course." Opal realized her selfishness had overcome her again and felt terrible. "Please be careful Rembeu."

"Of course, my child." He winked as his bright yellow robes swung through the door.

■　　■　　■

When Tarl finally woke he was staring up into those wonderful gray eyes. He managed a half smile. His throat still stung but it was easily bearable compared to the agony of earlier. As Tarl tried to sit up Opal pushed him gently back down.

"Please Tarl, you must rest. We will be ready to move on soon."

Tarl wanted to protest but no words came out. He swallowed and fire burned inside his throat.

"Shhh. Do not waste energy on talking just now."

But he had to explain; he had to tell her it didn't matter. A nasty sounding croak did not explain any of the things he needed to tell her.

"Tarl, please, I am asking you to protect your throat. There is a reason that your throat has been weakened." Opal could not understand why he kept trying to talk when it was obviously not possible.

Tarl felt so frustrated. All he wanted to do was to tell her to stop shushing him. This was just not good enough; he had to be stronger than this. He knew his body was constantly building after the Teachings but obviously it was just not enough. That was it. He was going to find a way to get stronger.

Opal noticed his annoyance and assumed it to be anger; anger directed toward her. Of course, he had every reason to feel this way. She looked away in shame. His hoarse whisper made her turn back.

Tarl was not going to give up. Opal was going to have to hear what he had to say.

"Listen to me." Tarl had sat himself up and was studying the compress in his hand. She waited, not wanting to hear; not wanting to know the depth of his resentment toward her. "You must trust me," the rough whisper grated from him. It was not what she thought he was going to say. "Opal, it doesn't matter. I don't care."

"But I..." Opal could not comprehend what he was saying.

"My turn to shush you," he tipped a forefinger toward her lips just brushing them with his fingertip. "Opal, you're so important to me... I cannot tell you how..." His voice was rising and falling in broken tones. He reached out to cup her looped hair in his hands.

She gazed up at him wondering how she could have gotten so lucky.

"For me is it the same."

Tarl's relief was clear.

They heard the jingle of Rembeu's key in the lock. Opal instinctively pulled away. Tarl remained unmoving for just a moment unable to believe his uncle's timing.

"Ah good then, you're awake." Rembeu bellowed too loudly as if aware that he had accidentally interrupted a private moment. He lay down several packets filled with food. Tarl nodded. Opal nodded. Rembeu nodded. "Goodness me, what have I walked in on?" Rembeu had hoped they had made some resolution regarding their conversation from the night before but there was something else going on. Opal blushed and dipped her head toward the ground hoping no one would notice. But it was Tarl's sheepish grin that triggered Rembeu's understanding. He remembered feeling just like that once himself a very long time ago and didn't want to embarrass them any further. "Right then, has Opal filled you in?"

Tarl shook his head. He tried a couple of words but after his last effort his voice had all but disappeared.

"Hmm, obviously you two are quite capable of communicating without speech." Rembeu laughed at his little joke and handed out the food packages. "Not entirely sure what some of these are, so I got extra in case some things are not to our taste."

Tarl was famished. His hunger was greater than the fear of painful swallowing. He opened one of the packets Rembeu handed him. The smell of steaming chili and honey wafted up to his nostrils. The aroma was amazing.

"Utensils," Rembeu was handing both Opal and Tarl two pieces of wood each. Tarl squinted back at him. "Like this," Rembeu demonstrated, "I saw the people doing it at the restaurant. They each copied.

"Well I certainly won't get fat eating here," Tarl whispered croakily as another vegetable piece slipped from its wooden clutches.

"He talks! Marvelous. Eat up, it will do you good."

Tarl's exasperation was obviously beyond Rembeu's comprehension.

Opal giggled. It was a combination of nerves and excitement.

■   ■   ■

After they had eaten Rembeu informed Tarl of their new found Lightworker. Somehow, Tarl wasn't surprised. No ordinary person could have helped him the way she had: How she had found him when he was trapped in his subconscious. That thought gave him an idea. He would have to think about how he could manage it but yes, he would figure out a way.

"Melik has informed us that the transfer point will be available to us early in the morning. He has also located the exit points of the stream we entered after Carny's little time borrowing trick."

"Right?" Tarl tried to make his gravelly voice sound confident.

"Oh, what on time's behalf am I thinking? You weren't conscious and Opal wasn't there. Right, well, Melik has discovered that the people of the path that I told you about, the one without anomalies, have a rather handy little skill. It seems that they are able to hold the paths directly adjacent to them at a constant. That is how they resisted extensive damage from Carny's world; very advanced and very powerful. Obviously they are aware of the different streams and are able to manipulate them but choose not to interfere."

"Unless it affects their reality stream?" Tarl's voice was just audible.

"Your voice won't heal if you keep straining it," Rembeu stated blandly. Tarl felt an unexpected desire to sulk but resisted.

Opal ignored the two of them. She needed to understand what Rembeu was talking about.

"In other words you think they wouldn't mind doing that again if they were benefiting the equilibrium of the paths?"

"Exactly, just like the alignment of a planetary conjunction."

"A planetary conjunction?" Opal was lost again.

"Yes! Very good." Rembeu was delighted at how well they were catching on. "They are quite capable of holding this path on a constant but we will have to make them aware of what we are trying to do. I am quite sure they know what has now happened on Carny's path and will be investigating our contribution. They obviously have full sensory abilities. Ultimately, they are going to help *us*. Because the path we exist on now is on its way into a new age, they should be quite capable of supporting this plane until these people wake from this destructive direction." He looked as satisfied as an inventor winning an award.

"But how do we initiate this?" Opal sensed there was something more.

"That is why we need a Lightworker." Rembeu beamed a smile in her direction. Opal shook her head.

"I still do not know what I am doing. You cannot possibly expect me to accomplish such a task?"

"Well not you alone, my child. This morning when I saw you with Tarl, I remembered what Umbra said when I rejected her idea of bringing you along."

"What did she say?" Opal had quite forgotten.

Tarl's throaty voice interrupted.

"Opal is our force of equilibrium."

"Goodness me. Is it that hard to stop talking for a little while?" Rembeu's frown was only fleeting and a delighted smile rose immediately after it. "However, yes, you're quite correct! What clever people I surround myself with." Tarl could only manage a sigh. Exhaustion was creeping up on him again. "Hhhmmm," seeing Tarl's face suddenly become pale again, Rembeu tried to calm his enthusiasm, "Yes, well anyway, the three of us need to act as a sort of bridge. By fortifying this 'bridge' we can then ensure their protection."

"A bridge? Is that to make the entry and exit points from this path to that one conjoin?" Opal asked hopefully.

"Yes, conjoin, lovely word that one. Well done Opal. Now, as well as that, we must work on building up the ethical and moral essence of the people here. This in turn will decrease the anger and negativity that is fostering violence. To do this we must cultivate the inner self of the people; send healing out into this world; remind them of what peace and the true freedom of self are like: Begin to tune them into the natural vibratory waves of light and sound."

Opal's enthusiasm was waning. She was not feeling terribly confident about any of this. Neither was Tarl.

"How will we pass through to the next path?" She asked tentatively.

"Don't worry. Melik has it all worked out. I know it sounds like a vast venture but it's the right way. Melik is however, still concerned about the fractured light. He says the fractures have been occurring for such a long time that the people will have to effect several significant changes before the rays can heal."

"Do we know how long that will take?" Opal enquired trying to remain alert. It was becoming more and more difficult to deflect Tarl's exhaustion.

Rembeu shook his head looking pensive.

"Unfortunately it could be lengthy. This world has been in turmoil for a very long time. Melik's analysis has shown that many ages ago there was a long period of harmony on this path but it did not last. Since then the people have fought over every imaginable thing. Ultimately of course, once the new spiritual force filters through and the people understand their relationship with this earth and the universe, this world will begin its restoration. Until then, the path they 'conjoin' with," he smiled at Opal, "will keep them stable."

Their tiny window allowed a little of the hazy afternoon light into their box-like room. Tarl glanced up at the polluted light. Dust particles streamed in like bright shards. The fan just churned the stale humid air around and around. Claustrophobia ebbed and the need to sleep hung heavily upon him.

Opal suddenly looked terrible. Her pale skin had become clammy and she looked as though she couldn't breathe.

"Opal, are you alright?" Tarl bent his head slightly to look in her downcast eyes.

"I think I need to go outside for a moment. I feel like the walls are closing in."

"Sorry Opal, that's my fault," Tarl croaked.

"How can it be your fault?" She was fingering her collar as if loosening it would enable her to inhale more air.

"I'm claustrophobic."

"You are? But …oh I see, I am sensing your feelings." Annoyance rose. She could sense Tarl's fatigue but she had not picked up on his claustrophobia. Her 'gift' was much too new to be trying it on such an important task. How was she going to do this?

"You see child. You can sense feelings." Rembeu was delighted.

"But I cannot stop this," she exclaimed as she buried her head in her hands. "I cannot even identify the difference between my feelings and Tarl's. And I didn't realize it was claustrophobia."

"It's alright Opal," Rembeu responded. "Listen to me. Close your eyes for a moment." Rembeu spoke gently, reassuringly. "Try to envision a light inside your head. Imagine it is flowing through your body."

She snuck a doubtful look in Rembeu's direction. Tarl was offering an encouraging nod.

"I do not think…"

"Just try, please." Rembeu said soothingly.

Opal closed her eyes and tried to see the light. Shapes shifted in the darkness behind her squeezed eyelids but no light shone. Trying to relax her face, she concentrated just on the light.

"I see it. It is bright and white. It looks like our moon."

"That's excellent Opal. Now just let the light flow." Rembeu smiled to himself. He knew she could do it.

"Oh. It is beginning to course through my body."

"Very good. Describe it to me."

"It feels… well…"

"Go on. Just say whatever words come into your mind."

"It feels like peppermint… sort of cool and fresh. It is turning into streams of colored iridescent light. It is so beautiful."

Tarl and Rembeu looked on amazed. Opal's entire body was surrounded by a lemon glow and her outstretched hands were projecting a yellow stream of light.

"Well done, my child," Rembeu spoke with awe, "now when you feel energized again allow the light to diminish."

When she finally opened her eyes she looked fresh and revived.

"How do you feel?" Rembeu asked.

"I feel… better. I feel …clear." She was looking at her hands turning them over as if she had never seen them before. "It felt like I was pure energy."

"Indeed it did." Rembeu laughed in Tarl's direction. Tarl's mouth was gaping.

"Tarl my young man, the lady doesn't want to see your tonsils." He slapped his knee. "Now that's done, perhaps you two should go for a walk. I'd like to offer fresh air but that's just not going to happen."

Strangely enough Tarl felt more energized as well. He nodded assent and offered Opal his hand. She smiled delightedly, placed her hand in his and rose from the mattress. Neither claustrophobia nor exhaustion overwhelmed her.

"Now don't go too far and keep to yourselves. And be back soon enough to get a good night's sleep. We have an early morning." He handed them two bags of dried fruit. Opal hesitated at the door.

"Should I not practice whatever it is we have to do tomorrow?"

"My child, you will be fine. I promise." Rembeu winked at Tarl, "and Tarl can vouch for my word."

"Now let's not get too boastful," Tarl whispered gruffly as he rolled his eyes.

"Young people these days: No respect." Rembeu teased as he moved toward the Voicer. "Go on then you two. And feel free to make fun of me behind my back."

"Like we have nothing better to talk about."

■　■　■

The earliest light of morning woke Rembeu first. He stretched and grabbed the Voicer.

"Melik? Melik do you copy, over?" Rembeu yawned and scratched his head. Silence. Rembeu kept trying but all he received was static.

Tarl roused and sat up. His normally straight dark hair was churned into a messy ball at the back of his head. Rembeu threw him a tiny mirror that he normally saved for scientific purposes. Tarl took the mirror frowning. Rembeu pointed at Tarl's head. Tarl squinted at the small reflection.

"It is still there," Opal yawned, her jaw widened but her lips stayed pressed together. Unlike Tarl's hair, her braids were still perfectly looped in circles.

"What's still there?" Tarl looked down at his front for whatever it was that was still there. His voice was still husky but the pain had eased considerably.

"Your head."

"Jokes so early in the morning?" Rembeu looked delighted.

Opal's self-consciousness didn't hide her amusement. Tarl ignored both of them. He combed his fingers through the back of his hair, passed the mirror back to Rembeu and stepped over to the sink to wash.

"Melik come in please. Over." There was no response.

"How long do we have until we begin?" Opal was trying to tidy herself. She waited patiently for Tarl to finish.

"Not long if Melik contacts us; very long if he doesn't," Rembeu answered drolly.

"Not funny," Tarl muffled through splashing water.

"Believe me, I am not laughing."

"Why isn't he answering?" Tarl turned around to face Rembeu.

"I don't really want to think about that." Rembeu lifted his Voicer and called for Melik's attention again.

Tarl and Opal exchanged worried glances. He moved away from the sink and Opal rose to take his place.

"Rem... signals get... cros... ver."

Rembeu breathed a sigh of relief and frowned in Tarl's direction.

"I think things are getting pretty bad up there for Melik. I hope that darn balloon holds out." Rembeu picked up the Voicer, "Melik we are only getting partial verbal. Try your tuner please. Over."

"How is that? Over."

"Better Melik. How are things going? Over."

"It's a little bit rocky down there. The forces are starting to penetrate the stratosphere. You should see the sky-show I'm getting up here. It's incredible. I can see your next path opening; it really is spectacular. Over."

"What is the countdown? Over."

"If you prepare yourselves now I'll count you in. Over."

"Nothing like leaving things to the last minute-turn. Over."

"Sarcasm has never suited you my friend. Get ready, entry and exit points are about to come into line. Over."

"Quickly, you two sit here." Rembeu was plucking several stones from his satchel. "Opal you need to be in the middle. Tarl you sit to her right." Rembeu sat down on Opal's left. "Now Opal, place the turquoise stone the woman gave you in your left hand and Tarl, the amazonite in your right." He pulled the Third and the Sixth Elestial crystals that Umbra had packed from his satchel: One pulsed bright yellow, the other azure blue. Their vibrations were very strong. He placed one in each of his palms. Now everyone place your palms together."

That was definitely something Tarl wasn't going to argue with. He placed his palm over Opal's and felt a tingling sensation.

Opal felt the tremor from his arm deep inside her. Her throat felt dry and sore and her head ached. Instead of fighting it she tried to do what Rembeu had described the day before.

"One minute-turn. Over."

Rembeu was about to explain to Opal again how to open herself to the life-force but was surprised to see she was already glowing. Her hands were radiating warmth and compassion; he could feel it surging up through his palms, then his heart, then his head.

Tarl's eyes were open but he could see far beyond the little room they sat in. When the warmth began to radiate inside him he felt as if he were no longer in a gravity-bound body but instead floating through many worlds as if riding a magic carpet. Opal's energy was flaring around her. White light shot from the top of her head and then expanded into rays of color. The rays then contracted into a bright yellow beam.

Rembeu could see it again. The beautiful world he had watched from the sphere when Tarl was unconscious. It looked so incredible that he had pangs of sadness that he was unable to visit. Tarl could not believe the incredible scene stretching out around him. Golden light glimmered across silken tents that rustled in a gentle breeze. People with beautiful smiles shone in their colorful saris as they made their way through the open streets. Amber carvings of dancers coiled their way across the rich fertile lands extending beyond the town. To Tarl, it looked like perfection.

It was time for Rembeu to do his part. He spoke slowly.

"The energy will make all the adjustments necessary. You have done so well Opal." He breathed deeply and then announced loudly, "To change this life you must change your minds. This in turn will change your hearts. Communication needs a voice. A voice is given through a strong mind. Open yourselves to the flow of life-force. Open yourselves to the universe. This will stir your awakening."

For the first time Opal saw a world beyond her imagination. As soon as Rembeu had spoken these words the people in the plane, with the perfect golden light, looked straight up at them. They too joined hands and raised their heads into the bright sunlight. Opal could sense the shift. It felt as if she were holding herself against an outgoing tide. She passed backward, away from this world and then felt the rush of the next path pulling her forward; the golden light flowing with her. The beach where she had found Tarl was now washed with creamy white sand which cushioned a sparkling sea-green ocean. She could see the incredible green emerald emerging from the roof of the castle and shooting high into the sky.

Then, she was being pulled backward into the present plane; golden light washing her. The presence of their little room returned but she could also see far beyond its walls: The sweeping planes below her consisted of an incredible mix of fertile, productive land and congested industry. Opal watched yellow light flood across the land and then ebb back until an explosion of energy burst within her. Sapphire blue light blazed from the crown of her head. It was this world's energy force. She had found it.

Tarl felt the incredible surge soar through him. The yellow beam of light had spun into a blazing ray of bright blue light. The blue beam then opened like a triangle above Opal's head. He could see Rembeu's hands pulsing with green light and his own were pulsing with blue light. Suddenly they were wrapped in a circle of colored streams like rings; one color atop the other. Then the rings fell, one into another until a simple circle of white light engulfed them.

"Hold on, you're going through. Over." Melik's voice called out to them.

A rush of wind whipped around them and they felt an upward force so strong it felt like they were being pulled from their bodies. The deep pitch of a resonating D# note hummed through them and reverberated in their heads.

"Hold on!" were the only words Rembeu could manage.

26

Light Ray Indigo

An image of the Wheel-Door spun in front of them, fading, intensifying and fading again. Colors flashed around them like a million dreams meeting. They were experiencing many different paths simultaneously. The Wheel-Door continued to revolve, its divisions luminescent. It shimmered in front of them just beyond their reach as they swirled upward, pulled by unknown forces. The energy they were experiencing made both speech and voluntary movement impossible. Images of other planes merged and disappeared. They were left whirling in a colorful nothingness until suddenly the Wheel-Door stopped spinning. Vivid rays of deep blue light shot from its center in a burst of energy. Instantly, they felt the pull: They were being sucked into the indigo colored light. Every cell in their bodies felt a surge of power until, just at the point of transference, all became calm.

The three of them were standing on velvety grass looking out across rolling silken meadows that glistened with tiny sapphire flowers. Cloudless delft blue skies arched above them and a cool breeze wafted across their skin; such a relief after the terrible humidity they had just endured. In the distance a huge lake reflected twinkling blues and purples and beautiful bird song swam toward them from flowering trees which scooped across the fields. A three-quarter moon still shone in the daylight sky. As they stood admiring the view Rembeu contacted

Melik. He kept his speech quiet, almost reverent. Melik had located their co-ordinates and asked to be kept informed.

"It is so beautiful," cried Opal her eyes wide with awe.

"Why thank you." A gentle, deep voice came from behind them. His wonderful accent and deep voice made his words sound rich and inviting. They turned to see who had spoken.

A tall man with silky smooth, toffee colored skin stared back at them. His big brown eyes gazed at them with a mixture of humor and interest. He wore a long midnight blue shift and his head was dressed with narrow sheets of linen wound up into a small mound. His feet were covered in golden ribbons.

In the distance, behind him, they could see many large and unusual buildings. The dome-like structures shimmered in the sun, their eye-catching designs of inlaid stone shining at their twisted peaks. Other narrower buildings had beautiful golden spires stretching up into the deep blue skies.

"Please, you can come with me." The stranger directed a hand toward the village. He then gestured toward their feet. "Please, make yourselves comfortable. You do not need shoes here. Removing them will protect the plant growth." His deep voice hummed out toward them embracing them in warmth.

They quickly removed their shoes. The grass was as spongy and soft as moss. Opal reached down to touch it with her hands as if she could not believe how delicate it was. The man smiled at her, his face filled with empathy, and then made long graceful strides toward the village.

"My name is Tarl." Tarl had to hurry to keep up. "This is Rembeu and this is Opal."

"I am very pleased to meet you Tarl, Rembeu and Opal," he nodded as he pronounced each name. "I am Shaief," his throaty voice rumbled.

"We are pleased to meet you too." For the first time in a long time Tarl felt excited to have transferred. It felt safe here. Even the shaking in his arm seemed less noticeable.

At the village entrance they passed through a large opening. The archway was encrusted with shining stones brilliantly shaped into geometric forms. Rembeu was surprised to see several moldavite stones looped around the stones of azurite and lapis lazuli. Moldavite was a very rare stone that came from the stars. Since it was a stone said to assist in communication with interdimensional energies he wondered if these people were also capable of interdimensional travel. This was going to be a very interesting visit.

Several of the dome buildings were joined by staircases that spiraled up the sides and across the crowns of the glittering structures. They all appeared to lead to a high platform in the center of the village.

Many people milled through the streets; their glossy tanned skin covered in similar loose fitting outfits. Some of the woman's shifts were angled at the hem line and many were embroidered with golden symbols.

The ground was covered in smooth tiles of different shapes, sizes and shades. Geometric forms were glazed into the tile's surface creating clever patterns that merged and stood out simultaneously. Opal spotted a row of curved glass walls that held different types of wares. They appeared to be shops but she could see people taking things without the necessary exchange. There did not even seem to be people minding the goods.

"These buildings are truly incredible." Rembeu was straining to see the shapes and symbols of inlaid stone that surrounded the tops of the domes.

"They suit our purpose."

"And what purpose is that, may I ask?" Rembeu sounded enthralled.

"These structures enable us to tune into our planet's vibrational energies. The spires help us to connect with the external and internal waves. We like to recline atop the platform and allow these energies to surround us while we watch the stars of the universe." Shaief's deep echo resounded out around them, each word rounded by his lovely accent. "Come, this way." He motioned them through a jeweled door into one of the larger structures.

Opal let out a small gasp. She could never have imagined such beauty. The curved walls were of meticulous design. Patterned stones swirled along the walls reaching up onto the ceiling.

"This is incredible," she exclaimed imagining these designs on her silks sails.

"This is our meeting room. It is rather more ornate than the others I assure you," Shaief replied rather solemnly. Taking pride in another's work was unheard of. He led them to a large round table where six members already sat. Three men and three women smiled up at them from high-backed chairs. All had sparkling brown eyes and glowing tanned skin. They wore similar blue shifts but their head wraps varied. The men's were differing shapes of plain cotton but two of the woman had golden ribbon threaded through their headpieces and woven into their long dark plaited hair.

The table they sat at had a segmented pattern of stones which reminded Tarl of the Wheel-Door. He ran his hands across the smooth bubbles.

"Welcome said one of the members. I am Mohmed, speaker of frequencies. We are most pleased you have found us."

Shaief saw the flutter of confusion on his visitor's faces. "Mohmed and I choose to concentrate our learning on adjusting the voice to other's frequencies. Each dimensional layer holds its own innate 'tune', if you will, and we have opened our own frequency to understand yours. We are able to communicate in the languages of many planes. I will be able to translate to our other members as they have taken other paths in their learning."

"Fascinating! Wait till I tell Melik." Rembeu remarked. "How have you managed to access these planes?"

Mohmed knew this question would come and prepared to explain the unusual story of his cultures evolution.

"Our quest has evolved over a very very long time. Many periods ago our people experienced a great catastrophe. This catastrophe resulted in extreme changes to our climate, turning our weather conditions to frost and eventually frozen ice. Those that survived were then faced with plague and starvation."

Shaief was quietly translating to the other members of the table, his voice sounding lighter; the words ringing out as if he were speaking an octave higher.

Opal turned when she heard footsteps behind her. A small woman, dressed in a cream cotton shift threaded with blue symbols at its hem carried two large platters of food. Her gentle face looked well lived but healthy. She smiled at Opal as she placed the platters on the table. Opal peered optimistically at their contents.

Tarl's eyes widened. The sight of food made him realize how hungry he was. The trays were generously loaded with small cups of thick vegetable soup.

"Please eat," Shaief said when he saw them hesitate.

Tarl watched Opal's face as she took a tentative sip. Her sheer delight encouraged him to indulge. The flavor was incredible and the texture was indescribable. Rembeu picked up a cup almost absently but when the liquid touched his tongue his eyes lit up as if someone had given him a rather pleasant surprise. He continued to take small delighted sips as he listened to Mohmed.

"Most of the population of other lands died. There was only very few who were able to resist death. Our history books describe the survivors as having developed another sense. Perhaps because of the plague or perhaps because of the terrible devastation they had to endure, they learned to survive in a way that did not rely on the methods we had previously understood to be essential for life." Shaief paused allowing the information to absorb. "We have continued to develop what we call our third eye and third ear: In a way we have learned to see with our ears and perceive beyond sight with our eyes."

"How does this help your civilization?" Opal was leaning forward, her fingers absently caressing the smooth stones of the table. She was feeling an overwhelming power build within her as if a light had been turned on for everyone to see. It was impossible to put the feeling into words but she felt like she belonged to something much larger; something intangible but nothing her mind could rationalize.

Rembeu was glad the question had been asked. He quietly pulled out his Voicer and switched it on hoping Melik would be listening. This information could keep Melik experimenting for a lifetime.

"There is much to explain," Mohmed's voice spiraled in the air toward her like a warm embrace. "One must allow the body to accept the waves of light and sound. Once one is accustomed, one can balance the natural electromagnetic flow of the body. This clears the 'sight' to perceive thought, emotion, even sound and allows the physical body to be touched without action."

"Can we learn how?" Tarl was eyeing the left over cups of soup.

"There are many ways to assist in this elevation of 'sight'. For example, we have learned to grow fruit and vegetables with positive energy. We use the energy of pleasant thought and the energy of sound to strengthen our crops. The greater the positive energy of the food consumed, the greater the positive force on our bodies and therefore, the more easily we are able to connect with the vibrations, our essence, our light. We are clearing the way to ascension. Ultimately we believe that our progress will ensure the protection of our fellow dimensions. We are here for the service of humanity; to guard humanity."

"So you can access other dimensions?" Rembeu knew it.

"Yes, we have opened the portals of your path also."

"Our path?" Tarl couldn't hide his surprise. "Have you entered our plane?"

"Oh no," Shaief interjected, "that is not the task of our people. We must not interfere. Just protect."

"We have been calling for you though," Mohmed continued, "we have seen your truth. You reside on one of the highest planes. Without your help we fear we will be unable to follow our truth: The alliance of paths. It is because of your plane's echelon that your dimension has felt the greatest influx of disturbances. You have seen the time clash in your skies; you have felt the quakes and storms. The ripples have affected the universal matrix and without your help, we fear we will be unable to accomplish our purpose."

"Please," Rembeu interjected, "what exactly is it that you have been unable to do?"

"We are missing the seventh entry key. Our greatest sadness lies with the inability to connect with our highest realm. We know they would be able to connect with us but we have been unable to open the portal from our side. As I said before, to accomplish our ultimate task we must be open to all frequencies."

"Have you any idea how this 'frequency' is opened?" Rembeu hoped that Melik was listening.

"Our House of Knowledge holds all the keys of the other paths. We assume this is where the final portal must be opened but we have been unable to decipher the code. It is a hyperdimensional code combining symbol, sound and vibration and electromagnetic radiation or rather light."

Rembeu needed to talk to Melik this was all very extraordinary. He wanted to ask so many questions but perhaps he should wait for all possible information.

"When would we be able to visit your House of Knowledge?" he asked.

"We shall wait for morning. It is growing late and we must align our energies with the sun before it sets." Mohmed's big brown eyes blinked toward his other companions.

"Yes of course," Rembeu uttered. He wanted very much to watch this process but felt inclined to give them privacy, he wasn't quite sure why.

"Shaief will show you to some accommodations for rest. You can perform any required ablutions before joining our people for dinner," Mohmed was rising from his chair. Their conversation was over.

Shaief allowed Mohmed and the others to exit before leading Rembeu, Opal and Tarl from the room. The empty streets were glossed with lilac light. The sun was beginning its descent toward the horizon. People were either already reclining on the large platform above them or were making their way up the staircases that curled around the domes.

Walking briskly toward a small building on the west side, Opal felt sad she could not spend more time looking around. Perhaps the next day would hold more opportunities. Shaief ushered them inside one of the smaller structures.

"I must leave you here for the moment. Please make yourselves comfortable. I will have someone collect you for dinner." He was obviously in a hurry to join the others.

"Yes, go ahead," Rembeu nodded his head toward the platform as if Shaief should hurry. "Thank you Shaief." Shaief smiled gratefully before beginning to climb the staircase at the side of their building.

The inside of this structure was very different from the one they had just left. The high domed roof was circled with a surround-window filling the rooms with light. The room was segmented by a crossed partition, rising only to head height, turning the one room into four separate areas and yet the area above the partitions remained open.

The most delightful part was the soft beds covered with sapphire blue covers. Tarl reached down to feel the fresh cool sheets. A waft of lavender met his nostrils. He wanted to curl up right then and there and drift into nothingness.

Rembeu wasted no time trying to contact Melik again. His Voicer had been opened on his own frequency for so long that he wondered if Melik had needed to contact him.

Opal wandered from one area to the next and stood on a small stool to peek her eyes over the top of her partitioned area.

"Well the accommodations are certainly more amenable." She peered down at Tarl's worn face. Dark circles rimmed his eyes and even his tanned skin was looking pale. She could sense his pounding headache. His pain was being caused by something way beyond her understanding. There had to be some way to help him.

Tarl smiled up at her. 'How lovely,' he thought. His terrible headache could almost be imagined away when he looked at her. He pretended to look surprised.

"Why, hello there," he took on a formal speaking voice. "Let me inform you of your facilities this evening. You shall be sharing one of our most exclusive dome-rooms with two of the most pleasing males you'll ever meet." Tarl swept an extended arm out around him. "I think you shall find it to your liking. Please note that our mattresses are actually raised from the floor and appear not to be covered in someone else's sweat. I would also like to point out, that the delightful window currently displaying a most dazzling sunset is not, in fact, covered with humid grime. I do hope, however, you are not prone to making too much noise as I don't think these partitions are even slightly soundproof."

Opal giggled, her gray eyes squinting upward. She raised herself on her tip toes trying to stick her nose over the partition.

"Well I'm certainly not the one around here who snores."

"Snores?!" Tarl feigned horror. "I'll have you know, I have never snored in my entire life."

"Oh, you mean your entire life until a few moon-spells ago." Opal tried to raise her head over the partition and lost balance. Tarl tried to stifle his laughter and went racing around the angled partition as he heard her thud to the floor.

Rembeu had made contact with Melik but he couldn't hear what Melik was saying.

"Would you two intrepid explorers of partitions please keep it down for a moment?"

"Oh sorry Rembeu." Opal's voice quivered as she tried to restrain from another spasm of laugher. Tarl unsuccessfully tried to suppress his amusement as he lay on the grass-matt floor next to Opal.

"I don't know, rude noisy neighbors that insist on poking their noses into other people's business." Tarl whispered into Opal's ear.

"You are so right. No respect these young people." Opal's impression of Rembeu was so good Tarl felt a whole new wave of laughter coming on. He quickly grabbed a pillow and smothered it over his face. This just encouraged Opal. She peered under the pillow. He turned away in fabricated horror mumbling something into the cushion.

Opal exhumed a last laugh and spread her arms out in exhaustion. She lifted the pillow again and spoke softly so that Tarl would have difficulty hearing.

"I wonder what our dinner will be." Her trick worked. The pillow was gone in an instant.

"Wasn't that soup incredible?" Tarl turned over onto his stomach.

"It was so wonderful I wanted to take another cup but I thought it would look rude," Opal said contentedly. "It made me feel wonderful... and the taste!"

"It felt like ...like light." Tarl's eyes were gazing into the memory.

"That is what I thought also."

"I wonder what exactly they are doing up there on that platform?" Tarl rolled over on to his back again.

"Me too." Opal inclined a forefinger into the air. "Shhh, I just heard Melik say something."

"Melik, finally," Rembeu's relief was obvious, "did you hear their conversation about vibrations? Over."

"I did. It's truly amazing that it hasn't been achieved here. I have been absolutely fascinated. I can't wait to have enough time to work on these possibilities. Perhaps they can teach you how they have achieved all this. Over."

"I will certainly try to find out but I get the feeling, each dimension must find their own way. They have made it clear that each path must each evolve in its own time. Over."

"Except when evolution creates destruction. Over."

"Of course, as usual, you are quite right. Well how are we fairing for time? As you heard we apparently need to open the next portal from this plane. Over."

"Yes, Rembeu that's interesting. I have been making assessments on the visuals from up here. I was going to wait until there was something positive to report but until now it has been looking rather worrying. Over."

Tarl and Opal lay very still trying to pick up Melik's next words.

"Just go ahead and give us any news you can. Over."

"Right. When the portals are open I have been able to see the time paths converging and clashing - as we did when you were up here. There appears to be only one more path that is pulling away. It seems that the resolution of this final path should facilitate your return home. You'll be pleased to know things are starting to quite down here. I've been picking up global reports of calming storms. People have even started addressing the destruction. Over."

Rembeu knew he wasn't being told something.

"Melik, it's me. What aren't you telling me? Over."

"Well," Melik hesitated, "It's probably just me being overly careful…but I'm worried that this calm is just a prelude to even bigger problems. Over."

Rembeu slumped. Somehow he knew it wasn't over.

"What's your take on the situation then? Over."

"Well, I fear it has all calmed down too quickly. Over."

"The calm before the storm hey? Over."

"Well, yes. You see the time disruptions are still occurring. You know my theories on fluid time. Well, I'm just saying that we can no longer be constrained by previous perceptions. If I'm correct, we don't have long at all. While the planet is calm it is storing energy, a time disruption could layer the energies causing catastrophic damage. Over."

"Have you calculated the intervals between time disruptions? Over."

"Yes, I seem to be able to pick them up before they strike me up here. The disruptions are traveling along waves from the planet out into the atmosphere. What I'm seeing up here indicates that when the next portal is opened the time will be equalized again but…"

The Voicer went dead.

"Melik? Come in. Over."

Nothing. Tarl and Opal moved over to Rembeu's partition and sat at his feet. He didn't look at them. His face had turned potato white.

"But what?" Tarl pressed his fingers to his forehead. His headache had suddenly swelled.

There was nothing Rembeu could think of saying that would make that expression on Tarl's face go away. He looked at Opal. There it was again. They wanted an answer.

"I don't know," he finally said.

"I am sure he will contact us again." Opal spoke up, sounding more positive than she felt.

"Yes, Opal, you're quite right. Worrying will get us nowhere."

"He's probably just thought of some grand idea and has just forgotten he was talking to us," Tarl tried, knowing how unlikely this was.

"Entirely possible." Rembeu didn't think it was possible at all but there was nothing he could do about it now. They had time - he hoped. "You know, perhaps we should have a look around this place before dinner."

"I would really like see how these people live. I saw some amazing shops nearby, I would very much like to look at them," Opal was trying to look excited. Negativity was not a choice at this stage.

"Marvelous idea," Rembeu said surprised at how glad he was that his companions chose to be optimistic. "You know I think I might have a look for this House of Knowledge they talk about. How about you Tarl?"

"I think I might have a rest before dinner," he lied.

"Another marvelous idea. Alright you two, I'll meet you back here before dinner."

Opal smiled sweetly at Tarl hoping he might change his mind and come with her. But he just smiled and feigned a yawn.

When Rembeu and Opal were safely gone Tarl began rummaging in Rembeu's bag. He pulled out the box of potions and the Sixth Elestial crystal that Rembeu had used to assist their transition into this evolutionary stream. He didn't know if this crystal had the same properties as the second Elestial crystal he had entered in Carny's prison cell but they had lost that one in transition. This one would have to do. The power of the crystal hummed in his hand.

One way or another he was going to remember exactly what he saw the day his mother died. The only thing he could not believe was that Opal's parents were responsible for her death. When he found the truth, no matter what it might be, he would deal with his own weaknesses. It was the only way he could think of to make himself stronger.

Tarl pulled out the sword Opal had given him at the fair; the memory seemed so long ago it could have been another lifetime, and then began mixing different potions. A powerful mixture would be needed, one that would give him access to a place more impenetrable than the Elestial crystal – his own mind.

Once the formula was made he checked outside the entrance: Neither Rembeu nor Opal were in sight. He climbed the outer stairway and made his way onto the platform. Only a few people still remained up there. After finding a quiet spot, he swallowed the tonic and lay back on one of the reclining seats. He placed the Elestial crystal over his brow and hugged Opal's sword close to his chest and then closed his eyes and tried to find the entry point to that place in his memory.

■ ■ ■

The sun had slipped away and the streets had darkened. Underfoot, random luminous tiles shone with early moonlight. Opal found the people incredibly welcoming. Their warm smiles greeted her and their kindness swam around her like waves. She felt strangely aware that they wanted her here; that she belonged here. The thought sat comfortably with her. There was a great deal that she could learn about herself and her abilities from these people. There was only one reason for not staying. Her heart beat a little faster with the thought of him. But Opal knew she could not help him. Not with what he was going through. What use was she to him if the one thing she had to offer was her Lightwork and it did him no good? Tarl had to help himself first.

Opal found herself staring into an open circular door. Boxes of beautiful stones glimmered back at her. Inside, trays of skillfully crafted jewels sprawled out around her. Filaments of twined gold circled bright shining tanzanite crystals and sapphires. Twisted head pieces of looped love hearts sparkled in the night glow. These people were artists in everything they did and their art work conveyed their feelings of unconditional love. What a perfect place to exist.

A cool chill caressed the nape of her neck. She must have been wandering around for a long time. Hoping she had not missed dinner, Opal began to wander back to their accommodations. Her hunger grew with thoughts of the soup they had earlier.

Opal looked inside their dome house but no one had returned, or perhaps they had gone to dinner without her. Not knowing where to look she decided to climb up to the platform to have a look from up there. The platform was enormous. Rows of reclining chairs lined the area. There were only a few people up there and most of them were off toward the west corner. Globes reflecting the light of the moon gave just enough illumination to reveal the geometric patterns of the tiles. They were truly fascinating.

She walked toward one of the chairs intending to gaze up into the clear purple night filled with prickling stars when she recognized Tarl's silhouette.

"Tarl?" she whispered so as not to disturb the others. He did not answer. "Tarl? Are you asleep?" Opal approached until she was close enough to peer down at him. The sight made her immediately panic. "Tarl! Wake up!" She started to shake him. The Elestial crystal fell from his brow. Opal called out to him again. Tarl started murmuring something indecipherable.

"Oh thank goodness. Tarl you looked…"

"What did you do!?" he suddenly shouted back as he began to rouse.

"I'm sorry but I thought you were…" Opal's shock stopped her from going on.

"Well whatever you thought, you thought wrong! I was so close. I can't believe you brought me back."

"Back from where?" She was still reeling from his attack.

Tarl sat up and placed his head in his hands. The pounding in his head was even more severe. Opal felt the same searing pain. And then much worse. She could see his arm shaking. The symptoms had finally externalized. He had grown much much worse.

"What is happening to you Tarl? What are you doing to yourself? Please, I want to help."

"I'm trying to go back," he cried, "I'm trying to go back to the day she was killed. Don't you understand!?" His fury was completely uncharacteristic. "I've got to see who killed her," he grabbed Opal's arms tightly, his face desperate, "I know it wasn't your parents, I just know it wasn't them."

She tried to hide the horror from her face. His grip was hurting her.

"Tarl you have got to stop this. You are fighting for something that you cannot fix. You want it to be different so badly that you cannot admit the truth. You must leave this alone," she looked into his eyes, "I have."

"*You* don't understand!"

"I understand that you are getting worse. I can *see* your tremor and I can sense your headache. You have to tell Rembeu."

Tarl looked down at his shaking left arm. He let go of Opal and clutched it in the hope he could stop the trembling.

"Opal there's something else I haven't told you. I've seen things, the same images several times…" He hesitated trying to put what he had seen in the Moon Gate and inside the mirror hall into words.

"Stop it right now Tarl!" Opal's frustration was getting the better of her. Tarl was obviously not going to listen to her. "You are jeopardizing everything, yourself included. What about us? Do you not care about what your uncle is going through?" She started to walk away but turned briefly back toward him. Her voice was a whisper, "And what about me? Do you not care what I am going through?" She turned away again and climbed back down the stairway.

Tarl felt like he was being torn in all different directions. The potion he had taken seemed to increase the pain in his head and now he wouldn't be able to hide his tremor from Rembeu. He knew Opal felt useless, unable to heal his pain but she didn't understand how much he wanted to ease hers. Maybe she wasn't going to admit it but he could imagine how much hurt she was harboring. He just wanted to fix it all. The universe was falling apart and so was he. He wouldn't make it. He knew that now. And he had yelled at her. Why did he yell at her? Why was he was messing everything up?

Tarl reached down to pick up the Elestial crystal and saw that it was damaged. He had sealed their fate.

■　■　■

Rembeu knew something bad had passed between his two companions. They were seated in an adjacent structure with about ten others for dinner. Rembeu was completely unsure of what to do with them. Neither was talking and neither was meeting the others gaze. Every question he asked was being answered with a head shake or a shoulder shrug. Tarl was even visibly shaking. What on time's behalf had gone on?

Surprisingly, Opal looked both hurt and hard. Rembeu could not for the life of him figure out what that meant. He feared Tarl had brought up Opal's past again. It was completely unfair that Rembeu could have cleared it all up if he chose to, but he couldn't divulge the truth just yet. It would ruin everything.

Rembeu's concern for his nephew had been growing for a long time now. Tarl had begun to show the signs that Rembeu was afraid of. The strain of this whole journey had been too much. How could they have expected him to suddenly cram the Learnings of a lifetime into such a short period? And worse, knowing what they had done to his mind after his mother's death. But he knew they had had no choice. They were just trying to protect him in the only way they knew how. For now he would pretend to ignore it. A pang of guilt stabbed him. Rembeu tried to rationalize his thoughts. He promised himself he would put things right. He just needed a little more time.

■　■　■

The incredible food was at least a delightful distraction. Rembeu sampled all the dishes: Beans fried in almond and sesame oil; grated potato as fluffy as an omelet; pumpkin stuffed with nuts and herbs; and apples marinated in honey and sprinkled with cinnamon and walnut. It was all delectable. The Altai would love this place.

Their companions seemed elated with their presence but did not feel the need to facilitate speech. Conversation was apparently not a requirement.

Rembeu watched his two travel companions eat the food as if it were cardboard. Ignoring them wasn't going to make them go away.

"Alright, what is the matter with you two?" Rembeu's voice commanded. They had no choice but to address him. Tarl shrugged his shoulders. "Oh no, body movements are not an answer. I want speech. Now." He waited in vain. "Opal?"

She hesitated throwing a quick glance in Tarl's direction before turning her face back toward her lap.

"Yes Rembeu?" she asked so quietly he could barely hear her.

"You two are obviously fighting. I want to know why."

Tarl began to interject in an attempt to refute the 'fighting' claim. Rembeu hushed him instantly.

"I have asked Opal as I do not wish to have a shoulder shrugging competition with my nephew." Tarl looked hurt. Rembeu covered his guilt well. He looked back at Opal with a demanding stare.

"Tarl is not well." Opal stole a glance at Tarl and flinched at the look of betrayal she received.

"Well I do believe I have eyes! I am quite capable of seeing that Tarl is unwell. Are you telling me you will not speak to him because you don't like people that are ill?"

Opal shook her head. Her big gray eyes swelled with inevitable tears. Tarl was distraught. First he had yelled at her and now his uncle was interrogating her.

"Rembeu! Stop it." Tarl's eyes flashed at his uncle. "If you want to ask questions, ask me. Now!" The censure Tarl returned shocked Rembeu.

"Alright then, *you* tell me."

"O.K. but you have to listen to me you have to let me explain." Tarl swallowed as he remembered the damaged Elestial crystal.

Rembeu nodded in acceptance. Opal shook her head. She got up to leave the table. Rembeu placed an encouraging hand on hers.

"Please Opal, perhaps we should both hear this?"

She slumped back into her chair and tilted her forehead into her palms.

"Uncle, I tried to tell you before, I have seen things. Much of it doesn't make sense and yet I seem to know what I am seeing but putting it into words is the most difficult way of dealing with it." He was getting away from what he wanted to say. "Please, I just wanted to have some proof."

"Proof of what exactly?"

"I don't know how I know this, I know I haven't got clear memories of that day, the day my mother was killed, but I somehow know Opal's parents weren't responsible."

Rembeu went cold. He tried to appear detached and nodded.

Opal could contain herself no longer. Her gray eyes looked up at Rembeu welling with tears.

"He must forget about it. It is over, gone, past. We cannot change it and he is just making himself sick over it. If he cannot accept it, I cannot accept it and I have had my whole life to learn to accept it." She looked harshly at Tarl, "and by the way I do not need a potion to do that."

Rembeu wondered what her last comment meant. He took one of Opal's hands. He hadn't imagined it would ever come to this.

"Opal, my child, I must agree with Tarl. If he is capable he must confront the darkest corners of himself. He must find those shadows and turn them into light; find his own code and decipher it for himself."

Opal could not have felt more betrayed. Rembeu had begun to respect her; treat her with kindness and compassion but when it came down to it he thought her opinions were invalid. She rose from the table trying to halt the tears flooding inside her.

"Well, you can figure this out by yourselves." Opal took a deep breath and prepared for the next statement, "I will be staying here anyway. I have nothing to go back for." She shot a look at Tarl that made him feel like he had been stabbed through the heart.

He could muster only one word,

"No."

■   ■   ■

Tarl watched Opal walk away feeling like she had taken his body with her. He sat dumbfounded, his head throbbing even more so and the tremor was now rising up through his arm and into his shoulder. He looked desperately at Rembeu.

"It's alright my boy. I promise it will be alright." Rembeu wondered why he was making such indiscriminate promises. It was definitely not going to be alright.

"Rembeu she can't stay here. That is what I have been trying to tell you."

"It's alright Tarl. You just need to talk to her. We have time."

"We don't have time. Has Melik contacted us back?"

Rembeu shook his head resignedly.

"But I know we have time."

Tarl nodded. He hoped his uncle was telling him the truth but in all honesty he knew it didn't matter. Everything good was disappearing. He hadn't wanted to say anything but since he had entered into the memory he had felt great fears about his father. The feeling was so bad that when Opal had tried to rouse him, he had woken believing that his father was no longer alive.

"I should try to explain to Opal."

Rembeu looked directly at Tarl.

"I believe you will need her help to see the vision you are trying to relive. I will only give you one warning. Do not expect relief from the truth. When you find out what it is you think you so desperately need to know you may wish you had done as Opal suggested."

"Do you know something that I don't?" For the first time in his life he felt wary of his uncle. Irritation twisted into anger.

"You know in your heart that the truth must be discovered by the person requiring that knowledge. Others cannot inform you of your destiny."

So Rembeu wasn't going to tell him what he knew. He was going to use wisdom to avoid confrontation. Tarl tried to calm the fury building in his chest. The reality was that he could course only one river at a time. The thought reminded him of the vision in the Moon Gate. He had to speak to Opal; convince her to come with them. It was imperative.

"I do think however," Rembeu began, "that you should give her a little time to calm down."

■   ■   ■

Opal couldn't go back to their room. All she could see was Tarl's face laughing from the other side of the petition. She climbed the stairway up to the platform and stood at a side rail looking at the illuminated tiles down below. A wistful smile rose as she realized that, from this perspective, the many separated symbols on the stones below created one large symbol. She had no idea what it represented but it was beautiful: A swirling pattern twisted like three rivers in and out of the shadows as if scooping up energy as it swam.

Opal breathed a huge sigh. Was she doing the right thing staying here? Or was she doing it to hurt Tarl? It was all so confusing. Lying on one of the recliners she began to feel completely alone. The stars glimmered down at her and she wished, against all practicality, that they would send her a message, a sign. But they just twinkled in the blackness as if there was not a care in the world. She crossed her arms trying to protect herself from the cool night air. She was so very tired. Her eyelids closed.

■   ■   ■

Tarl returned to the room. Opal wasn't there. He lay down on one of the comfortable mattresses. He would just rest for a moment and then look for Opal.

Rembeu had told him they were to be led to the House of Knowledge early the following morning. It all sounded very intriguing. Apparently their beliefs were intricately bound around the meanings of the sacred signs and astrology. In accordance, entry to this 'library' was only allowed at certain times. He wondered what they would find and hoped anxiously that whatever it was it would help them move on - with Opal.

The potion he had taken earlier made him feel as if he were fighting his own body. Emotions from opposite poles seemed to be battling it out inside him: Laughter fought tears; anger fought calm. He rubbed a palm across his stomach trying to quiet the demons. If he could relieve his headache, maybe he could think more clearly. He just needed to rest, just for a moment.

Rembeu returned to find Tarl sound asleep on one of the beds and Opal missing. He wasn't worried about her physical well being but he was certainly worried about her emotional state. And Tarl's express desire to suddenly address his past wasn't helping. But he knew it was a course his nephew would eventually have to explore. Tarl would never find his full power without first clearing the past. Rembeu just wished it could have been done before all of this.

Rembeu sat down to read the books Shaief had given him after dinner. They contained basic translations for the majority of the symbols that guided these people's lives. He positioned himself underneath one of the illuminated tubes and began to study.

"Rembeu, come in, over."

Rembeu dropped the book in his hurry to grab the Voicer. "Melik, thank goodness! What's happening up there? Over."

"Sorry Rembeu but I'm afraid I was right. I was hit by an electrical charge from one of the time distortions. The force of the magnetic flux density is strong enough to alter the direction of the magnetic fields. I've been able to ride this one out but the only reason we are able to communicate is because we reside on different paths. Over." Melik's anxiety was coming over loud and clear. Rembeu's heart felt like it was skipping beats.

"What does that mean for the planet? Over." Rembeu could feel his brow beading with sweat.

There was a slight hesitation.

"I can't assess what's happening down there. I am being buffeted through constantly varying time-storms. I can no longer calculate the interactions of kaon decays; I can no longer use time-measurements to calculate the portal openings. I am being played with like a toy. Over." Melik was defeated. Static was beginning to jam the connection.

"Are you saying you are in a different time sector to the planet? Over."

"Affirmative. O...r.".

"Melik, we're going to lose contact again, can you give me any information that might help?"

"I'm afraid, my dear friend, t...t it is up to you and Tarl now. I am s... ry, I c... n..." There was a sudden burst of static before Melik's voice could be heard again. "Oh no..."

"Melik? Melik? Please, if you can hear me, keep trying to make contact. Melik?" But Rembeu had an awful feeling that there was no one at the other end. He buried his head in his hands. "Melik," he whispered.

Rembeu decided he would tell no one until this whole thing was over. There was no need to cause more distress. Slowly he picked up his book of symbols and tried to read through a glaze of tears.

Tarl heard Rembeu's voice calling him. He was dreaming he was asleep and Rembeu was trying to rouse him. The more Rembeu called his name the closer he came to realizing he was dreaming reality. The familiar throb of his head reminded him of everything. His body jumped with a start. The warm glow of early morning sun filled the room and soft sweet birdsong spilled through the air.

"I must have fallen asleep." Tarl stared into Rembeu's eyes and looked around the room. "Where is Opal?"

"Now now, let's not start the day by traumatizing ourselves."

"No, you don't understand, I meant to go and talk to her last night."

"Not to worry. Nothing has changed I'm afraid, so you'll still have plenty of groveling to do." Rembeu forced a smile before turning round to pick up the books he had read all through the night and tried not to think about Melik. There would be plenty of time to grieve later.

"You've talked to her?"

"Yes, yes, she slept on one of those recliner chairs upstairs. I can't imagine that it would be very good for your back."

Tarl tried to hide his frustration.

"Did you talk to her? I mean did you try to explain?"

Rembeu turned back to face Tarl. His eyes were slightly squinted.

"You know that is something you must discuss with her. It is definitely not my place to interfere."

"Yes I know, I'm sorry, I just... I've just made such a mess of things."

"Mess?" Rembeu snorted in disbelief. "What absolute nonsense. How do you think we got this far?" He moved over to Tarl's side. "I have never been more proud of anyone in my life. Now come on, we haven't got time for self pity; we have answers to search for." He threw one of their packs at him and moved toward the door.

They met a group at the place they had eaten dinner the previous evening. Opal was waiting at the front of the crowd listening to Shaief give instructions. Mohmed and several of the members that had sat at the round table the day before were dispersed amongst the crowd also listening intently. Shaief made a motion that acknowledged Rembeu and Tarl's arrival. Tarl tried to maneuver through the crowd to get Opal's attention but Shaief had already begun moving them forward.

The lengthy journey took them past buildings of such intricate and incredible design that Tarl could feel his awe overpowering the conflicting emotions inside him. He hoped once the potion wore off he would regain some control. The side effects had been overwhelming.

Opal could feel Tarl the moment he arrived but chose not to acknowledge him at this stage. She still had no idea what she was going to do. Seeing his face would just make her more confused. She had felt him press through the crowd and then just linger far enough behind her that he could remain unseen. His hurt throbbed inside her chest like fire. Obviously he had mixed feelings also. Tarl's body was now wracked with clashing emotions and it ached with searing pain. Opal wondered how he could possibly function with all of that going on inside him. Guilt charged through her. She had tried to access him last night to alleviate some of his pain but it had felt like she was on another plane. It was impossible to reach him. Why couldn't she help him? That was what she was supposed to be able to do.

Rembeu was now starting to recognize the symbols represented on the pavement. He read as he moved over them. 'Life...force, ... two twisting structures...of living kind, ...joined by a third, ...to complete the power, ...the light...of seven, ...drawn in circles of enigma, the seven spinning wheels...of light, ...the ladder of hope,... the seven directions: North, West, South, East... Above, Below, Within, ...the enigma of time, ...the sound of planet, ...astral chords, ... the meeting of minds, ...the gateway to peace'. And on it went. Some he could not understand and he felt it important that he did. He moved over to Shaief to have him translate. What he didn't realize was that this information would be a crucial part of their next step.

The library proved to be a huge and magnificent building. A simple sandstone arch, engraved with symbols, gave entrance to a cavern that resembled the inside of an enormous geode. Hidden luminescent lights sparkled through the arched crystal-encrusted ceiling which displayed millions of hanging quartz clusters. The ceiling was so high that the clusters sparkled like stars. Polished opal walls swirled with color and hid carefully placed symbols which swam across the surface. The text was not only perfectly symmetrical, it was incredibly beautiful. Along these walls, in between the text, at equally spaced intervals, were solid crystal shelves holding numerous enormous ancient books. Huge raised quartz slabs stood like chess pieces along the west and east walls upon which sat bold examples of the natural symmetry of the seven crystal systems.

Scattered clusters of rising crystals rose from the floor in between a smooth path that traced from the entry to the far north side of the room. In the center of the path a huge crater-like hole fell beneath the surface, where deep inside, a prism of azurite stood protected by the crevice walls. The stone scattered light forward leading the eye toward something: And that something was indeed extraordinary.

At the far end of the path a tall oblong object made of double terminated crystals rose. They glistened with the refractions of the opal walls. Above them several very long quartz crystals hung on threads.

Rembeu noticed that as this device stood at the north corner, so too the south, east and west corners held smaller replicas of the impressive instrument.

As soon as Opal glanced at the surroundings she knew her difficult decision was made. This had to be her new home. When she sighted the crystal device at the end of the path she felt her heart swell with light. Words and music filled her head as if she were being called toward it.

Shaief spoke out softly but his voice echoed melodically around the huge room.

"This is our…" he seemed to have trouble translating the description. One of the other members said something to him with the same gentle tones. Shaief nodded. He decided to explain how it worked rather than defining it by one foreign word. "This instrument holds the music of light," he uttered reverently; "it is the catalyst we need to activate the portal to transcend this plane. It has existed from before our records of time. You see, when the Great Disaster destroyed most of this continent and killed nearly all the Masters of Knowledge, the people considered survival there only task. The hum of his voice resonated around them.

Rembeu tapped Tarl on the shoulder and whispered.

"Looks a bit like the Radiant, don't you think?"

"I was thinking the same thing. How *did* your Radiant lessons go with Umbra?" Tarl already knew the answer.

"Not so good actually."

"Didn't ever start them?"

"Well I did start them," Rembeu began, defiance coloring his words, "but… well, actually no I didn't." He looked a bit grumpy. "Umbra was so terrified I would mess up her vibrations she kept giving me ideas and encouraging me to do some scientific research on them." He looked guiltily at Tarl, "Well, you know what I'm like when I've got an idea." A sly look lit his face. "She must have spent all her spare time thinking up those ideas."

Shaief was still talking.

"Those that survived were the physically strong. The Masters of Knowledge were not able to endure the conditions. The few that did survive taught their bodies to hibernate for long periods of time. It is due to their incredible sacrifices that we have our population today. Unfortunately though, the Knowledge was lost forever.

"Many of us have spent our lives studying. We understand the basis of the symbols but there are several obstacles. First, the symbols continue to evolve." He gestured to a row of symbols along the west wall. "It is as if they were programmed to change but we have no conception of what this means. Secondly, the application of these symbols eludes us. We do know that there is a connection between each of the symbols and there is also a connection between the symbols and the musical vibrations of this instrument but it seems that a protective device has been put in place so that if the wrong vibrational code is activated it reverses the portal's potential. The more we try and fail the further backwards we go."

Rembeu turned back to the walls to regard the symbols more closely.

"Tarl look," he whispered.

"They're changing?" Tarl thought his eyes were playing tricks.

Rembeu quickly opened one of the books he had read from the night before but felt overwhelmed. Every symbol along the wall had begun transforming.

Tarl watched just one symbol carefully as it altered.

"Try to decipher what one symbol is conveying as it changes. Maybe each symbol is its own entity, you know, its own sentence."

"Good idea," Rembeu stood still as he focused on just the one symbol.

Opal walked slowly up to the beautiful crystal instrument and gazed at it in awe. Scattered around its base were several different sized crystal bowls polished smooth. To its left sat a table spilling with crystal wands. She looked up at the dangling crystals above her and then across the horizontal layers of the prisms. Her hands drifted above each layer but not touching them directly. Closing her eyes, she felt the musical vibrations grow inside her.

"Each layer of crystals represents the layers of existence; other planes and civilizations." Shaief moved nearer to Opal.

Opal's voice rang out around the room.

"There is a gap here. Something is missing."

Shaief followed her line of vision. He was amazed no one had seen it before.

"I believe you are right. Come Mohmed, look." Mohmed approached.

Opal lifted her hands toward the crystals dangling from the ceiling hoping one of them would be the missing one but none of them felt right. Her eyes scanned the rest of the room for the missing crystal.

Rembeu stood back in surprised satisfaction. The symbols were finally making sense. He leant over Tarl's shoulder and whispered thoughtfully.

"I think these symbols," he pointed to the path and then arched a forefinger in the direction of the entryway, "are out of sequence. Obviously they have been respectfully copied but, I think they have done so without true comprehension." Rembeu could feel the inkling of reason twinkling inside him. Possibilities were slowly forming.

"But why would they copy something they did not understand?"

"The seven keys!" Rembeu cried too loudly and winced as his voice resounded around the room. He had everyone's attention.

"Give me the pack Tarl, we need the Elestial crystal!"

Tarl's eyes widened in horror and then shut tight in fear. He remained paralyzed. The truth was about to come out.

"Come on boy, give me the pack." Rembeu reached over and slid the pack off his immobilized nephew's shoulder. "You look like you've seen a ghost."

Tarl began to stammer as Rembeu shuffled through the pack. "Oh uncle, oh I've done something terrible."

Opal thought Tarl was about to confess about the potion he had consumed and wondered why he felt the need to free himself of guilt right at this very moment but when she saw what Rembeu held in his hand and his horrified expression she remembered the damaged Elestial crystal. She ran over to Rembeu.

"Rembeu it wasn't his fault, I should have been more careful." Tarl's surprise at Opal's offering rendered him speechless.

Rembeu couldn't say anything either. The importance of this crystal was beyond his explanation. He held the crystal out to Opal as if he were a small boy who held his dead puppy in disbelief.

The crystal's energy engulfed her like a flaring fire. She looked down upon it amazed and curious.

"This is it," Opal said simply. "This is the missing crystal." She shook her head in wonder. "The damaged end has opened up another energy path," a smile rose on her face as she looked up at Rembeu, "this is the missing part."

"It's alright?" Rembeu frowned skeptically.

"It is better than alright, it is perfect."

"Very lucky." Rembeu's crumpled face had stretched into astonished delight. He patted a very surprised and unfathomably relieved Tarl on the shoulder.

Shaief conveyed the notable result to the other members who all looked very impressed. Rembeu passed the Elestial crystal to Opal and began the telling of his discovery.

"The first message," Rembeu began, "is that of the seven sacred directions: North, South, East, and West, Above, Below and Within." He faced the north end and pointed to the crystal device and then waved a hand to point out the replicas standing at the south, east and west corners. He pointed to the ceiling of crystal clusters. "Above," and he motioned toward the prism of azurite buried inside the crater at the center of the room, "and Below: Embodying the infinite universe and the finite world we stand on."

Shaief was fascinated.

"And Within?" he asked.

Rembeu gazed kindly at the crystal in Opal's hands.

"The Elestial Crystal. This stone carries the memories of time before humans existed. It holds the essence of all life and the memory of all death."

Opal cautiously carried the stone toward the crystal instrument. Shaief watched her unable to hide his fear. "Please be careful."

"It is all right Shaief. I can feel the harmony within the crystal. It will guide me. I promise to listen carefully." She gently pushed the crystal into the opening. She adjusted it slightly until it felt properly positioned. When she heard a small click she stood back unsure of what to expect. Slowly the Elestial crystal started to glow.

Tarl felt a strange shiver curl along his spine as a cool tingling began to disperse up the back of his neck. It pulsed across his skull and out across his brow.

"It is working," she whispered as though any loud noise may disrupt its function. Its warmth reached out for her. The vibration was welcoming. It whirred in her stomach and stretched out like growing wheel within her body.

The layered crystals began to glimmer and slowly each and every crystal in the room lit up glowing with blues and purples. The corresponding instruments at the corners of the room began to hum softly. It was the same melody she had heard in her head earlier.

"Look," Tarl was gazing wide-eyed at the wall to his left. Rembeu followed his eyes. Each of the symbols had changed to represent only one particular character.

"That's the first symbol I spoke of. It denotes The Seven Directions," he stated calmly.

"What is the second?" Tarl asked keen to continue.

"Yes, that also represents a combined significance. Seven golden keys each held within the segment of a circle. At the center of the circle there is a square divided into seven shapes. I believe the seven crystal systems must combine with the seven notes of the universal planes." He gestured toward the large examples along the walls of the seven crystal systems. "Perhaps each member could stand beside one of the crystal systems. Opal, can you feel this?"

She closed her eyes and raised her hands before feeling the pull of certain keys.

"Yes, it is quite strong," she answered. "I am ready."

As each member touched the crystal systems in turn, Opal played the corresponding key. The cubic system generated a 'G' note and then glowed in bold ruby, the hexagonal a 'D' which lit up like an emerald and so on. The beautiful sounds of the crystal instrument vibrated around them imbuing them with tranquility.

As the last note was played the symbols on the walls all transformed into the image Rembeu had just described. The combined notes continued to ring out softly. Tarl was feeling rather light headed. He wasn't sure if it was excitement or exhaustion. What he didn't mind was that although his arm still shook uncomfortably, his headache had all but disappeared.

"Right, the next?"

"Seven spinning wheels: One inside the other."

Shaief knew this one only too well.

"The seven systems of the body."

"Exactly right. But I think that the spectrum is also at its center. You see there: The seven colors of white light. Now let's have a look around to see what would correlate with that idea." Everyone scanned the room looking for spinning wheels. Eventually all eyes turned back to Rembeu. "Yes well that one is a little more difficult to decipher."

Tarl's eyes moved over to Opal. She stood calmly, her back toward him and her hands moving in undulating motions over the crystal instrument. He caught a reflection from one of the crystal bowls at its base. The bowls. Slack jawed he pointed at them.

"Of course! Opal can you access the centers by using those crystal bowls."

Opal opened her eyes and moved her hands down to the crystal bowls. As her hands passed over them they each turned a different color. Her hands then moved over the crystal wands piled on the table above them. Each had a corresponding counterpart. She ran the matching wand around each of the crystal bowls. High pitched notes rang out and their individual colors blazed brightly across the crystal lit room. The symbols changed again in confirmation.

"The next was, now let me think…" The silence was tangible. Now that they had activated this part of the system the symbols had stopped revolving. If Rembeu forgot their order they were stuck there, in limbo. "Oh yes, I like this one." Audible sighs were heard over the humming notes. "A difficult one. It combines the twist of two rivers joined by the rungs of a ladder inside a pentagram."

Tarl face was expressionless.

"What does it signify?"

"The meeting of body and mind," Rembeu continued, "the spiraling ladder represents life; DNA – present in almost every living thing. The mystic symbol of the five-sided pentagram represents life force – an awakening of consciousness." He walked over to the azurite crystal sunk in the center of the room. "I bet this… ahh, yes, see, it is centered inside a pentagram. We must be able to activate it somehow."

Mohmed walked slowly over to the large imbedded stone. He took a triangular object out of his pocket and placed it upon the apex.

"This has been passed down through many many generations. I knew it was invaluable but its secret was lost long ago. The center fits onto the apex of this stone but I have had no idea how to use it. It is the triangle of life."

Mohmed twisted the triangle until it fit comfortably and then removed his hand. The stone glowed bright blue and then suddenly a twisted helix grew upward within the center of the azurite. The spiral rotated as if it were beginning life all over again. They all looked over to the wall. The symbols changed once again.

"And the last?" Mohmed asked.

"Well actually I'm not entirely sure." Everyone remained motionless as though if they stood very still something would happen.

"But we'll be stuck here." Tarl tried not to panic but somehow he knew it was time. There was energy building inside him.

"Mmm, well I'm sure we will work it out together." Rembeu was thinking hard; only too aware of how little time they had. He pushed the memory of his conversation with Melik aside. "There are many other symbols. It seems to me that each of these other symbols corroborate the importance of the prime ones we have acted upon." Rembeu paused. "If I'm right, the final activating symbol is very interesting. I really don't know what to make of it. Many elements of the other symbols are contained in this one. This symbol is of a male encircled by a serpent. The same rings that circle within each other surround his head and above these rings is a kind of crown. A key is hooked over a finger on his left hand and he is surrounded by a divided pentagram."

The members of the council were all nodding in recognition of the symbol.

"Perhaps," Tarl thought out loud, "the serpent represents the helix?" He pointed to the shining blue azurite with its internal twirling spiral.

"I agree very much on that possibility," Shaief agreed with a nod.

"So do I," Rembeu answered, "any other thoughts?"

"It could also be the ascent of human life or growth," Tarl offered.

"Good Tarl."

Mohmed whispered to Shaief. Shaief nodded.

"Mohmed has reminded me of a saying: 'When the serpent awakes, the visions will call'."

"Where does that saying come from?" Rembeu knew this was important.

"There is a legend that has passed but it could be perhaps, nothing more than that?"

"Any information could spark someone else's thoughts."

Shaief nodded and went on.

"It is said there will be a boy child born of the sun. His image is said to have appeared after the Great Disaster apparently from nowhere. He spoke to the people and told them to have faith in themselves and said their survival was imperative for the future. Hope was given to those who did survive. He told the people he was a child of the Keeper; the Keeper of Light and promised he would return. When he did return he wanted the people to remind him of Truth and Light."

Rembeu went cold. His head turned very slowly to rest on Tarl. Tarl saw the movement from the corner of his eye and with a horrible feeling of apprehension slowly turned his head in his uncle's direction. The look in Rembeu's eyes was enough. Tarl slowly shook his head. And yet as he did so, something deep inside him was telling him it was alright; that he would know what to do. The tingling sensation in his neck and head grew stronger and now curved right around his forehead buzzing at his brow. It was not unpleasant; in fact it was strangely comforting.

Rembeu moved over to stand opposite Tarl. His words were simple.

"It's time," he said quietly.

"I know." Tarl's head began to nod.

Opal had managed to keep the vibrations emanating without using her hands. The sweet melody lingered and drifted through the air. She turned in time to see Tarl's frightened face become brave. Her heart felt as if it had stopped still.

"I have to find the portal don't I?" He asked Rembeu.

"I believe that will do the job." Rembeu smiled an uncle's smile and Tarl was grateful. He smiled back. Tarl began to move toward the Elestial crystal, looking into Opal's worried eyes as he passed.

"It's alright," he whispered to her almost believing it. "I'll need your help to maintain the present vibrations. My only concern is that I may upset them as I prepare."

"I know you can do it," she responded somewhat unconvincingly. That made him smile again.

Tarl stood in front of the Elestial crystal, took a deep breath and closed his eyes. The feeling inside him was growing more and more powerful like a tumbling snowball. He wouldn't even have to touch the crystal; it was just a means to empower his energy.

Opal stood in awe as Tarl quickly placed himself in some type of trance. She was finding it quite easy to control the instrument now and could observe her surroundings at the same time. She watched as rings of light expanded outwards around his head like a multi-hued corona. Checking his face, she tried to sense any discomfort. Only a feeling of divine serenity flowed through her.

The tingling in Tarl's head expanded outwards. Simultaneously, he was moving and stationary. His insides were twisting uncomfortably and he was unsure what was happening. In all the past meditations he had not felt his physical body at all. Perhaps he was doing something wrong. He tried to concentrate. The strange winding feeling moved more freely. It rose within him lifting his head in elation. And then he saw it. It was as if he were observing the beginnings of life: A cell, its division, the helix.

Tarl was turning; slowly at first and then faster and faster. But he realized now, it wasn't his physical body. The movement was only part of his energy, he was stationary. Finally he had achieved it. Without losing touch with his physical being, he was able to raise his energies. This was the culmination of all his Teachings.

Most of the people's eyes were transfixed on the rings of light around Tarl's head. They knew instantly that he must have been responsible for the image seen so long ago. But how? He was only a boy. This image had been seen before any of them had been born.

When a great noise rattled at the center of the room everyone shifted their attention toward it. The blue azurite at the center of the room was rising and turning slowly.

Shaief stared in disbelief. For so very long they had tried to activate the keys in this room. For so very long they had failed. He and his people were about to face the truth, whatever it might be. His eyes fluttered closed briefly as he silently begged for the truth that he had believed in all his life.

A beam from its apex began to twirl around the room like a light house. The beam then twisted up to fire directly at the ceiling before being sucked right back down into the center of the stone and disappearing. Everyone waited.

They were right to do so: The azurite, now standing at floor level and reaching nearly as high as the ceiling began to move. The stone divided itself into three segments. These three sections began to move outwards toward the edges of the surrounding pentagram. A spiraling ladder now emerged from within the stone and glowed bright with white light. And, right above it, at half the height of the room, began to spin a small seed of light. The light grew bigger as it spun, expanding colors out into a horizontal wheel.

"That is it. You have opened the portal." Shaief both knew he had been right and still could not believe it was happening.

"Indeed I believe you are right," Rembeu couldn't conceal his delight, "and I believe, you Shaief, should be the first to visit your neighbors."

Shaief quickly turned to Mohmed and the others to see if they also chose him to honor this moment. A sea of delighted faces greeted him. Mohmed also chose to follow.

Rembeu quickly moved over to rouse Tarl. Tarl placed the memory into the Elestial crystal so that the portal could be opened by whoever could play the crystal instrument. Opal felt the memory enter the instrument. He opened his eyes and followed Opal's amazed stare. He smiled to himself. It was all true.

"Quickly, Tarl come on we must climb the ladder to access the portal. You too Opal, the reverberations will keep it open for a while." Rembeu was beckoning with vigor.

Tarl and Rembeu began to climb the ladder behind Shaief and Mohmed. Tarl looked down to smile at Opal but she wasn't there. He froze. Below him Rembeu tapped one of Tarl's feet.

"Come on, let's not dawdle."

"Opal?" Tarl eyes found the beautiful watery eyed girl standing in the same spot, unmoving. He had a sickening feeling she really was going to stay. "Come on, it's alright, I know it is."

Opal slowly shook her head and swallowed, trying to get vocabulary back into her throat.

"I cannot leave. I belong here." Her eyes scanned the opal walls. "I have discovered that I can feel this instrument without ever having used one before. I can teach these people how to use it to open the portal. If I do not, they will not be able to open it again even though you have placed your memory energy into the Elestial crystal. I just know I'm supposed to stay."

Tarl couldn't comprehend what was happening. She was absolutely right. Without her knowledge they couldn't open the portal. There hadn't been time to think of that. But there was the vision in the Moon Gate. He couldn't leave her here and he couldn't stay; there was something higher directing him now and it was beyond his control.

"But you'll miss our next opening." Tarl's voice was barely audible but she heard him. "You won't be able to come home." Opal nodded her head, her eyes cast downward.

Rembeu's dilemma was two-fold. He didn't want Opal to stay here either but he didn't want Tarl to regret this moment for the rest of his life. He looked up at Tarl.

"Quick, go and say good bye." They both climbed down the ladder and Rembeu turned his head upward wondering what Shaief and Mohmed had found up there.

Tarl would have fought lions to make her come with him but the thought of forcing her was inconceivable. Destiny was a cruel power that even he couldn't reckon with. He should have told her what he had seen in the Moon Gate. Why had he waited? Looking into those sad gray eyes he tried to make a mental image so as never to forget them. He cupped his fingertips below her chin.

"You can't stay here Opal. There is something I haven't told you."

"I know Tarl. I have felt your vision." She placed a forefinger to his lips. I know that is why you have been in such a hurry to try to figure out your dream. But sometimes we must choose a path that is our final freedom. I know what you have seen and so I will try to avoid it," she smiled wistfully, "I will never forget you, ever." Opal fingered the locket that he had given her. That day seemed so long ago.

Tarl could no longer speak. Sadness welled to the top of his throat and constricted it painfully. He searched her face for any leeway. There was none. She had decided and he was no part of her decision. Slowly he leant forward, his lips moving closer and closer to hers. Her soft mouth touched his. She wrapped her arms around him and he pressed harder. There was nothing about her he would not remember.

"Tarl, the portal is reducing, we have to go."

He wouldn't let go. He would just stay there kissing her forever. But something more powerful than human emotion was pulling him away. He let go, turned and walked back to Rembeu who was half way up the twisted ladder. He climbed each rung as if he were weighted by leaden boots.

Tarl didn't look back; couldn't look back. His heart was being ripped in two. Why wasn't there blood everywhere? This much pain should surely cause blood?

Tears coursed down Opals pale face. Why was she doing this? And then she remembered. It was not all about her. Everything imaginable was at stake. She could help and she knew this was what she was supposed to do. Wiping away her tears did not stop their flow. Tarl had not even turned to make a last farewell. She watched him disappear into the swirling wheel vortex.

'Goodbye,' she thought.

27

Violet Ascension

Now, both Tarl and Rembeu were trying to hide their grief from each other. As soon as Tarl felt the familiar pull of the vortex, the thump of his headache returned. He was glad. At least physical pain would distract him from his emotions. He did notice though, that something about his body was very different; it felt somehow lighter.

The force grew stronger as they were pulled toward the next path and then suddenly they were being sucked through something viscous. For just a moment it felt as if they were deep under water until suddenly, light and sound rushed at them like a blast. They lay still for a moment adjusting.

Shaief and Mohmed were patiently waiting for their companions to arrive and were surrounded by several others. Once his eyes had focused, Tarl looked around. Surprisingly he found himself in a similar structure to the one they had just transferred from. The dome was much larger but similarly encrusted with clusters of clear quartz. He could see no books; instead the smooth crystal walls held assorted quartz prisms. The walls suddenly reminded him.

Panicked, he swung back to catch the last glimpse of the closing portal. What had he done? He reached out to the passageway but it had all but disappeared.

"Tarl," Rembeu reached a comforting hand out to rest on his nephew's shoulder, "Tarl there are people here who would like to meet you."

Tarl pulled himself into the present and tried to focus. What was done was done. He turned to face the people gathered behind him. At first he thought he was looking at angels. Both the women and men wore loose fitting silken pants and long sleeved over-shirts. Their skin was a creamy white as was their long hair. The only differences lay in the color of their eyes. Their irises varied from pale blue to green, brown, red and yellow. But the one uniting characteristic that filled him with awe was the incredible circle of light that surrounded each of their bodies. One shone with lemon light, another with violet. Several auras shared colors which altered slightly as they stood and watched him. He was mesmerized.

"I am Tarl, and I am most pleased to meet you." He was surprised at how calm his voice sounded.

"And we are pleased also." The female's voice was soft and high-pitched with an accent that slid across the words making them sound slanted. It reminded Tarl of a reflective lake.

"And you also Mr. Rembeu." The woman smiled serenely at him, her long fair hair wafting slightly as she spoke. "We have waited a long time to meet you". She said, her lacey voice sounding both calm and strangely familiar.

"Thank you," Tarl said not really sure if he was thankful.

"Please do come, follow us, it has begun to chill."

Indeed there was a coolness in the air but it wasn't like any cold Tarl had felt before. It was strangely comforting; emotional rather than physical. He didn't quite understand. He noticed that Rembeu, Shaief and Mohmed had moved ahead and hurried to keep up with them.

The people they followed seemed to move effortlessly in front of him as if their bodies were less affected by gravity. Tarl forced himself to put one foot in front of the other, knowing each step was further away from her: Trying to put Opal out of his mind felt like he was giving up on her forever. Everything felt so heavy. If only the crushing pain of her loss would ease so that he could breathe properly.

Shaief wanted to express how grateful they were for this impossible opportunity. He could not imagine how long it would have taken his people to succeed at the transfer and from the sound of the situation they would definitely have been too late. Shaief patted Tarl on the arm and spoke proudly, momentarily interrupting his thoughts.

"This is the day our history begins. We shall never be able to give you the worth of our thanks."

"You don't need to thank me Shaief."

"Oh but you cannot imagine; this changes everything," Shaief intoned as he gazed reverently at the surroundings.

The words stung Tarl. Everything had changed.

"Please Shaief," Tarl murmured as he forced a direct stare into Shaief's eyes, "please just make sure you take care of Opal."

"Of course Tarl, we will take care of her. I promise she will be safe," Shaief assured him, understanding how hard it must have been for Tarl to say goodbye.

"I shouldn't have let her stay," Tarl confessed without meaning to.

"Come Tarl, there are great discoveries to be made here," Shaeif was gesturing around him, "and of course, discovery always leads to the uncovering of knowledge."

Tarl had had enough 'discovery' to last a lifetime.

"Yes I understand," he replied.

"Tarl you are not listening to the meaning of the words. You have accepted your destiny without letting providence inspire curiosity."

"I'm curious," he said defensively.

"Think about it Tarl. Everything you are learning is because you feel you have no choice. You have courage, yes, but despite what you may believe; heroism will not help you increase your abilities. You are missing revelations because you are not looking for them. Looking for the truth in those around you is not going to uncover your own truth. When you find it you will understand. When you understand, there will be no barriers to your destiny."

"My destiny is already decided." Tarl was feeling very tired again and Shaief was forcing him to think.

"Never accept that there is no purpose you cannot change."

These last words found a place in Tarl's mind that hinted at ideas he could not form. The pain in his head made them disperse. He let them go.

"Thank you Shaief, I will consider your words," was all Tarl could manage wondering if he'd even remember them tomorrow.

They were being led onto icy streets where hundreds of people stood, evidently waiting for them. The huge expanse in front of them consisted of golden shimmering pavements dusted with soft snow. The buildings surrounding them were all pyramid shaped but varied in size and angle. White sleet had settled on their peaks making them look like snow covered mountains.

Slow claps began to rise rhythmically as the people's auras glowed brightly. No one could have asked for a more beautiful or welcoming reception. Although Tarl was slightly embarrassed, he enjoyed watching Shaief and Mohmed walk up to the people greeting them warmly. Rembeu also seemed to be enjoying himself.

Tarl's awareness of the cool air was increasing. Looking skyward he hoped he may see falling snowflakes but was immediately captivated by something even more incredible. The sky shimmered with a curtain of luminous colors. He had heard of auroras being attracted to the earth's magnetic fields but had never seen one. The surrounding stone pyramids shimmered with the refracted light. How Opal would have loved this.

It must have been much later in the day than Tarl thought because he could see a washed out sun beginning to descend. One of the men that had greeted them on their entry was watching Tarl's response to the surroundings.

"It is very peaceful here, come we want to explain," he motioned a hand over toward one of the far pyramids, "you will be comfortable here." Rembeu attracted the attention of Shaief and Mohmed and they followed a small group over to the west.

Rembeu followed trying to keep his mind on how incredible this place was but his thoughts kept returning to Melik. He wondered how he was ever going to be able to tell Tarl of Melik's demise. And how were they going to make the exit from this path without Melik's help? Perhaps they would not. Perhaps they weren't meant to. Rembeu was determined to do everything he could to get Tarl home again. Parvo wasn't going to be left to deal with the loss of his wife and the loss of his son. Rembeu had no interest in his own outcome: He had played his part; now it was time to make sure that Tarl was going to be saved.

Tarl must take his place as The Keeper of Light; the position his mother was to pass on to him.

The group was ushered into one of the smaller pyramid structures through a sliding gold door. A narrow ascending tunnel led them to a small doorway which opened up to reveal a huge granite surfaced room; the high ceiling lifting to a perfect point. In the center of the room a complicated three dimensional mosaic of a compass rose from the floor indicating that the entry was aligned perpendicular to True North. Other than this, the space was rather bare.

A floor of polished amethyst swirled in front of them as they followed the group toward the back of the area. Rembeu was surprised that the walls neither held intricate decorations nor were they adorned with symbols. Instead smooth granite blocks puzzled their way along the surfaces, each appearing to be slightly different; cut precisely for their particular location in the building.

They were directed to an area toward the rear of the room and sat on the long backed granite chairs offered them. Several small doorways punctuated the walls around them and all were curious as to where or what they led to. The seats were extremely uncomfortable but the inhabitants sat upon them without concern.

"Again, we welcome you". The sounds that they heard were real enough except that no one's mouth had moved.

Tarl and Rembeu exchanged amused glances while Shaief and Mohemed looked delightedly at each other.

"You are telepathic," Shaief enthused, "but you can speak also." He directed his attention to the woman that had initially made contact.

Her gentle smile rested on each of them.

"Indeed I have been nominated to conduct your introduction as I have spent my life studying speech in order to make you more comfortable." Her voice was lovely. It tingled in the air, hanging there for a moment before dissipating. "I see however, it is quite unnecessary," she gave Tarl a special smile as if she knew he preferred her voice to her thoughts, "as you are all quite capable of receiving our suggestions".

Tarl felt meanings enter his mind but he could not form thoughts from them.

"I shall continue to use voice speech for now, until I feel you are all comfortable and until I believe you can ascertain who the speaker is. It is good practice for me also. The surrounding members are able to understand speech but only a few have mastered vocabulary. Do not be offended that they do not enter the conversation. For much of the time I will just be transferring their thoughts to you. It is also asked that you not be offended by our lack of introduction. You see, we have no use for names. We are able to access minds without this precursory requirement."

Suddenly all sorts of thoughts rushed into Tarl's mind - thoughts that he would prefer she not be able to 'hear'. He pressed his eyes shut and tried to turn his mind into a blank. It wasn't working. His head thumped with pain. His life story was rushing in and out: Opal was waving goodbye; his mother was lying dead in his father's arms. Visions flashed frantically as if desperate to get out. Tarl's eyes burst open to cast a horrified look in her direction.

The woman breathed in deeply; her eyes closed, and her head bent slightly.

'It is alright Tarl; I already know everything there is to know about you.' Her thoughts were floating in his mind amongst the flashing visions. 'I am placing a calming thought upon your mind-plane. Do not be frightened, it will just help you focus on what is at hand.' She opened her eyes again. 'You will soon learn that thought transference holds more answers for you than you could possibly have imagined.'

No words had been spoken. Tarl realized he had received the message of her thoughts. He had no idea what that meant but he was aware that it was not important just yet. A strange feeling overcame him and he knew that in time, understanding would come. With this thought, his mind became calm and dark and felt quite peaceful.

The others had waited in apparent silence. Rembeu sensed a connection had been reached but chose not to question it. Somehow Rembeu knew that Tarl would discover the truth here. It was time to face the consequences of what he had done to his nephew. He hoped his nephew wouldn't loathe him for it.

"Firstly," the woman intoned, "we must express our pleasure at your arrival. It has been a very long wait." The surrounding members sat serenely without expression. She directed her gaze at Shaief and Mohmed. "Our neighbors." Then she looked directly at Tarl. "And the child of the Seventh Fate."

Tarl swung a look over to Rembeu who met his eyes just for a moment. They were completely devoid of expression. Tarl decided to keep his eyes from straying. No expression from Rembeu was worse than a bad expression.

"Our dreamer has long been having visions of your visitation. We have spent much time preparing for The Shift. We hope to make your visit as comfortable and time efficient as possible.

"I will begin with Shaeif and Mohmed." They both looked very pleased. "When the time is reached we must open the portal to your world again. We have many crystals in our library that you must take back with you. These contain many truths which will allow you to access the depths and realms of nature that you will be required as your race ascends. You are now ready to move forward. Our wheel crystal will assist you in activating the acoustic centers of the brain. This will allow adjustment of the body's magnetic field which will enable you to use your crystal harmonizer."

Tarl couldn't believe what he had just heard. If the wheel crystal was all they needed to work their harmonizer then Opal would have no purpose there. He knew she shouldn't have stayed. He had to get her back but trying to get Rembeu's attention wasn't working. The woman's words were spellbinding.

"You also will learn to tune these crystals to your own path to recapture your missing past. So long as these crystals are honored you will find they will be an immeasurable source of information and enlightenment. You will even find that light energies will become apparent around your bodies as is ours. We have very little time. Your return must be tomorrow. Unfortunately, because the portal was opened in such unstable circumstances, it is only viable for one rotation of our moon.

"Although we shall see each other again, it will not be for a very long time. When we meet again, you shall have all the knowledge required to freely open the portal at any time you wish. And always remember, reciprocal knowledge is the key."

Tarl was suddenly renewed with hope. The portal would be open tomorrow morning. Somehow he would have to convince Opal to come back with him. The more time that went by made him realize how wrong it was to let her stay there. The visions from the Moon Gate flashed in his mind again. He pressed his eyes closed. He just wouldn't let it happen; couldn't let it happen.

The woman nodded toward Rembeu and Tarl.

"As you may have already guessed, we are Light Bearers. We have evolved beyond the restraints of the realities of the material world. Yes, we remain in human form and yet, we are able to move beyond these bodies." She smiled at Tarl as if he would understand.

"Human emotion, after all, is of great value. If it is used properly it can resolve karmic patterns. However, there is much greater possibility beyond the human form. It will not take long for you to begin sensing much of what is available." Her soft pale face rose to the ceiling as if she were receiving a message no one else could hear. "Yes, it is your way Tarl."

More people telling him he should know things he didn't. But he wasn't perturbed. It seemed when he needed to, he could find what it was that was required. This place was affecting him too. A strange feeling of being very far away and very close at the same time was starting to disturb him.

"You must prepare yourselves for the shift. We do not have long. We have to alter our plane to open the gateway to all that is flowing in and out of the continuum. A metamorphosis will begin to occur shortly that you may have difficulty understanding. Don't try to. Just let the energies flow through you. And don't allow fear to become part of the process.

"You have traveled through these evolutionary paths always spiraling upward, pulling these paths with you to balance the tearing universe. And you have woken here: The place of *your* awakening.

"We know you have seen wars caused by greed and the results when one sex tries to dominate the other. You have seen the desire for power destroy, and what insecurity can cause. You have seen overpowering technology emitting electromagnetic radiation which has disrupted the natural rhythm of the human, polluting the world and altering the energy fields: The long term exposure affecting thoughts, emotions and physical health; and damaging the planet's auric field. All these reach out and damage our cosmos creating the disturbances you have been trying to fight. Never forget that every thought that goes out will mould the universe.

"Such a strong light energy has lain dormant within you for so long now you have forgotten how to access it. But it is there, I promise."

From the corner of his eye Tarl saw Rembeu shift uncomfortably.

"Do not allow your previous rules to inhibit your abilities. Your imagination is only the beginning of what is possible." Tarl thought that wasn't much of a beginning.

"There is no light in negativity," she said with a knowing smile.

Tarl started to feel self-conscious and then stopped himself. If this was true he wanted to know what exactly was 'inside' of him. She looked pleased and raised her head again to open herself to a message.

"Now we acknowledge the contributing power of three, the triangle of expanding life. Karmic patterns have brought you together. You must be able to feel it?"

Tarl had no idea where this was going but without wanting to be ungrateful he tried to put pictures of food in his head so she would recognize his very human hunger. If she did she wasn't confessing.

"You are in tune with the galactic language of energy Tarl, so too is your female."

Tarl immediately lost interest in food. Was she talking about Opal?

"Yes, Tarl, together you make the key and key hole. You should not have allowed her to stay behind. You let fear influence your acceptance."

"But you are opening the portal tomorrow," Tarl's said, his heart jumping sickeningly. "We can get her to pass through."

For the first time her serene face dropped. She laid her sad eyes upon Tarl's.

"Movement through the portal can be only one way now Tarl. Greater understanding is required before the polarity can advance beyond its primary system."

"But," Tarl wanted to protest; threaten to go back with Shaief and Mohmed; to not return; to leave them all to find their own 'inner kingdom'. But it was pointless. If he didn't help these people it would not be long before there was nothing to go back to. Or for that matter, exist in.

"The third twist of the rope is your uncle – he ties the web to its stabilizer. He is the inception of your understanding and the teacher of your growing strength."

Tarl didn't appear to be impressed. Anger was building inside him again and he didn't know how to control it. Trying to think calming thoughts didn't help. All he could see was Opal pummeling her hands against a closed portal crying out as she realized her mistake.

"Tarl you must concentrate," her delicate voice resounded in his head. It was uncannily soothing. He forced his aching, hungry body to pay attention.

"Now, our world has only one anomaly left to fight: Time. Brevity must be addressed. The time distortions on all planes have become increasingly apparent."

Rembeu thought of Melik. He wondered what indeed they would be going back to when and, indeed if, they returned.

"Do you have any information on the damage?" asked Rembeu.

Tarl thought this a strange question. Why hadn't he just asked Melik? His thoughts were interrupting his concentration again. He tried to focus as she continued.

"Your travel through each plane has smoothed those worlds for a while; however, your plane and this final path have suffered concerning time clashes."

"Our path?" Tarl had a terrible feeling about his father. What was happening to him?

"Indeed. Perhaps it has been the most devastated. And conceivably that is because you belong back there."

"Why would where I belong make a difference?" Tarl thoughts were fading again.

"You haven't any idea?" It was more a statement than a question. Tarl shook his head.

"Have you not wondered why the time clashes appeared in your world first?" The question was guiding his thoughts. "Perhaps you can think about this and we shall discuss it tomorrow. I know you require sustenance. We shall meet in the evening room and have further discussions over supper."

Tarl's relief was clear. His body deflated in resignation as several of the members rose easily from their chairs. His legs were tingling with impending numbness and his back took a few moments to straighten. How did these people use these chairs? He and Rembeu traipsed behind them as they made their way outside.

The deep purple sky fell around them like a comforting blanket. High above them the colored rays of the aurora shimmered. They walked the snowy streets passing exquisite ice sculptures of prancing animals and, higher beyond their heads, were sculptures of flying birds; wings outstretched, heads held high. A moon-dial stood in the center of a hidden courtyard catching the icy moonlight and spilling a triangle of light across the snow covered pavers.

Tarl enjoyed watching his steamy white breath roll from his mouth. He scuffed a sandal at the icy ground. It was definitely snow. He could feel it; feel the cold and yet he was not cold. Rembeu also appeared to be fascinated by the phenomenon. Tarl waltzed up to his uncle.

"It's obviously below freezing and yet no one appears to be cold: Me included."

"Indeed. It really is quite remarkable. I have been wondering if it has something to do with energy. I have read of an ancient civilization that uses an energy form called TUMO that helps people withstand subfreezing temperatures. Apparently the initiate would have to perform a series of exercises while they were naked and wet at altitudes much higher than our Mt Atlas. They apparently learnt to generate heat of such intensity that it could melt snow. Perhaps with telekinetic powers these people have been able to generate the energy to encompass a few of their guests." Rembeu nudged Tarl in the ribs.

"Well hopefully that means they like us." Tarl's joke came out flat.

"What, you think there is something they're not telling us?"

"No. I don't know. No. I'm just hungry."

"Just a big growing boy, aren't you." Rembeu had to raise an arm to ruffle Tarl's hair. "I tell you what though; you could do with a bit of a haircut."

Tarl patted the thick straight hair behind his shoulder blades. It needed to be brushed. He thought of Opal's lovely long shiny hair braided with silk.

"Yeah," he said trying to keep up his uncle's good spirits. Something was holding him back about telling his uncle about his plans to bring

Opal into this plane. Remaining silent, he walked beside his uncle trying to understand all these new strange feelings.

■　■　■

The supper room was extraordinary. It was another triangular roofed creation that was augmented by intricate designs flowing upward from floor to ceiling. On the east facing wall, the colors worked in such a way as to imitate sunrise and on the west facing wall sunset was displayed in the same striking manner. Interspersed along the center, large candles, shaped in animal forms, glowed softly.

The woman's voice chimed in the sonorous room.

"The design that appears to be sunrise is based on the Kundalini fire. It represents the heat which extends from the base of the spine to the crown. Rembeu your thoughts are correct."

"So no thoughts are sacred?" Rembeu asked laughing.

"Of course thoughts are sacred. Unfortunately for you I have been attuned to your thought vibrations and am unable to return my focus to others until we have completed our quest."

Tarl thought it wasn't so long ago that he would have been delighted to be told he was part of a quest. Now, however, the word made him feel exhausted.

Several round tables were scattered across the room. Rembeu chose one near the center of the room. At least it was quiet here. All he could hear was the crackling of the burning candles; a gentle echo in the vast room. Speech seemed to be an unnecessary disruption.

"You are merging Tarl, you adapt well," her comforting voice rang out around him.

Small plates of a thick bright green soup were placed in front of them. Tarl hesitated. It was too small to be a main meal. He assumed it was an appetizer. He looked around to see what his companions were doing.

Shaief and Mohmed were deep in conversation with each other and did not even seem to be aware that food was sitting waiting for them to consume. The members of the other tables gazed reverently at their plates. It seemed appropriate to wait for a signal.

Her beautiful voice raised his attention. It was so familiar and yet he couldn't place it. The memory of those sounds teetered at the edge of his mind teasing him.

"There is a matter of the utmost importance that we must discuss."

They listened intently, waiting as she scooped a golden spoon into her mouth. Tarl gratefully followed. The dish had the tang of sweet green peas. As he swallowed he felt a warming light flood through his body.

Rembeu's curiosity was buoyed as Melik's last words drummed through his mind.

"And that matter has to do with the time disturbances?" he asked.

"Time disturbances are a contributing factor. However it is more complicated than that. As you know time disturbances have altered awareness in regards to the corresponding paths. You have activated six of the seven energy wheels of the universe and by doing so have exacerbated the time disruption."

"There is only one more energy wheel?" Tarl's voice was filled with frustration. They had only one more path before being able to return home and Opal had come so close.

"This has resulted in time passing slightly differently in each alternate plane and this will continue until you activate the seventh and final energy wheel of the universe.

Tarl was wondering what time his father was experiencing; and Opal. If time had jumped forward in Opal's plane wouldn't that mean that the portal would not open?

"Tarl, the portal-opening is being directed from this plane. That is why we must form the coordinate-bond from the time on our path."

Melik's strained words were coming back to Rembeu.

"We only seem to have experienced several slight forward jumps. Are the other planes experiencing only forward movement?"

The woman appeared to wait for a message.

"You must try to understand that time in fact is fluid. It doesn't exist as you have previously believed it did." She looked directly into Tarl's eyes. "You may have flashes of things that you understand as being your future, for now you will just have to accept that this is not necessarily so. You will come to understand before you leave here."

The vision in the Moon Gate was confusing enough. Now he didn't even know from 'when' the vision was supposed to represent. It didn't make sense, how could things have happened in his past without him knowing about it? And how could he have experienced a future and not remember it?

Rembeu realized Melik had been on to something revolutionary. A sharp pang struck him in the chest but tried not to clutch at it. The pain seared for a moment and made it almost impossible to breathe. It subsided just as quickly and Rembeu took a deep breath. Quickly he glanced at Tarl but thankfully he hadn't noticed. After supper he would need to make himself a potion. Ignoring the signs was not going to help anyone. All these plane transferences in such unstable conditions were a lot for an 'old man' to take, he thought. A memory of Cymbeline ran across his vision. They were very young. She was beating him in a race: The older brother losing to his sister because of a weak heart. The irony was not beyond him. He wondered if the pain of missing her would ever fade and then realized that he hoped it would not.

Tarl was glad to see more small plates being placed in front of them. One was topped with a swirl of deep purple paste. When the smooth mixture touched his tongue he thought his auric field may be becoming visible. Checking his limbs, he was disappointed to see no discernable difference. Rembeu, did not appear to have any glow around him either.

"Our food is grown within these pyramids." The woman had been observing Tarl and could not hide her humor, "Most of our generative pyramids are made from granite. Its minerals act like a conduit, harnessing rising energy. We have discovered that these high intensity fields not only allow early sprouting and fast growth but the plants harness energy and light, which we then absorb as we eat. "Eating this food will help you reconnect with your guides on even higher planes."

"There are even higher planes than this?" Tarl was fascinated.

Her laughter was like softly ringing bells.

"Yes, of course, but you do not need to access them yet. You have already been guided through the first dimensional barrier."

"Please, tell me about them."

"They exist in different dimensional fields to us. Beings in these fields are able to mutate and change form. Their advancements allow them to consciously occupy infinity. They are able to move amongst time and are interconnected with all other dimensions.

"They can change from the human body?" Tarl liked that idea.

"It is difficult for you to comprehend beyond your three dimensional perception, but eventually you will be able to access these planes. Just being here, you are discovering multidimensional consciousness."

More food was produced. He eagerly dipped his small golden spoon into a tall crystal glass. A creamy white mixture was layered upon a fluffy base of deep orange. He found the taste indescribable and irresistible. The food seemed to ease his headache, although his left arm had become practically immobile.

When Tarl and Rembeu finally went to bed in another simple structure close by, their minds were reeling with information.

By a burning candle shaped like a dove they talked until they fell asleep.

"You know I've heard that granite can help direct intergalactic communication." Rembeu was smiling across at Tarl.

"Have you now? Well, that would be even more fascinating to me if I could understand what on 'time's behalf' that means." Tarl raised his eyebrows.

Rembeu laughed. It had been a while since they had shared a joke. He so wanted to say something funny but couldn't think of anything.

"That's alright Rembeu, there not a lot to make us laugh at the moment."

"I didn't say anything Tarl. Did you just read my mind?"

"I don't know, did I?"

"Indeed I think you did!" He rested a proud gaze upon his nephew. Perhaps Tarl could fight it; perhaps he and Parvo had not made such a terrible mistake after all.

"Think something else," Tarl was feeling rather excited.

"O.K." The next thought that came into his mind wasn't one he wanted to project. Guilt followed and then he tried to cover it with a childish joke he used to tell Tarl when he was little.

Tarl's unconvincing smile revealed that he hadn't done a very good job of covering up. Apparently Opal was on both their minds.

"I'd forgotten that joke, I used to love it when you told me that joke didn't I?"

Rembeu nodded, his face dissolving into the wistfulness of the memory.

Tarl didn't want either of them to be sad, not right now.

"Hey hey, don't start getting all mushy on me now," Tarl said.

"Mushy? Where do you pick up this dreadful language?"

"Oh, I've been around. And I'll have you know I intend to pick up some intergalactic words while I sleep."

"Well, hopefully whoever transcribes this language will have better pronunciation than the 'mushy' people."

Tarl tried unsuccessfully to keep a straight face. They both started quivering with the kind of laughter that has no real foundation; it just feels too good to stop.

Finally, just as Tarl was about to drift into sleep he murmured.

"I will get her back Rembeu, I don't know how, but I will get her back."

Rembeu wasn't so sure.

■　■　■

Tarl's night was filled with the dream he had tried unsuccessfully to re-enact in the last plane. This time however, he dreamt it over and over again; each time another segment of memory opening up to him.

A voice inside him cried out.

"The image will keep replaying until you have discovered the truth." Tarl tossed and turned not sure he wanted to know the truth any more. The final image came just before dawn.

Tarl woke with a jolt. Slick with sweat, his body ached like never before. Turning to tell Opal what he had seen, he remembered she wasn't there. He had to get to her. His urgency was electric. As he tried to get out of bed his body felt as if it were weighed down with pain. He had given up on trying to move his left arm. It was of little use to him now.

Rembeu woke with the sound of Tarl's grunts.

"Tarl," Rembeu murmured, "what's wrong?"

"I saw it, I saw that day, I saw them shoot her."

Rembeu went cold. It was as if he had lost whatever it was that had previously protected him from the freezing temperatures.

"What exactly did you see?" He pulled the blanket up around his shoulders but it didn't help.

"I'm not sure exactly, but I did see them shoot my mother. I can't believe I was wrong. I was sure Opal's parents weren't responsible." Tarl fought the pain and struggled to sit up.

"And that is all you saw?"

"Yes, I think so," Tarl nodded slowly as if trying to grasp a missing piece.

Rembeu sighed. Perhaps now wasn't the time to be concerned about all of this.

"Come on, we should go and find Shaief and Mohmed; perhaps breakfast with them before they return."

Tarl lifted his head in agreement. Fear started to prickle at him. If he was so wrong about something this important, how could he trust his instincts at all?

They found their two companions wandering the icy streets in the early mauve light of dawn admiring the simplicity of the buildings.

"We will miss you both," Shaief said as he moved to greet them inclining his elegantly rolled turban.

"We will miss you also." Rembeu returned their welcoming smile.

"Are these not beautiful buildings?" Shaief asked with admiration.

"Indeed they are, however I do believe your buildings encompass great beauty also." Rembeu stated. Tarl nodded.

Both Shaief and Mohmed were thankful.

"Well, now that we have a greater understanding of our symbols we will be able to feel a part of their beauty rather than feel overpowered by them," Mohmed replied humbly.

Tarl's mind was in fast forward. How could he retrieve Opal? The portal would be opening soon and he would have to act quickly. Going in would be easy but coming out needed more thought. At least knew one thing for sure; if he could find her again he would forget about what Opal's parents did or did not do. He should have left it alone in the first place. It was time to just let some things go.

The four of them walked toward the supper building and shared breakfast. When it was time for Shaief and Mohmed to take their one way journey back through the portal, Tarl had still not come up with a plan. The portal opened and began to spin. Shaief and Mohmed waved their last goodbyes and dissolved into the swirling tunnel. He took a step forward, she was so close now. He took another.

Rembeu saw how close Tarl was to the portal entry. He called out Tarl's name, his voice carrying threatening undertones. Tarl didn't even hear him. What he did hear however was a very familiar voice vibrating in his head.

"Acceptance is a very hard lesson to learn."

Tarl stopped dead still. Finally he had placed that voice. It was his mother's. An image of his mother at the kitchen table explaining how to make orange tea 'properly' skimmed through his mind. But how was this woman, who looked nothing like his mother, making the sounds of his mother's voice?

'Not similar Tarl, the same.'

He shot around to find her. She was looking directly at him. 'I know you're not her. Why are you doing this?' He tried to express anger in his thought.

'There is no need to form angry thoughts Tarl; I can see your face.'

That's why he had felt so comforted by her voice. How could he not have recognized it straight away? How dare she manipulate him like this?

'Why do you have her voice?'

'Tarl you have done well receiving and transmitting information but your anger and fear are restricting you.'

'Well, you caused my anger.' That was childish and he knew it.

'Tarl, listen carefully. I am not pretending to use your mother's voice.'

'I don't understand.' Tiredness was overwhelming.

'You're not trying.'

Rembeu could tell that there was an exchange between them going on. He had no telepathic abilities but so long as she stopped Tarl going back through that portal he didn't really care what was being said.

Tarl moved closer to the woman and stared into her beautiful green eyes. He hadn't noticed their color before.

'Is a person what you see on the outside?' she put the thought in his head.

'Not entirely.'

'Perhaps just their eyes? I believe you say that eyes are windows to the soul?'

'But you're not her, I don't understand.' Burning tears welled.

'Again Tarl, you must try to accept without understanding.'

'Right.' He was trying to.

'Your anger has subsided slightly Tarl, but your fear has grown. You are holding on to it as protection but fear can only be destructive. You must release it to ascend.'

The portal had closed without even the tiniest sound and Rembeu walked over to check on Tarl. He might not have been telepathic but he knew something was wrong and he didn't care if he was interrupting.

"Tarl, are you alright?"

Tarl broke his gaze and turned red-eyed to face Rembeu.

"I'm alright, Rembeu."

"He is not alright Rembeu."

Looking over to the woman, Rembeu's pained expression showed he already knew this.

"Rembeu, it is time for Tarl to know the truth. You know as well as we do, you should not have allowed Dormancy to be enacted."

Tarl didn't know what 'Dormancy' meant. He wondered where all this had come from. Couldn't he just be left to try to comprehend one thing at a time?

Rembeu nodded gravely and turned to face his nephew. How he had matured in this short time. His face, nut brown and now slightly gaunt, flexed a strong jaw and dark unfathomable green eyes. His baby nephew had turned into a complicated young man. Perhaps if he hadn't performed the Dormancy, it wouldn't have been so difficult for him all these years.

"Tarl," Rembeu's voice revealed a slight tremor, "there is more to the dream than you have remembered."

"What do you mean?" Tarl didn't understand.

"Tarl, your father and I were unable to help you in such terrible grief. You remember, you came to live with me for a long time after your mother passed?"

"Yes." Tarl nodded.

"You stayed with me because we were worried that you may be the target for further attacks?" Tarl nodded again. "Well, that wasn't because we were worried about renegades attacking you," Rembeu's voice wavered, "we were worried other gypsies may attack you or that you might even harm yourself.

"Other *gypsies?*"

"Tarl, think hard, in your dream last night, what happened after you saw these people point your mother?"

Tarl closed his eyes and tried to recall the horrible dream scene by scene.

"I saw the same two people struck by pointers. They fell down before I could get to my mother."

"O.K. Tarl keep your eyes closed. Try to go back to the scene just after your mother was pointed. Try to remember it a little slower."

They wanted him to watch his mother being struck and dying? This was macabre and cruel. He shook his head.

"Tarl, something else happened. I know it seems cruel, and I am so sorry to make you do this but you have to try to remember."

Tarl closed his eyes again; fear drumming in his ears. He saw the pointer shoot through his mother's chest and looked up at the two people running toward her. His father was leaning over his dying mother. Were the two people taking aim again? He opened his eyes suddenly to stop the vision. Shaking his head; his eyes pleaded with Rembeu to stop this.

"I can't do this Rembeu."

"You have to keep going Tarl, please. When you see the gypsies fall, you must look down at your hands."

Reluctantly he tried again. The gypsies were running toward his father. He watched them fall: One and then the other. Pointers had pierced both their hearts. Tarl looked down at his hands. Now he was confused. His right hand carried a bow but his left hand had no pointers. At his feet, strewn across the ground, were a whole pile of them; enough pointers to fill a sack. As he slowly opened his eyes an image flashed in front of him. Horror took the place of disbelief.

"No!" Tarl was shaking his head violently. "No, no, I didn't! I couldn't have!" His whole body began to tremble. His left arm started to ache so badly it felt as if someone were trying to wrench it from its socket and his head felt as if it were going to explode. Tarl dropped to the ground on his knees.

"Tarl you acted out of shock. Someone had just killed your mother."

"I killed them." Quiet whimpers of agony escaped his throat. Somewhere amongst the pain came a lost and tired voice. "I killed Opal's parents...And by killing them I...by killing them I killed their children."

"Not Opal, Tarl, not Opal."

Remembering last time Rembeu wrapped his nephew in his arms to console him. He had already seen Tarl go through this and it was just as cruel the second time.

Of course, when Tarl had found out that the orphaned children of the gypsies, who waited quietly in their cabin for their parents to return, had been killed by renegades as an act of revenge for the death of his mother, Tarl's guilt was bottomless.

At the time Tarl's self destructive manner grew worse and worse until they had found him gripping broken mirror shards; blood pouring down his left arm: The arm that fired the pointers. That's when they had decided to enact Dormancy. It would take away the memory of pointing the gypsies and blur the moment of his mother's death. It just meant putting his pain to sleep for a while, giving his body time to breathe again. Neither Pavo nor Rembeu had mentioned it again.

What Parvo had never told Rembeu was that not long after the incident he had found out that one remaining child had lived. After returning from the forest to find food, she had come home to a slaughterhouse: Her brothers and sisters, waiting for her to bring home their dinner, now lay dead at the kitchen table. They had never even found out that their parents had been killed moments before them.

The watchers had found Opal collapsed in the forest after she had tried to outrun the horrific vision.

Worried for her safety they took the small child, only nine, into protective custody where she remained until Parvo learned about her situation. At the time Tarl was with Rembeu, and Parvo was looking for some purpose that would take him away from his memories. He brought Opal home with him and she stayed until Tarl was due to return home. Reluctantly, Parvo arranged for her adoption with Mr. Tzau but he had never told Rembeu or Tarl about Opal for fear of raising the Dormancy. Parvo had told the Watchers that renegades had killed both Cymbeline and the gypsies. Against every principle he had ever stood for he lied and lied easily. Perhaps if he had acted as quickly as his son his wife may have still been alive.

The day after the Dormancy, Tarl had woken like a new person. He had still grieved over his mother but he was able to cope, able to experience each day. Finally they knew, at least now he would survive. As time went on, it seemed more and more unnecessary to awaken the memories. So no one ever did.

Tarl couldn't reconcile the conflicting emotions. The only person he wanted to be with right now was Opal but he had just remembered that he'd killed her parents and may as well have killed her brothers and sisters as well. The memories were bursting within him like a dam of fetid water.

Finally, he understood some of what he had seen in the Moon Gate. But there were still the scenes with Opal that he couldn't explain. He couldn't think properly.

"I need to sleep," were the only words he could mutter before he passed into oblivion.

When Tarl woke he felt as if he had slept for several moonspells. Although groggy, he was able to sit up comfortably. He found himself alone in some kind of small rectangular chamber, lying on a beautifully carved wooden base with no blankets or pillows just a simple golden shawl covering the middle of his body. The walls appeared to be pure gold and there were no windows. He could not understand how light was obviously filtering into the room as it was not at all dark.

Rolling his left shoulder he discovered that the tremors in his arm were gone. His arm was moving comfortably. There was no pain. His head no longer thumped, his arm no longer shook. He felt good. Adjusting his legs he pushed himself off the bed and realized he was naked. Wrapping the long shawl around his body he began looking for a doorway amongst the smooth golden walls.

Two steps in any direction revealed small openings. He ducked into a narrow tunnel that moved around a corner before descending. Now it was dark. Unable to see anything, he was surprised not to be consumed by claustrophobia. Feeling along the walls, Tarl came across another tunnel opening. He had no idea which way to go.

Imagining the woman's face with her lovely green eyes, and pale honey hair, he sent out a message and waited.

'I am awake, I am in the tunnel and I would like to know which way to go.'

'I see you. We are glad you are awake. Please follow the tunnel to your left.'

As soon as he turned left a light shined up at him from below. Tarl walked toward the light.

28

Broken Promises, Broken Dreams

As soon as Opal saw the portal close she knew she had made the wrong decision. Desperately, she tried to pull it open again. The others saw her panic and tried to help her but it was too late. Her shock was so great that she fell to her knees, covering her open mouth with her pale fingers.

"Why can we not open the portal again?" She desperately asked one of the council members. He shook his head.

"This is the first time we have seen the portal open. We have to wait for explanation."

"What have I done? I'll lose them forever! I promised I would stand by him and now..." her voice was disappearing into a whisper. "I promised..."

The council member gently lifted her by the elbow and led her on the long journey back to the city center. Somehow her feet just kept moving one in front of the other. Opal looked down at them as though they were foreign; not part of her body or party to her will.

The bright clear sapphire sky stretched above her and beautiful bird song swelled around her but it all felt empty. She had broken the connection. No longer could she feel Tarl. What consequences would there be?

The return journey seemed to take much longer than their passage that morning. How she wished she could turn back time. They seated her in the dining area and placed a bowl of steaming broth in front of her. Even though she was not hungry she knew how this food made her feel. Each mouthful warmed her deep inside. But nothing could replace her loss.

Opal's mind was reeling. How could she have been so selfish? Her reasons for staying lacked altruism. It was as simple as wanting Tarl to be sorry for being angry with her. And now who was sorry? A glistening tear rolled into her soup. The remaining broth looked bottomless and her spoon seemed too heavy.

Ever since violence had taken away her family she had managed to steel herself against the world. Now, she realized, she had just existed amongst people she had never let herself get involved with. If Parvo had kept her, things may have been different, but when he organized her adoption, the rejection went deeper than she could cope with.

Since then, she had told no one her story and no one had ever asked, although she suspected Mr. Tzau would have known. Tarl was the first person to hear the words from her own mouth and he had accepted her anyway. He had only wanted to believe her parents had not committed such a crime to relieve her of guilt, not because it made a difference to him. Why was she seeing this all so late?

One of the members at her table signaled to a small lady and she quickly turned up at Opal's side with a package. The two members sitting beside her lifted her from her position and guided her back to her sleeping accommodations. Outside the sky was beginning to darken. Time seemed to have passed more quickly than she felt it should.

They handed her the package and ushered her into the room. There was no resistance left in her body. Staring blankly at the empty room, she wondered what incredible discoveries Tarl and Rembeu had made, and sat down on the bed feeling exhausted. The package held several pieces of small fruit and a very old book. The book was the translation of their languages. She sighed. At least this was a distraction – if she could concentrate.

Opal tried to focus. Unsuccessfully she attempted to reflect any other thoughts that invaded. At some stage tiredness overcame her and she sank into a fitful sleep.

In the middle of the night an extraordinary sequence of visions woke her. Their importance was just beyond her comprehension.

29

Dreams broken, Promises wakened

As Tarl emerged from the passage, Rembeu could hardly believe what he saw. Tarl's tanned skin was shinning and his face was relaxed and glowing. He even appeared to be taller and was certainly moving with the grace only confidence affords.

"I see you are feeling better," his uncle smiled as he eyed the golden shawl, "delightful outfit, I'm sure the ladies would love it."

"Ha ha. Actually it's very soft on the skin." Tarl tried to look nonchalant as he swaggered towards his uncle. "Where is everyone?"

"They have left us alone for a while so we can relax together - for the time being anyway. There are clean clothes over there and plenty of fresh food on the table behind me." Tarl moved over to the clothes and began to dress.

"How long have I been asleep?"

"Long enough." Rembeu said gesturing to the table laden with food. "Eat."

Tarl reached for a plate with his left hand. It moved painlessly. He looked at his arm strangely, as if it were an alien part of his body. How had the pain disappeared? Opal had been the only one to give him some kind of relief and he couldn't even imagine how far away she was now.

Rembeu watched Tarl turning his hand from one side to another. He felt ashamed that he had allowed Tarl to go through all that pain knowing the cause. He could see how much better Tarl was now but he would never be able to take away the tinge of sadness that stung his nephew's eyes. Rembeu turned away not wanting Tarl to see his own regret.

"I assume there's a plan?" Tarl seated himself on one of the uncomfortable chairs to eat. "Let's hope it doesn't have anything to do with lengthy seating arrangements."

"Actually I think you may want to take that statement back."

"And why is that?"

"Well I hope I misunderstood actually."

Tarl wasn't expecting that.

"How bad is it?"

"Well, you are on the path to actualization now that the Dormancy has been lifted. I'm not sure what they did to you in your unconscious state but I'm told your body accepted their Teachings with gratitude, as if you had been an empty vessel waiting to be filled." Rembeu's brow creased.

"They taught me things while I was unconscious?"

"Indeed. So you must have the knowledge within you now."

"The knowledge to do what?" Tarl was involuntarily calm.

"You must activate the seventh wheel."

"Oh." The time had come: The final ascension. Tarl didn't know how he knew, but this was it and yet something was missing. "You're not telling me something."

"It sounds like there is some kind of metamorphosis involved."

"Some kind of what?"

"It sounds like…"

"I heard what you said. What kind of metamorphosis? Whose metamorphosis?" The questions were coming out but Tarl knew what Rembeu was implying: He was going to have to change his physical body – in the physical world.

Rembeu grimaced. He didn't need to say anything.

"I've got to make some kind of transformation? That's ridiculous! I mean, I've altered myself in different states of awareness but that's not real, I mean, physically real."

Rembeu shrugged.

"Maybe it is?" The pain in Rembeu's chest sparkled again. He flexed his hands.

Tarl shook his head.

"Will I turn back?"

"I certainly should think so! You must return to your own path with the same energies you left it with. Your return is vital to this whole situation." Rembeu was horrified that he might have to bring back his nephew as some unimaginable creature.

A thought flashed through Tarl's mind. If he turned into some kind of spirit maybe he could retrieve Opal. The foolish thought was quickly dismissed.

"That is not what we had in mind Tarl," the woman's voice swirled behind them. Rembeu and Tarl turned to face her. Her green eyes swam out toward him.

"Are you going to tell me what you *do* have in mind?" Tarl's voice held strength but not anger.

"Of course, Tarl. Now you are well: You have rested in the great chamber and have eaten plenty of our food we can discuss your task."

Tarl thought she made it sound like he would just have to do some house chores: mop the floor; rake the yard. He stopped the rambling thought processes. Putting his plate down beside him, he threw a wink at Rembeu.

"Alright then let me hear it."

30

Light Seeks Truth

Opal continued to have strange visions even while she was awake. She held onto them as if they were a life raft in rocky seas. How they were being received wasn't important to her. Even though she could no longer feel Tarl apparently she was still capable of receiving his messages. It felt comforting and confusing simultaneously.

Mohmed and Shaief brought her further desperation. She had missed the reopening of the portal. When they went on to explain that the polarity of travel was only one way and that Tarl was distraught at not being able to retrieve her, she was convinced that he was sending her these messages. After finding out about the wheel crystal in the next plane she felt like a fool. Thinking she would be invaluable to these people was childish. In fact, she was an unnecessary responsibility. Suddenly, everything within her, craved Tarl's presence. Without him she felt empty and lost, as if all purpose had dissipated.

Opal used the information Shaief and Mohmed passed on to her regarding their visitation to make some sense of her visions. Explanations to her new companions didn't offer any help. Finally she decided there was no choice but to return to the library and wait for a further sign – hopefully that sign would be Tarl himself. With permission from Shaief she took plenty of supplies and made the long journey back to the library by herself. Through all the difficulties in her life, she had never felt quite so alone.

The library was as beautiful to her as it had been the first time she saw it. Dropping her supplies, she ran her fingers across a cluster of crystals. Incredible augmenting notes rose around her and echoed across the space. At the center of the room, where the portal had opened, she sank down onto the floor. What if he could not come for her and that was what the messages were about? What if she were to stay here forever? How could she have been so rash? When she had found out that the portal wasn't supposed to open again anyway until these people were ready, the folly of her situation felt as if it would crush her. There was no reason for her to be here at all.

The journey had worn her out but there was no comfortable place to rest. She curled up into a tight ball and tried to drift into sleep. Maybe she could find him there? Just before sleep encompassed her she called out Tarl's name.

The strange visions came again, closer and more vivid and this time she could feel the emotion involved. There were two gypsies aiming pointers that pierced right through a woman who sat beside someone familiar…Parvo! She was watching the death of Tarl's mother. But who were these gypsies? Again they took aim, but before she could feel the extreme panic that was about to befall her, she saw Tarl's arm rise and expertly release two pointers, piercing both of the gypsies. So Tarl was right, her parents had not killed his mother.

But Tarl had pointed the people who had. Why did he not just tell her that? Would he rather she live believing her parents had killed his mother than tell her, he in fact, was a killer also? Suddenly another vision stung her. She felt Tarl's overwhelming horror as he fell to the ground unconscious. That was when the greatest surprise came. The frantic faces of Opal's parents were visible in the distance. They had come to warn Tarl's parents. How did she know that? This was not part of Tarl's message. How was this happening? Her parents were hesitating with panic but she held on tight to their image. She was not letting them go now. They began to run back to the forest, toward home, but another familiar face stopped them. Pressing her memory she tried to place that face.

"You must run!" he cried to her parents, "They have all been killed. Your children have all been killed." Her parents protested vehemently but the man went on.

"I heard the strange sounds across the way at your home; I went to look and see if everything was alright. I opened the door," the man began to cry; "they were all dead. I do not want you to see them. Arleur will take care of their burial I promise, you must run, run quickly, all of you must or they will kill us all. You must find new refuge. Tell all the gypsies. We knew we could not trust the Keeper Council."

So they had to run again; leave or die. And all those that believed in them would have to disappear also. Her parents were forced to leave, their children lying dead and alone, without even being able to bury them.

What would they have done if they had known one child was still alive?

Opal's eyelids fluttered open again just long enough to see a shimmering vision of Tarl standing over her.

"Wait for me, please," she heard his wavering voice as if it were being spoken from under water.

Opal sat bolt upright and reached out to him but his image was gone before she could comprehend what she had seen. Perhaps she was just going mad? It was all too much for her.

"Please, Tarl, if you can hear me, I am waiting right here for you! I will not move until you come for me." Desperately, she hoped it was true. And then the most amazing thought struck her: Her parents may still be alive.

31

Truth seeks Light

Tarl knew what he had to do. It was just a matter of figuring out how he could activate the seventh wheel and fulfill his own promise to Opal. The wheel was to be initiated the following day. One final teaching - they attempted to translate as 'osmosis'- was to be given in the Great Chamber after which he was to rest for the night. There simply wasn't enough time to figure out how he might accomplish these tasks but he knew it was imperative he succeed. He would just have to find a way.

After this, if everything worked out correctly, they would return home; back to their own path, and hopefully to a world that was not destroyed.

When Tarl finally woke from the chamber the next morning he felt ready. The teaching of the night before had strengthened him even more. The 'osmosis' was a strange feeling; as if his very essence were being sucked out of him and expanded within him at the same time.

He hadn't known what they were going to do with him or what they might think was necessary to enable him to absorb their knowledge. But the one thing he didn't expect was the thing he ultimately needed. His instincts had been right all along: The Divine Sources had been mistranslated. There was only one person that hadn't been living a lie and it wasn't himself or Rembeu.

When it was finally over they left him to sleep. That was the last thing he was interested in doing. There were too many other thoughts to occupy him.

Tarl met Rembeu and followed the members out into the streets. The bright white ice reflected the colored sky-ribbons and charged him with energy. They strode toward the center of town where the moon-dial hid within the small courtyard. One of the men strolled up to the device and twisted the pointer on the graduated dial. Slowly a huge glistening structure began to ascend from the ground just north of them. Tarl threw a glance at Rembeu who looked suitably impressed.

The sparkling coiled structure twisted upward: A series of rings joined into a spiral.

The green-eyed woman was staring at Tarl intensely.

'Diamonds,' her voice moved across the sand-drifts in his mind, 'they will enhance your ability to open up to the higher planes and find the ultimate flow of energy.

'It's very beautiful,' he returned with thought. The spiral stopped rising but continued to twist.

'Yes, it is also very powerful.' Her smile brimmed inside him. It was a new aspect to his sensory perception since being given the osmosis. Turning to look at her he noticed the energy from the diamond rings was swelling. Everyone had moved except the three of them.

"You may enter the spiral," she spoke softly as she nodded to Rembeu and Tarl.

"Yes, wonderful." Rembeu looked delighted at the prospect.

'I will remain here to hold the third point until you have succeeded.' Her thoughts were flowing into his mind easily.

"Are you ready Tarl?" Rembeu pressed a palm onto his shoulder just before he entered the spiral.

Tarl nodded. Surprisingly, he *was* ready. Pushing any niggling doubts aside, he concentrated on positive thoughts. At this stage there really wasn't any choice. A single doubt could destroy what he was trying to do. He stood outside the pulsating coil about to look into places and times he could not yet imagine.

'Remember Tarl, at your center lies the secrets of life; of light. It is your key, use it. The electromagnetic fields must be controlled to create the time-storm. Use them to transform your reality; use them to ascend. Where you are about to go, time will be irrelevant. If we were able to access this energy field we would be able to tell you more. Good luck,' her thoughts drifted away.

Tarl stepped under the lowest rung of the spiral and Rembeu followed. He turned to take a last look at the lady with the green eyes but the light from the diamonds was too bright to see her. Suddenly panic shot through him. Why had he left her without trying to understand her existence? Tarl's unexpected need to discuss this with her erased everything else from his mind – except her voice.

'Tarl, concentrate, you will see me again, I promise. I am right here in your mind. Now, focus.'

Her voice soothed his fears. Closing his eyes he reached for Rembeu's hand. Gradually his entire body filled with energy. The rings of the spiral lit up with all the colors of white light spinning from burning red to bright orange, golden yellow to deep sea green, and then blue, indigo and thrilling violet. They swam in the colors with wind whipping up around them. It was extraordinarily beautiful.

Rembeu felt the sparkling energy whisking up inside his body. His chest felt like it was caving in, as if hundreds of iron filings were being zapped around a magnet inside him: Needles prickled the back of his neck and it felt as if his consciousness was being sucked out through his ears. Wondering how long this would take, he questioned whether he had that long. He knew what those pains were and it wasn't good. Gripping Tarl's hand he gritted his teeth and prepared.

Tarl felt the power building until he thought his body could no longer stand the pressure, and then abruptly the wind died and the world felt like it had stopped. Everything was perfectly still. When Tarl opened his eyes again, he squinted into a perfect white sky. The spiral had become invisible and he looked toward those outside. They fought thrashing winds, their arms raised about their heads in protection. But the lady with green eyes stood firm. Her long hair lashed about her face but she remained calm, never taking her eyes off him.

As he watched, millions of small opalescent ice 'bubbles' began to rise from the icy ground into the air. The green-eyed lady smiled.

"What are they?" Rembeu managed, relieved the pressure had dissipated.

'They have acted as our protectors for many thousands of orbits.' Her voice even penetrated Rembeu's mind. 'They helped us remain balanced. I am sure they hold many secrets. Watch them.'

The scene beyond them was altering. The woman's image had begun to shimmer. Tarl raised a hand as if it would stop her from disappearing but he could do nothing to change what was happening.

'You have activated our rebirth Tarl, keep going.' Her thoughts were kind, gentle. Tarl forced himself to concentrate. 'After a time our planet will be covered with a blanket of white energy. And then our world will warm again, cleansed and renewed. Eventually we will be able to...'

Her voice had drifted into nothingness like snowfall. They watched her fade; the others long gone. For the briefest moment Tarl was sure he saw his mothers auburn hair and beautiful face shimmer in the distance but in the very next moment he witnessed an incredible flash of light and watched the ice bubbles in the sky burst into a thousand colors. Snowflakes fell from them twirling to the ground. The time-storm had opened.

The power he had felt before was still growing but emotionally he had somehow surpassed it. All darkness of thought slipped away as he felt his body dissolve into what initially felt like numbness. A voice spoke to him, deep and somber. It was a voice he had never heard before.

"Tarl, you have passed through your own blackness. You have found and fought your deepest fears. Now you must wake."

It was too soon to hear this voice. He wasn't ready yet. Everything was moving too quickly. Trying to slow the momentum, he grabbed Rembeu's arm. In a flash he sensed Rembeu's illness. Why hadn't he noticed anything before? Ashamed, he realized that he had been too wrapped up in his own dilemmas. Tarl flung a look in his uncle's direction. His pale face looked sicklier than Tarl could ever remember.

Rembeu saw Tarl's expression. He winked at his nephew encouragingly.

"I'm alright, Tarl. Just keep doing whatever it is you have to do to open the seventh wheel."

Tarl nodded.

"Just got to make a couple of brief stops first. Just hold on for me, OK?"

For some reason Rembeu wasn't at all surprised.

"We are not riding a wind-ship here Tarl."

"No, even better, we're riding a time-storm. Hold on."

Rembeu felt himself twist in the stillness. The sickening lurch made him feel as if he were moving in slow motion, as if he were dislocated from time and reality. And then he saw the image. He should have guessed. Opals flickering reflection sat in front of Tarl.

"Wait for me, please," he called out to her but her image faded again.

Rembeu had no idea how this was happening but he was most impressed.

"Interesting! What's the plan?" Rembeu tried to concentrate above the pain.

"I can't explain everything now. You have to trust me, and not because of the Divine Sources. I have to go back to the time after the Great Disaster and give the people the message they say I left. And then I have another little trip to take. I'm holding you here. You won't even know I've been gone."

"How long will that take?" Of course he trusted his nephew.

"Just hold fast. I promise I'll get you back."

Rembeu knew Tarl had to do it, or had to try. He held onto his pain as if it were the very thing that would keep him alive. He also held onto his faith in his nephew. If he made it back, he would never underestimate anyone again.

Tarl's image vibrated. He was traversing unfathomable distances and yet unshifting in his form. Rembeu's image hovered as if frozen in stolen time. The ancients of the Great Disaster surrounded him. Words came without design, without glory. Tarl gave them hope and told them who he was, promising to return. And when he did, the people must remind him of Truth and Light. It was all over in an instant. Rembeu hadn't even noticed he was gone.

And then Opal's image shimmered in front of them once more. Tarl tried to steady their position so that he could retrieve her.

"Opal," Tarl cried out.

Opal was reaching out to him. Tarl could see her mouthing his name but he could not hear her. She began to fade again. Her horrified face disappeared. Tarl could feel her screaming his name but he could no longer see her.

"I can't steady it. We've got to go back!" Tarl closed his eyes and focused. It wasn't working. He was getting farther and farther away. "Rembeu! I've got to get back!" His fists were bunched at his forehead; the upper part of his body rocking with agitation.

"Tarl," his uncle began gently, "Remember, Opal is the force of equilibrium. She is part of this process. We may not be able to make it without her. Try to tell her to use her light to pull us back; steady us."

Tarl calmed down immediately. Rembeu was absolutely right. He sent the message out to her repeating it over and over again. Much to Tarl's shock her image returned but her body still appeared as a faint shimmer.

"Tarl you can do it, pull her in, she will feel you, she will make it."

"Opal. Keep trying." Tarl was yelling as loud as he could even though he knew that volume was going to make no difference whatsoever. "Please hear me," he whispered. As he felt her words fill his mind, her image began to focus.

"I am right here," Opal cried.

He reached out for her.

Opal was ready this time and reached out for him. Tarl's hands clasped around hers firmly before a rush of wind and then total stillness.

"You came back for me," her gray eyes peered up at him fighting tears of relief. He couldn't believe he had really done it. His eyes looked down into hers intently. Opal was really here.

"Well apparently," Rembeu said weakly, "you're a little too important to leave behind," the depth of his expression belied his humor, "some kind of karmic connection apparently," he managed a distressed smile.

Tarl was afraid to let go of her hand.

"Never do that again. Please," he uttered as he hugged her to him. All she could manage was a purposeful shake of the head.

"I think we're running out of time Tarl," Rembeu pointed in front of them. He refrained from clutching his chest but the pain was squeezing so tightly he was having trouble breathing.

A figure stood before them just beyond their invisible spiral and a voice began again.

"You have made the the triangle of spirit, now you must prepare. You will find no limitations in the light. You must clear your emotional bodies. Your polarity is about to alter; reflect forward and back. You will feel the transmutation take place slowly. Let the light body ascend."

"No, it's too soon. Go away." Tarl was yelling at the strange figure that seemed to pay no attention to his defense.

"Tarl, I don't think that's someone you can argue with. He appears to be your own creation: Your first key." Each word Rembeu spoke carried a weight that hung heavily upon Tarl. That was when Opal sensed Rembeu's pain. Immediately, she let go of Tarl and held onto Rembeu.

"Tarl, Rembeu is very ill, we have to…"

"I know Opal, I'm sorry but this is my only chance." His senses were overwhelming him. Both of them could see how much he was struggling.

"Tarl," Rembeu began, "You cannot change the past."

"Who says?" he was sounding defiant. "I could fix everything." Tarl was attempting to spin time backward again, away from the figure, but the image kept following.

Rembeu could no longer stand. Slowly he sank to the floor. Opal would not let go. Pressing a hand across his aching chest, she tried to source the light.

"Tarl there is no time. Please," Opal begged.

Tarl heard the hurt in her voice. And then they all saw it. He had spun time back to when his mother was alive. They could see her blurry image laughing in the distance.

"Tarl!" Opal screamed. "Tarl there is no pulse!" He looked down to see Opal's horrified expression and Rembeu's limp body. Something inside him took over. He reached out his arms and closed his eyes.

The voice came again.

"You must face your most difficult of tasks: To just be; to accept the fact that you are part of a whole bigger than even you could imagine;

that in holding onto the pain, you are allowing instability in the universe. Remember who you are and what you hold – the keys to the universe. Forgive the graveness of the past and find honor in yourself. Look beyond the light; access truth. You will be surprised at what you find. It is time to activate the seventh and final wheel."

The figure swelled into a starfish of light and as it burst they found themselves floating within the spiral surrounded by a black sky swirling with pin pricks of starlight. Opal was fighting overwhelming panic as she gripped Rembeu's hand. Just as she looked up at Tarl a searing pain enveloped her torso. It felt as if her body was being slowly crushed. The feeling was excruciating, but it was not Rembeu's pain she was feeling. In shock, she cried out. Tarl knelt down and took both Opal's and Rembeu's hands.

"Everything is going to be alright," he said as he felt the heat rise up within him. Lifting his head, he let the eruption take him. It burst through his body like an explosion. The light crashed around the three of them, knocking Opal unconscious.

Tarl had risen like a pyramid and for a brief moment he experienced all existence: A universe inside him had expanded until it exploded into pure white light. He was all knowledge; infinite and indefinable; he *was* light, traveling at inconceivable speeds without destination being significant; he was the stars and their source; he was the planets and their skies; the clouds, the rocks, the water and the wisdom. The support of the surrounding planes buoyed around him. In an instant he felt all time and realized that life as he had known it was but one journey; one existence. There were many more waiting for him.

In that moment of recognition a swirling colored light moved slowly toward them. He looked at it curiously, wanting to reach out and touch it but realized he had no human parts to do so and smiled at it unafraid. Before he could comprehend its purpose the images from the Moon Gate flashed in front of him and the last sound he heard was a high struck note from the Radiant.

32

An Altai Welcome

Opal blinked her eyes open first. Dust drifted from her lashes. A huge crash boomed in her ears and a tumbling of rocks fell down a side wall threatening to crush her. For a moment she did not remember anything. Looking around, she tried to make sense of the scene. A terrifying rumbling was building in the distance. Nothing seemed familiar. And then it all came flooding back. Desperately, she looked for Rembeu and Tarl. Thick dust blanketed the surroundings but she could make out a figure a little further ahead. Crawling across chunks of rubble Opal cut her silk dress and slashed her left calf before feeling Rembeu's still body.

"Rembeu. Rembeu, I am here. Can you hear me?" She was not going to accept that Rembeu had not survived but he didn't move. Opal reached for a pulse. There was a very slight beat. "The light burst must have restarted your heart," she whispered in shock. "Hold on."

Several hurried footsteps were coming toward her. Small blurry figures were racing in her direction, their hazy silhouettes obscured by the rising dust. Panicking, she laid her body sideways across Rembeu hoping to protect him but the figures started shaking her.

"Mr. Rembeu, Mr. Rembeu, must move Mr. Rembeu. Place falling down. Miss Opal must move. Please, must hurry!"

Opal recognized the voices immediately. The Altai. They were back in Atlas Mountain!

"Please, you must help Rembeu. He has had a heart attack. He is not conscious."

"We helping, we helping!" Several of the Altai scattered around Rembeu and surprisingly managed to lift him without much effort.

"You too, Miss Opal, coming now! Please!"

"I cannot see Tarl, help me find Tarl!" The dust screen was getting worse. She could barely see which direction the Altai were running off in. "Wait! Some of you have to help me find Tarl." But she could neither see nor hear the Altai any longer.

Breathing was becoming difficult. Shifting aimlessly around in this mess was not going to help her find Tarl. She would have to find fresh air but without knowing which way to go she stopped crawling on the broken ground and gasped for air.

A huge roar soared up in front of her and the air began to vibrate. Terrified she turned in the opposite direction and scrambled as fast as she could. There was a hazy light ahead and she moved quickly toward it. The light became brighter and she realized she had found the entry. Just as she climbed through the opening an enormous crash echoed behind her. A huge slab had fallen from the top of the mountain. It would have crushed her if she had still been in there. It would have crushed anyone that was in there.

"Tarl?" she whispered almost to herself. She started to move back into the passageway but something was tugging on her feet. A pleading Altai looked back up at her.

"Please, Miss Opal, no time now. No good. Must come safety. We keeping you safe. You not worry there." She realized the Altai was risking his own life to come and get her. Taking a last glimpse of the dust filled passage, she slowly turned away. If she could make sure the Altai went back to safety, maybe then she return.

At that moment her life seemed useless.

The Altai started running toward the canal and jumped into a boat waving at her frantically to hurry up. There was only one last boat behind them which she jumped into. Rowing quickly, she tried to catch up.

The trip felt surreal. Rocks were crashing down behind her in the main cave and here she was rowing through the still waters of the caverns. Opal followed the boat ahead of her around several turns until the awful sounds of injured and frantic Altai trebled toward her across the water. A strange feeling crept across her shoulders. It felt as if someone was behind her but there was definitely no one there. After all, she had taken the last craft.

The docking platform was overcrowded with boats but she found a small dock to squeeze into and ran up the steep stone incline to find a vision of tragedy. So many Altai were laying injured and dead that she had to try to stop herself from reeling in horror. Several tents looked like makeshift hospitals. Somehow she would have to help.

A familiar voice called out her name. She turned toward it and could not believe her eyes.

33

Home too far away

Blinding white light surrounded Tarl. He blinked, trying to focus his vision. There was no pain but he was aware of feeling intangible as if his body was displaced. The white light stretched outwards like an open door and he moved forward. He could see a figure moving in the dim light ahead of him. It crawled through a dusty rubble strewn passage and disappeared through a tunnel of light. Tarl moved after it calling out for it to stop but it wouldn't.

As he moved through the tunnel he realized he was back in Atlas Mountain. Why was it so bright? Why wasn't there any noise? Squinting into the light, he finally made out a familiar figure as Opal's scrambling movements came into focus.

"Opal! Opal!" Tarl was screaming with all his might but she wasn't stopping. Maybe she was rushing after Rembeu. Tarl chased after her. Now she was jumping in one of the boats and was starting to row into one of the caverns. Why wouldn't she stop?

The inside of the mountain was a wreck. Sections of the walls had collapsed and fragments of stone were sliding down the sides creating rivers of smoke as they did so. The Crystal Radiant was partly intact but a considerable amount of crystals had fallen and smashed onto the ground. *Where was everybody?*

Tarl reached one of the last two boats just in time to see Opal row off into one of the tunnels on the left. Constantly calling ahead in the hope she would hear him and afraid he might get lost amongst the myriad channels, he tried to hurry after her. His boat moved swiftly, not even seeming to make any ripples.

Opal was making hasty progress as if she were being chased by death itself until finally, several more turns later she pulled up at a large cove. There was no beach here just a platform to dock at. There were many many small boats already docked there but Tarl managed to squeeze into a berth and jump onto the platform in time to follow Opal up a long rise of stone steps.

When he reached the top he could not believe what he saw. There were injured Altai everywhere. All Tarl's offers of help were ignored. Perhaps custom did not allow others to interfere in their healing. Realizing he could no longer see Opal, he began to run frantically amongst the injured trying to find her, or Rembeu, or anyone that he might be able to help.

Inside him, a cry was welling. It was hurting and yet he had no injury. The pain was growing in intensity until it became overwhelming.

Dizziness washed over him as he pulled away from the scene. He tried to fight it, tried to commit to the scream inside him, but the scene was getting farther and farther away and everything he was watching was becoming smaller and smaller. Confusion overcame him. A deep anguished cry burst from his lungs but no one even turned around to look at him.

"Don't be afraid Tarl," her voice hinted warmth and comfort. The pain immediately eased with her soothing tone and the scene dissolved. Tarl was back in the white light. She looked just as she had done the last time he had seen her alive. Her soft face smiled upon him; her green eyes gazing kindly. Her long auburn hair flowed down behind her shoulders and her arms reached out to him.

"Mum?"

"It's alright Tarl."

"How are you here? Am I dead?"

"Essence is far more complicated than we can imagine."

"I'm so glad you're here. I don't understand what's happening."

"I know Tarl. That is why I am here." She took his hands in hers.

"Was that woman with the green eyes you?"

"Part of me – when you pass from this life to the next you become part of the whole once again – as you have just experienced. If you choose to return to a form, part of your previous being returns and part stays within the whole.

"What is the whole?"

"It is all knowledge; everything; all the questions and answers."

"But I don't have any of the answers."

"But you have found solutions; they are keys."

"I remember feeling like that was a possibility but it's gone now. I can't feel it any more."

"Of course not. It is not required in human form."

"But I'm not human, no one can see me."

"You are simply in transition. You have accomplished what no other human ever has."

"Where am I then?"

"For the first time perhaps you should just 'be'. No questions. No answers."

"Doesn't that defeat the purpose of having gone through this?"

"Would you rather not have gone through this?"

"What would have happened if I hadn't?"

"I believe that is a *question* Tarl," she smiled at him as if he were a naughty child again. It felt wonderful. "But I think you know the answer to that already."

"I would have done anything to see you just one more time."

"I know my child, I know. And we have had our moment together."

Tarl felt himself pulling away.

"No I can't go yet, please don't let me go. I don't even know where this is, where you are."

"Remember Tarl, the journey never ends. You should feel no need to know *where* I am but rather *that* I am. Even you have many other forms to take. Now, you are my beautiful child, but there is much that awaits you and I will be there to guide you each time. You have many more great things to accomplish and so you must return. My love for you is infinite. I am so proud of you." A warmth surged within him that could only be matched by the explosion of white light he had felt between worlds. As Tarl watched her image fade, he felt finally, free of sadness.

34

Stories from home

"Parvo?" Opal ran toward Tarl's father. His muscular frame looked enormous beside the Altai. His brown skin was ruddy with dirt and smeared blood. It looked as though he had ripped his clothes to use as swabs. Amazed she reached for his arm. "You are really here!"

He laughed for the first time in a long time and scooped her into a hug.

"I'm so glad to see you. I've been so worried."

"I was told you were caught in the mines; that you were…"

"That is a long story but I made it out." Parvo breezed his hands up and down his body, "Obviously." He would never tell her the whole truth: That he had been badly injured when a shard of stone had pierced down through the top of his shoulder narrowly missing his heart. He was lucky to be alive; not so for many of his men.

"Oh no. Rembeu! The Altai took Rembeu." Opal had pulled herself out of the embrace and was frantically searching for Rembeu.

"It's alright I helped them carry him to that far tent," Parvo pointed to the one in the distance, "he is going to be alright. They have administered a tonic. Right now he just needs some rest."

Opal's relief was palpable.

"How did you get here? How is Calatia?"

"I will answer all your questions, I promise, but please just tell me where Tarl is," Parvo said.

The expression on her face made him feel like his heart had stopped.

"I could not find him," she looked ashamed, "the ceiling fell in behind me. I took the last boat. Even if he had survived he will not be able to find safety," she shook her head as tears welled in her eyes.

"Where exactly did you arrive?" Parvo was gripping her shoulders, his stare full of gravity. He was not going to accept anything had happened to his son. He just couldn't.

"Inside the Wheel-Door."

"Stay here and help the Altai," his eyes were wide and burning with fear.

"Parvo," Opal's voice was quiet, "the mountain is falling down in there. It is collapsing around us."

"All the more reason I have to find him."

"Then I want to come with you."

"I understand that Opal but I need you to stay here and help the Altai. Rembeu told me about your healing powers."

"But Umbra will be able to help," her eyes were pleading with him.

Parvo's brow creased. He held Opal's face in his hands and slowly shook his head.

"Umbra can no longer help anyone here I'm afraid," Parvo said quietly.

"Umbra?" Opal shook her head in disbelief. "Umbra is…"

Parvo patted Opal's hair.

"The radiant was struck by a tremor and part of the wall smashed to the ground. Umbra was crushed beneath it. I'm sorry."

Opal's thoughts jazzed in front of her. The pain Umbra had felt seared through her body again. It was the pain she had felt when they were transferring back to Atlas Mountain. How was she sensing Umbra's pain? There was no connection.

"But Umbra is not…"

"Opal I really need to hurry." Parvo was nodding hoping she would understand his urgency.

"Oh yes Parvo, of course, you must go. I will wait here and try to help." Her mind was reeling; her eyes begged him to return. Summoning the courage to ask one more question she grabbed Parvo's arm.

"Mr. Tzau?"

Parvo shook his head. His voice was just above a whisper.

"The Maker, Mr. Tzau died in his silk factory. I'm afraid Maiji was there also. The silk factory was destroyed. I'm sorry Opal, I couldn't save them."

Umbra, Mr. Tzau, her best friend and her work: all gone. Just like that.

"Is Mrs. Tzau…?"

"Thankfully she and the children survived. I have been asked to to build another silk-house." There was more but this wasn't the time. He felt terrible having to tell her all this bad news. There must be something positive he could tell her. "If you had stayed you would have been killed too." That didn't sound as helpful as he had hoped.

Opal nodded slowly without raising her eyes lest they overflow with tears.

"You must go now. Find him. Please Parvo, find him."

His large rough hand skimmed her chin.

"I will," Parvo said as he dashed off toward the dock.

35

Atlas at last

Rolling notes vibrated around him, dragging Tarl from unconsciousness. The heaviness of his body was overwhelming and he felt incredibly small. His last memories broke open like an emptying egg: His mother's face; his experience in the light. The feeling had been so overpowering he wanted to go back there. He wanted to feel the incredible peace and timeless reverence.

As he tried to sit up, his head felt as if it weighed more than bullion. Moving his hands out across the ground he could feel only rubble. Where was he now? Would he be able to find the others?

The floor beneath him was strewn with smashed rocks and he shifted uncomfortably around them. Dust rose all about him and thunderous echoes boomed above his head as rocks crashed to the ground. Squinting helped him focus and he managed to roll into a position that he could push himself up from. An agonizing pain spun inside him making him clutch his stomach.

A terrible rumbling sound echoed through the passageway vibrating all around him. The dust was everywhere and he unsuccessfully tried to refrain from coughing. The action caused the stabbing pain in his stomach to surge like fire. It appeared he was lying just inside the Wheel-Door; the exact same position he had thought he was earlier. Shutting his eyes, he begged this to be real; begged to be heard; to be seen. He heaved himself from the floor and stumbled down the corridor.

All around him walls were cracking and crumbling. The dust was so thick it was difficult to see his outstretched hand. It looked as though the mountain had taken an awful pounding. If this place had suffered so badly what would Calatia be like?

Through the grainy air he saw light ahead of him. Tentatively, he staggered toward it.

A black silhouette appeared to be approaching toward him. Tarl stopped dead still.

"Hello? Can you hear me?" Tarl's voice echoed in the din.

"Tarl! Son is that you? I can't see you."

Tarl now knew he was in some other strange dimension: One where he was visiting his dead father. Despair hit him like lead. His father hadn't made it either. He was an orphan.

"Tarl! Oh Tarl! I can't believe I found you. I knew you weren't dead, I just knew."

His father knew *he* wasn't dead?

"Dad?" he whispered in shock. "You're not dead?"

"Not yet," Parvo said with a sad smile and then wrapped his arms around his dust covered son so tightly that Tarl just crumpled in his arms. Parvo grabbed his son and pushed him toward the entry of the cave. He barely recognized his own child: Tarl had grown so tall and broad; his face was gaunt and his hair had grown long. What had his son been through?

"Dad?" Tarl's voice was weak.

"Yes, Tarl."

"Opal? Rembeu?"

"Shhh Tarl just let me get you to our sick bay."

The weight of existence dragged Tarl back into unconsciousness.

■   ■   ■

Parvo carried his son to the same tent Rembeu had been sent to: The one for serious emergencies. Tarl's stomach wound looked very bad. Parvo hadn't been able to stop the bleeding and Tarl hadn't returned to consciousness yet. Parvo wasn't sure if the latter was good or bad.

When Rembeu saw the state of his nephew he told Parvo to find Opal immediately. Parvo forced himself to leave Tarl and went looking for her. Opal was healing an Altai when he found her. An arc of light spun above her and colored rays shot down through her arms and into the Altai. As preoccupied as he was with Tarl's injury, this sight reminded him of something he had seen a very long time ago and he realized he was in the presence of a Lightworker; a rare talent indeed, but there was an unmistakable clue that she was more than that. No Lightworker he had ever heard of could use light with refractions the way she did. Opal was no gypsy! She had to be a child of a Spirit Warrior. But that ancient reign of royalty had suddenly disappeared without a trace. And yet she was influencing the light like…

Shock struck him like a thunderbolt. How could he not have seen this before? Her parents weren't gypsies at all. If she had been born of a Spirit Warrior and a Lightworker she would have had to have been protected. The abilities she may be capable of were unfathomable. Thoughts began to fall one at a time.

Words formed from memories. It had been suggested that her family had gone into hiding. What better people to hide amongst than the gypsies? And she was the only one left. The rest of her family was dead. Just as the last thought hit him, he saw Opal look in his direction. Her expression changed from welcome to horror.

Parvo was staring at her with a look of overwhelming alarm. Fear blazed in her heart. Tarl must have been … No she couldn't deal with it. Her head was shaking from side to side in disbelief not wanting to know what he was about to say.

"No, Opal," Parvo pulled himself back to reality. He remembered why he had come to find her. "Tarl is still alive but he is very badly injured. You have to hurry. He's with Rembeu." Parvo watched her run frantically toward Rembeu's tent. This wasn't the time to bring up such questions. He wondered if she would even have the answers.

Opal ran to Tarl's side. Tarl's life force was slipping away rapidly. She reached for the opal and crystal locket that Tarl had given her a lifetime ago and placed it over his stomach with her hand hovering above it. Then, raising her other hand up above her head, she pointed her fingers toward the sky.

"After this I guess we'll be even," she whispered into his ear. A small tear rolled down her cheek and dropped onto the bridge of his nose. A blaze of light shot out from her raised fingers like a rainbow and sizzling white light circled below the hand that floated over his stomach. Taking a last look at Tarl's handsome face, she then closed her eyes and twisted the hand above her head into a scoop directing her fingers onto the top of her head. Blazing colored rays shot down into the centre of her skull. The seizure that followed was agonizing.

Parvo looked on horrified. This wasn't right. The healing a Lightworker performed should not harm them. He looked over to Rembeu whose painful expression confirmed his own. Opal was giving up her life-force to save Tarl.

Parvo lunged forward and pushed her away. The force of the light hit him with such power he was nearly knocked out as his head slammed onto the ground. He raised himself ready to go again but the connection had been broken. Opal lay on the ground, her face as gray as her unresponsive eyes.

Tarl made a groaning sound and Parvo ran to his side.

"Tarl wake up, it's urgent," his voice was intense and commanding. Tarl forced his eyes to open. He stared into the horrified eyes of his father and then followed their gaze to Opal's still body.

Tarl scrambled over to her, wincing with each movement. He felt something fall and caught the reflection of the locket. He picked it up and placed it on her middle. Opal was trying to fill her lungs with air but there was no energy left inside her to continue. Tarl spoke to her softly as his mind traversed hers.

"Opal you must listen to me. I know what it all means now. There is such a thing called the Divine Sources. It reveals seven predictions. I didn't tell you because I didn't believe they were true. I should have trusted my instincts. I now know they were mistranslated. Rembeu believed I was some kind of savior but he was wrong. The proper translation is 'protector'; 'Protector of Truth'. Think about it Opal: 'Truth and Light'.

Sounds were forming inside her head. Consciousness was brimming like foam on the shore. A memory stirred deep within her. It just reminded her of fear and the strange man in the forest that thrust the treble key into her hand. She pushed the image away.

"Opal, the Divine Sources are about you and me. I am of 'higher understanding': Truth; and you are 'true energy': Light. You are a Lightworker born of a Spirit Warrior. You are the 'balance': The force of equilibrium.

It didn't make sense. She was not the child of a Spirit Warrior. She was born to gypsies: Gypsies that ran and hid and left their only surviving child alone.

"Opal, just listen, I know how hard it is to believe but it's the truth. Listen. 'The child of the seventh line,' that's me, 'will thread two answers on that fateful day,' that's both of *us* Opal. Our connection was meant to happen on the day of such tragedy for both of us. The tragedies were supposed to bring us together. I was supposed to help protect you. And if I didn't find you that day, it says: 'so much more tragedy shall follow'."

Opal's eyes fluttered slightly. She tried to speak but no sound came out. Tarl obviously believed whatever he was talking about. If she believed in him she would have to try and comprehend what he was saying. Why couldn't her mind focus?

"Both of us are born of the seventh sign and both of us lost our care-giver under that same zodiacal sign. Together we are the bridge. You are the seventh source. Opal, you have to fight; you have to find the energy or this will not end. The destruction will be complete. *I* am here now to protect *you*. You are the tuner, you speak the language of the Radiant and yet you have never been taught. You are a child of a Spirit Warrior. You hold the Spirit Warrior's memories. I have seen it in the Moon Gate. Now I finally understand. What I thought was death was just *transformation*." He rubbed his forehead in desperation. He could feel her listening to him he just couldn't get her to come back to him.

Opal felt like the world was far far away. Everything Tarl was saying was bubbling across to her on a shiny lake; each word popping and disappearing. Maybe he had seen death, maybe this was it.

Tarl had to make her believe. If she didn't they were doomed.

"I was told in the Great Chamber of the last path," he stated, pleading for her trust. "That's why I had to come back for you. Think about it. You never sensed any power until I left Calatia. And even through my Teachings I did not develop my ability to feel thought until your energy came to me. That's what Umbra meant when she told

Rembeu to re-read the Sources. She must have known. We still need to find the seven colored flames, and then we will find the Protector's Throne."

Opal could feel Tarl trying to answer her thoughts. She could not believe what he was saying. Why was he doing this? He should just leave her alone.

"I was told the seventh source in the Great chamber. It says that the two shall be one; the Light Worker and Receiver of Truth shall share the light and bestow harmony upon a timeless shield. We haven't finished yet Opal." Tarl could see she was giving up. "Your parents had to protect you. Look what happened when the Keeper Council found out about you. They tried to kill you, all of you." The shame flooded through him again, "And I helped."

But it wasn't true. She had to tell him. A pain like stabbing ice chips filled her lungs. Tarl watched her gasp.

"That's it, Opal, come back to me please."

"It wasn't them…" her voice was barely audible.

"Don't try to speak." He swallowed the hurt lumping in his throat.

"It wasn't them…" Opal's eyelids flickered and she managed to keep them open long enough to see the confusion on Tarl's face. "You did not kill my parents. I do not know who you pointed, but they were not my parents." The effort exhausted her and her eyes rolled back in her head as she slipped into nothingness. Tarl was too shocked to react.

Rembeu was unable to move from his makeshift bed but he had heard it all. How was it possible for him to have been so wrong? He hadn't had a clue how important Opal was and he hadn't listened when Tarl had protested about the Divine Sources. And now Tarl was saying the Keeper Council was responsible for Opal's family's deaths. How could he have not trusted his nephew? Why didn't he listen to Umbra? He had failed. If he hadn't felt so impossibly tired he would've told Tarl he was sorry, but instead his eyes closed and was pulled into the darkness of sleep.

Parvo called out urgently to several of the Altai checking patients behind him. One ran to Rembeu the other to Opal.

"She be alright Mr. Parvo. She need resting now but she be good after."

Parvo grimaced at the look on the Altai attending to Rembeu. He shook his head.

"Mr. Rembeu not so good. I stay and help."

"Thank you," Parvo replied trying to hide his distress. Wrapping an arm around his son, he realized that what he had concluded about Opal, was indeed true. She was one of the reasons he had made the journey here. But how could Tarl have known about what the Keeper Council had done? It was time to confront his son. The other complications could wait.

Tarl was trying to process all this information. So he had not pointed Opal's parents? Then who did he point? And if Opal's parents weren't dead, where were they and why hadn't they come back for her? And then he realized: They thought she was dead too. He would have to find them. When all this was over he would definitely find them. Right now though, he had to figure out a way to stop these quakes.

"I have to go back to the Wheel-Door," Tarl was thinking out loud.

"No Tarl, you can't it's too dangerous." Parvo was waving an emphatic hand.

"I've got to stop the tremors." Tarl was shrugging his shoulders. He had to do something but he had no idea what.

"Tarl, I think I know why the tremors have not stopped," Parvo said.

"What do you mean?" Tarl wasn't sure he wanted to hear.

"The Radiant was badly damaged. It needs to be repaired. The vibratory waves must be equalized to correct the bioelectrical meridians and energies." Parvo was surprised to hear himself repeating words Cymbeline had taught him so long ago.

"There was so much dust I..." Tarl suddenly realized he had not seen Umbra. He had had so much to think about that she had not even entered his mind. "Where is Umbra?" He asked, alarm rising in his voice. "She will have to tell me what to do. I don't know how to work the Radiant."

Parvo let go of his son and tried to keep his voice steady.

"Umbra will not be able to help you Tarl."

"Why?" Tarl knew something was wrong. He searched his father's face for clues. A sickening dread lurched and the stabbing pain in his stomach returned. "Is she injured?" But he already knew the answer.

"Tarl, she was crushed under debris. It was all very sudden. She would never have left the Radiant even if the Altai had tried to drag her away." Parvo could see the shock fall across his son's face.

Tarl knew his father was right: Nothing could have made Umbra leave the Radiant. It was her sight, her heart, her existence. Its function was everything to her. Tarl stifled burning tears and tried to think.

"*I* can't work the Radiant… but Opal can."

"Opal?" Parvo exclaimed "Of course, she's a Lightworker."

"Yes," Tarl said rather sadly, as if giving up her right to be normal, "yes she is."

"We have to rouse her," Parvo said grimacing slightly.

"But I can't move her now!"

"I don't think we have a choice Tarl. And I don't think we have a lot of time either. The Altai will be able to administer a stimulating potion that should last long enough…"

"Long enough? But I don't even know what we can do?"

"Once the Radiant is balanced we should be safe. Then Opal can spend time recuperating." Parvo hated having to compel either of them to go but it wasn't a choice.

Tarl had no alternative. He instructed the Altai to do as his father suggested.

"I'm coming with you." Parvo's voice rose up, defiant. He wasn't going to let his son risk everything now. Not when they were so close to resolution.

"No," Tarl turned to face his father trying not to allow the bitterness he felt about the Dormancy to influence his attitude. This was just how it had to be. He had never said no to his father before but he wasn't a vulnerable little boy anymore. The shock on his father's face stirred his guilt but the feeling flowed through him and released. "I'm sorry dad, but you need to stay here. We'll be alright. We can do this, together."

Parvo couldn't hide his surprise. The young boy that flew away on the Orbitor was now a man. Parvo couldn't protect him anymore. Acceptance was harder than he could have imagined. Holding his breath, he slowly nodded before wrapping Tarl in his arms.

"How's your stomach?" Parvo asked Tarl as he reached for the bandages around his middle.

"It's better. Opal must have almost healed it before she was interrupted." A grateful smile crossed his face. "I'll be fine dad."

"Please Tarl, please be careful."

"Of course." Tarl looked his father in the eye. "*I* have someone to protect now." He glanced in Opal's direction.

Parvo tried to smile at his son but he couldn't hide the terrible feeling of loss. His boy didn't need him in the same way anymore.

"I am so proud of you Tarl."

■　　■　　■

Opal and Tarl arrived at the entrance to the main cave and climbed off their small boat into chaos: Thunderous noises greeted them; tumbling rocks fell from the splitting walls; and dust rose up around them like a blanket. The air had become considerably cooler and Opal shivered involuntarily. Tarl could see she was still weak and had gotten paler since leaving the cove. He would have to watch her carefully.

"We need to make it to the island but the path has crumpled over there," he stated, ignoring the piercing twinges in his stomach. Tarl pointed to the collapsed bridge, shouting to be heard and was surprised to see the Radiant dull and lifeless. He had never seen it like this before. Dread rose within him.

"We could go around the edge, close to the wall?" Opal suggested.

"It's too dangerous. There's too much debris falling from the walls. And the dust is thicker there."

"Then we will have to go through the center and swim across the river." Opal shrugged her shoulders.

Tarl looked at the huge boulder sitting at the center of the cave. If it had fallen while they crossed, they both would have been crushed instantly. There didn't seem to be any other choice. Nowhere was safe. He nodded to her.

"Just make sure your feet land evenly on the ground and try to move as swiftly as possible," he said.

"I will be right beside you." Opal was frowning into the distance. Tarl raised a hand and turned her face toward his. He winked at her. A slight blush turned her face toward the ground.

"Come on."

They moved as fast as they could across the rocky floor dodging the rain of falling debris. The dust hung low and made it difficult to see where they were stepping but they managed to scramble across to the river.

"It looks like a mud bath," Opal said as she looked down into the murky water.

"Supposed to be good for your skin." Tarl was hesitating too. Drowning wasn't his favorite thing to do. A huge crack struck the air behind them and they both jumped into the brown river. The icy water punched at their skin and slowed their movements.

The island was less damaged than the rest of the cave and even the Radiant, did not seem to be as badly damaged as Tarl had thought. Quite a few of the larger crystals had fallen from several stories high and now lay fractured upon the ground. Opal ran over to them and knelt beside them as if they were dying birds. Tarl looked at the massive blocks of debris that lay beneath them. The thought of Umbra's body lying under there made him feel a sense of urgency. Opal must have felt the same way.

"Tarl we must hurry!"

"What do you want me to do?"

"We have to get these crystals back into the Radiant. They will die without the source."

"But they're broken." He picked one up and it crumbled in his hands.

"No!" Opal became frantic and started sifting through the fragments of crystal. "We must return them."

"Careful." Tarl said quickly, pulling her out of the way of some falling fragments. He closed his eyes in relief.

"Oh," Opal said in surprise, "thank you."

Tarl started sifting through the shattered crystals not knowing exactly what he was looking for but something caught his eye. At first he couldn't tell if it was real or imaginary. Placing his hand over it, he felt a vibration. Immediately he knew he had grasped something extraordinary and in the instant he sensed it, a thousand colors blazed from it. He raised it from the dusty floor. The light caught Opal's eye and she gasped at the object in his hand.

"You've activated a phantom crystal," she uttered reverently.

"Is that good?" Tarl carefully opened his palm. The image of a small crystal, a replica of the one that lay broken beneath it, hovered in the bright light.

"That is the heart of the broken crystal. It holds all the information of the larger crystal; all those lifetimes of learning; everything."

He looked down at the pulsing crystal ghost in his hand.

"A new beginning." The smiles they exchanged were filled with hope.

"Tarl, there must be others!" Opal cried, searching anxiously.

"What do I do with this one?"

"I have found one also. Look." As Opal's fingers made contact with the crystal, colors flashed out toward them. When their eyes finally adjusted again they could not believe what they were seeing.

"There is so many of them," Opal gasped. "Look."

"It seems you have activated all of them." Tarl was looking across the floor of shattered crystal trying to guess how many there were.

"How did that happen?" Opal asked, filled with amazement and delight.

"Well if a job needs doing…"

Opal let out an exhilarated laugh.

"Tarl. You make jokes at the most inappropriate times."

"Why thank you." He nodded in her direction. "But we still don't know what to do with them."

"No," she closed her eyes and tried to concentrate, "it would make sense that these crystals would be used to replace the larger crystals, but the cavities where they should be placed have been destroyed. They need to be connected to the source."

"Opal…" Tarl's voice sounded as if he had seen a real ghost.

The strange tone in his voice made her open her eyes. The crystals strewn across the ground had altered their light force. Their blazing colors were now focused into pointing arrows of light.

"That, I did not expect," she said as she looked ahead to wear the light pointed.

Tarl was already staring dumbfounded.

"Nor that," he said. They were staring into a crevice between the vertical crystals just ahead of them. "But that is just a solid limestone wall behind those crystals," Tarl stated.

"I do not know how I know, but I know these crystals need a source. And the limestone is not it. I think we need to go inside that crevice." Still holding the pulsing crystals they silently crept forward.

The triangular fracture was too small for either of them to fit into so Tarl began to carefully move one of the large vertical crystals aside. As he did so, the phantom crystal came into contact with it. A humming tone resonated out around them. They exchanged surprised glances.

Opal's eyes suddenly lit up.

"I remember!"

"Remember?" Tarl asked, confused.

"I do not know how this is happening but thoughts are coming into my head and somehow I know that they are memories… memories that are not mine." Opal wondered if Tarl had been right. Maybe there was more to her being here than she could have imagined. It was true that after Tarl came to get her, her experience in the white light seemed to have amplified her senses; as if her abilities were finding more and more volume. She had no difficulty sensing the hurt of the Altai or of healing them. Her abilities now seemed like a natural extension; something she no longer needed to question. Even when she collapsed after tending to Tarl's stomach wound she had felt a strength growing within her; something undeniable and powerful. For all her desire to be 'let go' there was an equal and opposite need fueling her to go on.

Tarl wasn't going to argue with anything that might help.

"What are you remembering?"

"I can see a family: not mine. It is some kind of meeting… they are discussing something about tonal patterns," she could not explain to Tarl that she was feeling the words rather than hearing them, "I think I am being told about an ancient belief…"

"Go on try to tell me what you are hearing," Tarl urged her.

"Well… they are saying that every being holds their own musical vibration," she frowned at Tarl trying to explain, "It is like a seed held within us. Feeling the same frequency born within us is like tuning an instrument to a tuning fork." She tilted her head as if trying to hear a far off sound. "I think...I think it's Umbra. Umbra's memories are held within these crystals."

"How can that be?" Tarl wanted to understand.

"Think of your wind ships and their frequency devices," she tried, "the basalt has to be struck with a frequency that aligns with the stone, enabling it to levitate."

Tarl nodded.

"Yes, did dad tell you that?"

"This is the basis of all life." Opal went on, getting more and more excited as the information became clearer. "That is our karmic connection."

"We share the same frequency?" Tarl tried to understand. "Is that unusual?"

"I do not know," she smiled delightedly at him, "maybe."

"Well my introduction would have been a lot easier if I had known that," Tarl said with a nod. Opal ignored him and went on with her incoming thoughts.

"That is what links us, definitely." She rubbed her ghost crystal across one of the large crystals by her side and nodded for Tarl to do the same. A deep hum rose around them and a light began glowing within the dark crevice. Opal smiled and then disappeared inside. Tarl hurried to follow her, dodging falling debris as he did.

They stood inside the center of the small cavern. The limestone wall was covered by the blazing colors. The crystals' arrowed light drew their vision upward toward a stream of bright white light roaring from a hole in the center of the roof. Along the floor the colors were merging into a column and shooting upward, out of the cave into the sky beyond. And then, as their eyes adjusted, they saw seven glowing colored pillars standing separately around them.

They walked into the center of the pillars; the circular floor lighting up with their steps. An edging of triangular opalescent tiles worked their way toward a white pearl center. The white light shimmering from the roof was causing luminous reflections.

"The source!" Opal stared reverently at the white pearl circle.

"How do we access it?"

"I do not know. There must be something, something close by..."

Tarl peered into the glowing light of one of the pillars.

"Look, there's some kind of imprint on this one."

Opal followed his gaze and then studied the other columns to see if she could find anything on them.

"This one has one too." Opal was looking at the opposite column. "Put your hand on it," she enthused. He did. Nothing happened.

"Put yours on that one," he said nodding toward her. She did. Again nothing happened.

"They are too far apart for the same person to place their hands on them together," Opal wasn't sure what to do next.

"Let's try and place our hands on each of the markings at the same time," Tarl said.

"Alright." Still nothing happened

"Wait," Tarl had a thought. "Hold the phantom crystal in your right hand. I'll place my left hand on this print and you place your left hand on that one," they turned themselves around to face each other, "and then touch the two crystals together over the pearl center." It was worth a try.

Opal had a strange feeling that she was about to experience something incredible. The moment the phantom crystals touched, a shaft of bright white light shot from the pearl center up through the crystal points and into the dazzling light at the center of the ceiling. They felt a rush of static flash through their bodies followed by an electric wind swirling around them. Their bodies lifted very slightly from the ground raising them on tiptoe.

"We are in the energy." Opal was laughing with delight. Music from the Radiant began to swell. Harmonies rose and fell in perfect synchronization. "The Radiant is awakening. It has activated again."

"Opal, look!" Tarl cried.

Opal turned her head to see a river of rainbow light gliding along the floor from the outside of the crevice. The light rolled in toward the white pearl center and was sucked into the white light stream.

"The energy from the phantom crystals is re-entering the Radiant," Opal said reverently.

"Was that what you meant by the 'source'?" Tarl managed in his awe. Opal just nodded unable to form words.

"That's it!" Tarl cried out. "The fifth prediction of the Divine Sources states that 'one born of the source and the other its love, moon

and sun meet to bear forth the power'. You are born of the source and
I grow from your ability - together we create great power."

"I do not know how I can be a part of these Divine Sources you
talk of, I have never heard of them."

Tarl wanted to tell her all about his experience in the Great Chamber
but he was fighting hard to not be pulled toward the light. Opal didn't
seem to notice its strength.

"See what happens when we let go," Tarl suggested. They released
their connection and Opal felt her full weight pull her back to the
ground. Tarl did not. The drag pulled him in toward the pearl center.
Opal watched in horror trying to comprehend what was happening.

"Tarl! What are you doing?"

"I'm not *doing* anything. I'm being pulled in." As much as he did
not want to be sucked into the light it was an incredible feeling. It was
as if he was falling forward and backward at the same time and yet
equally feeling that there was no definable physical movement at all; as
if things were passing over him.

"Grab my hand." Opal was squealing now in panic.

He reached out to clasp her outstretched hand but just brushed her
fingertips before being pulled inside the white light stream. In shock
she watched him dissolve into the surging light.

"Tarl," she whispered as she lost sight of him. Opal tried to move
as close to the light-stream as was possible but the energy coming from
it pushed her away. How had this happened and more curiously, why?
She had no idea what to do next. Stepping outside the crevice she tried
to make sense of what was going on. The light continued to blaze and
the Radiant continued to play. But no one was instructing it.

Although the thick blanket of dust still hung heavy in the air,
the thunderous sounds had stopped and debris had ceased to fall.
Shattered crystals still lay strew across the ground but she could see
none of the phantom crystals glowing anymore. Feeling quite lost, she
looked around the cave half expecting Tarl to be standing in a pocket
of clearing dust waiting for her.

When she turned back around to look at the Radiant her jaw
dropped in shock. The phantom crystals had begun to grow in the
same places the old crystals had fallen from and now pulsed with
new life. But, most astonishingly, circling the Radiant, strode seven

dazzling colored columns like the ones they had discovered inside the crevice. They pulsed in synchronized fashion to the harmonies of the Radiant acting like some kind of protective device. It felt as if they were somehow alive: Emotion seemed to be pouring from them. In the next horrifying minute she realized she could also feel Tarl. It was as if *he* were pulsing through these protective columns.

"Tarl?" Opal called out. "Oh no, Tarl. What should I do? Where are you?"

His words filtered into her head and she simply turned her eyes up high above the Radiant. There he was, just inside a small opening in the limestone wall. Bright white light shone around his body and seven rays of light rose around his head like a crown. He looked down at her serenely. Opal nearly collapsed in relief.

"Tarl. You are alright?"

The minute these words were spoken Opal felt a strange rush surge through her body. She tried to keep her voice steady. "Tarl, come down. Please come down here. I think you should come down here now."

"I don't think I…" His smile was escaping and confusion was brimming.

"You have got to come down Tarl, NOW." Opal tried to be forceful without alarming him.

"I don't think I want to," Tarl said slowly.

Now Opal felt frightened. She could run to find Rembeu but she did not want to leave Tarl here alone.

"It's true," he said simply.

"What is true Tarl?"

"These must be the Seven Colored Flames. I understand now."

"What do you understand?"

"My destiny."

"And what destiny is that Tarl?" Opal kept her voice even.

He quoted from the sixth prediction of the Divine Sources.

"'The one that comes before the seven colored flames cossets the ultimate sacrifice of becoming inner light.' I am the protector. This is what I must do." Tarl's face was calm.

"What must you do?" Opal did not like the sound of this. Something was definitely wrong. But what? Why was she so sure it was not Tarl up there and what would she do if he did come down anyway?

Tarl laughed. He was mocking her. Opal turned ice cold. A sudden loss hit her that was so overwhelming it was like someone had sucked the very life out of her. Tarl was gone, she had lost him to some other place and this was all that was left behind. Her misery shot through her almost blinding her. Weakness overtook her, dissipating any strength she had gathered. She crumpled to her knees, her fingers clasping her aching forehead.

"THE LIGHT OF THE INNER THIRD HAS BEEN RAISED."

The booming voice broke her silent horror. Opal lifted her head and peered over her shoulder to see Rembeu standing straight and tall behind her; his eyes rose toward the likeness of Tarl. Grateful beyond words, Opal felt her body melt with relief. Surely Rembeu would know what to do. Scooping herself up, she moved over to him but he held a defiant hand out to her and without meeting her eyes gestured over to his right. Parvo stood there waiting for her to come to him.

"YOU HAVE HAD TO FACE THE DARK TO COME THROUGH THE LIGHT. BUT INSTEAD OF CONFRONTING THE ENEMY, YOU HAVE ALLOWED IT TO ACQUIRE THAT WHICH IS NOT HIS. TARL! YOU MUST LISTEN. YOUR FEELINGS OF FREEDOM HAVE FORMED WITHOUT TRULY UNDERSTANDING WHAT THAT FREEDOM IS. EVERYTHING YOU HAVE BEEN THROUGH HAS BEEN LIKE AN INITIATION. YOU HAVE DEVELOPED INCREDIBLE POWER. I KNOW THAT IT IS A LOT TO BEAR BUT YOU CANNOT GIVE IN NOW."

Words drifted toward Tarl from a far off place. They were disturbing his numbing peace. He was floating in a life-raft of light; drifting without aim; glowing in the nothingness. For the first time in his life he was free: no emotion; no questions; no need for answers; no need for thought. It was wonderful. No, it was better than wonderful, it was perfect.

"I KNOW YOU FEEL ABOVE EVERYTHING YOU HAVE EVER KNOWN BUT YOU MUST UNDERSTAND THIS IS ONLY THE TRANSITION. IT'S A TEST TARL! AN EGO DRIVEN BEING CAN NOT BE SUSTAINED WHERE YOU ARE."

"But…" the image of Tarl floating high above them appeared to be fighting confusion. "I am not just ego. I am the protector. It is my destiny."

"YOU ARE RIGHT: IT IS YOUR DESTINY TO PROTECT BUT DESTINY IS DIVIDED. TARL YOU HAVE TO CHOOSE THE RIGHT PATH. YOU KNOW WHICH ONE IT IS. YOU'VE FOUGHT THE DARKNESS BEFORE. YOU CAN'T GIVE UP NOW."

Opal was gripping Parvo's hand so tightly his fingertips were going white. Parvo didn't even notice. He was staring intently at 'his son' trying to find something recognizable in him.

"I don't understand why this is happening?" Parvo declared.

"I am just so glad you came. How did you know to come?" Opal asked.

"As soon as I felt the rumbling stop I went to follow you. Rembeu was falling in and out of consciousness but he insisted on coming with me. He has taken some very strong potion but I don't know how long he is going to be able keep this up.

"That's not really Tarl up there is it?" Parvo asked not sure he wanted an answer.

"He has had a lot of fighting to do: I do not think he ever let me in enough to know just how difficult it has been for him," Opal sighed at her inability to get him to confide in her, "I would not blame him for giving up."

"No," Parvo whispered, "he can't give up."

"TARL," Rembeu was trying to control his fear, "TARL! THIS IS IT. YOU'VE FACED YOUR MONADIC SELF, YOU'VE DEALT WITH THE POLARITY OF WHO YOU ARE AND WHAT YOU'VE DONE; FACE THIS; FIND YOUR MIND'S THIRD – THE REBIRTH OF KIND." There was no recognizable response. "STOP THINKING ABOUT YOUR DESTINY," Rembeu tried to find another way to get to him. "WHAT WOULD YOUR MOTHER DO?"

"What?" The image faltered and then strengthened again. "She was a K-keeper…" there was a detectable stammer. "She would be proud." The statement was unconvincing.

"What would your father do?" Rembeu's was struggling to keep his voice strident. His energy was draining.

Opal looked desperately over toward Rembeu. The man had just had a heart attack. How was he doing this? Parvo rubbed Opal's shoulder in an attempt to reassure her but this was all too much.

"M-my father would be …proud?" He was speaking as if he didn't know his father was watching him.

"What? Can't find any new words?" Rembeu was attacking now. "What about Opal? What would she think?"

"Wha…?" the image faltered again and his voice became very quiet, "I can't hear her from here."

It was the breakthrough Rembeu had needed. Tarl's voice, wherever he was, had broken through. Rembeu resisted the overpowering urge to slip quietly into sleep. His body was so tired, so heavy but he forced his eyes to stay open. Just this and then he could rest. He gestured to Opal who unwillingly released Parvo's hand and moved over to Rembeu.

Rembeu's face was pale and slick with sweat. How long he could keep this up? Rembeu seemed to read her thoughts and whispered in her ear. She nodded.

"Tarl, Opal wants to send you a thought," Rembeu's voice still held strength despite his increasing fragility.

"I…I… want to hear her. I can't hear her. I can't feel her anymore."

Opal did as Rembeu told her.

Pressing her eyes shut tight, she pushed the only thoughts she could be sure of holding onto, to the front of her mind where they hung thick with emotion.

Rembeu and Parvo watched as the image looking down at them faltered again. The 'crown' around his head was dissolving. A strange look of bewilderment covered his face. Opal remained very still, her eyes shut tight as she continued to press her thoughts out to Tarl. In the back of her mind she could see a waterfall falling, shining with color, like a backdrop to her thoughts. It felt comforting as if she were being answered.

Just as it appeared as if Tarl was about to speak, they heard a rush of water behind them. Both Rembeu and Parvo turned their attention away from the image and toward the lake. The still murky waters behind them began bubbling. The bubbling turned into rolling waves. Something was rising from its center.

The point of a huge crystal broke through the surface rising slowly, causing cascades of waves to wash across the shore where they stood. Opal felt the rise within her and encouraged it with her thoughts.

Rembeu recognized the crystal. It was the Rainbow Crystal that his family had waited for generations to see and been sworn for those generations to protect. He had been told it was here somewhere within the mountain, secreted from the world, but he often doubted its existence. Again he had been wrong.

With a stab of sadness Rembeu thought about Umbra. She had never given in to the idea that it did not exist. Now he knew Tarl had done it. The seventh prediction had never made sense to him until he had overheard Tarl's translation to Opal: This must be the Protector's throne; the seat before the seven colored flames; The Protector of the Light. Tarl was the protector of Opal. So his family had just been Keepers of the Light; Keepers until the rightful Lightworker came to them.

The realization was sobering indeed. He guessed that now, the Keepers would no longer be required; would cease to be relevant. Perhaps a new line of Protectors would begin? Or perhaps there would be no need for titles. Rembeu's feeling of loss was overtaken by a new feeling of reward: Cymbeline's hopes may at long last be fulfilled.

Rembeu wondered what it was like to be in the light. As much as he relished formulating ideas and devising theorems, he did not envy anyone who could voyage the light. That took more than a teacher could manage: An old teacher at that. Rembeu decided that he would like to be called a Teacher from now on.

He turned back to see the image of Tarl, high above the Radiant, melting like liquid wax. Something inside Rembeu had become very still. He knew that the image wasn't Tarl but if that were true then where was his nephew? As Rembeu went to turn back to the rising crystal he caught the look of shock on Parvo's face. Parvo was running into the murky water. Rembeu looked back at the crystal and horror overtook him. Lying there, wet and unmoving, was Tarl. He lay across the seat of the Rainbow Crystal: The Throne of the Protector.

Parvo snatched Tarl from its pew and swam back to the water's edge, dragging Tarl with him. Tarl's skin and clothes shone with viscous liquid as if he were encased by it. Parvo began to try to revive him but Opal, now very quietly kneeling at the edge of the water beside Tarl, moved her hands out across his chest.

"It is alright. He just needs to wake."

"But he's not breathing!" Parvo was out of breath himself.

"She knows what she's doing," Rembeu tried to reassure Parvo who forced himself to stand back and let her help.

"Come on Tarl," she said gently as she placed one hand on the top of his head and directed the other toward the crown of hers. "It's time to breathe in life. You have been in the Source. You have raised the throne, now we must link light. Do not be afraid any longer; remember what I have just told you."

Tarl suddenly gasped. It felt as if he were taking his very first breath, as if no amount of air were enough to fill his lungs. He gasped again and again but it did not seem to help. He tried to speak, to tell them he couldn't get enough air but there was no room for words in his fight.

Opal pressed down on his chest and as she did so water bucketed from her lungs. She began coughing, having as much difficulty breathing as Tarl. Rembeu panicked.

"Do something!" Parvo was unable to control himself any longer. But Opal held up her hand.

"It is alright. I think you shall find he can breathe now."

"S…okay," Tarl managed after another copious inhalation.

His relief was obvious. Opal released Tarl. The effort to sit up was immense.

"How do you feel?" Parvo was trying to help support Tarl's back.

"mm…" he wasn't really sure how he felt but he was glad that he did, "better." They wouldn't want to know what he had just gone through: From the light he had had to fight the darkness to come back. Floating in the impenetrable blackness had felt like he was nothing, non-existent in the most awful way, unable to reach out or to be reached. And yet, even in the numbness, he knew a part of him existed beyond the black hole. He couldn't feel or hear anything until Opal's words formed within him somehow. They were like a light in the terrible darkness.

Now, her words moved soundlessly through his mind again and he raised his eyes to hers. She caught his stare, her expression serious. Tarl knew this wasn't the place to discuss it but he gave her a look so intent that it took all her effort to meet his eyes without turning away. And then he saw something incredible.

"Opal, your eyes," Tarl said in awe.

Opal felt it. She did not even need an explanation.

"I know," she said simply.

"They're beautiful." Tarl stared into her soft gray eyes, now flecked with sparkles of silver. "They remind me of…"

"Umbra, I know." Opal felt his thoughts. "I do not know how, but I think our heritage is linked. I guess we have more questions to answer."

Tarl just nodded in amazement.

"What is the last thing you remember?" Parvo was gripping Tarl's shoulders now staring into his face as if he were hiding something.

"I remember being inside the Radiant… and then there was white light and then blackness…It felt as if I were both pulled upwards into light and downwards into…"

"The source pulled you in," Opal's head was directed at Tarl but her eyes focused on Rembeu, "Rembeu was right, it was a test."

"It's alright Tarl," Rembeu said, looking relieved, "I don't think you'll have to revisit that place again." Rembeu realized that the image of Tarl was just a manifestation of the past that Tarl had been unable to let go. The 'Source' had given him the ultimate test: Put all the bad into the light and all the good into the dark and see what or whom, wins.

"Yes, I think it's alright now." Exhausted, Tarl tried a smile to reassure his father. As he did, he saw, behind his father's shoulder, the huge crystal jutting from the lake. "O.K. I'm pretty sure that wasn't there before," his eyes gestured toward the monolith.

Rembeu smiled.

"I think you will find, my nephew, that that is the Rainbow Crystal. I think you know it now as the Throne of the Protector: Your throne Tarl.

"The…Throne? It's real?" Tarl was blinking widely as if he were not seeing properly. "It's really real?"

Rembeu didn't need to answer. It was beautiful and it was *very* real. The huge stone captured a shimmering rainbow inside it which scattered ribbons of color across the still trembling water.

Parvo didn't understand.

"The Protector's throne? Tarl's *throne*? But I thought Tarl was the ..."

"Tarl was right about the mistranslation of the Divine Sources," Rembeu admitted, interrupting the inevitable question. "Even Umbra must have known. I wonder why she never told me?"

"You wouldn't have believed her," Tarl said matter-of-factly.

Rembeu smiled at his nephew.

"Well just come on out and say whatever it is you like then."

Tarl laughed and pushed himself into a standing position. He gazed down at Opal who was still kneeling by the shore, and offered her a helping hand. But Opal's stare was fixed on the crystal throne.

"Opal it's alright. I think Rembeu is right about what it is." But Opal wasn't moving. "Opal, what's wrong?" Concern had crept into Tarl's words.

Opal was shaking her head slowly. Her expression was one of disbelief. She turned her head toward Tarl, her eyes not wanting to leave the crystal.

"My parents talked of this stone, I am sure of it." Her eyes finally met Tarl's. "It is part of my family's history. My parents spent their lives searching for it." It didn't make any sense. Could they still be searching for it now? Her eyes sparkled with hope.

"What do you know of it?" Rembeu was fascinated.

"My parents called it the Diviner's Stone: A Crystal which holds the memories of our ancestors, maybe even all ancestry. My parents said it could protect them; protect our lineage. I am afraid that they never gave me much detail. I assume that was because they did not know a great deal about it but they did say it was hidden in a great mountain under tranquil waters protected by people of pure thought, and that it would not be revealed until two equal powers had become one."

"The seventh prediction," said Tarl simply. "It's not a throne by which to rule, it is a seat for the protector to watch over his Lightworker." He smiled at Opal.

Rembeu wished he had understood this earlier.

"What does that mean, exactly?" Opal had no idea what she wanted to hear but she had a strange almost overwhelming feeling of needing to belong to these people. It was a feeling she had denied herself for most of her life.

"I think it is what it is. We have found out the truth about our lives, our connection, and now we need to honor those truths," Tarl said quietly.

"How do we do that?" she asked, secretly hoping for more.

"How have we done any of this?" Tarl replied.

Opal was suddenly looking very tired and Tarl realized that the three of them hadn't slept for a long time.

Opal felt exhaustion creeping up the back of her skull and clutching her brain.

Parvo had been watching them all fight off exhaustion.

"We all need sleep. At least here the destruction seems to have stopped. Nothing more can be solved without rest."

"Mmm," Tarl felt fatigue fall down upon him like a heavy blanket.

"Come on, let's head back to the caves and let the Altai know everything has calmed here." Rembeu mustered all his energy to make it back to the boat. Parvo traipsed behind him and Tarl and Opal followed.

"I think it's finally over." Tiredness drew out Tarl's words. Opal nodded, obviously overcome herself. Tarl reached out and clasped her hand and her head dipped toward the ground as weariness took over. He pulled her in close to him and held her slight body tightly.

"I am so tired," her voice was just a whisper.

"Opal..." he hesitated not sure if this was the right time, "thank you... for what you told me before. I don't know how you did it but I know you brought me back." The memory of her calm words came back to him. "And I will find your parents no matter how long it takes."

"We will find them together," Opal replied. Her eyes rose up to meet his. They were filled with a sureness that showed him she believed his words.

His heart beat a little faster.

"You can rest now. Everything is going to be alright. I promise," Tarl said.

Somehow she knew he was right.

36

Peace by Piece

Atlas Mountain had taken many moonspells to clean up and there was still large cracks in the limestone walls that needed fixing. The Altai had worked constantly trying to return the cave to its former dignity.

When finally they could clean no more, a memorial ceremony was held for Umbra, Melik and many of the Altai. Tarl was devastated on hearing the news of Melik's death. It didn't seem possible that someone brimming with such enthusiasm could just be gone. Rembeu had told Tarl that Melik wouldn't have wanted to go any other way but it wasn't very reassuring.

Beautiful polished crystal coffins were rowed along the rivers garnished with orchids. Rembeu, Parvo, Tarl and Opal followed the many boats filled with Altai. The journey was long and slow with reflections from the crystal coffins sparkling across the arching walls like flames. The ceremony was held in a huge grotto that Tarl had never visited before. The center of the cavern ascended almost as high as the mountain itself and white sandy beaches rose from the glimmering blue-green water. Rembeu's sad words filled the cavern before each of the crystal coffins were rowed to the far side of the lake and were sunk into the wet quicksand.

When they finally returned to the main area of the cave a feast was held that rivaled any gastronomic experience Tarl had ever had. A considerable amount of apple wine was consumed which led to a lot of toasts and shared memories. Eventually most of the Altai left the dining area to spend the time with their families and, save for a handful of intoxicated Altai at the far end of the table, Parvo, Rembeu, Tarl and Opal sat alone.

Tarl felt like it was the right time to ask.

"If I didn't…" Tarl prepared himself to use the next words, "If I didn't point Opal's parents, then who did I point? And why did they want to kill my mother?" His mouth had suddenly gone dry.

Parvo tried to hide his discomfort. He knew this conversation would come soon enough. Rembeu and Opal swapped worried glances.

"I was going to tell you Tarl, there has been so much happening that I thought I'd wait until you were ready," Parvo said.

"Well I guess I'm ready now." He wasn't sure he was.

"I have been investigating this for a long time. There was a lot that others tried to cover up, as you can imagine. I only just found out the whole story recently." Now that he had started to tell Tarl it seemed a lot easier than he had thought.

"So you found out that it wasn't Opal's parents?" Tarl asked.

"Yes, because of the secrecy of the gypsy people the Watchers had no way of identifying them. They had been given the name of Opal's parents by one of the gypsies that had chosen not to run. The Watchers had no reason to believe it was not them."

"But didn't they wonder why they tried to kill her?"

"Because the act was toward a Keeper the matter went straight to the Keeper Council. That's where the all the cover-ups began. Without the permission of the Keeper Council the Watchers could not continue an investigation." Parvo took a deep breath and tried to get the information across to Tarl without too much emotion. "I'm afraid the Keeper Council was corrupt; has been for a long time. The Keeper, Deneser, is undergoing interrogation now after several members of council rallied against him. Apparently," Parvo gripped his hands tight, "one of the council tried to give a gypsy couple a great deal of gold to 'remove' Cymbeline. Now it seems that those gypsies were Opal's parents."

"No, it couldn't have been," Opal interrupted, shaking her head.

"No Opal, you don't understand. Your parents refused to co-operate. That's why whomever was responsible on the Keeper Council had your brothers and sisters killed."

"They were killed by the Keeper Council?" The news seemed too much for her to bear. They had done nothing wrong except try to help. The pain that she had denied herself for so long suddenly came flooding back. She wrapped her arms around herself to hold it all in. And then a thought came to her. "But they were there," she looked across to Tarl her eyes brimming with controlled tears, "I saw them in your dream. They were in the background."

"It appears they had come to warn us...too late." Parvo's voice broke and he stopped talking for a moment to regain his composure.

"But then...?" Opal was trying to keep her thoughts together but Parvo interrupted.

"However, two other gypsies did agree to assist the council and they are the ones you..." Parvo couldn't bring himself to say it. But everyone knew.

"But why was she such a threat?" Tarl's mind was moving too fast to worry about the fact that his father couldn't say the words 'kill' and 'Tarl' in one sentence.

"Tarl, your mother was the most wonderful person, please never think otherwise, but she was also a strong leader. Cymbeline believed that the rules governing the separation of councils were wrong, outdated. She wanted to change them, make the councils integrated. Her idea was to have a world where there was one large governing body, a Grand Council that contained several members of each council in the one committee. It was a revolutionary idea..."

"And," Rembeu's voice was filled with pain, "very threatening to the highest council, which of course, is the Keepers."

"Exactly. The Keeper Council was the only one to oppose. Without full agreement between councils there was no possibility of change." Parvo's face had paled. He took another sip of apple wine as if that might give him back some of what he was missing."

"So she died for nothing?" Tarl's voice was hard and bitter.

"Well, no that's not true. Now that the investigation is being performed and most of the corruption is being expunged several of the Keeper Council have voted to go ahead with a merged union. They all want to be free of the long standing dogma and are willing to give up their positions to create this new council." Parvo paused momentarily as his eyes flicked to the table. He twisted his glass between his fingers. "They have asked me to be a part of it... can you believe it? A Maker on the Grand Council."

"Well that is truly good news!" Rembeu slapped his palms on the table and sat back in surprise. "And a marvelous councilor you will make."

"Thanks Rem," Parvo nodded in his direction and chanced a look at Tarl.

Tarl was still absorbing all this information. Opal could see Parvo was waiting for him to say something. Why was Tarl sitting there silently?

"Parvo, I think it is wonderful news. Congratulations," Opal said. "It will be good to know you are my representative. I am so glad something so positive has come out of this," she reached across to clasp his free hand between hers.

"Actually there is something else I have to tell you Opal." Parvo's face was quite serious and she withdrew her hands as if she might need them to steady herself.

"What is it?"

"Mrs. Tzau has asked that when you return she would like you to run the silk factory. We all know that you were the most beautiful artisan there. It is only appropriate after what has happened that you take over."

Opal could not believe what she was hearing. Her life in Calatia seemed like another lifetime ago. She had not even thought about going back but now she realized that that was what she would have to do. No one had offered her any other choices and yet somewhere deep inside her she had imagined there was one. Being a Lightworker had given her more life than anything she could remember. Loss strode over her so wholeheartedly that her vision momentarily went black.

Tarl heard the words but couldn't comprehend their meaning. Back to Calatia? Opal couldn't go back there. She belonged here with him. But then did he belong here? There was no way he was going back to Calatia after all of this. All he knew for sure was that he could not be separated from Opal. After all, he was her protector. He was sure he could feel her crying out to him but he didn't know what to do. This couldn't be the way it was supposed to end.

Opal realized how generous the offer was. She owed her very existence to her adoptive parents and she wanted to show her gratitude. Perhaps this was a way she could thank them. It would be very hard work, much harder than her previous position but what else could she do? There was no way out. After everything that had happened, everything they had been through, this was how it would end. Bowing her head, she accepted the offer.

"It would be an honor to partake of such a generous proposal." She was amazed at how steady her voice remained.

"Opal can't go," Tarl blurted out. The sound of these words caused Opal such relief that she sank her face into her open hands.

In his confusion Tarl took this as a sign that she must want to go. And then suddenly he remembered the words that had swum out to him in the black nothingness of the Source. She had begged him not to leave her. She told him he was the only one she had allowed herself to care about in all these years. Without him she would give up and had reminded him of his promises. She had said she loved him.

Tarl started to make a further protest but it was Rembeu who spoke up.

"I believe that would be a terrible waste of Miss Opal's abilities."

Opal looked across at Rembeu, confusion and surprise lighting her face. Tarl looked desperately at Opal eyes pleading her to stay. Parvo was equally surprised assuming that this offer would be greeted with all round congratulations. After all when Opal returned to Calatia he assumed that she would at least take back her old position.

"Parvo, together Tarl and Opal have re-balanced our evolutionary paths. They have opened the Source; shared the Light. They have developed powers beyond our comprehension. Tarl is now the Protector of the Light - Opal's Protector." Rembeu waited for Parvo to take this in. "They both must take these abilities to the next level. Whatever that may be."

"But surely… you are a Keeper…" Parvo's voice wavered slightly.

"I *was* a Keeper, Parvo. There is nothing for me to 'Keep' any longer."

This was not what Parvo wanted to hear but he knew that Rembeu spoke the truth. He had known about the Divine Sources since Tarl was born. It didn't make it any easier to let him go. Parvo had watched Cymbeline pass on the Keeper position to Rembeu so that she could marry and have children. He knew that Rembeu had sacrificed any kind of life so that Cymbeline could live hers. And now it was Tarl's life. His son was the child of the seventh line. Tarl and Opal had succeeded in repairing the path discrepancies, and so, had now changed history. The following generations would not suffer the cruelty of a death due to Boundary prejudice as they had. And now Parvo's life would change again. His only son would not be coming home with him.

"Opal is the child of a Light Warrior," Rembeu went on, "she can work the light just like Umbra."

With Rembeu's words, Opal's mind made the sudden connection.

"It was Umbra. Umbra was the one who was calling for me in Calatia," she said.

"Yes, Opal I am sure you are right. Umbra told me many times that there was another who would take over the Radiant workings and that I should be as true to that person as I was to her. Opal has learnt to work the light and now she must discover her true potential."

A feeling of wonder rose inside Opal. She could stay. She could harmonize the Radiant and learn more about her new found abilities; abilities that had been denied her so long because of her parent's fear; a fear that achieved nothing except loss. It did not matter now. When she found them she could tell them it was safe for them to be who they really were. The world had changed and she had helped change it.

"I was sent another message when I stayed behind to teach the harmonizing device," Opal said more self-assuredly. "At first I thought it was Tarl trying to send me his thoughts but it did not feel like him. Now I realize it was Umbra."

"What was her message?" Rembeu wanted to hear anything that might bring her memory back for just a moment.

"Umbra told me to follow my heart because my heart spoke the truth and if I followed the truth I should be born into myself. It did not make sense at the time but now I realize that I am meant to stay. I have much more to learn and I can only do that here."

"That sounds like her." Rembeu smiled wistfully.

"I can still hear her you know. She told me to say what was in my heart when I lost you in the Radiant." Opal was looking at Tarl as if he might suddenly disappear at any moment. "I can feel her in the Radiant when it is harmonizing."

"Umbra chose well," Rembeu uttered the words as if they meant 'goodbye'. "Yes, very clever indeed. I don't know how she found you but she must have sensed the karmic connection…" Rembeu's words trailed off with his thoughts.

The last remaining Altai were staggering off in the direction of the kitchen. Rembeu assumed, to get more apple wine or perhaps even indulge in one of their custom brews. Having never managed to develop a taste for it he was unsurprised that they did not offer him any. He watched them disappear through the kitchen door and smiled to himself as he heard something smash on the floor. His thoughts turned back to Opal.

"The Radiant will continue to play now because it has been balanced," Rembeu said softly, "but occasionally adjustments will still need to be made." His eyes rested gently on hers.

Opal knew what he was asking of her.

"So actually Parvo," Opal was speaking confidently now, "I thank you very much for passing on the offer but I believe my new duties will keep me here." Opal's smile just confirmed she could work the light.

Tarl couldn't hide his delight. He knew his father was terribly upset by this but guilt was no longer an option. This was where he belonged too, with Opal. Tarl faced his father.

"Me too."

37

Parting ways again

The night had stretched into dawn as they sat talking around the dinner table. They had all felt that if they kept talking nothing would change. For just a while, they could pretend that Parvo did not have to return to Calatia to help rebuild the town and that Rembeu would stay in here in Atlas Mountain instead of journeying off on what he said would be the 'scientific endeavor' he had been planning all his life: A life that he could finally start to live.

Tarl and Opal had asked him to stay but he had assured them that they would cope with their new duties with considerable skill. After resting here for a while Rembeu said he would leave them in the hands of the Altai and promised to return 'sometime in the foreseeable future'. Tarl made sure that Rembeu knew it would always be his uncle's home and that he was only a very proud guest. His uncle was touched by the gesture but he couldn't deny that sometimes it had felt like a confinement rather than a home and now that he was free, for the first time in his adult life, he would enjoy being able to come and go.

Parvo's departure was more difficult than Tarl could have imagined. Tarl wasn't sure how he felt. Watching his father disappear, so soon after seeing him again, was wrenching at best. He had stood waving at the disappearing Orbitor II until it was only a speck in the sky – just as his father had done when he had left Calatia. Opal stood beside him until his arm was too tired to keep waving.

Then he had counted down the time until Rembeu was to leave. He and Opal tried to squeeze as much information out of him as possible until he made a flippant comment about being glad to get away from his little tagalongs. Their feigned hurt had made him feel terrible, and so, instead of an apology, Rembeu organized lots of workshops, experiments and learning programs for them to complete before his return. When they confessed to exaggerating their hurt, he huffed and cursed and then laughed, claiming he should have known them better. It was definitely time for him to go.

As usual there was a feast the night before Rembeu's departure and more apple wine and Altai brew came out. They talked about everything. Stories about what they had each felt during particular times along the journey and thoughts about the future.

The night stretched into early morning and when Tarl woke he realized he had fallen asleep by Opal's side on one of the cradles in his now familiar cavern. His neck hurt and his stomach panged. Raising himself gently, he looked down at her lovely face. Opal's pale cheeks were dashed with color. Tarl smiled gratefully as she stirred.

"Good morning," he said gently.

"Is it still morning?" Opal's long lashes fluttered several times before her sparkling silver and gray eyes opened. She pushed herself up and brushed her long silky hair with her hands.

"Probably not. How do you feel?" Tarl had a big grin on his face which made her feel self conscious.

"Did I miss something?" Opal asked self-consciously.

"Not missing anything," his grin didn't falter. "In fact you're rather perfect." That made her blush.

"I cannot believe Rembeu's leaving today." Opal was instantly sorry she had said this when Tarl's grin disappeared. Tarl nodded.

"We should go and find him. He's probably waiting for us to say goodbye." Tarl stood and held out his hand to help her up.

"Thank you." A timid smile crossed her face and his heart melted. She was such an unusual mix of vulnerability and strength.

"Very welcome," his grin had returned.

"Why are you looking at me like that?" Opal was feeling embarrassed again. Tarl laughed and pulled her down the incline toward the boats. "What is so funny?" She asked. By now she did not really care what it was that was making him laugh, she was just glad he was laughing.

Tarl strode the paddle through the still clear water spraying swirls of glowing surface-bugs around the boat. Opal sat behind him and rested her head upon his back. The warmth of her body made his heart hammer.

At the Wheel-Door they found Rembeu lugging a huge bag of goods for his journey. Several Altai swarmed around him making suggestions and reminders that they thought he might require.

"What on times behalf? Would you lot give me a bit of room!" Rembeu made a swirl with his arms as if it would shoo them away. "Oh there you are," Rembeu said as he caught the forms of Opal and Tarl moving toward him. "I'm glad you could make it."

They ignored his sarcasm.

"Oh, are you leaving today?" Tarl replied straight faced.

"Yes, yes, very funny. Come and help your uncle with all these bits and pieces." He pulled a bag from one of the Altai and passed it to Tarl. "It's alright Zwet! You've already got too much to carry. Huffedy me!"

"And you said *we* were annoying tagalongs," Opal reminded him with a sweet smile. Several of the Altai made horrified grunts.

"Oh you two are just so amusing. Honestly! A bit of peace and quiet won't do me any harm at all. No Zneez! I think you're very helpful." Rembeu rolled his eyes at Tarl and Opal. "You're all very helpful, thank you," each word was stressed as if he was talking to children.

A chorus of the Altai version of 'you're welcome' followed with several self-congratulatory nods. In their distraction Rembeu managed to free himself from the circle and traipsed into the outdoors.

"Right now, that's enough. You don't all have to follow me to the solar sail. I've a hand trolley here somewhere."

One of the Altai obligingly located it.

"Right, good then, put it all in there," Rembeu ordered.

"Uncle, if there's any news will you…?"

"Yes Tarl of course. Anything I find out about Melik's …" Rembeu couldn't say it, it still didn't seem real. "If I find any evidence at all I will let you know. Hopefully there will be something left of his balloon that will give me some clues."

"What will you do after that?" Opal inquired.

"You know what? I don't know. I have many ideas. Did I ever tell you about the Sletartem Tribe?"

"O.K. then," Tarl quickly interrupted, "you must be planning on staying because that story takes a while." Tarl raised his eyebrows teasingly.

"Oh huffedy me no! I know when I'm not wanted."

Tarl winked at Opal.

"Alright then, we'll walk you to the solar sail," Tarl said.

"No no, I've never been much good at goodbyes. Let's just say it here and I'll be on my way."

"Please Rembeu, keep in contact, even if you do get distracted by some marvelous endeavor." Opal was trying not to cry.

"Oh my girl there's no need for that, of course I'll keep in contact." Rembeu was surprised at how emotional he felt.

Tarl thought how amusing it was to hear Rembeu refer to Opal in the same way Umbra had referred to him.

"Be careful uncle, please."

"I'm always careful!"

Tarl raised a challenging eyebrow.

"Rembeu."

"Oh alright, 'I promise I will be careful'. How's that?"

"Better."

"We will miss you so much," Opal went on, "I can't believe you're going."

"Now now, you and Tarl probably won't even know I'm gone. I'll tell you all about the Sletartem Tribe over the Voicer."

Tarl thought this the perfect exit.

"We will both look forward to that." His eyes twinkled with cheek.

"Honestly, a bit of interest please!"

"Goodbye uncle."

"Goodbye Rembeu." Opal was curled up close to Tarl as if he were helping her to stay standing. Tarl wrapped an arm around her and smiled.

"Goodbye my warriors." Rembeu enveloped them both with a vigorous hug. They were both surprised and delighted. And then instantly he let go, turned away, and grabbing his hand trolley strode on toward the solar sail as if he could walk the distance back to Calatia.

Watching Rembeu leave was nearly harder than watching his father leave. Now everyone was gone; indefinitely: Except Opal. For some strange reason he was reminded of the Teaching where he faced his older self and smiled with the knowledge. There was still a lot to accomplish; a lot to plan but knowing his future with Opal was just beginning was the most fulfilling feeling he could ever have imagined. Warmth spread inside him that felt like morning sunlight. He realized he was feeling Opal's love.

Tarl turned around to gaze into her beautiful sparkling eyes. After everything, here she was, right beside him. Opal was looking up at him in a way that made it hard to breathe. He reached his hand down to cup the back of her neck and slowly leant in to touch his lips to hers. It felt as if he had waited his whole life for this moment; a moment more incredible than he could have imagined. He wanted to stay right here forever but the sudden churning of machinery diverted their attention. Rembeu's solar sail was in full lift-off mode and was rising high above them. They lifted their heads to watch it disappear overhead. If they could have seen Rembeu's face they would have seen a large grin of freedom riding every moment.

"Oh by the way," Tarl said casually, "there's something I've been meaning to tell you." He returned his gaze to her.

"And what is that?"

"I promise to never leave you; I will keep my promise to find your parents..." he paused before tucking a loose strand of her hair behind her ear, "and I love you too."

ABOUT THE AUTHOR

Mardi Orlando lives in a coastal region of Victoria, Australia with her husband of thirteen years. After studying psychology she worked with many associations whilst continuing to indulge in her two passions: Science and New Age Philosophies. She has also travelled extensively and has found an open mind essential in all walks of life. Mardi is also the author of 'The Life Expectancy of Wind', an illustrated book of poetry, and 'The Wishall', a children's adventure story.